SA

MW00561460

By Kelly Elliott

Cover photo take by Rutheah Rodehorst
www.bluehousefotos.com

Cover design by Sarah Hansen www.okaycreations.net

Editor - Jovana Shirley www.unforeseenediting.com

ISBN- 13: 978-0-9887074-3-6 eBook

ISBN- 13: 978-0-9887074-5-0 Paperback

Thank you…

Arianna Niknejadi - You are not only being my BFF, but you have supported me and helped me so much along this journey. Thank you, Ari, for answering my endless questions in the beginning about Fragile X, thank you for sharing your personal stories with me, and most importantly…thank you for allowing me to share a piece of your precious Logan with the world. Thanks also for reading Saved and giving me your feedback. For yelling at me when I was on Facebook and should have been writing or doing edits. Thank you for helping me write the blurb when I was just stuck. You truly amaze me in all that you do…from being a wonderful friend, to an amazing mother. You rock you bitch!

Gary "Leo" Taylor –I swear I get at least ten messages a day saying how you are the perfect Gunner. You truly are…but you're more than that. Your determination is awe inspiring, your heart is genuine, your smile is infectious, and you might have been told this before…but you take one hell of a good picture cowboy. You're a friend who I admire and can count on. Thank you for just being you and always having my back and making me smile.

Molly McAdams – As I write this I'm having Molly withdraws 'cause we haven't had lunch in like…*Two weeks!* Thank you Molly for *always* making me laugh. You have no idea how much I look forward to our weekly lunches. You're an amazing friend…*a kick ass author*…(Can I just say……oh my god I can't wait for Stealing Harper BTW) and a beautiful person inside and out. Thank you for everything! Love you girl! P.S. Gus, Rose, Fergie and Pumpkin want another sleep over!

Sarah Hansen – Thank you for another beautiful book cover. I'm so proud to say that you've done my book covers. You rock and are the best!

Rutheah Rodehorst – You are an amazing photographer. Your pictures have truly brought to life these books. Thank you for allowing me to share your work on the cover of my books.

Jovana Shirley – Girl…you amaze me! You did a *fabulous* job on editing Saved. You made me smile numerous times throughout.

For that…I thank you from the bottom of my heart! Now on to Faithful we will go!

Kim Bias, Lisa Kane, and Denise Tung – Thank you girls SO MUCH for your support. It means more to mean than words could ever say.

Heather Davenport, Jemma Scarry, JoJo Belle, Rosa Saucedo – Thank you so so SO much for helping with Saved. I love you girls and I love how you have my back. I'm just so damn blessed to call y'all friends. Rosa my photo pimp….LOL! I love you!

Amanda Orozco – I can thank Gary for bringing you into my world. I'm so glad we have become friends. Thank you so much for answering all of my questions about horse breeding. I love you girl and would do anything for ya! Keep sending me those couple pictures!

Sue Sunderlin – Girl you know I love you! Thank you for being there for me….your friendship means so much to me. Thank you for letting me use you and Mark as my inspirations for Ari's parents.

Alexandra Louk – Thank you for sharing your story with me. Thank you for being my inspiration and teaching me that it just takes touching one person's life to make a world of difference.

Stacy Borel – I'm so damn glad we have become friends. You make me laugh...you help me find smutty music so I can write sex scenes and you know what candy apple means! I love you!

Liz Aguilar – You are amazing. The things you do for me just blow my mind. Thank you will never be enough!

My street team, Kelly's Most Wanted- Holy shit…I don't even know what to say to y'all. Thank you will *never* be good enough. I wish I could name each of you but you know who you are. I'd be lost without you girls…please know that. I love each and every one of y'all.

Dedication

This book is dedicated to my husband Darrin, my daughter Lauren, and my mother.

First I need to thank you Darrin…for reading your first ever book and making that book mine! I hope you see the bits and pieces of us together in these books and smile. Thank you so much for supporting me in this journey, even when it's taken me so far away from you. (BTW I really am listening to you talk…it just *looks* like I'm not) Thank you for letting me share a bit of you also with the world. I love you more than life itself…always have….always will. Thank you for yet another star wish too! LOL! You are my true romancer Darrin. I love you *more*.

Lauren – Oh. My. God. You're growing up before my eyes. I'm not gonna lie… some of our "adult" conversations on the way to and from school…yeah they freak me out just a little bit. You make me laugh, you make my cry, and you make me mad as hell sometimes…but I look forward to your smile every morning. Never change who you are to make someone else happy. You're a beautiful person inside and out…stay that way. I love you so much Lauren and I am so proud of you.

Mom – I wish you were to see all of this. I hope you would be proud of who I am. I miss you.

***

In this story you will meet a young man named Matthew Peterson. Matthew is a very special little guy and is very near and dear to my heart…he has Fragile X Syndrome. Matt was based off of my best friend's son, Logan Howard.

For those of you who don't know, Fragile X Syndrome is a genetic disorder that causes mental impairment, intellectual disability, poor eye contact, hand biting or flapping, learning and behavioral challenges, sensory processing disorders as well as anxiety and attention deficit hyperactivity disorders. It also happens to be the most common known genetic cause of Autism.

Fragile X syndrome can range from moderate learning disabilities, typically seen in girls, to very sever intellectual disabilities typical found in boys but some girls as well. It can cause physical features such as a long face, velvet soft skin, large ears, hyper flexible joints, as well as connective tissue problems, and seizure disorders. Children and adults with Fragile X are visual learners and learn best from peer models. It's imperative that they are exposed to typical social situations to develop strategies for appropriate social interactions.

Fragile X syndrome is detective by a simple blood test, screening for this is strongly recommended as 1 out of 260 females and 1 out of 800 males carry the FMR1 permutation gene which can cause Fragile X syndrome. The genetic test is also strongly recommended to those who have received diagnoses of autism.

Approximately 1 in 3600 males and approximately 1 in 4000 females are born with Fragile X.

Carriers of the Fragile X gene can experience Fragile X related disorders such as FXTAS (Fragile X –associated Tremor/Ataxia Syndrome). The tremors have similar symptoms as Parkinson Disease, FXPOI (Fragile X Primary Ovarian Insufficiency Prevalence), which can cause early menopause and failure to conceive.

The silver lining to all of this is that children and adults with Fragile X tend to be loving and empathetic with amazing senses of humor. They have a strong need to please others and can light up any room when they walk in. They are great with any visual technology such as tablets and smart boards. They love to sing, play and laugh just like everyone else. Never under estimate a child or an adult with Fragile X because they will surprise you at every turn…

For more information on Fragile X Syndrome:

Please contact the National Fragile X Foundation

www.Fragilex.org

or

800-688-8765

PROLOGUE

ARI

10 Years Old

I couldn't believe my parents were taking me away from all my friends. *I'll never forgive them for this.....ever! I'm never going to talk to them again.* They totally ruined my life.

I'm just going to sit here and keep sighing.

"Arianna, you'll make new friends, sweetheart. I know you will." my mom said.

I rolled my eyes in the backseat because I knew my mom couldn't see me.

"Don't roll your eyes at me, Arianna!"

What? How does she do that?

"This is *so* not fair! You're the worst mother ever! Why would you take me away from all my friends?"

My mother turned around and looked at me.

Oh, I think I went too far that time.

"First off, young lady, I'm not the one who is moving us to Austin for a new job. That would be your father sitting right here next to me." Mom looked over at Daddy who was smiling.

"Second, if you ever talk to me like that again, you'll be very sorry because I... I..."

Daddy looked over at Mom and waited for her to tell me what torture she would put me through. It seemed like he was enjoying all of this.

"To quote the great Katharine Hepburn, 'I could peel you like a pear, and God Himself would see the justice in it.' I'll do it, too, young lady, if you keep pushing me!"

Daddy laughed, and I just stared at her.

What does that even mean? Why is she always quoting Katharine Hepburn? Oh no!

She was going to make me watch another one of her movies. Just great! *Why can't I learn to keep my mouth shut?*

"I will never meet another friend like Katy, Mom. Never!" I closed my eyes and fought to keep the tears from falling. *I will not cry!*

Turning off the main road, we started to drive through our new neighborhood. It was cute, really cute. There were all kinds of houses in different sizes. *Thank God!* I hated our old neighborhood. All the girls were into English riding, and they teased me because I liked to barrel race. *Ugh, and all the stupid tea parties I had to go to! Yuck!*

As we drove by one simple looking house, with nothing extra special about it, I noticed a girl who looked to be around my age playing with an older boy out front. I sat up to get a better look. *Oh, he's cute!*

"Mom, are we close to our house?" I asked.

I looked out the back window, watching the boy chase the girl around the yard. *God, I hope that's her brother.*

"We're a few blocks away sweetheart. We have twenty acres, so we're at the end of the road."

I turned back around and smiled. *Perfect.* I could ride my bike by their house. Maybe it wouldn't be so bad here after all. As I continued to think about that boy, I wondered about what I should wear for my first bike ride through the new neighborhood.

CHAPTER ONE

ARI

Jeff stood at the door of the hunter's cabin, I could tell he'd been crying, and my heart broke at the sight of him. I couldn't believe it, I just stood there and stared at him.

He came for me.

"Ari, I know you told me not to come tonight, but."

I jumped into his arms, wrapped my legs around him, and kissed him like there was no tomorrow. I thought he was in a state of shock because it took him a few seconds to start kissing me back.

He pulled away from me with a confused look on his face. I didn't care that some bitch could possibly be carrying my future husband's baby. *Okay, that's bull shit. I do care.*

Even if I might not be the one to give Jeff his first child, she was *not* taking him from me. I was going to fight with every goddamn ounce of energy I had to make sure she knew that he was mine.

That bitch wants a fight? Well, she's got one!

"Ari, I just couldn't let you walk away from me again. I love you too much to lose you again, baby."

I smiled down at him. *He's mine.* I wrapped my legs around him tighter.

"You came after me, Jeff. I love you so much. Now, get your ass in here and make mad, passionate love to me before I change my mind."

Immediately, he smiled at me, but then it faded. I knew what he was thinking. I ran my hands through his beautiful, soft hair.

"We'll worry about it Monday. Right now is only about you and me."

Smiling again, he walked into the cabin and looked around.

"I wish I could have seen your face when you saw all of this."

"It's beautiful, Jeff; I couldn't have asked for anything more perfect. I love you baby, so much."

"Oh god, Ari, I love you, too."

Jeff kicked the door shut and then pushed me up against it. He started to kiss me with so much passion that I thought I was going to explode. I wanted him so much that I could practically feel myself willing him to do as I wished. I pushed my hips into him, trying to ease my need, and that was when I felt it.

The ring box! Oh shit! Is he still going to ask me to marry him? I started to feel like I couldn't breathe. I pulled my lips away from his, and I just stared at him.

Do not cry, Arianna. Do not.

"Baby, I'm so sorry this night was ruined for you. I had it all planned out, and I'm so pissed right now!"

With my legs still wrapped around him, Jeff walked us over to the bed and then slowly sat me down onto it. He stood up, pushing his hands through his hair. I didn't know what to say. For once in my life, I was...

Speechless. Holy hells bells.

"Um..." I stalled, still trying to figure out what to say.

Jeff looked around the room, and I noticed when he moved his hand up to his front pocket.

Just do it! I didn't even care anymore about how he did it. *Just fucking ask me to marry you!*

Then, he did the one thing I'd been dreaming about since I was ten years old when I first laid eyes on him. He reached into his pocket, took out the ring box, and got down on one knee.

His beautiful green eyes captured mine, and he smiled. My tears were falling like rain. *I love this man with my whole being.*

"Ari, I don't even know where to begin to describe how much I love you. I can't even tell you how long I've loved you. I've dreamed of this moment since I was sixteen years old. I always thought that I'd just get down on one knee and say 'marry me,' but, baby, that's not what I wanted to do with you."

He shook his head, and I could tell he was trying to keep from crying.

Jesus, Mary and Joseph he's really asking me to marry him!

He cleared his throat and then started talking again.

"You've believed in me and stood by me through all the craziness that's my life. I can't live one single day of this life without your love, Ari. I was lost before you, and I would forever be completely and utterly lost without you. Your love saved me. I promise you, Arianna, with every ounce of my being, I'll do nothing but love you and cherish you. I'll do everything in my power to make you happy every day for the rest of our lives. Arianna Katherine Peterson, will you do me the honor of becoming Mrs. Jefferson Michael Johnson?"

Jeff opened the ring box and took out the ring.

Oh.My.God. It was breathtaking.

"This ring, Ari this ring is a symbol of my love for you. I will *always* love you and *only* you."

I just stared at it. It was a vintage-style platinum ring with a round-cut center diamond. Round baguette diamonds surrounded the center diamond. The band was amazing. Two bands extended out from the prongs holding the center diamond on both sides and then molded into one as the bands completed the circle. I'd never seen such a beautiful ring in my entire life.

I looked up at Jeff, who was staring at me.

I couldn't talk. *Holy shit! I can't talk.*

"Um, Ari I'm not really sure, but I think this is the part where you tell me yes."

My dreams were about to come true. *I'm going to be Mrs. Jefferson Johnson. All those years of practicing my signature on my school notebooks was finally going to pay off!* As I felt a tear roll down my face, Jeff reached up and brushed it away.

"Jeff, I would be honored to be Mrs. Jefferson Michael Johnson."

Jeff let a smile that stretched from ear to ear. He shook his head and started to laugh.

What the hell?

"Why the hell are you laughing, dickwad? Are you trying to ruin my perfect moment?"

Jeff threw his head back laughing harder. He stood up, reaching out for my hand, and then he pulled me up to him. The look in his eyes was enough to drive me crazy. Right now in this moment, I wanted nothing more than to be with him. I wanted to forget all about crazy-ass Rebecca and the child that she was carrying. I wanted Jeff to save me from the nightmare that my father threw at me tonight.

"*Me* ruin it? It took you long enough to answer me, Ari, I was starting to get worried."

I giggled and reached up to kiss him. Placing his hand on the back of my neck, he pulled me in and deepened the kiss.

Holy hell! My head was spinning.

I was engaged to the man of my dreams. Sure, he was a pain in the ass, but fuck me, he sure could kiss.

Jeff barely pulled away from my lips as he smiled down at me.

"Ari?"

I could hardly talk.

"Yes?"

"Will you let me make love to you, baby?"

Oh. My. God. The Butterflies were taking off and going nuts in my stomach.

"Um sure. Why not?"

Jeff laughed against my lips. The heat from his mouth was driving me insane. I'd never get tired of being with him.

"Have I told you today how beautiful you looked? I had to catch my breath when I saw you walking down the aisle, baby."

"That's not what I heard from the preacher. All I know is that when the preacher pulled me to the side to tell me that my boyfriend needs to come to service tomorrow, I had to wonder what the hell was going on up there with you and Gunner."

Jeff laughed again. As he slowly pulled away from me, his eyes travelled up and down my body. I swore that every time he looked at me, it was like he was seeing me for the first time. When his eyes landed on my mouth, I couldn't help but lick my lips. He let out a small moan that traveled through my whole body.

I would do anything for this man. *Anything.*

CHAPTER TWO

JEFF

Holy shit! The moment Ari said yes, my heart started beating a mile a minute. It sure as shit wasn't going to slow down anytime soon while I looked her body up and down. So *fucking perfect*. She'd always been perfect. Now, she was going to be truly mine.

When she licked her lips, I let out a moan. *Shit.* I wanted to be inside her, I wanted to forget the last few days ever happened. I just wanted to be alone with the only girl I would ever love.

"Ari…"

She smiled that damn smile of hers that could bring me to my knees and make me do anything she asked.

"Jeff…"

She slowly turned around and then looked back over her shoulder at me with those beautiful green eyes of hers. *Damn!* I started to unzip her dress, and I couldn't stop my hands from shaking. I felt her body shiver the moment I touched her, and I swore that it felt like my knees were about to give out on me.

Holy shit, this girl is going to be the death of me.

Moving my hands slowly back up her body, I placed them on her shoulders and gently pushed off the dress, letting it drop to the floor at her feet. She stepped out and turned to face me.

Mother-fucker. I'd never seen anything so beautiful.

She was dressed in a pink lace bra with matching pink lace panties. I had to catch my breath from the sight of Ari in nothing but her lace underwear and cowboy boots. Taking a step back, I thought back to the first night we ever made love.

***

Brad and Amanda's wedding

Four Months Earlier

"Holy shit!" Gunner and I said together.

Gunner turned to me at the same time I looked at him. I quickly glanced back down the aisle to see Ari walking toward me with a huge bouquet of roses. She was the most beautiful thing I'd ever laid eyes on. As she stepped closer, I got a better look at the dress she was wearing.

Mother fucker. Her breasts were practically falling out of it. *Why the hell would Amanda have them wear that? Oh hell no! She was going to have to change or put on a jacket.*

Thank God, Gunner was the best man because I didn't hear any part of the ceremony. I couldn't tear my eyes away from Ari. *My Ari.* Tonight I would finally make her one-hundred percent mine.

I was still pissed at Gunner and his fucking romantic ways while they were at the hunter's cabin. Ellie had told Ari all about it, and I had to listen for a week about how passionate Gunner was.

I turned to look at Gunner, and I gave him a fuck-off look. He just raised his eyebrows and then smiled. *Bastard*

"Jeff, what the hell is wrong with you tonight? Your mind is in another world for Christ's sake." Ari said while she danced in my arms.

I held her closer and took in a deep breath. *Vanilla.* She always smelled like vanilla.

I looked over at Jenny, who gave me a thumbs-up. I lifted my hand and returned one back to her.

Damn. I'd never met someone who worked as hard as she did. Gunner and Ellie were so happy with how Jenny had decorated the cabin the night he'd asked her to marry him.

Tonight was costing me a fortune, but making it a night Ari would never forget was worth it.

Pulling away, Ari looked up at me. Tilting her head, she slowly let that damn smile play across her face.

My god, I love her. I couldn't believe that I'd almost let her go. What a stupid mother fucker I'd been. Tonight it was all going to change. I was going to make love to her for the first time.

Oh shit. I feel sick.

"Jeff? Are you okay? You look like you're going to be sick!"

I smiled down at Ari, I lifted her chin up toward me and kissed her. She deepened the kiss and let out a small moan.

After a few seconds, she pulled away. "You want to get the hell out of here and go back to my place?" Ari asked as she wiggled her eyebrows up and down.

Oh shit…here we go.

"Um…actually, I had something else planned for us tonight."

Ari looked at me and smiled.

"Oh, yeah?"

"Yep, but it's a surprise."

Just then, Brad and Amanda walked up to us.

I slapped Brad on the back. "Congratulations y'all."

"Thank you both for being in the wedding and helping out with so much. I couldn't have done it without your help, Ari," Amanda said.

She gave Ari a hug and then turned to hug me. Ari pulled up the top of her dress….*again*…. and smiled at Amanda. She'd been screwing with that damn dress all night. I almost got into it with three guys just for staring at her a little too long. *Bastard pricks.*

"You wait until I get married, you bitch. I'm *so* going to make you wear this same fucking dress. I can't even breathe in this bitch."

Amanda let out a laugh and hugged Ari again. "I love you, Ari! I hope that you have a wonderful evening. We're heading out in a few minutes, so I just wanted to say thanks and good-bye."

Ari and Amanda both got tears in their eyes. Brad and I looked at each other. Brad just shrugged his shoulders, and smiled.

After Brad and Amanda said their good-byes to everyone, Ari and I found Gunner and Ellie. They were talking to Heather and Josh.

"Oh my gosh, wasn't that such a beautiful wedding?" Heather gushed.

Ari rolled her eyes and screwed around with her dress some more.

"It was beautiful. Amanda did a great job and I was surprised she was able to keep it on the small side with Brad's mom so involved with the planning." Ellie said as she looked over at me and winked.

Fucking Gunner! Can't keep is goddamn mouth shut. I was sure he'd told Ellie what I had planned for tonight. *I'm never telling him anything again.*

"So, Josh and Heather….you two looked comfy on the dance floor tonight," Ari said nudging Heather with her shoulder.

I thought Heather was going to kill Ari. I'd never seen that girl look so pissed-off in my life. Josh just smiled and leaned in to say something to Heather. She turned and glared at him.

Oh shit, that's not a happy look.

"If you'll excuse me, I think I'll be heading home. Now that Amanda and Brad are gone, I need to get out of this dress. And no…you *cannot* help me, Josh!"

Everyone let out a laugh except for Josh. Poor bastard had it bad for Heather, but he seemed to always say the wrong thing to her. Gunner and I had tried to tell him that she wasn't like the bitches he'd slept around with and that he needed to take things slow with her to win her trust. *Stupid bastard.* He was always making sexual comments to her and all that did was push her further away.

Ellie and Gunner said they were taking off as well. As we all walked out to the main lobby of The Driskill Hotel, Gunner and I talked a bit about the ranch while Ari and Ellie talked about school.

"You okay, dude? You look like you're going to hurl," Gunner said as he threw his head back and laughed.

"Fuck you, asshole! If I remember right, you were a walking mess all Christmas day. Don't even start with me."

Gunner smiled and turned me away from Ari and Ellie.

"Jeff, dude, just relax. She's gonna be surprised, and she's going to love it. Ellie and I ran up to the room to take a peek after Jenny was done. It's beautiful. Just…just take it slow. Remember that this is for her dude. Be honest, Jeff. Be real."

Motherfucker. I'd never been with a virgin, and my hands were shaking already. *What if I hurt her? What if she hated it? What if-*

"Jeff, stop. I see the fucking wheels turning in your head, dude. It'll be fine. Trust me."

"Yeah, take it slow…it's her night….not about me. Holy shit Gunner. What if I hurt her? Do you know how long I've waited to be with this girl? What if I turn into a crazy man? Oh shit, maybe I should have waited longer. What if she's not ready?"

"Jesus, Jeff. You know that she's ready. She's more than ready. I think if you wait any longer, she's going to be the one to attack you. You won't go crazy. I'm not going to lie though. It'll be fucking hard to take it slow."

"Fuck Gunner! You just gave me a damn visual. What did I say about that? I'm done talking to you."

I turned and walked over to Ari and Ellie. I leaned down and kissed Ellie good night and told her that I loved her. While Ellie and Ari hugged and said their good-byes, Gunner handed me the key to the hotel room I'd booked.

I grabbed Ari's hand and started walking towards the stairs.

"Wait, where are we going, Jeff? I'm so ready to just go home and get out of this dress."

I stopped and turned her to face me. She had a questioning look on her face.

I leaned close to ear and said very softly and slowly, "I need to show you your surprise, baby."

Ari's head snapped up, and she looked into my eyes. For a second, she looked scared. Then her eyes immediately softened, and she smiled.

She turned away and walked over to the stairs and started to head up them at a rather fast pace. I had to let out a laugh. *Goddamn, I love this girl.*

I slipped the room key through the slider and looked over at Ari who looked like I felt, sick to my stomach. I should have come up to the room first to make sure everything was okay.

"Jesus H. Christ, Jeff, just open the door!" Ari said stomping her foot.

Yep, I loved this girl. I was pretty sure that I was going to die and go to heaven tonight.

I opened the door, and Ari just about pushed me out of the way as she made her way into the room. She stopped dead in her tracks and let out a gasp. The room was filled with LED candles everywhere and Roses were covering every possible surface. The bed had petals spread all over it with one single red rose lying across the pillows.

Next to the bed was a huge plate of chocolate-covered strawberries and a bottle of Veuve Clicquot Brut Champagne, Ari's favorite.

Yep, Jenny was worth every damn dime I paid. Gunner was now forgiven.

Ari turned and looked at me.

Oh shit. Tears were running down her face. I walked over to her and wiped them away as I leaned down and kissed her.

"I love you, Ari. I love you more than anything in this world, baby."

"Jeff....I don't. I don't even know what to say! It's so beautiful. It's....it's perfect!"

Our room was on the historical side of the hotel facing 6th Street. Ari walked over to the balcony doors, threw them open and walked outside. I could hear music coming from a bar not far away. The song sounded like it was "Dirty Dancer" by Enrique Iglesias. I smiled when her hips started moving to the beat. Damn, the girl loves to dance.

I took off my tie and jacket, set them on a nearby chair, and made my way out to her. I wrapped my arms around her and felt her moving her hips as she pressed into me. *Fuck me! Please don't let me lose it like a damn sixteen year old boy.*

As I moved my hips with hers, she threw her head back up against me and let out a small moan. I about lost it right then and there.

"Jeff?"

"Yeah, baby?"

"I'm scared."

Holy shit. I just about dropped to my knees. I'd never in the 9 years I'd known Ari, ever heard her utter those words. She was the strongest person I knew.

Gunner's words came back into my head. *Be honest, Jeff. Be real.*

"I am, too, baby."

Pulling away from me, Ari turned to face me with a shocked look on her face.

"What? Why would you be scared?" Ari practically shouted.

"I mean, why are *you* scared Jeff? For Christ's sake, it's not like you've never had sex before. I've never done this before. What if...what if I don't...."

"Ari, stop. First off, baby, I'm scared because I'm going to be making love to you for the first time. I might have had sex, before Arianna, but I've *never* made love to anyone before. I've dreamed about this night with you for years. I just want this to be perfect for you, Ari, I want you to always remember this night."

I watched as a tear rolled down her cheek. I brushed it away with my thumb and leaned down to kiss her. She stepped back away from me. I was confused by what she was doing until she turned and walked back into the room. I followed her in and shut the doors to the balcony.

She turned back to face me as she stepped backward until her legs touched the bed. I could hardly move my legs, but somehow, I managed to walk over to her. She looked at me with that smile.

"Can I ask you something, Jeff?"

"Yes, of course you can, Ari."

"Will you please get this mother-fucking dress off of me now before I explode in it?"

I let out a laugh and nodded my head. Ari turned around. I could barely hold the zipper while I slowly unzipped her dress with trembling hands. She let out a sigh when I had it unzipped all the way.

Motherfucker. Her back was so soft and beautiful. I thought about the day at the ranch when I was trying to put her bikini top back on in the river. I ran my finger down her neck to the bottom of her back. Her whole body shivered, and I smiled, knowing that my touch affected her like this.

She turned around and had her hand clutching the top of the dress. Smiling, she let the dress fall.

If I died this very second, I would die a happy man. I let my eyes travel up and down her body. She was perfect. She wore a strapless white lace bra with a matching thong on her flawless hourglass figure. Her skin was glowing with just a slight tan.

My heart was beating a mile a minute.

She held out her hand for me to help her step out of the dress. She stood there, just letting me look at her. I realized then, that I'd never just stopped to really look at her. In the past, when I'd given her an orgasm, she'd only been totally nude a few times. Afterward, I'd always ended up waiting for her to fall asleep, and then I would take care of myself in the shower. She'd practically begged me the other night to let her give me a hand job. Now, I was about to see her nude and I would be able to really take her all in.

She's about to be totally mine.

"Do you like what you see?"

I couldn't talk. I just stared at her lips that she was now licking. I watched as her hands moved to her bra, and the next thing I knew, it was gone.

"Ari…I think I'm going to pass the fuck out."

Ari threw her head back and laughed. "Good! I was hoping for a reaction like that."

I just looked at her and smiled. Her smile faded as she glanced at the bed and then back at me.

"Can I undress you, Jeff?"

What did she just ask me? I looked her up and down again. "Huh?"

Ari laughed as she walked up to me. She slowly started to unbutton my shirt, and each time she undid a button, she kissed my chest.

"I don't know if I hear your heart beating or mine!" Ari said with a giggle.

"Both maybe?"

"Hmm…maybe."

She pushed off my shirt and then took her time staring at my chest. Her fingers started to trace my tattoo. My whole body shivered, making Ari smile. She reached down and unbuckled my belt. After she unbuttoned and unzipped my pants, she leaned over and began taking off my shoes. As she slowly stood back up, I slipped my pants off and then looked back at her.

The way Ari was looking at me caused me to say another silent prayer I would last at least five minutes. She looked down at my boxer briefs and then moved her eyes back up to mine. She placed her hands on my hips, and I swore my dick got so hard that I thought I was going to die. She slowly slipped them off, and then she stood back up and stared at my dick.

"Do you like what *you* see, baby?" I asked with a smirk.

Ari looked at me and smiled, but I could tell she was getting more nervous. Taking her hand, I guided her onto the bed. She sat down and slowly started to lay back. Her whole body was shaking. I kneeled on the bed next to her and started to take off her thong.

"Jesus, Ari…you're so fucking beautiful. I could just stare at your body all day."

I watched as a blush spread across Ari's cheeks.

I leaned over her and kissed her with as much passion as I could. She moaned into my mouth, and I felt it travel throughout my body. I reached my hand down and ran it along her stomach to her thigh. I gently nudged her legs apart, and she practically jumped from my touch.

"Jeff…"

"I love you, Arianna."

"I love you…so much Jeff."

Moving my hand to caress between her legs, I placed one finger inside of her, and she just about came on the spot. *She's so fucking wet.*

"Fuck, Ari. You're so ready, baby."

"Please, Jeff."

I slowly added two more fingers while my thumb rubbed against her clit. Ari started pushing her hips into my hand, and I could tell she was close, so I stopped moving my hand.

"Jeff! Why did you stop?"

I softly kissed her neck, and then moved down to her chest where I started to suck on her nipple.

"Oh, Jeff."

God, I just wanted to make her feel special and loved. As I continued kissing down her stomach, I felt her body shake. A small smile came across my mouth, knowing my touch was driving her crazy. Moving lower, I kissed her hip and then over to the other. When I started to kiss down her leg, I heard her moan.

"Oh god, Jeff…please."

I slowly made my way over to her inner thighs. When I blew on her clit, her whole body jerked as she grabbed the bed-sheets with both of her hands. I looked up at her and almost lost it. Her eyes were closed, and she was chewing on her bottom lip.

I gently put my fingers back into her as I started to kiss her clit. Her moans were driving me fucking nuts. We had never done this before, and I was afraid that she would stop me.

It didn't take long before she was calling out my name as she ran her hands through my hair. I had given plenty of girl's oral sex before, but with Ari, it was so much more. Her taste and how she felt on my lips….was beyond perfect.

"Holy hell, do that again!" Ari said after she caught her breath.

I moved up her body, feeling her chest rising and falling with each deep breath, and I smiled at the sight of her flushed face.

"Baby, I want you to come again, but this time, with me inside you. I want to see you fall apart when we're making love."

I started to lean over to get a condom out of my pants, when Ari grabbed my arm and shook her head.

Oh fuck. Why is she saying no?

"Ari, I have to wear a condom, baby. I've never had sex without one."

"You don't have to, Jeff. I'm on the pill. I started taking it right after Thanksgiving…you know, just in case. I don't want anything to separate us, Jeff."

I just stared at her. *Oh shit, I'm not going to make it past two minutes.*

I slowly parted her legs as I moved closer to her. She closed her eyes when she felt me against her opening. Putting my hands on the sides of her face, I leaned down to whisper in her ear.

"Baby, keep your eyes open. I want to watch you."

Her beautiful green eyes opened and captured mine. "Okay," she whispered.

I gently started to move inside her. I felt her tense up, and I stopped.

"Are you okay, baby? Does it hurt?"

"S'Okay Jeff. Please don't stop. Please just don't stop!"

I pushed myself in a little more, and she winced. *Shit! Do I go fast? Do I go slow?* I just didn't want to hurt her, so I inched into her only a little at a time.

"Jesus, Mary, and Joseph, Jeff, how much more?"

I had to laugh. *Ari and her damn mouth.*

With just one slight push, I would be all the way in. *Holy shit, she feels like fucking heaven.* I almost wanted to pinch myself to make sure I wasn't dreaming.

"I'm in baby, all the way. Are you okay, Ari?"

Ari smiled and wrapped her legs around me. "I'm more than okay. I think I'm dreaming!"

I slowly started to move. I could tell at first it was not pleasant for her, but after a minute or two, her facial expression softened and she smiled.

"Oh god Jeff. That feels so damn good."

"You feel like heaven, baby." I could hardly catch my breath. I was trying so hard not to come before she did.

"Can you go faster?" she asked, pushing her hips into me.

Fuck yeah! I moved faster, and I could tell her climax was building. She arched her body into mine and closed her eyes for a second before she opened them again and looked into my eyes.

"Oh my god, Jeff... oh god."

Motherfucker. Ari, please hurry! I wasn't sure how much longer I could take it. *Jesus, I can't believe I'm willing her to come fast. What the fuck is wrong with me?*

Ari started to move her hips with mine and as she called out my name. I couldn't pull my eyes away from hers.

"Oh my god! Jeff! Yes! Oh. My. God!"

I called out Ari's name as I had one of the most intense orgasms of my life. It felt like I was coming forever. I couldn't believe we came together. It was so perfect.

Propping myself up on my elbows, I ran my hands down the sides of her face. We were both having a hard time catching our breath. After about a minute, she gave me that beautiful smile of hers. My breath caught in my throat.

"Jesus, I thought you worked out every damn day. Why the fuck can't you catch your breath?"

I just looked at her. She busted out laughing, and then she kissed the shit out of me.

"I love you, Jeff. Thank you so much for making all my dreams come true."

"God, Ari…I love you so much, baby. I hope that I've only just started making your dreams come true."

***

We made love three more times that night.

It was the best night of my life.

\

CHAPTER THREE

ARI

Jeff stood there and just stared at me like he was seeing me for the first time. His eyes traveled up and down my body.

I couldn't believe that I was going to be his wife. And she was going to have his baby.

"Jeff?" I asked, trying to get his attention.

He looked like he was lost in space. *What is he thinking about?* I shook my head to wipe away the thoughts of Rebecca. *I won't let that bitch ruin my night anymore!*

"Um, Jeff? Hello? Earth to Jeff."

Jeff slowly picked up my left hand and kissed the engagement ring. His beautiful green eyes caught mine. My heart was racing a mile a minute, and my knees felt weak just from that simple kiss.

"You're so beautiful, baby. I love you so damn much. The sight of you just takes my breath away. I want to make love to you, Ari."

Oh.My.God. *Can he be any more perfect? Damn him!* He was going to make me cry. Dickwad.

I stepped forward and placed my hands on his chest. He had already taken off his jacket and tie, so I started to unbutton his vest. He looked so damn handsome in those black Wranglers and boots. I'd never get used to seeing him in Wranglers.

"I'd like nothing more than for you to make love to me, Jeff."

I slowly started to open his shirt revealing his massive chest. I leaned into him and kissed his chest softly as Jeff sucked in a deep breath. I loved how my touch still affected him so much.

I took off his shirt and threw it to the side. I lowered myself to my knees and started undoing his pants. As I took off his belt, I looked up at him and let out a small gasp. I was frozen in place from his stare. The way Jeff was looking at me, made me want to push his ass on the bed to have my wicked way with him. He hadn't looked at me like that since the first time we made love.

Jeff reached down and grabbed my shoulders and pulled me up to him. He gripped his hand behind my neck and crushed my lips to his. He kissed me with so much passion that I could feel it running through my veins.

"Take off your boots, Ari."

"Okay."

I'd never taken off a pair of damn cowboy boots so fucking fast in my life. Something in Jeff's voice had me panting with need.

He turned me around and started to undo my bra.

"I can practically hear your heart beating, Ari."

"Yes," I whispered.

He slipped off the bra and started to kiss all the way down my back. My body was shaking in response to his touch.

"You're so beautiful, baby."

He turned me around and lightly kissed me on the lips. Then, he dropped to his knees and started to kiss my stomach. He reached up and began taking my panties off.

Oh, holy hell. I think I could have an orgasm right now.

Next thing I knew, I felt his breath… down there.

"Jeff…"

"Ari, lie down on the bed."

Why does this feel like our first time all over again? I could hardly move I was so nervous. It wasn't like we hadn't had plenty of sex before tonight, but something about the way Jeff was talking to me moved through my body like a bolt of lightning.

I sat on the bed and slowly moved back. I watched as Jeff started to take his boots and jeans off. My breathing became heavier as I watched him undress. He picked up a remote and Christina Perri's "A Thousand Years" started playing. Then, he just stood there, looking at me.

God he has the most amazing body. Seeing him stand there completely nude was driving me insane. I was so wet that I swore I could feel the sheets dampening beneath me.

"Wh...what are you doing?" I could hardly talk because I was so turned on.

"I just want to look at you, Ari. You're so beautiful. I just can't believe that you're mine."

"Jesus H. Christ, Jeff! If you don't get over here soon, I'm going to start without your ass!"

Jeff threw back his head and laughed. Moving onto the bed, he was over my body so fast that my head was spinning from his instant heat. He grabbed my hands and placed them near the sides of my head as he pinned down my arms with his.

"Have I ever told you how much I love your smart-ass mouth, Arianna?"

"Um...."

Leaning his head down, he brushed his lips against mine. I pushed up my hips against him, prompting him to move or do something. He just smiled at me, and I melted. He started to softly kiss my neck.

Moving over to my ear, he whispered,

"I love you, Ari."

"I love you, too, Jeff...more than you know."

Releasing my arms, he slowly made his way down my chest. As he sucked on my nipple, I felt like I was going to explode. I ran my hands through his hair. *Oh god.*

His hand gently stroked along the side of my stomach until it rested between my legs. Everywhere he touched me felt like an electric shock. As he kissed my lower stomach, he slowly started to push one finger in at a time inside of me while his thumb pressed against my clit.

"You're always so ready, baby."

"Don't stop Jeff. Please just make me forget everything."

Before I knew it, his mouth was on my clit as I called out his name. I swore it felt like the most intense orgasm I'd ever fucking had. I didn't know if it would stop? *Oh shit, he's so good at this.*

I felt like I'd left my body for a few seconds. It took me a good two or three minutes to catch my breath.

When I opened my eyes, he was just watching me. He smiled and moved back up my body.

He was inches from my face.

"I only want you to think about us, baby. It's only the two of us Ari, always and forever."

I felt him push my legs apart as he slowly entered my body. I arched my body from the instant pleasure he gave me. As we made love, I wanted nothing more than to give him everything I had. I wanted to give him all my love, my trust, and my dreams.

I thought about how badly I wanted to give Jeff a child. *Would I ever be able to give him that? Would Rebecca be the one to do that?* I felt a tear slowly run down my face.

Jeff looked at me and kissed away the tear.

"Please tell me you're happy, Ari. Please, baby, tell me you're not crying because you're sad."

I held him as tightly as I could.

"I've never been so happy in my life. Please just let me lose myself in you."

With that, he was able to make me forget everything but us.

The next morning, I walked into Emma's kitchen and saw my mother talking to Emma. My heart started beating so fast. They both looked up at me and smiled.

"Good morning! So, um, wow, they sure are taking things down and cleaning up pretty, fast aren't they?" I said.

I walked over to the coffee pot and poured myself a cup. I glanced out the window and saw Josh standing against his truck, talking to one of Gunner's cousins. *Lynda...I think that's her name.* I wondered what she was still doing here. I thought Gunner's other cousin Shannon had told me that they were all staying at a hotel in Austin.

I turned around to see Emma and my mother staring at me. *Motherfucker, here we go.*

"Okay, did someone die? Jesus, with the way you two are looking at me."

"Arianna, dear, I'm going to guess by that ring on your finger that you and Jeff worked things out?" Emma asked me before she looked over at my mother.

I could so feel a damn Katharine Hepburn quote coming from my mother any second now.

I sat down and let out a small sigh. I turned to Emma, who was giving me that damn sweet-ass smile of hers. *Fuck I loved this woman.* Ellie was very lucky to have gained Emma and Garrett as family when she married Gunner.

I smiled at Emma and took a sip of coffee.

"Yes, Emma. We worked things out, but, the light of day has my head spinning. My thoughts are racing."

Emma reached over to take a hold of my hand.

They must know about Rebecca. Great, I can't even have five fucking minutes to enjoy my engagement.

"Alright, Mom, let it out. I can see you're holding something in."

My mother sat up straighter in her chair and took my other hand.

Oh Jesus, Mary, and Joseph.....this is going to be bad.

"As the great Katharine Hepburn said, 'Life is hard. After all, it kills you.' It'll all work out somehow, Arianna."

What the hell? That's the best she can do? I just looked at her as I watched a smile play across her face.

"Really, Mom? That's the best you've got?"

My mother glanced over to Emma, and then she looked at me confused. "What were you expecting me to say, Ari?"

"I was expecting you to tell me that it's all going to be okay, Mom. I wanted you to say that this Rebecca bitch, sorry, Emma, is not carrying Jeff's baby and that my dad didn't really ruin my engagement night by dropping the biggest fucking bomb on me ever! Sorry again, Emma."

Emma smiled at me as she squeezed my hand tightly. My mother removed her hand from mine as I reached for my coffee. As I took another drink, I noticed my hand was shaking. *Shit!*

"I'm sorry, Ari. I wish I could tell you it'll all be okay, sweetheart, but I'd be lying to you. I'm not sure if it will. Have you and Jeff talked about this?"

I shook my head. Then, I felt tears welling up in my eyes. *Do not cry, Ari.*

"Mom..." My voice cracked.

"*I* wanted to be the one to give him a baby. I wanted that more than anything, and I keep telling myself that if this turns out to be his baby, I'll be okay but...but..."

Emma squeezed my hand.

"Ari, I think that it's time you got tested," my mother said matter-of-factly.

I snapped my head up at my mother. *Why is she bringing this up now?*

"Tested? Oh my, Ari, is something wrong?" Emma asked, looking back and forth between my mom and me.

"No, Emma, nothing is wrong with Ari. Ari, if you want to even consider having a baby with Jeff, then you need to be tested to see if you're a carrier of the gene. Emma, remember how we spoke last night about Matthew and how he has Fragile X?"

Smiling, Emma nodded her head. "I don't think that I will ever forget that sweet boy finding my mop and bucket and asking me if he could mop my floors. Every time he comes over, he asks to do it again."

I let out a laugh.

That sounded like my little brother Matthew. He'd been diagnosed with Fragile X when he was eighteen months old. My mother and father had been concerned because he was not sitting up or meeting his other developmental milestones when he should have been. After endless tests and going to see the best doctor's money could buy, they had finally gotten their answers. I would never forget the day they had found out. The first time I'd ever seen my father cry was when I was thirteen years old. My mother had given herself a day of sadness and then she bounced back full force. She had found the best occupational, speech, and physical therapists around.

I looked over at my mom and smiled. If I could only be half of the mother that she is, then I'd be so happy.

"I know that I need to find out if I might pass Fragile X onto any children that I might have. I've been putting it off for years, but I think you're right, mom. I need to know."

"Does Jeff know that you could possibly pass this onto your kids?" Emma asked as she gave me the sweetest smile.

Jeff, he was so good with Matt, and Matt just loved Jeff. Matt would follow him everywhere and would do anything to make Jeff laugh. Once he would figure out what made Jeff laugh, Matt would do the same thing over and over again, and Jeff would laugh every time. Jeff has never once lost his patience with Matt. Jeff had even stopped by the house at least once a week to play video games with Matt. Sometimes, Gunner had even tagged along with Jeff to hang out with Matt. Both of them treated Matt like a regular boy and not a mentally impaired one. This just added to the list of reasons of why I loved Jeff so much.

Just thinking about the way Jeff was with Matt made my heart melt. "Yes, he knows, and it doesn't matter to him either way. He says he would love our child no matter what. He adores Matt, and Matt adores him. Speaking of, where is Matt Mom?"

Emma and my mother both laughed.

Emma turned to look behind me. "Jeff stopped by and took Matthew down to the stables to see the horses. Of course, Jeff didn't have to ask twice," she said.

The thought of Jeff spending time with Matt just made my heart hurt even more.

Fucking stupid-ass Rebecca. That bitch was lucky she had a damn restraining order out against me because all I wanted to do this very moment was kick her ass.

Then, Heather walked into the kitchen with her perky-ass morning voice.

"Good morning, Sue and Emma. My gosh, Ari, you look like you're ready to kick someone's butt."

I just glared at her while she poured herself a cup of coffee.

Emma stood up and smoothed her hands down her dress. "It's such a beautiful morning, ladies. Let's drink our coffee outside and watch all the young men take apart the tents."

We all looked at each other and busted out laughing. *I just loved this woman.*

As we walked out to the porch, Heather saw Josh talking to Lynda, and she stopped dead in her tracks.

"What the fuck is she still doing here?"

I turned my head to look at Heather. "Holy shit! Did you just say *fuck?*"

Heather gave me a go-to-hell look that made me laugh.

"Yes. Yes, I sure as shit did! That woman would not leave Josh's side during the whole wedding. I mean, she was really hanging on him while she flaunted her stupid breasts in his face all night."

I looked down at Heather's chest and then back up at her. Out of all of us, she probably had the best boobs.

"Heather, flaunt what the good Lord gave ya. I keep telling you that. I know you like Josh, and according to Jeff, Brad, and Gunner, Josh likes you. So, do something about it for Christ's sake!"

I watched Heather look back over at Josh and Lynda, and I could practically see the steam coming from her ears. Emma and my mother were deep in conversation about Fragile X. Another item on my to do list, get tested for Fragile X.

"She stayed last night did you know that?" Heather said as she glanced back at me.

"What? Who stayed last night?"

"Lynda. She claimed that she was feeling sick. She said the ride back to Austin would just make her feel worse, so she stayed here last night. She bunked with me in my room and talked about Josh all darn night. I don't like her. Something about her just sits wrong with me."

"Oh, holy hell, Heather you're fucking jealous!" I laughed loudly throwing my head back. When Josh saw us, he took two steps away from Lynda and smiled at Heather. I heard her mutter something like asshole under her breath, and then she turned and walked towards Emma and my mom. Josh's smile faded when Heather walked away. He turned and said something to Lynda before he headed down to the barn.

Interesting. Very interesting.

CHAPTER FOUR

JEFF

"Where is Ari's horse, Jeff?" Matt asked.

"She's not here, buddy."

I saw Josh walking into the barn with a concerned look on his face. I looked down at Matt as he was trying to sweep some hay away from one of the barn doors.

"Hey, Josh."

Josh looked over at Matt and smiled, and then he looked at me as his smile faded. *Shit. I know that look. Something must have happened with Heather.*

"What's up, dude? Hey Matt buddy, you helping Jeff clean up?" Josh asked.

Matt smiled at Josh and held out the broom for him to see it.

Then, Matt turned to face me again.

"Where is Ari's horse, Jeff?"

"She isn't here, buddy. What's going on, Josh? You look like someone just kicked you off the playground." I said with a smirk.

Josh rolled his eyes and gave me the finger.

When I laughed Matt looked at me.

"What's so funny, Jeff?"

"Nothing, buddy, Josh rolled his eyes at me, and it made me laugh."

"Do you like that, Jeff? I can do that, too! Jeff, where is Ari's horse?"

"She's not here, buddy. Want to pet Rose?"

"Yes!"

Josh walked into Rose's stall, put a lead on her, and brought her out. I picked up Matt and carried him over to Rose.

Matt loved being around the horses, even just the mention of seeing them got him all excited. Ari and I had taken him to some stables around Austin a few times. *I just loved this little guy.*

I started to think about Ari and how badly she wanted kids. She'd been worried about having kids. Now, with the whole Rebecca shit, I knew it was going to be on her mind again.

"You like her, Matt?" Josh asked. He was giving Rose some oats while Matt was running his hands along her back. "You want to sit on her, buddy?"

Nodding his head at Josh, Matt smiled the biggest smile I'd ever seen.

"Keep a good hold of him, Josh," I said.

"I know what I'm doing, asshole."

"Assmole!" Matt yelled out.

Josh and I lost it, and we both started laughing. This only caused Matt to say it over and over again.

"Assmole! Assmole! Assmole!"

Holy shit! We couldn't stop laughing.

"Assmole Jeff!"

Oh hell! I needed this laugh.

Josh had tears running down his face. I think the fucker even snorted.

"Huh? Jeff, why is my little brother saying a bad word?"

Josh and I both looked at Ari, and instantly stopped laughing. Matt smiled at Ari as she walked up to him.

"Hey, buddy! Do you like sitting up there on Rose? You want to go for a ride with me, sweets?" Ari asked.

Matt nodded his head, and I held my breath because I knew what was coming next.

"Assmole!" Matt yelled again.

Ari was so good with Matt. Instead of laughing, she just went on about her business.

She started to pull out a saddle and harness while she talked to Matt.

"Matt, we're going to ride Rose for a little bit while Josh and Jeff talk about using the proper language because swearing is not nice.

"Ah, that's the pot calling the kettle black, Ari." Josh said with a laugh. Ari turned and shot Josh a go-to-hell look.

"Where is Ari's horse, Jeff?" Matt asked again.

"She's not here buddy. Remember I told you a little bit ago that she wasn't here."

Ari turned to me. "Be specific Jeff, he needs a real answer, babe."

Oh shit! I always forget that. I'm just so use to him repeating his questions to me. *Damn.*

"She's down at another stable, buddy, and then she's going to come live on our property at our stable," I explained.

"Oh...cool," Matt said.

And that was it. Question was answered, and he was satisfied.

Damn. Where was Ari twenty-five minutes ago when he first asked me that question?

"You want me to go riding with y'all?" I asked while I helped Ari saddle up Rose.

Something was off with her today. Last night had been so perfect, but this morning it was like she woke up with the world on her damn shoulders.

Rebecca.

"No, I'd rather be alone with Matt if you don't mind. I think you need to make a phone call. Don't you?" Ari said with sarcasm dripping from her mouth.

"Um, yeah I guess so, but I was kind of hoping to take care of it tomorrow when we're back in Austin."

Josh lifted Matt and put him in the saddle while I helped Ari get seated behind the saddle on Rose.

"Can you hand me that helmet for Matt, Josh?" Ari asked.

Then she turned and looked at me. The look in her eyes as they filled with tears about gutted me.

"No. Take care of it now."

She put the helmet on Matt and started to ride off.

"Ari, what about your helmet?" I asked.

She just rode off without an answer and never looked back at me.

Fuck.

I jabbed my hands through my hair and looked up at the ceiling. *Motherfucker.* Josh slapped me on the back, bringing me back to reality.

"Jeff, she's right. Call Rebecca and set up a time to meet with her. You have to get this shit taken care of. I still can't believe that you're the one who got the baby daddy phone call." Josh said with a laugh.

"Yeah, douche-bag assmole! You should be the one with about twenty-five girls knocking on your door."

"Fuck no. I have three fuck rules."

Did he just say fuck rules?

"One, always use protection and buy the most expensive-ass condoms you can get. Two, never have sex drunk, and three, *never* have sex with a girl who is clearly in love with or obsessed with you."

I just stood there, staring at him. *Bastard.*

"Fuck off, Josh!"

Josh threw his head back laughing, as we walked out of the barn. He stopped dead in his tracks, grabbed my arm, and turned to walk us in the other direction.

"Jesus, Josh, I'm not in the mood for a romantic stroll with you. I've got to go call a crazy bitch who claims to be pregnant with my kid."

Josh picked up the pace and made his way around the other side of the barn. *Shit.* He was almost in a dead jog. *What the fuck is he trying to get away from?*

"Josh! What the fuck, dude? What are we doing?"

"Shit, Jeff, keep your voice down and just walk, dude. I'm trying to get the fuck away from Lynda, Gunner's cousin." Josh whispered.

I wanted to laugh at him but, considering what I had going on with Rebecca, I didn't need any bad karma.

Throughout the wedding reception yesterday, Lynda had spent most of the evening hanging all over Josh. Every time Josh had looked for Heather to dance, Lynda somehow showed up and talked him into dancing with her.

"What is she still doing here? I thought Gunner's cousins went back to Austin last night," I said.

"They did! Lynda claimed that she wasn't feeling well, and get this, she ended up staying in the same room as Heather last night. God knows what the fuck she said about me to Heather."

"Wow. That's messed up dude. What's going on with you and Heather anyway? Are you ever going to ask her out on a real date?"

Josh stopped and looked at me. I almost laughed at the face he was making. *Damn. I've been in his shoes before. I should really be a better friend.*

"I have asked her Jeff, like twenty times. Every time I ask her, she says no. I've done everything I can think of. She's driving me crazy. One minute, she acts like she can't stand me, and the next she looks pissed because I'm talking to another girl. Do you know when the last time I had sex was?" he said, clearly frustrated.

"Ah, no, and I don't care to know, so don't share that shit with me!"

"Four fucking months, Jeff! *Four.* I haven't had sex in four months, and it's all her fault!"

I just stood there and looked at him. *Holy shit. He really liked Heather.*

"How the hell is it her fault?"

"She has me all tied up in knots. Every time I get ready to have sex with someone, I can't do it. I have to get dressed and leave. All I can think about is her."

As Josh and I made our way towards the house, I saw Heather with Emma, Garrett, Mark and Sue sitting on the porch.

Shit. I didn't want to face Ari's parents just yet.

Heather looked over and gave us a small smile before she turned to Garrett and Emma.

"Well, I guess I better get ready to head back to Austin. Thank you, Garrett and Emma, for allowing me to stay here last night with you. I truly appreciate it." Heather said.

Just then Lynda, came walking up calling out Josh's name. I saw Heather's body stiffen at the sight of Lynda going up to Josh as she placed her hand on his arm.

"Josh, do you think I could get a ride back to Austin with you? I thought Jeff and Ari would be heading back sooner, but Ari said they weren't heading back until this afternoon. I really, really need to get back," Lynda whined.

Josh looked so confused. *Poor fucker.* Heather just stood there, waiting to see what was going to happen.

"Um… yeah sure. I mean, I wasn't really planning on leaving anytime soon, but if you need a ride I guess."

Lynda let out a small yelp and jumped into Josh's arms. "Oh, thank you, Josh! You're my hero. I'll go get my things."

After Lynda let go of Josh, she thanked Emma and Garrett for letting her stay the night, and then she headed into the house. The smile she gave Heather was loud and clear. This girl was digging her nails into Josh and holding on for dear life.

Just then, my cell phone beeped with a text message. I was surprised it came through because I usually didn't have a cell signal at the ranch. I pulled out my phone and saw the message was from Ellie.

Ells: *Hey, big bro. I am dying here. How did it go last night? Can't get a hold of Ari ☺ Gunner just told me that we're going to Belize! Eeeeppp! Love you, Jeff. Give Ari a hug and kiss for me.*

I smiled as I read her text. I still couldn't believe it. My little sister and Gunner…married. *Fucking bastard with his carriages! Damn that romantic bastard!*

"That must have been from Ellie," Emma said with a smile.

I swore that this woman could read minds.

"Yeah, she wanted to talk to Ari. I guess Gunner let her know that Belize was their destination. To be honest, I'm surprised that Ari didn't give it away."

Just then we heard Ari and Matt riding up on Rose. I turned to look at them as they headed our way. *God she's beautiful.* She was leaning down, saying something in Matt's ear. He started to laugh, and she looked up at me and smiled. My knees about buckled.

Shit! Will she always have this effect on me?

Emma, Sue, and Mark walked past me.

Emma stopped and smiled at me. "Yes, Jeff, she will always make you feel weak in the knees." She gave me a wink and then made her way over to Rose, taking the lead from Ari.

Jesus H. Christ, she does read minds!

CHAPTER FIVE

Ari

I was feeling so much better from just being alone with Matt and not thinking about Rebecca or Jeff. The moment I saw Jeff standing there though, my heart started to beat faster.

"Ari! There's Jeff!" Matt said as we got closer to the ranch house.

"Yep, buddy, there he is. I bet the next time you visit, Jeff will take you for a ride on his horse. Would you like that, bud?"

"Yes. He's an assmole, so is Josh. They are assmoles." Matt said, laughing.

Oh, fuck a duck! I tried so hard not to laugh. I leaned down and told Matt not to say that word in front of Mommy and Daddy because that was a special word only for Jeff, Josh, and me. Matt nodded his head, then his smile grew bigger the second he saw Jeff.

Our mom walked up to greet us. "Did you have a good ride, my little man? You like spending time with Jeff, Ari and the horses?"

"Yes! Jeff is an assmole, Mommy!"

Oh shit. My mother and father turned away from Matt and me. *Bastards!* I saw their shoulders moving up and down from laughing.

Then my dad turned to look at Jeff. "The jury is still out on that, buddy."

Jeff looked shocked, and I really started to laugh. Dad helped Matt down. He told him that they had to get ready to drive back home and that Matt's iPad was all charged and ready to go.

I jumped off of Rose, and Emma started to take her back to the barn. Just then, Dewy walked up and told Emma he would tend to Rose.

"Thank you, Dew. She deserves some extra oats. She's so gentle when Matt is on her," I said.

"You got it, Ari," Dewy said with a wink.

I looked over at Jeff. He looked like he was going to be sick. I started to walk over to him.

We hadn't talked since we'd woken up. I knew that I'd been in a mood this morning. I had tried to sneak out of the cabin, but failed big time. Jeff had woken up the minute I'd tried to get out of the bed.

I stopped right in front of him and attempted to put on my best smile. I stood on my tippy toes and leaned in to give him a kiss. He bent down and pulled me to him. *Holy hell!* He kissed the shit out of me right in front of everyone.

He pulled away from my lips slightly and smiled. "I missed you."

"I just went for a short ride. What are you going to do when I'm in school this fall, and you're here?"

Jeff pulled away from me and looked shocked. *Yep.* This was another thing that we hadn't talked about.

"Have you called her yet?" I asked.

"Ari, do we have to talk about this here?"

I looked around and noticed the only person sitting on the porch now was Garrett. Josh had walked with Dewy down to the barn to take care of Rose. Heather must have gone inside to pack up to leave, and Emma had walked off with my parents.

"No, Jeff, let's not talk about it and just keep putting shit off. Let's just pretend that none of it matters." I replied sarcastically.

I turned to walk over to the Jeep. I was ready to leave. I jumped in and started it up. Jeff had driven his truck back down to the ranch house this morning.

I looked back at Jeff. "I'm going to get my things. I'll meet you back here in a little bit. I'm ready to head home."

Jeff started to walk toward the Jeep, but I took off. I let myself look in the mirror, and I saw Jeff running his hands through his hair. *Shit!* I did it again. I ran away from him before we could talk. I hit the steering wheel so hard that my hand felt like it was broken.

***

When I got back to the hunters cabin, I walked in and the first things I noticed was the smell of lilies, it was amazing. I leaned against the door, and I finally allowed myself to cry as I slide to the floor. *Oh god. What if this turns out to be his baby? Mother-fucking son of a bitch.*

After ten minutes of endless crying, I finally got up and started to pack my stuff. I needed to suck it up and deal with this. I had to be strong and fight for what was mine. Even if this was his baby, Lord I prayed it wasn't, I would not let her take Jeff away from me. *Never.*

Just then, a damn Katharine Hepburn quote popped into my head.

As one goes through life, one learns that if you don't paddle your own canoe, you don't move.

Damn my mother!

I packed up my stuff and loaded it into the Jeep. Then, I went back into the cabin and cleaned up a bit. *Shit, who's going to clean all of these flowers out?* I wanted to bring them all home with me. Knowing Jeff, he probably paid Jenny to clean it up.

I walked over to the kitchen table and pulled out my phone. Good I had a strong signal. Looking through my calendar, I went back to last November, thinking of the day Jeff and Rebecca would have been together. By my calculations, she would be about thirty weeks. I searched the Internet for a pregnancy calculator and found that mid- August would be her due date.

Just then, I heard Jeff's truck. I jumped up and started to make my way to the door to leave. Before I could get out the door, I knocked over a bucket with Stargazer lilies and bluebonnets. *Shit!* I ran and grabbed some paper towels to clean up the water. I worked as fast as I could before Jeff could walk in.

I hurried and threw away the paper towels. As I turned to leave he walked in the door. He gave me that damn smile of his, and I stopped dead in my tracks. *Okay, Ari, time to grow some fucking balls and just face this shit.*

I smiled back at him. He walked up to me and hugged me. I almost started to cry. *No! I will not shed anymore tears over that bitch.*

"Ari. I love you, baby, so much. Please tell me what's bothering you."

Really? I wanted to laugh out loud. *What a stupid fuck.*

"If you have to ask me that, Jeff, then I certainly don't feel the need to tell you the answer."

He closed his eyes, and leaned his forehead against mine.

"Ari, I'm sorry. I didn't want this weekend to be like this, baby. I wanted it to be special for you. I'm so sorry."

"Me too, Jeff, I just can't seem to forget the fact that you might be a father in two months. That one little problem just seems to be a fucking thorn in my side."

"How do you think I feel? I don't want to have anything to do with Rebecca. She's nuts. You should've heard her just now…"

Oh my god. He called her. My whole body started to shake. *He talked to her on the phone. What did they talk about?* I couldn't breathe.

"Ari, are you okay, honey? Ari?"

I shook my head and held up my hand. I needed a minute to process this.

"You talked to her?"

"Well, yeah. You were the one who told me to fucking call her!"

I know that! Dickwad!

"I know. What did you talk about?"

Jeff stepped away from me and ran his hand through his hair. "I, um, I talked about meeting her for lunch tomorrow. I asked if you could come, and she said no. I couldn't talk her out of the restraining order. I'm sorry, baby."

Oh, gag me. I wanted to throw up at the thought of him having lunch with her.

"S'okay. Where are you having lunch?" I asked, trying to act like none of this was bothering me in the least bit.

"Um, we're meeting at Hula Hut. I guess she's been craving for their Hawaiian fajitas. I'm meeting her there around 11:30."

I had work to do. I needed to get back to Austin. *Now.*

"Okay. Well I have a few errands that I need to run tomorrow, so I'm really ready to go home now. Can we leave, please?"

Jeff tilted up my chin so that his eyes captured mine. I wanted nothing more than to just strip down and spend the rest of the day in bed with him. I tried so hard to give him a normal smile.

His eyes lit up when I smiled. "I love you, Arianna, more than anything. It's all going to be okay. I know this baby isn't mine."

"I love you, too, Jeff, and I pray to God you're right."

***

After Jeff took out my stuff from the Jeep to put into his truck, he headed back to the main house. I took the Jeep back to the barn and started to walk up to the house. I noticed Jeff and Josh were standing at Heather's car with the hood up.

Heather looked like she was going to be sick.

"Hey, what's going on?" I asked noticing Heather trying to hold back tears in her eyes.

"This stupid dumb-ass new car of mine won't start. I bought a new car, thinking it was reliable, and then it fucking breaks down on me!" Heather yelled.

Wow! We all snapped our heads over to Heather. She never swore unless she'd had a few drinks in her.

"What? I'm mad! How am I going to get back to Austin? I have to go to work tomorrow."

I noticed Lynda was sitting on the front porch, looking pissed-off beyond all get out. "What's up with Lynda? She looks pissed," I whispered to Heather.

Heather glanced over at her and then shrugged her shoulders.

"Don't know. I guess she's ready to leave as well, and Josh is her ride. She needs to get back to Austin too."

Jeff shut the hood to Heather's Toyota Camry. "Heather, I think you need to take it to the dealership."

"*What?* That means having it towed to Austin!"

Josh walked up to Heather and took her into his arms. "Don't worry princess. The dealership will pay for it since the car is still under warranty." Josh said.

Heather was now in full-on crying mode. Lynda jumped up and started to walk toward us. Just then an idea popped into my head.

I blocked her route to Josh. "Lynda, Jeff and I are heading to Austin right now. Why don't you ride back with us?" I smiled sweetly at her.

At the same time, Jeff, Heather, and Lynda all said "What?"

The only one who didn't say anything was Josh. He was too busy being in heaven from holding Heather.

Jeff tugged me off to the side. "Ari, we really need to talk, and we can't do that if Lynda is in the car!"

I just glared at him. Then a black BMW pulled up the drive. Gunner's Uncle Jim got out and started to walk over towards us.

"Daddy? What are you doing here?" Lynda asked.

Jim smiled at each of us, but he gave Heather a small frown. I guessed it was because he could tell she'd been crying.

"I drove back out here to pick you up. I didn't think anyone would be heading back into Austin, so I thought I'd better come get you." Jim explained.

I knew Lynda was pissed because she couldn't ride back to Austin with Josh. I could see it all over her face. I was pissed now because I had to drive back to Austin with Jeff alone, and I knew he wanted to talk about Rebecca.

Jeff shook Jim's hand, and they spoke for a few minutes. I helped Heather move her overnight bag and a small suitcase into Josh's truck.

"Ari, why can't I ride back with you and Jeff?" Heather practically begged.

"Heather, Jeff and I really need to talk about this whole bitch Rebecca bullshit."

Even though I wanted to jump at the chance to have Heather to ride with us, I wanted her to get closer to Josh. If it meant driving in a truck alone with Jeff back to Austin, then so be it. The tension between Heather and Josh was getting unbearable.

Heather let out a sigh and gave me a quick hug good-bye. Josh avoided Lynda like she was the plague. He jumped in his truck so damn fast that I had to giggle. I watched as his truck disappeared down the gravel road.

When I turned around, I saw that Lynda was also watching the truck. I instantly got a very bad feeling about this girl, considering the way she'd been hanging all over Josh last night and now today. I knew this would not be the last we saw of Lynda.

After packing Lynda's things into his car, Jim said his goodbyes and drove off. I was going to have to ask Ellie about this Lynda chick.

Jeff and I headed inside to let everyone know that we were leaving. After we said good-bye to Emma, Garrett, my parents, and Matt, we started to make our way to Jeff's truck. Before we left, I noticed when Jeff stopped to say something to Matt. The smile that played across Matt's face gave me butterflies in my stomach. He loved Jeff so much, and Jeff loved him in return.

The ache in my chest grew stronger as I started to get a terrible feeling. For once, I actually feared that this baby was really Jeff's. Then, Jeff walked over to his truck and opened the door for me. I took one last look at my parents and Matt. The urge to cry was growing stronger by the minute.

As soon as he pulled out to the road, Jeff turned on his iPod.

Huh, looks like he's in no mood to talk either. Fine by me.

I leaned my head back, and the next thing I knew, I was dreaming about Jeff holding a baby wrapped in a pink blanket. The smile on his face was like none I'd ever seen before. He looked so happy. Then Rebecca walked up and kissed him on the cheek as he told her he loved her.

I woke up, not realizing that I had just screamed out "no" in my sleep.

"Jesus H. Christ, Ari! You scared the fuck out of me. Did you have a bad dream or something?"

It took me a few seconds to process what I'd just dreamed about. My head snapped over to look at Jeff. *Did I have a bad dream? Really?*

"Ah, normally, when someone wakes up screaming, it's from a bad dream, dickwad!"

Jeff stared straight ahead, but I saw the muscles flexing in his jaw. I wasn't sure why I was being such a bitch to him.

"Maybe you should go back to sleep since you're in a pissy mood."

"Yeah, maybe," I said as I looked out the window and did the one thing I'd told myself I wouldn't do. I cried.

CHAPTER SIX

JEFF

I didn't know what the hell was wrong with Ari. Ever since she had woken up, she had been in a piss-poor mood. It had gotten worse when she found out that I'd called Rebecca. *She's the one who wanted me to call her.*

Fuck this is not how this weekend was supposed to be. Twenty four hours ago, she was so happy, and today it was like she couldn't stand to be around me. On top of all this, I had to go and deal with Rebecca tomorrow.

The first thing I needed to do was work on this restraining order. I knew Ari would be pissed if I kept seeing Rebecca alone. I wanted to slam my fist on the steering wheel. *Why the hell is this happening to us?* We were finally together.

I looked over at Ari, and I swore if I'd not known any better, I'd think she was crying.

"Ari, baby, are you crying?"

She just shook her head and kept staring out the window. *Fuck me.* This whole thing with Rebecca must be tearing her apart inside. *I'll be so glad to meet with Rebecca and get this shit over with. No way is that kid mine. No way.*

***

We drove the rest of the way to Austin in silence. Ari never once looked at me. I wished that I knew what to do to take away her pain. I was dying inside. I needed to take her out tonight or something.

"Hey, baby, you want to go out to dinner and maybe some dancing at Rebels?" I asked as I reached over and took her hand.

I glanced over at her as she turned to me. *Holy shit. H*er eyes were bloodshot from crying. She shook her head and then attempted to smile at me. My whole damn world just shattered at the sight of her upset.

"Ari, I promise you, this is all going to be okay. You have to trust me."

"How do you know that it's all going to be okay, Jeff? Please tell me if you have some inside information that you haven't shared with me yet. I can't possibly see how you think it's going to be okay. You're having a baby. You're having a fucking baby with *someone else,* and we just got engaged. She will forever be in our lives, Jeff. I'm sorry if that freaks me the fuck out."

"Let's just wait and see about tomorrow. Okay, baby? I just want to get back home and crawl back into bed with you."

"I want to go back to my place for awhile," she whispered.

I snapped my head over to look at her. *What the hell?*

"What? Why? For Christ's sake, Ari, we just got engaged, and we've barely even spoken to each other. Now you want to stay at your place tonight?" I was so pissed that my hands started shaking.

"I just need to go home for a few hours Jeff. That's all. I need to think about a few things and get my head wrapped around this whole thing. I'll come back to your place later tonight. I'm going to need my Jeep anyway since you're meeting..." Ari's voice trailed off.

Jesus, now she can't even say her name. This was so fucked up, and I had no idea what to do about it. I should have talked to Garrett this morning. *Damn it!*

"Okay, as long as you plan on coming back tonight, Ari, I don't want to be away from you. I need to be with you."

Ari smiled at me. We drove in silence until I pulled up to her place. I helped bring her bags into her house, and then I watched as she collapsed on the sofa. I knelt down in front of her, and she leaned forward putting her forehead up against mine.

"I love you, Ari. I'll always love you, baby, and no one or nothing is going to get in the way of that."

She sucked in a breath and pulled away from me. The tears rolling down her face about gutted me right on the spot.

"I hope you're right, Jeff. I really hope that you're right."

CHAPTER SEVEN

JOSH

The moment I jumped into my truck the excitement I felt about Heather riding back to Austin with me vanished in an instant. I looked over at her, and I swore that if looks could kill, I would be long gone. I tried to give her a smile, and I noticed when she somewhat relaxed.

We both reached for the radio at the same time, our hands bumping into each other. *What the fuck?* There goes that damn feeling throughout my body. Every time this girl touched me or smiled at me, it was like an electric bolt ran through me. I'd never felt this before with anyone.

"I'm sorry. That was rude of me. It's your car." Heather said before turning to stare out the window.

For some reason, the idea of ever hurting her sickened me. All I could think about was trying to cheer her up from the sour mood she was in. I knew that fate was on my side when her new car wouldn't start. Luckily, Lynda's dad showed up when he did. I almost wanted to jump for joy when I saw him get out of that BMW.

"Don't worry about it, Heather. What type of music do you like?" *Shit*....I realized then that I really didn't know much about Heather at all.

The only time we had ever really talked was a few nights ago at Gunner's bachelor party after the girls crashed it. Even though Heather had been pretty drunk, we had mostly talked about her parents, who passed away a year ago.

"Um, I really like all kinds of music. I'm pretty fond of country, but Christina Aguilera is probably one of my favorites," she admitted.

I wanted to laugh at the memory of Heather and the girls getting wasted while painting those damn pails for the s'mores. Heather and Ari had been dancing to Christina Aguilera's "Red Hot Kinda

Love," and I had sworn that it was Heather's crazy way to flirt with me. *Shit if it didn't work, too.* I had to take three goddamn cold showers that night after every time I'd thought about it.

I had bought the whole damn CD the next day.

I smiled at her and reached down to get my iPod to play the album. After a quick search, that song started. Heather snapped her head over at me, and the blush that moved up her cheeks caused me to smile at her.

"Why are you playing this song?" Heather asked.

"I thought you just said that you liked Christina Aguilera." I turned my head back to watch the road, and I did everything I could not to laugh.

"Josh, I'm not stupid. I know why you played this song, you asshole!"

"Holy shit, Heather. I'm going to have to wash your mouth out if you keep swearing like that." I said with a laugh.

"Why did my car have to break down?" Heather said barely loud enough for me to hear her.

What's her problem anyway?

"Why are you so against me, Heather? What have I ever done to you to make you hate me so much?"

Heather sucked in a breath. "You think I hate you?"

I let out a small laugh. "Yeah. What else would you call it, Heather?"

I watched as she turned back to look out the window at the passing fields. She stayed quiet for a few minutes, and then she startled me when she started to talk again.

"Josh, I don't hate you. Really, it's the opposite. I've had a lot to deal with in my life this past year. I just can't...I can't let anyone in right now. I don't think I could stand to lose another person I cared about."

My heart was beating a mile a minute. *What the hell is this girl doing to me?* I couldn't even think straight to form my next words. *What did she mean? It's the opposite. Does that mean she...oh holy fuck...she can't love me ....can she? She pretty much just said she cared about me. Didn't she?*

"Okay, Josh, I see the wheels spinning in your head. You can stop over-thinking what I just said. I only meant that I like you… a lot..um, as a friend only."

"Well that deflated my hopes a bit. Why only as a friend Heather? You have to know that I'm interested in more than friendship."

Heather let out a laugh and looked at me. "You? Interested in something more than friendship? What like fuck buddies or something? Not gonna happen with me, Josh. Ever!"

"Jesus, Heather, I would never think of you like that. I can't even believe you just said that."

"Please, Josh, don't act all shocked that I said that. I know how you are, and I know about all the women you've been with. Well, no, thank you. I don't intend on being another notch in your belt. So, I think we need to keep this strictly friendship only. That's all I'm interested in."

I sat there, stunned. I'd never heard Heather utter a hurtful word to anyone in the last year that I'd known her. When I looked over at her, I was pretty sure that I saw her quickly wipe away a tear. *Fuck me.*

"I'm not really sure what to say after your declaration of what you really think about me, but I would never think of you in such a disrespectful way. I mean, I haven't even had sex in… anyway, it's been awhile since I was even out on a date. I know that I've made some bad choices, but really, none of those girls…"

"Josh, please. Can we just talk about something else or just not talk at all?" She looked out the passenger window, sighing loudly.

Son of a bitch, I think things just got worse between us. I leaned over and turned up the music just a little louder. The silence in the truck was almost unbearable. The sick feeling taking over my stomach had me wishing that I had just driven Lynda instead of Heather back to Austin.

***

After driving for almost an hour, I got an idea. "Are you in a rush to get back to Austin?"

Heather turned to look at me, and I had to catch my breath at the sight of her beautiful blue eyes.

"Well, no, I'm not really in a big hurry. Why?"

I smiled at her, and she slowly let a smile come across her face.

"I thought that maybe we could take a small ten-minute detour and head into Marble Falls for lunch. Maybe we could grab a bite to eat at the Bluebonnet Café?"

Heather's smile faded for a quick second, but then it appeared again. Her eyes seemed to fill with tears before she let out a small laugh.

"I love the Bluebonnet Café. My parents used to take me there all the time, especially when I was younger. My dad loved their coconut cream pie. I can practically smell it, just thinking about it. He always wanted to retire in Marble Falls. They both loved it there. They were…, well, they were actually heading to Marble Falls to look at land when they had their accident."

Heather's voice trailed off before she attempted to smile again at me.

Oh God, I just brought up all those bad memories for her. I am such an asshole.

"Shit, Heather, I'm so sorry. I had no idea. I just thought that since we were so close, we could stop there. I used to love going to Marble Falls when I was a kid. I haven't been in so long. I thought that a Chocolate Meringue pie sounded pretty damn good, but I completely understand if you want to pass."

"No! I would love to go. I think it'll be good for me. I've been trying so hard to push away memories of my parents, but I really think this is just what I need to help me move on. I love the idea of stopping in Marble Falls."

I was pretty sure that Heather saw the breath I was holding in as I slowly let it out. I thought for sure that I'd really fucked it up with her after she'd mentioned that her parents had been killed on their way to Marble Falls.

***

I turned onto Highway 281, making our way into Marble Falls. Traffic was a bitch and I quickly saw why. It looked like there was a street fair on the main street of the town. I was lucky enough to find a parking spot right behind the restaurant. I jumped out of the truck and jogged over to Heather's side. I think I caught her off guard when I opened her door and helped her out of the truck.

She let a small smile spread across her face, and I swore that it felt like my knees were going to buckle out from underneath my ass. This shit was weird. No girl had ever had this type of effect on me.

The moment I reached down to take her hand in mine, I felt a jolt run from my fingertips to my toes. I was shocked that she let me hold her hand as we started to walk into the restaurant. I glanced down at her, and as she looked up at me, she smiled the sweetest goddamn smile. Even if nothing ever came out of this whole thing with Heather, I knew that I would forever remember this moment, walking into one of my favorite restaurants while holding hands with the girl of my dreams.

The girl of my dreams. Where the hell did that come from?

CHAPTER EIGHT

HEATHER

Sweet Jesus…. I thought just coming to Marble Falls was going to make me nervous, but, the moment Josh took my hand in his, I knew that I was beyond nervous. I was scared to death. He looked down at me with his beautiful green eyes, and my heart just melted. I couldn't help myself. I had to smile at him. *Why did he have to take my hand?* I'd been fighting my attraction to him for a year now. I couldn't let him into my heart. *I can't, and I won't.*

Once we stepped inside the Blue Bonnet Café, the memories came flooding back. I could almost hear my dad saying he couldn't wait to have a piece of pie as my mother laughed that sweet and gentle laugh of hers.

I miss them.

Josh must have sensed how I was feeling because he squeezed my hand a little tighter as we waited to be seated. When I looked up at him, I had to catch my breath. His smile was just amazing. He had a single dimple on the right side of his cheek. Even if he barely smiled, you could still see it. In Ari and Ellie's words, he had a panty-melting smile. *Yep, he sure does.* His laugh sent tingles throughout my whole body while I felt butterflies in my stomach. I'd never been this attracted to a guy before.

Why does he have to be such a man whore?

"You hungry?" Josh asked.

I didn't think I was up until this moment. "Yes, actually, I'm starving."

Josh looked up to the hostess as she walked toward us. Her face lit up like a Christmas tree when she got a good look at Josh. *Is she blushing? Oh, for Pete's sake, he's just another guy, lady.*

Okay, well, another guy with an amazing build, a beautiful smile, green eyes you could get lost in, and light brown hair that you just want to run your hands through.

Oh my god, what the hell is wrong with me? I'd been around Ari too long these last few weeks. She'd gotten me drunk three times, and one of those times resulted in me dancing and flirting with Josh. I was still embarrassed as hell thinking about that night.

"Hey there, y'all. Welcome to the Blue Bonnet Café! Will it just be the two of y'all today?" the hostess asked, her voice purring as she stared at Josh the whole time.

Ugh, Josh turned to look at me and let out a small laugh.

"Yep, just me and my *friend* here," he said giving me a wink.

Bastard.

"Well then, follow me, and I'll show y'all to your seat."

She turned, leading us to our table, and I swore that she couldn't have shaken her ass more if she tried. I glanced up at Josh, who was looking everywhere but at her ass.

Once we sat down, our waitress came over, and it was a repeat of what the hostess just did. She stared, she flirted, and he ignored her while he just looked at me. *Oh brother. What would it be like to go on an actual date with him?* I'm sure he has girls all over him no matter where he goes. Every time we had ever gone to Rebels, he had usually danced the night away with fifty different girls. During the last few times though, he had pretty much turned down every girl while he just sat at the table talking to me.

"Hey y'all. What can I get ya to drink?"

Josh just smiled at me and then turned to the waitress. *Good Lord.* The smile he flashed her caused *my* panties to melt, and from the look on her face, she was having the same reaction. *Bastard!*

"I'll just have a glass of water, please. Heather?"

"Diet Coke, please."

The waitress asked if we were ready to order but, Josh asked for a few more minutes.

We sat there in silence while we each looked over the menu. My heart was beating like crazy. *Damn it, why does he have to be so gosh darn cute?*

Man whore. Just remember he's a player, Heather.

I glanced up and saw him staring at me. Oh dear Lord. His eyes were so beautiful, I could get lost in them. I smiled at him, and he smiled back at me with the sweetest smile I'd ever seen. *Yep, I'm so screwed.*

"You ready to order princess?" Josh asked.

Princess?

"Ah, yep. I mean if you're ready, then I'm ready."

Josh smiled and I couldn't help but smile back.

Our waitress came walking back up and turned to face Josh. "So what will it be, handsome?"

What the hell? Oh. My. God. What a bitch. I peeked over at Josh and noticed he was, yet again, looking at me. This time his smile...*oh, holy shit.* I'd never noticed he had a crooked smile. *Deep breaths, Heather.* This was a mistake. *Breathe in.....breathe out....do not look at him.*

I looked down at my menu as Josh began to talk to the waitress.

"I'll have the catfish plate two fillets with okra, mashed potatoes, and a side salad with ranch."

She slowly smiled at him. Practically purring, she said, "Perfect choice, handsome."

Oh, gag me. I had to clear my throat just to remind her that I was sitting here. I honestly believed that she would've walked away, never even bothering to take my order. Josh laughed a little, and that just pissed me off even more.

"And for you?" the waitress asked, barely glancing at me.

I rolled my eyes at Josh and looked up at her. I really wanted to pull an Ari and tell her to back the fuck off, but I did what I always did. I kept quiet.

"Yes, um…I'll have the grilled chicken breast sandwich."

"You want fries?"

"No, thank you. I'll take a side salad with ranch, too."

With that, she gave Josh one last smile and walked away. *Jesus, is this how it is everywhere he goes? Girls just falling all over him trying to get his attention.* Another reason it could never work.

Good Lord, that was a joke," I mumbled.

Josh was still smiling at me as he shook his head. "What's a joke, princess?"

That was twice he had called me princess, and each time, it sent my stomach into a nose dive. *What the hell, Heather? Pull it together. Damn Ari for not letting me drive back with her and Jeff.*

"The way she was flirting with you, I'm sorry but we could actually be on a date. It was just rude. That's all."

Josh laughed again, running his hand through his hair.

Oh my god, it's getting hot in here. Look away, Heather. Look. Away.

"Can I ask you something, Josh?"

"You want to make this a date?" he asked with a smirk.

"No, I do not!"

Josh sat up straighter, and his face turned serious. It was almost too serious.

"Heather, you can ask me anything you want anytime you want."

"Why do you keep calling me princess?"

Josh let a smile play across his face as he reached across the table, taking my hand in his. Everything in me was screaming for me to pull my hand away, but I couldn't. It felt so nice to feel someone's touch. Ever since my parents passed away, I longed for someone to touch me in a way that made me feel safe and loved.

"I call you princess because you deserve to be treated like one," he said softly.

Holy hell. I was not expecting him to say that. *Just when I think I have him figured out, he goes off and does something so...un-Josh like.*

I could feel the heat moving into my cheeks. Josh reached up and ran his hand down the side of my face. The warmth from his hand was driving me crazy.

"You're so beautiful, Heather, both inside and out. I've never met anyone in my life that always puts her friends first, and would do anything for them. You amaze me."

"Josh...I."

Just then, the waitress walked up and reached between us grabbing Josh's glass.

"More water?"

I pulled my hand out from his and glared at the bitch. She totally did that shit on purpose. I looked back over at Josh, and he looked pissed off. His hand was running through his hair again. I wanted to do that so damn bad. His hair looked so soft. Then, Josh did something I had not expected him to do.

"Listen, um.. Josh paused, looking at her name tag. "Casey, we really need some privacy, I hate to sound like a prick, but, maybe after our food arrives, I'll just flag you down if we need anything. Okay?"

She just stood there in shock. If I didn't have the urge to laugh, I totally would have kicked him for being so rude.

"Well, of course. Can I get you another Diet Coke, miss?"

I just nodded my head. Even if I tried to talk, I knew that I would lose it and laugh my ass off. I couldn't even look at Josh. I could feel the heat from his stare. Once she walked away, I looked up at him.

"Oh my god, Josh. Asshole much?" I started to giggle.

Josh reached over and took my hand in his again.

Okay, so no harm can come from us holding hands, right? Friends hold hands.

***

After we ate, we both ordered a piece of pie. I got the apple pie, and Josh got the coconut cream pie. With my first bite, the memories were almost too much to handle.

Josh asked Casey about what was going on in town. She told us all about Meet on Main. They had dancing, live music, and shopping. Josh asked if I wanted to check it out. I really didn't want this afternoon to end, so I said yes.

We walked a few blocks over and spent the next thirty minutes walking around, visiting all the booths and shops.

Memories of my mom and dad kept flooding my mind.

I missed them. Even a year later, the pain was still so raw. *Oh god, maybe it was a bad idea coming to Marble Falls.*

Josh must have sensed how I was feeling. As we walked past the band, he took my hand and led me out to where everyone was dancing. The band was playing a cover of Jason Aldean's "The Only Way I Know". It didn't take long before Josh was spinning me around on the pavement. I hadn't had that much fun in… I don't know how long. *My god, this guy knows how to dance!*

After Josh and I cut up the dance floor through two more songs, the band took a break. They switched it over to music so that everyone could keep dancing. Blake Shelton's "Over" started to play. Josh just smiled at me and pulled me into him. Even though I was only five foot three and he was six two, we fit together so perfectly. The warmth of his body made me feel so safe.

I relaxed in his arms for the first time in more than a year. I never wanted this feeling to end, but I knew that it had to. As much as I wanted, there was no way I could ever let Josh Hayes into my heart. *Never.*

CHAPTER NINE

ARI

I woke up from a terrible nightmare. *Fuck a duck!* If I had one more dream about Jeff and Rebecca, I swore that I would never go to sleep again. I looked over at the clock. It was 6:30. Jeff must already be up and out for a run.

I picked up my cell phone and called Amanda.

"Hey sweets. What's up?" Amanda said. She sounded like she couldn't breathe.

"What the hell is wrong with you? Oh god! Are you having sex?"

Amanda laughed. "No! I'm at the gym, running on the treadmill. It's something you should be doing, Ari."

"Yeah, whatever, bitch. I need you today. Are you free?"

"Yep, Brad is helping his dad out, so I'm free the whole day. Why? What's up?"

I took a deep breath and then started to tell Amanda about my plan.

"Holy hell, Ari! Are you fucking nuts?"

"No, I'm not nuts. I really don't think this baby is Jeff's. I have to see her, Amanda. I have to find out why she picked now to tell him that she's pregnant. I need to see her with my own eyes. Manda…please do this for me," I begged.

"Gesh, Ari. Damn it. Okay. What do I need to do?"

"Meet me at Haylcyon in thirty minutes. I found out yesterday that Crysti is working this morning. Then, you and I are having lunch at Hula Hut today."

"Oh shit. I have a bad feeling, Ari, a very bad feeling about this."

"Just shut up, and get your ass over to the coffee shop. Parking is a bitch, so just pay to park."

I hung up with Amanda and started to get dressed. I didn't have time for a shower, so I just threw my hair up in a ponytail and tried to make myself look somewhat presentable. Thank God I kept clothes over at Jeff's. I picked out a pair of black capri pants, a light blue tank top, and flip flops. Now, I was ready to get to the bottom of this Rebecca mess.

Just as I was walking into the kitchen to grab a bottle of water, Jeff came through the front door.

"Hey, baby! What are you doing up this early? I thought that maybe we could continue with what we started last night," Jeff said as he walked up and wrapped his arms around me.

Even sweaty and stinky, he smelled like heaven. The warmth from his arms relaxed me immediately. He would freak out if he knew what I was going to do today.

I let out a small laugh. I had to catch my breath. *Damn, he's so handsome.* I reached up on my toes and gave him a kiss, filling it with as much passion as I could. I wished we could just go back in time and admit how we really felt about one another instead of acting so stupid. Rebecca wouldn't even be a second thought right now.

"Wow. What did I do to deserve that?" Jeff asked kissing the tip of my nose.

My heart was breaking. *Please, God. Please don't let this baby be his.*

"Nothing. I just wanted to kiss you. Do I need a reason to kiss you now?"

Jeff threw his head back and laughed. "Nope! Feel free to kiss me anytime or anywhere you'd like baby."

I giggled and reached for my purse. "I have to go. I'm meeting Amanda for breakfast, and then I think we're going shopping."

Jeff's smile disappeared as he ran his hands through his hair. I knew he was so torn about meeting Rebecca on his own, and I couldn't be mad at him. He needed to meet with the bitch to get this over with. My hands started to shake.

"Ari, I really don't want to meet with her today. You believe that, don't you?"

Holy hell. I wanted to throw up just thinking about him seeing her again.

"Of course, I know you don't want to meet with her, but….but you have to. You have to do this and just get it over with. I'm sure that it's gonna be okay. Just meet with her, hear her out, and then we'll take it from there. If she's seven months now, then she's due around the middle of August. We just have to wait until the baby is born, and then we can find out for sure."

Jeff looked like he wanted to say something, but he stopped himself. I was sure that he was about to ask what would happen if the baby was his. *Jesus, Mary, and Joseph, please don't even say it, Jeff, or I'll puke.* I tried to smile, but I was sure that it was a bad attempt at looking happy.

"I love you, Ari. I love you and only you. I always have, and no matter what happens, I always will. We're moving out to the property in a few weeks, so it'll just be you and me, baby. *You and me.*"

He pulled me into him, and I did everything I could not to cry. I pulled away, smiling, I reached up to kiss him again.

"It's going to be alright, Jeff. Don't worry. I really have to run. I love you. Try to have a good day and…well, good luck with your lunch."

Jeff kissed me with such sweetness that it was all I could do to get out the front door. I jumped into my Jeep and backed out of the driveway as fast as I could.

After I got a block away, I pulled over and cried my eyes out. I had a very bad feeling that things were not going to turn out how I so desperately wanted them to.

After I dried my tears, I headed over Halcyon.

As I was walking up to the coffee shop, I saw Amanda was waiting outside for me.

We hugged, and Amanda held me tightly for just a few more seconds than usual.

Then, she whispered in my ear,

"Don't worry. We'll kick her fucking ass the moment the baby is out."

I had to laugh. I missed Ellie. My heart started to ache from thinking about it all. All this shit was going on, and my best friend was thousands of miles away. She called last night, but I acted like everything was perfect. Perfect engagement, perfect life, perfect everything. Pesh.

The moment we walked through the door, my eyes caught Crysti's. Her smile faded instantly, and I felt a bit of excitement, knowing that I was the last person she expected to see this morning. My morning was working for me, she was working the counter. Amanda and I walked up to her, and I acted surprised to see her. She seemed much more shocked to see me, and I noticed when she looked down at my engagement ring.

"Crysti right? You're Rebecca's friend, aren't you?" Amanda asked.

Crysti pulled her eyes away from me. She smiled at Amanda nodding her head.

"Ah, yeah. You're, um, Jeff and Gunner's friends right?"

Oh Jesus. I wanted to laugh at that one.

"Well, I'm a friend of both yes, Ari's engaged to Jeff," Amanda said smiling as big as she could.

"Engaged? Didn't you get married this weekend?" Crysti asked, clearly confused.

This just got very interesting.

"What made you think that I was getting married this weekend?" I asked.

"Oh, well… I mean one of the guys from the football team was here last week, and he mentioned a wedding. I heard your name and Jeff's, so I guess I just assumed y'all were getting married."

I was so going to have fun with this. "Nope, that was Gunner and Ellie who got married. Jeff asked me to marry him Saturday night after the wedding." *Ah! Chew on that, you little stupid blonde bitch.*

"Wait. *What?* Gunner got married? Oh, wow… I mean, I guess I just never thought he was the kind to settle down."

"Yep, well, when you meet the love of your life, you tend to change your ways," Amanda said. "By the way, can I get a salted caramel mocha frapp?"

Yeah… well, I guess so. Wait a minute. Did you say that Jeff asked you to marry him on Saturday night? Even after he knew about the baby, he still…" Crysti trailed off, not finishing her thought.

Oh. My. God. That lying bitch. Rebecca thought Jeff was getting married, so she decided to pull out the last-ditch attempt.

I always thought that Crysti wasn't the brightest one of the group, and she certainly didn't let me down. Unfortunately, she realized her mistake before she finished telling us about Rebecca and the baby.

Amanda looked back over to Crysti while I held my breath.

"So, was that why she called Jeff last week? She was making some last-ditch effort to get him back? I would think that she would've told him about the baby as soon as she found out," Amanda said.

Crysti looked around and then back at me. "Listen, I don't know why Rebecca waited so long to tell Jeff. The baby is his though. She knows that for a fact. She was, um…she was just scared. She was really scared when she found out, and she was waiting for the right way to tell him. She thought that he should know before he got married, but, looks like he isn't married yet. Now, is he?"

Amanda stepped between Crysti and me. It was a damn good thing she did because I was ready to leap across that counter to knock the shit out of this girl.

"Listen here, Crysti. You tell your friend, Rebecca, that there is no way in *hell* she is ever going to keep Jeff and Ari apart. If you were smart, you would probably refrain from saying shit like that around Ari. There's a reason your crazy-ass friend put a restraining order out against her," Amanda said.

Moving around Amanda, I glared at Crysti with a smile. "I don't think we'll be staying for coffee. Thanks Sweets. You've been *very* helpful this morning."

I turned and started to head out the door. *Why do I feel like I'm about to cry?* This was a whole new game now. *So, that bitch wants Jeff? Well, she's going to have a goddamn fight on her hands.*

Amanda was pissed. "Jesus H. Christ, Ari I wanted to knock the shit out of her. Are you thinking what I'm thinking?"

"That crazy-ass Rebecca panicked when she heard Jeff was getting married? Yep, I'm thinking the same thing, Manda. Come on, let's go shopping for a few hours. I have a lunch date that I can't be late for."

***

Amanda and I spent the next few hours shopping at Barton Creek Square, and then we headed over to Hula Hut. I bought a hat to hide my hair, in hoping that neither Jeff nor Rebecca would see me.

Jeff and the bitch should be there by now.

Amanda walked in first and asked the hostess about a pregnant girl who was suppose to meet someone here. The hostess knew who Amanda was talking about and remembered that she and her boyfriend were sitting outside. I so wanted to scream that he was not her boyfriend. Knowing me so well, Amanda gave me *the look*, and I just smiled instead. We asked to sit close to them but not where they could see us because we wanted to surprise them. We explained he just came into town, so we didn't want to interrupt their reunion until after they were done eating. After that long bullshit story- it was true...kind of.

The hostess finally sat us near them. We were still inside the restaurant, but we had a clear view of where they sat outside.

"Okay, so what's your plan now?" Amanda asked before she took a sip of her tea.

I looked over and saw Rebecca smiling. After she said something, I watched Jeff put his hand on her stomach. The smile that spread across his face gutted me. I was going to throw up. *Motherfucker.*

"Oh, that bitch is good, isn't she? Ari...look at me."

I pulled my eyes away from Jeff and turned to look at Amanda. "Oh my god, what if it really is his baby Amanda? Oh. My. God. I can't do this. I think I'm gonna be sick."

"Ari, look at me. You and I both know that's not his baby. Reach down in yourself and pull out that bullshit your mother's always feeding you. You're going to beat this bitch at her own game."

"How, Amanda? Should I get pregnant?" Actually, the idea was not far from my mind. With everything that has happened in the last few days, I had forgotten to take my birth control pills again. The last time I took them was on Thursday. I started adding up the days in my head. *Four days with no pill? Shit!*

"No, I'm not telling you to do that." Amanda tilted her head and looked at me.

"Holy hell, Ari! Please tell me you didn't."

"I didn't what?"

"Did you do something to get yourself pregnant?"

Some friend she is. "Bitch you know me better than that! Gesh, Amanda. I do have a small problem."

"And what is it?"

"I haven't taken my birth control pills since Thursday. I just remembered this morning."

Amanda's mouth dropped open. "What the hell, Ari!"

"I know, Amanda, I know. I'm making an appointment with my doctor for…" I paused as an idea hit me. I looked back over to where Rebecca and Jeff were sitting, and I saw Rebecca's iPhone sitting on the table. *Perfect!*

"Amanda! I need you to go over and say hi to them."

Amanda looked at me like I just asked her to take a piss in front of everyone at the restaurant.

"Excuse me? What did you just say?" she asked, clearly confused.

"Okay, listen. I need you to go over there and say hi, place your napkin on the table over her phone. Then, pick up the napkin with her phone when you leave."

"Oh. My. God. Are you fucking crazy, Ari? Ellie is getting back soon 'cause I can't handle you alone."

I glanced over to their table again and saw Jeff laughing. *Yeah, he really hated this lunch. Bastard!* I looked back at Amanda and sat up straighter.

"Amanda, I need her phone. I need to see if she has any appointments in there. I need to find out who her OB is. Please do this for me. *Please?*"

When Amanda peeked back at their table, she saw Jeff smiling at something the bitch was saying. Amanda shook her head and turned back to face me. Fire was burning in her eyes. *God how I love my friends!*

"Okay. I'm only doing this because somehow that witch is getting him to laugh, and he looks too goddamn comfortable sitting there with her. Bastard!"

Yep, I love my friends. I watched as Amanda went through the door, heading outside to their table. As soon as she walked up to their table Rebecca's smile faded while Jeff sat up straighter and looked around. *Yeah, you better look around at who's watching you. Jerk.*

Amanda put her napkin over Rebecca's phone as she leaned over to say something to Jeff. They talked for about another minute before Amanda turned to Rebecca to say something to her. Rebecca smiled and nodded her head. Bending down a little, Amanda touched Rebecca's stomach while she used her other hand to scoop up the napkin and phone.

Yes! I almost jumped up and shouted. I did a small fist pump and smiled at Amanda as she walked back in with a shit-eatin' grin on her face. She avoided our table and went straight to the other side of the restaurant. *Damn, she's good!*

I looked back toward Jeff and Rebecca's table, and sure enough, he was watching Amanda walk back in. Turning, he looked at the bitch as she just smiled at him. I watched them talk while I waited for Amanda to get her ass back to the table. It sure did look like they were having a cozy little conversation. Then, their conversation seemed to shift. Jeff didn't seem to be smiling or laughing, and Rebecca's face turned white as a ghost. *Shit! I wish I could hear what they are saying.*

"Hey, sorry about that," Amanda said, finally returning to the table.

"Jesus, Mary, and Joseph you bitch! You scared me half to death, Amanda," I yelled, trying to catch my breath.

Amanda just shook her head and handed me the phone. "Here. I can't believe that I just did that! Oh man, it felt so damn good being so bad. I really should get into private investigation. I think I would kick ass at it. Wait until I tell Heather and Ellie what I did. They won't believe it!"

"Well, expect both of them to give your ass a lecture. Okay, let's see what this bitch has down on her calendar."

Amanda was trying to lean over the table to see what I was looking at and it was really annoying.

"What the hell, Mand? Do you mind?"

Amanda sat back down, and I started to look at Rebecca's appointments.

"Oh. My. God! She goes to the same doctor as me," I said looking at Amanda's shocked face.

"No way, Ari. No freakin' way. When is her next appointment?"

"Almost two weeks. This is perfect. I know exactly what we have to do."

"Oh dear god. Do I even want to know, Ari?"

Smiling at Amanda, I handed her the phone. The next thing on my list was to make that appointment I kept putting off with Dr. Wyatt.

"And how do you propose I give her back the phone?"

"Just simply say that you picked it up by accident."

The waiter came with our bill, and I paid in cash, telling him to keep the change. Amanda got up and walked back outside. I stood over by the door and watched. Rebecca looked pissed off when Amanda handed over her phone. I had to let out a laugh when Amanda just shrugged her shoulders before she turned to walk away.

Rebecca's eyes followed Amanda as she headed straight toward me. Immediately, Rebecca spotted me, and I did the only thing that came to my mind. I took off my hat, let my hair fall down, and I held up my middle finger. I smiled sweetly at the bitch before turning around to leave.

By the time I made it out to the parking lot, Amanda had caught up to me. I knew we only had a few minutes before Jeff would be coming after me. I had no doubt in my mind that Rebecca would tell him I was there.

"Ari! Jeff yelled.

Yep, stupid bitch is playing right into my hands. I turned around and smiled as Jeff jogged up to me.

"What in the hell are you doing here, Ari?"

"I was having lunch," I said as I gave him an innocent smile.

Jeff looked over at Amanda and then back at me.

"Oh my god. Y'all took her phone on purpose, didn't you? What's your game, Ari?"

What? He did not just say that to me.

"What's my game, Jeff? My game? What's yours? For someone who can't stand that girl, you two sure did have a nice little lunch. You were all laughing and smiling and touchin' on her stomach. Did you enjoy yourself, dickwad?"

"Ari, I can't believe you were spying on me, and the worst of it is that you might have made Rebecca upset."

"Holy hell," Amanda said as she took two steps away from Jeff.

"*I* might have made *Rebecca* upset? Are you kidding me, Jeff? You're an asshole." Turning away from him, I started to walk off.

He reached for my arm and spun me around.

"That's not what I meant, Ari. It's just that she said she can't get upset. It's something about being at high risk for going into labor early. That's why I was trying to be nice and not jump down her throat. Listen, can we just talk about this later when I get back home?"

I could not believe how fucking stupid he was. *She couldn't get upset. Lying bitch.* She was setting the whole thing up, so she could have the baby early.

"Let go of me, you stupid fucking-twatwaffling dickwad."

"Ari, please wait."

I jerked my arm out from his. I couldn't believe how stupid he was being. "You know what, Jeff? You can believe whatever that lying bitch wants to tell you. I thought that you were smarter than that. Did you ever think that she came up with that whole "high risk" bullshit so that you would play nice with her? Why don't you ask to go to her next doctor's appointment with her? How about that? Now that Daddy is in the picture, I'm sure she wants you to go to all the appointments with her."

I was so upset that I started shaking.

Amanda walked up and took my hand in hers. As she glared at Jeff, she said, "Really, Jeff, I can't even believe you. Let's go, Ari."

"Ari, please wait, baby."

I stopped dead in my tracks closed my eyes, and took several deep breaths. Opening my eyes again, I slowly turned around to look at him.

"Baby, can we talk about this when I get home?" Jeff's voice almost sounded like he was pleading.

"Why don't you stop by my place on your way home? I'll be staying there tonight. I need time to be alone and think."

The look in Jeff's eyes about gutted me, but all I had to do was remember his smile as he touched Rebecca's stomach.

"Sure... yeah... okay, Ari. I'll stop by your place. Are you going straight home now?"

"No, I have a few errands to run, and then I'm taking Amanda back to her car. I'll be home in a few hours. You better get back in there. You wouldn't want to upset the baby mama."

***

As Amanda and I started to walk up the hill to the parking lot, I felt my legs getting weaker. Amanda pulled me up and kept me walking.

"Just wait until we get in the car, Ari. Then, you can let go."

The moment I sat in the car and shut the door, I let out a scream so loud that I thought Amanda was going to jump out of the car.

"Better, sweets?" Amanda asked after unplugging her ears.

"If only a scream could make it better, Amanda. Did you see how big she is? There's no way she's only seven months pregnant."

As I looked over at my friend, I let the tears fall.

The last time I had felt this sick to my stomach was when Jeff and I had first kissed at the ranch, and he'd told me it was all a mistake.

"Ari, don't give up now. The fight has only just begun."

I smiled at Amanda and wiped the tears from my eyes. I picked up my cell phone and scheduled an appointment with Dr. Wyatt for next Monday at 2 p.m.

I was not giving up. Jeff was mine. I would not let some lying bitch take him from me, even if I thought that lying bitch might actually be telling the truth.

CHAPTER TEN

JEFF

As I stood there watching Ari walk away from me, my heart was breaking. *Shit!* Shoving my hands through my hair, I turned to walk back to the restaurant. *Why the hell did Ari come here? Does she not trust me? Does she want to get put in jail? Damn it!* The moment Rebecca had seen Ari, she about flipped out.

Rebecca was on the phone when I walked back up to the table.

"Listen, I can't talk. I'll call you back. Yes, I know, I heard you, Crysti. You said it's important. I'll call you back later."

I sat down as she was hanging up.

She put her hands on her stomach, and started to fan herself.

"Oh, wow. It sure is hot out here. Do you want to go next door and get an iced coffee or something?"

I shook my head no. *Maybe Ari's right, and Rebecca has been playing me this whole time.* There was only one way to find out. Just get to the point, Jeff.

"Listen, Rebecca, I'm re ally done with this whole let's play-nice bullshit. We need to talk about this baby. I'm telling you that there is no way this baby is mine."

"Well, Jeff, I'm telling you that you're the father. You were the only person I slept with during that time frame, and afterward I found a piece of the condom in my panties."

She let a smile play across her face, and I just wanted to slap it off. Just then, I looked down at her stomach, and I could see the baby moving. My heart jumped at the sight of it. *What if this baby is mine?*

"Fine, Rebecca, if this is the game we're going to play, then let's play it. When is your next doctor's appointment?" She sat up a little straighter in her chair and started to fiddle around with her napkin.

"It's in two weeks."

"I want to go with you. Since you waited until you were seven months to drop this on me, I think it's only fair that I get to come to all your appointments from now on."

"Um, okay…sure Jeff, that's fine. I don't have the doctor's information with me, so can I just text it to you later?"

"You don't have the doctor's info in your phone, Rebecca? No number or nothing?" I asked skeptically.

She let out a nervous laugh. "Of course, I have Dr. Wyatt's number, Jeff. I just meant that I don't have the address. I'll text you the day and time of the appointment along with the address this evening. Do you want to pick me you up, so we can drive there together? Maybe we can grab dinner afterwards?"

Oh shit, here we go. "Rebecca, I need you to know that I asked Ari to marry me last Saturday night. I love *her*, and I'll always love her. Even if this baby turns out to be mine, Ari is going to be a part of this child's life."

Rebecca had a stunned look on her face. "Wait…what do you mean you asked her to marry you? I thought…"

"You thought what?" I asked.

She started to look around frantically.

"Um… I don't know what I was going to say. You asked her to marry you even after you found out about the baby? I'm not so sure that I'm okay with Ari being involved in any way, shape, or form. I mean… look, she came here today to spy on us! You have to see that she obviously does not trust you, Jefferson."

"She trusts me. It's you she doesn't trust."

"Well, ouch, that hurt. I'm not dropping the restraining order until after I have the baby. I don't trust her, especially after the stunt she pulled today, and I'm beginning to think that her little friend didn't accidentally pick up my phone either."

I held back from laughing. The moment Amanda had brought back the phone, I had known something was up. It had Ari written all over it.

"It doesn't matter why they were here. Ari is a part of my life, and you need to accept that." I looked down at her stomach when I saw the baby move again.

She followed my eyes and smiled. "Do you want to feel again? He's moving around a lot today."

"He? You already know the sex of the baby?" I couldn't help but reach out to feel the baby.

Rebecca let out a laugh. She glanced down at my hand on her stomach and then looked back up at me.

"Yes, I was too excited to not find out. I'm going to start painting the baby's room and then try to put the crib together."

I knew what she was doing. She was trying to get me to volunteer to help her. I knew that I had to talk to Ari before I started doing shit like that.

I pulled my hand away from her stomach and then laid some money on the table. I needed to get out of here.

"Well, I need to get going. I'm getting ready to move out the ranch so I need to go and pack up."

"Wait! You're moving out to the country? Isn't that place like three hours away? What if something happens with the baby?"

"Rebecca, you made it this far without me. You'll be fine with me being two-and-a-half hours away. If you need something, you can just call me. My cell phone works off and on out there, so, after we get a land-line I'll give it to you."

"We? As in you and Ari? Is she moving out there with you? Are y'all moving in together?"

I stood up and threw my napkin down on the table. *What is she, my fucking mother now?*

"Listen, what happens between Ari and me is none of your business Rebecca…at least not until we have a test done after this baby is born, so we can find out once and for all if he's mine or not."

She looked up at me with tears in her eyes. *Son of a bitch.*

"Of course, Jeff, I'm sorry. It really is none of my business. May I ask when you'll be moving?"

"After Gunner comes back from his honeymoon, we're going to start moving, so we should be totally moved out to Mason in about three weeks. We have to be out of the house by the middle of July. Speaking of dates, I asked you earlier but you never told me. When is your due date?"

"Wait a minute. Did you say when Gunner comes back from his honeymoon? When did he get married?"

"He got married to my sister this past Saturday."

The look on her face was pure shock. She turned white as a ghost as she started ringing her napkin. More than a minute passed before she seemed to get her composure.

"Are you going to tell me the due date, Rebecca?"

She let a small smile come across her face. "Jefferson, Jr. is due on August seventeenth."

Holy fuck! Jefferson Jr.? This girl is nuts. "Yeah, well, I'm not so sure on that name, Rebecca. We can talk about it later. I have some shit I need to take care of, so I'll talk to you soon. Don't forget to get me that info on the doctor."

She nodded her head and stood up. She started to reach over to give me a hug, and I took a step back.

"Right…I'm sorry. Well…okay, it was good seeing you. I'm sure this is all going to work out for the best, Jeff. I'm sorry you missed out on the first few months, but now that you are here, you can start being a Daddy to Jeffer um, to the baby."

I nodded my head and turned to walk away. I had to shake this feeling I was having. The moment I'd seen and then felt the baby move in her stomach, a small part of me had hoped that this baby was mine. I was not okay with thinking this way. I only wanted to have children with Ari, not some crazy-ass bitch who has been obsessed with me for the last three years.

Once I got in my truck, I finally relaxed. I put my head down on the steering wheel, and I swore that I just wanted to cry. *Why is this happening to me?* The last thing I wanted to do was hurt Ari more, but I couldn't walk away if this baby was mine though. *Damn it, I wish Gunner was here.*

I pulled out of the parking lot and headed back to the house. Maybe packing up would help keep my mind off of shit for a while before I head over to Ari's place. My biggest fear was that she wasn't going to move out to the ranch with me. My life might as well be over if Ari wasn't in it.

***

After three hours of packing, I called Ari.

"Hey," she answered.

"Hey, baby. Are you home?"

"Yep, I'm here and just sitting in a hot bath right now."

Jesus, this girl can make me hard with just the sound of her breathing.

"Can I come join you?" I asked, smiling.

"How fast can you get here, cowboy?" Ari said with a laugh.

"I'm on my way now. Wait for me?"

"Okay. Be careful driving. Jeff?"

"Yeah, baby?"

"I love you."

My heart just about dropped to my stomach. *I love this girl so damn much.*

"I love you, too, baby. Be there in a few minutes."

CHAPTER ELEVEN

ARI

I placed my cell phone on the bathroom floor and just sat frozen in the bathtub. I could hear the hurt in Jeff's voice. I hated Rebecca with every ounce of my being. *Why is this happening to us?*

After we'd left the restaurant, Amanda and I had tried some shopping therapy. The whole time we had walked around Emeralds, I couldn't get it out of my head how big Rebecca was. Even with her sitting down, I could tell she had to be further along than seven months. I was going to get to the bottom of this, but if this was going to work, I needed my girls to help me.

Jesus, Mary, and Joseph, maybe I am losing my damn mind. Am I really going to go through with this? Yep, I really am. I closed my eyes, trying to picture what it would've been like if this whole Rebecca thing had never happened this weekend.

I wasn't sure how long I'd sat there with my eyes closed. I heard the front door open, and I could hear Jeff walking to my bathroom. My heart started to beat like crazy. Just the idea of being with him had me almost panting with excitement. The sounds of his footsteps stopped.

I slowly opened my eyes to see him standing in the doorway. His eyes immediately captured mine. As I looked down his entire body, I lost my breath from just the sight of him.

"Hey, Baby," he said huskily.

All I could do was smile. He walked over and kneeled down by the tub. He brushed the back of his hand down the side of my face. My breathing was louder and faster now, but I didn't care. I just wanted to forget everything. He was here. He was here with me, and that was all that mattered.

"Jeff."

"Shh, let me love you, Ari."

Oh my god. I wanted nothing more than for him to do just that. He stared into my eyes like he wanted to tell me something so desperately. He almost looked…lost. *What if he wants this baby to be his? What if- no I have to stop asking what-ifs and start talking to him about this.*

"Jeff, maybe we should talk first." *Shit, I can't believe I just said that.*

"I don't want to talk, Ari, I want to make love to the only girl I've ever loved, and will ever love."

"Jeff…I."

The next thing I knew, he was sliding his hand behind my neck as he brought my lips to his. He kissed me with so much passion that I swore I was going to explode. He pulled away, reaching over to pull the towel off the rack. He got up and held the towel open for me. As I slowly stood and stepped out of the bathtub, I heard him suck in a breath of air.

I smiled at him. "You're not getting tired of me yet, I see."

Jeff let out a small laugh and shook his head.

"Baby, hell would freeze over before I ever got tired of seeing your body."

He wrapped the towel around me and then pulled me closer to him. "I missed you today."

"Really? Cause you looked pretty happy at lunch with your baby mama."

Fuck! Why did I just go there? Oh my god, what is wrong with me?

"I'm sorry, Jeff." I said.

He ran his hand through his hair.

"What is up with you these last few days? Why are you being such a bitch?"

Oh no, he didn't.

"What? Are you really asking me that, Jeff? Because if you are, then maybe you need to just leave!"

I pushed him out of the way as I made my way into my bedroom. I was so mad I was shaking.

"Ari, what do you want me to do? *Tell me* what I need to do!"

I spun around and just glared at him. "Well, for starters, stop calling me a bitch. Do you know what it's like to be told that your boyfriend, the love of your goddamn life, is having a baby with another woman? To have your engagement night totally ruined because all you can think about in the back of your mind is how you will *never* be the one to give your future husband his first child? To have to know that you're going to be at her beck and call for the next few months until this baby is born? Shit, Jeff...I might not ever be able to even give you a baby like she can. And you think I'm being a bitch? Fuck off, dickwad." I quickly wiped off the tears from my face before I turned away from him.

"Ari, I'm sorry I called you a bitch. I really am, baby. I would do anything if I could turn back the clocks and never even lay eyes on Rebecca. I promise you that, this is not going to come between us. Baby, we'll have kids. I know we will, and."

"It *is* coming between us, and you don't know if we'll ever have kids, Jeff. If I'm a carrier of Fragile X...I don't....I don't know..." I stopped talking and did the one thing I swore that I would never do. I felt sorry for myself. My body slowly started to sink.

The next thing I knew, Jeff was reaching for me and trying to pull me into his arms. That was when the anger hit me like a brick wall.

I pushed him away.

"Just go, Jeff. I need to be alone. Please just leave."

"No. I came over here to be with you, Ari. I want you," he said, his hands still holding me.

I let out a laugh. I wasn't really sure why because none of this was funny. I tried with all my might to shove him away, but all he did was hold me closer. Then, he pushed me up against the wall. As he lifted me up, I instinctively wrapped my legs around him. He grabbed me by the back of the head, pulling on my hair, as he slammed his lips onto mine. My head was spinning. I wanted him so badly, but at the same time, I was scared to death.

"Ari, please…just let me in baby."

With that, I completely relaxed in his arms. As he pushed me harder against the wall, I felt him pulling off my towel. *Oh sweet Jesus.* I put my arms around his neck, and I kissed him back with as much passion as he was giving me.

He almost seemed desperate as he moved away from me just long enough to pull his shirt over his head. The sight of his chest still gave me butterflies in my stomach. I placed my right hand on his chest, feeling him shudder under my touch. I wrapped my legs around him tightly as he moved us away from the wall and to the bed.

As he laid me down, my heart was pounding so hard that I could see my chest rising and falling. The sight of him, just staring at me, was turning me on more than I could stand. As he slowly started to take off his pants, I pulled my eyes away from his to watch him. *My god, his body is beyond perfect.*

"Ari, you look so beautiful, baby. Your skin is glowing."

I couldn't even form words. I'd never before had this overwhelming feeling to just be with him. It was almost like I would die if I didn't feel his touch.

He moved over me, bent down, and pulled my lower lip between his teeth. A small moan escaped my lips as Jeff closed his eyes. When he opened them again, he had such passion in his eyes that I almost sucked in a breath of air because it surprised me so much.

Just when I didn't think I would be able to stand it any longer, he propped himself up on his elbows and then his hand gently started to move down my face. I felt my body tremble under his touch. He let a small smile come across his face, and I couldn't help but smile back at him. Then, he moved his hand down my neck to my chest, which was moving up and down so fast from my erratic breathing.

"Do you want me, Ari?"

"Yes, more than anything," I said with way too much desperation in my voice.

Jeff's smile got bigger as he moved his hand further down to my lower stomach. All I wanted to do was yell at him to get on with it, but it almost felt like we needed to go slow. We both needed this moment to feel wanted and loved by each other.

"Open your legs for me, Ari."

Holy fuck. I'd never heard such seduction in his voice before, and I swore that the moment he touched me, I was going to come.

He moved his body between my legs as I stretched them open. Then he kissed me, but pulled away to fast. He ran his tongue down my chest and then sucked one of my nipples into his mouth. As he started to slowly pull on it, I let out another moan. *Yep, I'm going to explode any second now.*

Then, I felt his hand moving down the side of my body, coming to rest between my thighs. My body jerked when I felt him touch my clit. He slid his fingers into me one by one, and I arched up against him as hard as I could.

"Jesus, you're so wet, Ari. I want you more than anything, baby."

"Oh god, Jeff...please...I want you, too...so badly."

He started to move his hand faster as he moved up to capture my mouth with his. I never wanted this moment to end. This was probably the most sensual I'd ever felt, and each passing second was getting better and better.

I could feel that familiar build-up in my body, and all I wanted to do was push harder into his hand.

"Ari," Jeff whispered in my ear.

That was my undoing. I called out his name over and over before he caught my cries with his mouth.

I slowly came back down to earth, but Jeff never let up on his kissing. I almost needed to pull away from him to catch my breath. Before I knew what he was doing, he was slowly kissing down my neck again…to my chest…down...my stomach. *Oh, holy fuck!*

I grabbed onto his hair the moment I felt his hot breath inches away from my already sensitive nub. The moment he started to kiss it, I rocked my hips into him. *Shit!* I just needed more. It was only a matter of seconds before I was arching my back and calling out his name again.

My head was spinning, and I was barely aware of him moving up my body. He kept kissing me ever so gently. *Holy hell, this is unreal.*

He started to kiss my neck and continued up until I could feel him breathing in my ear. "I'm going to make love to you now, Ari."

Oh. My. God.

I'd never felt such pleasure like when I felt him enter my body. He made such slow and passionate love to me that I totally forgot about everything, except for him and our future together.

CHAPTER TWELVE

JEFF

As I lay in bed, I listened to Ari breathing as she slept. She kept moaning in her sleep, and it seemed like she was having another bad dream. She had been having them the last three nights. I would do anything to take away all her worry.

Just then, I felt her jerk awake.

"Bad dream again, baby?"

She lifted her head from my chest and looked at me. The smile she gave me just about stole my breath away. *God, I love her.*

"Actually, no. For once, I was dreaming about something nice. Very nice!"

I let out a laugh and pulled her closer to me. I felt her stiffen in my arms, so I slowly started to move my fingers up and down her back.

"Mmm that feels so good," she said.

We laid there for another few minutes in silence before Ari took a deep breath.

"Jeff, we need to talk about it."

"I know we do."

"When's her due date?"

"She told me August seventeenth. She also said that she's having a boy."

Ari snapped up her head, and I saw the tears welling up in her eyes.

"How do you feel about all of this, Jeff? I saw you smiling when you were touching her stomach. If this is going to work out, you need to be honest with me right now.

Holy shit. What am I supposed to say? A small part of me felt something when I'd felt the baby move. Oh Ari. There was no fucking way was I going to hurt Ari that way. I only wanted kids with her. There was no one else for me.

"Ari, it's hard not to smile when you feel a baby moving around in anyone's stomach. Something weird did happen though. She seemed shocked when I told her I'd asked you to marry me last Saturday. She couldn't believe that I asked even after I'd found out about the baby, but it wasn't just that. When I said that Gunner got married, she was really surprised. I think she thought it was us getting married."

Ari quickly sat up. She pulled the covers over her as she tucked her legs up to her chest.

"Don't get mad."

"Oh shit, Ari. What did you do?"

"Well, I had a feeling that her calling you right before the wedding was all too coincidental. I just had a feeling. So, Amanda and I went to Halcyon this morning, and Crysti happened to be working. She also seemed surprised that we hadn't gotten married. Turns out she overheard someone talking about a wedding. When she heard your name and mine, she thought it was us getting married. My guess is that she called Rebecca to fill her in with what she'd found out. I think Rebecca came up with this whole baby thing to keep us from getting married."

Wow. When Ari puts her damn mind to something, she goes one hundred percent at it.

"Well, what are you thinking?"

"It's possible. If she was lying though, why would she offer to let me go to her next doctor's appointment?"

Ari's face turned white as a ghost.

"She did? Did she offer or did you say that you wanted to go?"

"Does it matter Ari?"

"Yes, Jeff, it matters a lot! Did you ask to go or did she offer?"

I had to really think about it.

"I think that she offered. No, wait…I told her that I wanted to go since I'd not been a part of the pregnancy for the first seven months."

Ari turned her head and took a deep breath. *What is she thinking?*

"Okay. Did she give you the appointment date, time, and doctor? What information did she give you?"

"Um, well, right before I came over, she sent me a text with her appointment time and directions to the doctor's office."

Ari jumped up, reached for my phone, and then handed it to me.

"Can I see it?"

I nodded my head. "Of course, you can see it."

I opened up the message and showed it to Ari. She made a face and then handed the phone back to me.

"Is she going to drop the stupid-ass restraining order against me?"

Oh hell, here we go.

"No, I asked twice. She feels like it would be…safer for her to keep it up until the baby is born."

"Okay, she's a weirdo. Does she think I would actually hurt her? Holy hell! What else did y'all talk about?"

I laid there for a moment, thinking about if there was anything else I left out. I really just wanted to put the whole thing as far out of my mind as I could.

"Well, we talked about her having a high-risk pregnancy. She can't get upset and that kind of shit. She talked about painting the baby's room and putting up a crib. Ah shit, I don't know Ari. I wasn't even listening to her through half the conversation."

Lying back down under the covers, Ari moved slightly away from me. *Shit! Not again.* After we'd just spent probably the best night of our lives together, she was pulling away from me again. I couldn't believe how much I'd wanted her earlier. She'd looked so unbelievably beautiful, her skin glowing, as her eyes filled with love.

"Ari, please don't pull away from me again, baby."

She rolled over to her side to look at me. "You can't let her pull us apart, Jeff. Promise me that you won't let that happen."

I pulled her closer to me, and she put her head on my chest. I started to run my fingers through her hair. She smelled so good. Something was making my heart pound hard in my chest. Maybe it was just this whole bullshit with Rebecca. I was so afraid that I was going to lose Ari over this. *I can't let that happen. I won't let that happen.*

"I promise, baby. She won't pull us apart. I promise."

Ari reached up, putting her hand on my chest, and then she kissed me gently on the lips. I wanted her so badly again. I deepened the kiss as I rolled her over, climbing on top of her.

"Jeff." She moaned.

"I love you so much, Ari."

I started to make love to her, my cell phone started to ring.

"Ignore it," Ari said as she pushed her hips up into me.

No problem.

My voice mail notification went off.

"God, Ari, you feel like heaven, baby."

Ari smiled at me, and my heart melted. I would never get tired of seeing that smile. She rolled us over, so she was sitting on top of me. *Pure fucking heaven.*

"So, what are our plans today, cowboy?" she asked as she moved her hips.

I started to laugh, thinking about all the packing that we had to do.

"You really want to talk about our plans for the day…now?" I groaned.

She slowly lowered her lips to mine and whispered, "No."

She took my lower lip between her teeth and let out a moan.

Then, my cell phone went off again. We both ignored it. When it went off a fourth time, I started to get worried. *What if something happened to Gramps or Grams?*

"I have to see who it is, Ari. What if something happened to Gunner's grandparents?"

Ari moved off of me as I reached for my cell phone on the night-stand. *Holy fucking shit!…* The four missed calls were from Rebecca. Not good.

"Who was it?" Ari asked.

"Um…it was Rebecca."

"Are you kidding me?" Ari let out a laugh. "Nice. It didn't even take her twenty-four fucking hours." She jumped out of bed, grabbed her robe, and walked out of the bedroom.

Son of a bitch! I can't believe this. I listened to Rebecca's message. *What the hell?* She was just trying to give me the information for the doctor's appointment. I sent her a text message, telling her to text it to me, and to only call me from now on if she had an emergency. *Bitch.*

I got up and headed into the kitchen where Ari was making coffee. I walked up behind her and pulled her into my arms.

"You don't want to finish what we started?" I whispered into her ear.

Turning, she looked at me and gave me the weakest smile. I knew she was trying, and I loved her for it.

"I'm sorry. The mood is kind of…gone." She turned back around and pulled out two coffee mugs. "Do you want anything for breakfast?"

"How about we go out for breakfast?"

She glanced at me, surprised. "What about your run? You never miss your morning run."

I smiled at her. Reaching down, I scooped her up in my arms and carried her back to the bedroom. There was no way that I was going to let Rebecca win.

"I have something more important to take care of, like making love to my future wife."

Ari let out a laugh and started to kiss me as I brought her back into the bedroom.

"Well, if you insist on giving up your run for sex, who am I to complain?"

The passion between us was unbelievable. It was like we couldn't get deep enough into each other. *I can never…ever…lose Ari.*

I would rather die than not have her in my life.

CHAPTER THIRTEEN

ARI

This had probably been the longest week of my life. Rebecca had managed to text Jeff every day at least three times a day. I'd been trying to let it go, but today, I was on my last nerve.

Then, his phone went off again. *What the hell is it this time?*

"Jesus, Mary, and Joseph! Really, Jeff?" I yelled.

Jeff pushed his hand through his hair while he looked at his cell phone.

Josh was standing there with a pissed-off look on his face.

"Holy shit, dude, is she fucking watching us? Every damn time we're trying to move something heavy, your fucking phone goes off!"

I had to let out a giggle as I looked around. It wouldn't surprise me if she were watching us. *Crazy bitch.*

Heather walked out of the house, carrying a box, and she seemed to be struggling. I'd never seen Josh move so fast in my life as he took the box from her. Even on the football field, the bastard had never run that fast. Heather and I were planning on going out to dinner tonight in Mason, and I couldn't wait to drill Heather about her trip with Josh from Mason to Austin. She'd been avoiding me like the plague all week. Something must have happened, and I was going to get to the bottom of it.

I watched as Heather thanked Josh. *Holy hell.* She was blushing as she looked away from him. He said something to her that made her laugh. She looked over at me, and I smiled at her. Her smile faded as she walked back into the house.

Damn it. Why is she fighting this thing with Josh so much? What the fuck is wrong with this group of friends?

I looked back over at Jeff, who was now pacing back and forth on the phone. My heart stopped for a moment. *Oh shit. What if something happened to the baby*? I mean, I couldn't care less about that bitch, but I would never want something to happen to that innocent child. Poor thing was going to have a nut-case for a mother.

Just then, my cell phone started ringing. I pulled it out and looked at it. *Ellie?*

"Hey! What the hell are you doing, calling me on your honeymoon?"

"Hey, sweets. Um…Gunner is talking to Jefferson right now. We're in Miami, waiting for our next flight."

"What? I thought y'all weren't coming back until next week."

"Yeah… well, Gunner got a call late last night. His dad had a heart attack."

"Oh my god, Ellie! Oh no. Is he okay?"

"I guess. His mom, Grace, called last night and said she was at the hospital. His dad was stable. The doctors told him that he needed a serious amount of rest and relaxation. Somehow Grace was able to talk him into going to the ranch to visit his mom and dad."

"No shit. Wow. Well, you know when something life-changing like that happens, you tend to think of things differently. You know what I mean?"

Ellie let out a small sigh. "Yeah," she paused for a moment.

"Ari, how are you?"

I sucked in a breath of air. She knows.

"When did you find out?"

"A couple of days before the wedding, I knew something was wrong, and made Gunner tell me. I'm sorry that I didn't say anything to you. I felt like it wasn't my place."

I felt the tears coming again. *Shit!* "S'okay, Ellie. I know it had to have been hard for you to keep that from me. You won't believe how I found out though."

"Will it make me hate my own brother?"

I let out a laugh. "No, but you'll hate Rebecca even more!"

"Yeah, like that's possible. I'm ready to choke her until she spills the truth."

"Glad to hear that! I'm glad you're coming back. I actually need to talk to you about a few things."

"Okay…well, we should be in around four. Are y'all heading out to the ranch?"

"Yeah, Josh and Jeff have the whole house almost cleared out. We're making a trip out there now. I think Josh and Heather were planning on staying the night. We can all catch up, that is, if y'all aren't too tired by the time you get in. Heather and I were going to go into Mason for dinner. Do you want us to wait?"

"Hell no, I won't be too tired! I can't wait to see you. It feels like I've been gone forever. Why don't y'all go ahead and eat? There is a bar on Main Street I think. I'm sure Jefferson knows about it. Maybe we could all just meet up there? Damn it, they're calling our flight. I'll see ya in a few. Love you sweets. Kiss and hug Jefferson for me. Hang in there. I'm almost home."

The moment I hung up with Ellie, I could feel my stress lifting away from me. Things would be so much better when she got here. I'd felt so alone this last week. Even with Jeff and I being so close, it still felt like I was lost.

Jeff walked up to me. He hugged me so tightly that I felt like I couldn't breathe.

"Was that Ells?"

"Yeah, she told me about Gunner's dad. Is he going to be okay?"

"Gunner said he should be. He said that his dad probably needs to retire from the Army. His mom is doing everything she can to talk to him about it. The fact that she got him to go to the ranch for a few weeks blows my mind."

"Well, it'll be good for both Gunner and his dad. They need to work on repairing their relationship, especially with Gunner being married now. I don't think his dad wants to miss out on having grandkids someday."

I looked up and smiled at Jeff. The smile he gave me in return melted my panties.

"I sure as shit wish Josh and Heather weren't here," Jeff said as he wiggled his eye-brows up and down.

Giggling, I glanced toward the house. Heather was carrying out another box while Josh was on her heels, asking her to put it down.

"Maybe we should make Heather ride with Josh again," I said looking back at Jeff.

He threw his head back and laughed.

"If she wants to come out to the ranch, she either has to drive her car or go with Josh. I have the truck packed full of shit."

I had to laugh. Heather had just gotten her car back from the dealership. There was no way was she planning on driving out there again.

I looked over at her as she started to walk up to us.

"Ellie is on her way back," I said to Heather.

She came to a stop with a confused look.

"Gunner's father had a heart attack, but he's okay." I explained.

Heather's face turned white as she brought her hand up to her mouth. She leaned over, like she was going to be sick.

"Heather... honey, are you okay?" *Shit.* I didn't even think about what I was saying. I suddenly remembered that Heather's dad had a heart attack while driving and that's what caused their car wreck.

Heather spun around and ran right into Josh.

"Hey, what's wrong? Heather, look at me, princess. What's wrong?" Josh asked, concerned.

Heather just broke down and cried. Josh pulled her into his arms, and she completely lost it. This was the first time that I'd ever seen her cry about her parents. Trying to figure out what was going on, Josh looked over at Jeff. Jeff mouthed *her parents* to Josh.

Jeff walked up to Josh, leaning in to whisper to him. Jeff must have told Josh about Gunner's dad and Heather's dad. Josh closed his eyes. Then, turning around with Heather still in his arms, he started to walk with her into the house.

"Jeff, I honestly believe this is the first time that girl has cried since her parents died. She's been holding it in for so long. I knew that one of these days, the damn was going to break."

Just then, Jeff's cell phone rang. He pulled it out of his pocket and answered it without even looking at who it was.

"Oh, hey, Rebecca."

Jeff mouthed *sorry* to me. I turned and walked toward the house. The last thing I wanted to do was have to listen to him to talk her.

"Um... well, we're kind of getting ready to take a load of stuff out to the ranch. My truck is packed up, so, I can't help you with that."

Before I walked in the front door, I turned to look at Jeff. He was watching me, so I just gave him a smile before I headed into the house. Since there was no furniture left anywhere in the house, Josh and Heather were sitting on the floor in the living room.

I sank down on the floor next to Heather. She seemed to have calmed down. I reached for her hand, and she smiled at me.

"Where's Jeff?" Heather asked.

"Talking to Rebecca."

"Bitch!" Josh and Heather said at the same time.

We all started to laugh when the front door opened as Jeff walked in.

"What's so funny?" Jeff asked as he bent down to look at Heather.

"Nothing, dude. Nothing at all." Josh said with a smirk.

Jeff gave Josh a dirty look. He turned back to Heather. "Hey, are you okay?"

"Yeah, Jeff, I'm fine. I just wasn't expecting that. Josh actually made me feel a lot better with his stupid jokes."

Jeff smiled and then looked at me, and his smile faded just a little.

"Ari, do you think I could use your Jeep for about an hour?"

"I thought we were getting ready to leave for the ranch, Jeff. Man, we've got a lot of shit to get unpacked in both the cabin and your place. Where the hell are you going?" Josh asked Jeff.

"Rebecca's car won't start, and she's tried to call everyone she could think of to give her a jump."

"Can't she just call a tow truck or something for Christ's sake? How the hell has she managed without you for the last seven months, Jeff? This is getting insane." I said as I stood up.

Jeff stood up and ran his hands through his hair and then down his face.

"What am I supposed to do, Ari? Just leave her stranded? What if something happened with the baby and she needed her car?"

"Come on, Jeff, even I can see this for what it is. You mean to tell me that this girl couldn't find one person to come and help her. Jesus, dude, you're not that stupid," Josh said as he stood up, holding out a hand to help Heather up.

I reached into my purse and threw Jeff the keys to my Jeep before I headed toward the back door.

"What the fuck are we supposed to do while you rescue Rebecca?" Josh asked, annoyed.

As I walked into the backyard, I had to lean over and rest my hands on my knees, because I couldn't catch my breath.

I felt someone's hand on my back. I stood and turned around to see…Heather.

"I'm sorry, Ari. He left to go help her."

"Motherfucker, I can't believe it. He left? He went to her?"

Heather had tears in her eyes again.

I stood up straighter. "Don't you dare shed a tear for that bastard, Heather. Do you hear me?"

I stepped around her to go back into the house. Josh was looking out the front window. I walked up next to him, and he bumped me with his shoulder and gave me the sweetest smile.

"I'm sorry, Ari. I hate to see that bitch coming between you and Jeff."

I looked over at Josh and smiled at him. "Who are you? And what have you done with Josh-the-man-whore?"

Josh threw his head back and laughed. "Well, I guess it's time to grow up and find someone worth being faithful to."

"Really? Do you think you found that person?" I asked bumping my shoulder against his. He looked down at me and gave me the sweetest smile.

"I think so. It's just a damn shame that she doesn't feel the same way."

I turned around to see if Heather had come back into the house yet.

"Josh, give her time. I know she likes you. Just…give her some time to let you in."

"Shit, Ari, I'm trying. I'm trying to do everything that I can think of to prove to her that I've changed, but she just keeps saying that she only wants to be friends. I don't really know what else to do but wait."

I took a deep breath in and let it out slowly.

"That's all you can do. Wait."

CHAPTER FOURTEEN

JEFF

I knew Ari was going to be pissed when I got back. I shouldn't have left without talking to her. *Fuck!* I slammed my fist on the steering wheel. By the time I got to Rebecca's apartment, a friend had gotten her text message for help and showed up. Right as I was pulling up, I got a text message from Rebecca, saying she didn't need me. *Too fucking late now.*

I parked and started to get out of the Jeep.

"Jeff! I'm so, so sorry, honey. I tried to send you a text as soon as I could. I hope this didn't cause too much trouble for you," Rebecca said.

"No, it's okay." I looked over at the guy who was doing something to Rebecca's battery. I started to walk over and he slammed the hood shut right before I got to it.

"It's okay, dude. I took care of it. Nothing that a little bit of Coke on the battery posts won't fix."

I just looked at the guy. He seemed nervous. I turned back around and looked at Rebecca, who had a huge smile on her face.

"Well, since you're here do you want to see the baby's room?"

Fuck me. "Sure, but I really need to leave in like two minutes, Rebecca. Everyone is waiting on me."

Smiling she hooked her arm with mine and led me into her apartment. After we walked through the living room, she opened up the door to a room that was pretty much filled with boxes and shit that looked like it needed to be put together.

"Wow, what the hell is all of this stuff?" I asked.

Rebecca let out a giggle and started to walk into the room.

"Well, it's the crib, basinet, changing table and other things like that. I have a hard time leaning over and such, so I haven't had a chance to put it together. My brother was going to help me, but he never seems to have the time."

I looked around. There was a ton of shit. The walls were white, and I remembered her saying that she wanted to paint them.

"Don't you need all this stuff out of here to paint the walls? Who's going to move all of this? You can't do it, Rebecca."

When I turned to look at her, the smile on her face was almost one of victory. I was beginning to think that Josh was right. She'd planned for this to happen. This was all just a way for me to get over here to see all this shit and feel sorry for her. *Fuckin' A.*

"I know I can't move it, Jeff. That's why I was hoping that you would be able to help me. The sooner, the better before the baby comes."

"Well, you have until the middle of August. It's just the middle of June, so you have two months."

Rebecca frowned. "Yes, I know, but I don't want to wait until the last minute. I'm getting bigger by the day. I need this taken care of, like, soon. Are you free sometime next week, maybe?"

I hate this. I was so torn. For the sake of the baby, I wanted to help her, but I knew Ari was going to flip the fuck out.

"Let me talk to Ari, and I'll get back with you. I really have to go."

As I turned to walk away, she grabbed my arm.

"Wait a minute, Jeff. This is *your* baby. What do you need to talk to Ari about? I mean, is this how it's going to be? If we have a birthday party, are you going to have to ask Ari if it's okay for you to be there? This is not going to work."

I just stood there looking at her. *Is she serious?*

"Listen, Rebecca, you dropped a huge bomb on me last weekend. My whole goddamn world has just been turned upside down. What I thought was going to be my future has just possibly changed. So, yeah, Ari is a big part of my future. My goal in this life is to not hurt her. If that means talking to her about any decisions I make regarding this baby until it's born then so be it."

"I'm sorry, Jeff. I didn't mean to seem insensitive to Ari. Of course, I understand your need to talk to her, but for fuck's sake, we're talking about painting and putting together some baby furniture. I'm not asking you to move in with me. I feel guilty for not including you in things up until now. I mean, you missed out on feeling the first kicks, the sonogram, and discovering that it was a boy. I'm just trying to make it up to you by including you in all of this. If Ari can't see that… well, I hate to say this, but that's her problem. If she was more secure in your relationship, then she would understand."

"Ari is not insecure in our relationship, Rebecca. Listen, I really have to go. Let's plan on doing the baby's room next week. I have someone coming out to the ranch to take a look at the horse stables. I'm not sure what day he's coming. After I find out, I'll get with you, and we'll plan something."

Rebecca smiled. Reaching her hands up to my shoulders, she kissed the side of my cheek. "Thank you, Jeff. It really does mean a lot to me to have you a part of this. Again, I'm sorry you made a wasted trip over here."

***

I walked out to Ari's Jeep and jumped in. I looked over at my phone on the seat and saw my notification light blinking. *Shit.* I picked up my phone and noticed I had four missed calls and one voice mail from Ari.

She had called about three minutes ago. I listened to the voice mail. She said they were giving me another ten minutes and leaving. *What the hell?*

Immediately, I called her back.

"Hello?"

"Hey, sorry, I left my phone in the Jeep. I'm on my way back right now."

"Whatever. We have everything loaded in both vehicles. Do you want me to just drive your truck? Josh is getting bitchy, and we're ready to leave."

"No, I'll be there in a few minutes. Just wait for me."

"Fine." She hung up.

Jesus. Waiting for this baby to be born was going to be a long two fucking months.

***

I pulled up to the house and parked on the street behind the trailer that was hooked up to Josh's truck. After tying something down, he jumped off the trailer.

"You think that pussy truck of yours is going to be able to pull that trailer?" I asked.

Josh gave me a dirty look and turned back to his Dodge truck.

"Fuck you, Jeff. Just because I don't have a diesel-eating truck doesn't mean she doesn't have power."

"Yeah, whatever you say Josh. Your truck has no balls, dude. I'm just saying."

Just then Ari and Heather came walking out of the house each carrying a small box. Ari's eyes caught mine and her smile instantly faded. By the time she walked up to me, she had nothing in her eyes but anger.

"Can I please have my keys back? Heather and I are going to head out now. We'll just meet y'all at the deer cabin."

I handed her the keys, and she snatched them out of my hand and pushed past me. *Yep, this was going to be a long two months.*

"I thought we were going to drop off your Jeep at your place, so you could ride with me," I said.

"Well, that changed the moment you dropped everything and everyone for Rebecca. I don't want to be stuck while you're running back into Austin whenever she needs you."

"Ari."

She turned around and held up her hand.

"The time to talk about it was right before you decided to walk out that door. I'm sick of talking, thinking, and listening. I'm done Jeff. If I hear about her and that baby one more time, I'm taking off this ring, and that will be the last thing I throw at your ass."

So, it looks like I won't be bringing up the whole baby room thing anytime soon.

* * *

The drive out to Mason by myself sucked. Gunner called and said they had landed earlier than they thought. They were going to head straight out to the ranch. *God, I can't wait to talk to him.* I was at a complete loss as to what to do.

We all pulled up to Gunner's grandparents' house. Garrett and Emma came walking out with Ellie's dog Gus running behind them. He headed straight to Ari's Jeep. Ari bent down, giving him hugs and kisses. Ari's laugh moved through my body, and I couldn't help but want her again. Emma walked up to Ari and held her at arm's length. She smiled with a questioning look, and Ari smiled back at her. Gus won't leave Ari alone as he kept jumping up at her.

"Afternoon, Garrett. Have y'all heard from Gunner?" I said after I was finally able to pull my eyes away from Ari. She looked so damn beautiful. I couldn't keep my eyes off of her this whole week. There was something so different about her. Maybe it was because we were engaged now. I shook my head to clear my thoughts.

"It seems like you've got some heavy shit on your mind, Jeff," Garrett said with a straight-as-hell face.

"You never were one to beat around the bush, were you?" I said as I shook Garrett's hand.

Josh walked up and slapped me on the back before he shook Garrett's hand.

"Back to your question, Jeff. Yes, we heard from him a little bit ago. They're only about an hour out," Garrett said.

"Yeah, we would have been here sooner, but…um, I had some shit to take care of," I explained.

Josh let out a laugh and shook his head at me. *Bastard.* He should be the one with the damn crazy-ass pregnant girl, not me.

"Yeah, well…sometimes we have to step in the shit to move past it, Jeff. Did Gunner give you the key to the cabin?"

What the fuck does that mean? "Um…yeah, he gave it to me. I guess we'll head over there now. Josh's truck has Gunner's stuff since he put most of his stuff in storage. I think Ari and Heather were planning on heading into Mason to grab something to eat."

"No, we decided to stay here. Emma made a King Ranch casserole that sounds yummy. Plus, I want to be here when Ellie gets back," Ari said, walking by arm and arm with Heather.

I watched as Ari, Heather, and Emma made their way into the house with Gus jumping on Ari the whole way. He would not leave her alone. She kept yelling down at him. She looked so damn cute, trying to be all stern with him.

***

Josh and I emptied the trailer on his truck, and then we brought my truck and trailer over to my place. By the time we were done, I was starving. Somehow, I had gotten a text message from Ari, saying Gunner and Ellie were back.

Josh and I headed back to the ranch house. The moment I saw Gunner's truck, it felt like a ton of bricks had been lifted off of my shoulders. We got out of the truck as Gunner came walking out of the house. *Man, that bastard looks fuckin' happy.* He walked up to Josh first and gave him a hand-shake and slap on the back.

Then he walked up to me. He shook my hand but pulled me in toward him.

"What the fuck did you do to Ari?"

I pulled back and looked at him, confused.

"What the hell kind of greeting is that? I didn't do anything to her. Why?"

"Grams and the girls didn't hear us pull up. When we walked in the door, Grams was holding Ari while she was crying her goddamn eyes out. Ari brought us up to speed about everything that had happened. She can't stop crying, Jeff. Man, why the fuck are you not using your head with Rebecca?"

Holy shit. I couldn't believe it. I was getting the same damn lecture from the one person I thought I would be able to talk to. I threw my hands in my hair and started to walk down toward the barn. I needed to get away.

"Jeff, hold up, dude. Talk to me," Gunner said as he came up behind me.

"What do you want me to say, Gun? I'm losing my goddamn mind. I thought, out of all people, you wouldn't be the one jumping down my throat because Ari is hurting. What about me? How the fuck do you think I feel? I don't want to have a baby with Rebecca. I want to have a baby with Ari and only Ari. I'm being pulled in two different directions. If this baby is mine, I'm not walking out on it like my good-for-nothing father did. I want to be here for him, even if Rebecca is the mother. I don't know how to make Ari understand that. I don't know how to take away her pain, Gunner. There's nothing I wouldn't do to keep her from hurting. I just seem to be making it worse. Rebecca isn't helping with her needy-ass self either."

Gunner sat down on a hay bale and looked up at me. "Jeff, have you told Ari all of that?"

I sat down on the bale next to him and put my head in my hands. "No, not in those exact words."

"Well fuck, dude. Don't you think it would help her to understand your need to jump when Rebecca says how high? You owe her the truth, Jeff. If you don't tell her, she's just going to keep thinking the worst. Right now, to her, you are putting Rebecca above her. It needs to be Ari first. Find out if this baby is even yours. If he is, then be the best damn Dad you can be. Just remember who your world is right now, dude."

I lifted my head and looked at Gunner. I knew he was right.

"What the hell, dude? Marriage made you smarter."

Gunner started to laugh. "Something like that."

"I'm sorry your honeymoon got cut short. How's your dad?"

Gunner's smile faded some.

"When we landed, I talked to my mom, and she said that he's doing better. It was a mild heart attack, but she said it scared the shit out of him. I still can't believe that she talked him into coming here. Gramps and Grams are celebrating their fiftieth anniversary in a couple of weeks. I know Grams is really excited about her boy being here. They were already planning on a big party, but now, I think it just turned into something bigger."

"That's good, Gunner. How was your honeymoon? Did y'all have fun?"

The smile that lit up Gunner's face was so infectious. I had to smile back at him.

"It was amazing. I never in my life thought that I would be as happy as I am with Ellie. We had a blast. Did you know that she is deathly afraid to swim in the ocean?" Gunner said with a laugh.

I laughed with him shaking my head. "I thought she would be okay with it since the water is so clear. She won't swim if she can't see in the water."

Gunner nodded his head and then looked at me. His smile faded as he glanced down at the ground.

"Jeff, I'm sorry this shit is happening with you and Ari. I really want y'all to just be happy. I really think you need to talk to Ari and help her understand the position you are in. I've never seen Ari so emotional, and it really freaked out Ellie. She told me that since she's known Ari, she has never seen her cry that much. Grams ended up taking Ari to her bedroom.

"Fuck. She's been so emotional the last two weeks. I really fucked up when I told her she was being a bitch about it."

"Oh, holy shit, Jeff." Gunner pushed his hands through his hair as he stood up. He started to walk toward Big Roy's stall. "Dude, you need to stop blaming this on Ari. Man up, asshole, and go talk to her before something else happens. If you keep your feelings in, Jeff…you're gonna lose her. I'm pretty sure that if you do lose her again, you might not have another chance at getting her back."

I grabbed a handful of oats and walked up next to Gunner. I knew he was right. I needed to talk to Ari, and I needed to do it soon.

CHAPTER FIFTEEN

ARI

It felt so damn good to just cry. I hadn't wanted to fall apart in front of Gunner because I knew he would tell Jeff, but I couldn't help myself. *What the fuck is wrong with me?* This whole Rebecca pregnancy thing was really throwing me for a loop. Emma brought me into her room, so we could be alone.

After I got my crying fit over and done with, I looked up at Emma, who was just sitting there, waiting for me to get my shit together.

"Ari, honey, I need to ask you something."

"Of course Emma, ask me anything." I said, trying to give her a smile.

"Arianna, are you pregnant?"

What the hell? Holy shit, where did that come from?

I had to laugh. "No, Emma. Rebecca is the one who was is pregnant." I said as I looked down at my stomach. *Wait. When was the last time I had my period? Holy fuck!* I didn't get it last month, but I thought that was just from the stress of Ellie's wedding and thinking about Jeff asking me to marry him. *I'm on the pill. I can't be pregnant. Oh. My. God.* I missed a few pills a month or so back.

I snapped my head back up at Emma. She was smiling at me like she knew already. Her powers seemed to know no bounds.

I gasped. "Oh. My. God."

"Ari, I need you and the girls to go into town."

"What for? Why now? Emma! You can't plant that seed in my head and then expect me to just go buy you butter in town for Christ's sake!"

Emma started to laugh as she wrapped her arm around my shoulder, holding me close.

"Ari, the moment you stepped out of that truck today, I knew. You have a glow about you, darlin'. Your skin looks beautiful. The fact that you are so emotional is another dead giveaway. I need you, Ellie, and Heather to go into town and buy a pregnancy test."

Holy hell! My head was spinning. Just then, there was a knock on the door. Emma called out for whomever it was to come in. The door opened, and it was Jeff. *Oh shit.* I looked at Emma with a pleading look in my eyes. She smiled at me and nodded her head.

Standing up, Emma said, "I'll leave you two to talk."

As she walked out the door, she gave me one last look with a smile. I tried to smile back, but now, my whole body was shaking. I looked at Jeff. *No, this is not happening.* I still needed to be tested for the Fragile X gene. I couldn't even think straight. How will Jeff feel about me being pregnant?

"Ari, baby, we need to talk." Sitting down next to me, Jeff ran his hands through his hair and down his face. He was clearly frustrated.

His cell phone started ringing. That was weird because it was so damn hard to get a signal out here. He pulled it out, and I saw Rebecca's name on the screen. I instantly felt sick. I stood up to leave but he grabbed my arm and pulled me back down.

"Damn it, Ari! Please stop running away from me." Jeff sent the call to voice mail and tossed his phone behind him onto the bed.

"I'm not running Jeff. I just don't want to be in the same room when you talk to her."

"Well, I'm talking to you, not her. I need you to understand something, Ari. You need to know the reason why I feel the need to be there for Rebecca."

I started to laugh. "I didn't realize you had a need to be there for her, Jeff. I thought you were doing it for the baby, and that's all," I said with as much sarcasm as I could.

"That's not what I meant, Ari. I'm not there for *her*. I'm there for this baby. I don't want to start off being a dead-beat father by not being there for this baby. I don't want to be like my dad."

"I get that, Jeff. I really do. But you don't even know if this baby is yours! I mean, you drop everything for her, and it always turns out to be some excuse just for her to get you to be with her. The baby isn't even born yet! What's it going to be like when it is born?"

"When he is."

"What?"

"The baby....you said it. It's a boy, so I was just saying when *he* is born."

I just rolled my eyes at him. "Fine, Jeff, you do what you feel like you need to do. I'm getting sick of talking about this. I have too many other things that I need to deal with. I can't worry about Rebecca and her twisted ways."

"Fuck, Ari, I don't want you to just keep brushing this off. I need you to know that you're my world. You're my number one, baby. I only want to make you happy, Ari, and I feel like you're so damn sad. I don't know what to do to make it better. I don't want this to hurt you, Ari."

Oh shit, here came the tears. If I'm pregnant...and Rebecca's baby turns out to be his...what if mine is.

"Jesus, Ari. Why are you crying? Baby, please talk to me."

I was able to get myself under control. As I wiped the tears from eyes, I decided this was it. I needed to be stronger.

"It's okay, Jeff. I understand. Really, I do. I'll try to be more patient with everything. You're going to the doctor's appointment, right? So, you will be able to find out if August is her due date, right?"

"Yeah, I'm going with her in a week and a half. You still think she's lying about her due date, Ari? I mean come on, that would be pretty hard to do."

I shook my head at him. *Stupid ass.* I was so done talking about this.

"Well, I guess you'll find out soon, won't you? Listen I need to run into Mason with Ellie and Heather. We need to pick something up for Emma."

"Do you want me to go with y'all?"

"No!"

Jeff let out laugh and pulled me onto his lap. "I take it you want to spend some time with the girls.

"Yeah, something like that."

"Ari, are you going to stay here at the ranch with me this summer? Or are you going back to Austin? I really want you to move out here with me. I know you still have school, but I don't want to be apart from you, especially with me starting up this new business and all. I need you with me, baby. You know more about horses than anyone else I know."

I smiled at the idea of living in the little ranch house on Jeff's property. He wanted to tear it down and start on a new house from scratch. I thought the house that was there was perfect. It was a two-story white ranch house with a wraparound porch on the first floor. The views from the porch were amazing. Jeff had already remodeled the kitchen, and it was perfect.

"I want nothing more than to move out here with you, Jeff. I already signed up for online classes, and I was only planning on taking a few classes in Austin next semester. My mom and dad are somewhat pissed, but at least I'm still going to UT. I think I'll only have to stay a few days a week in Austin, so I can go to class, but other than that, I was planning on just moving out here."

Jeff smiled and pulled me in for a kiss. It quickly turned into a much more passionate kiss, and I had to pull away.

"Um, I'm not sure how Emma and Garrett would feel about us making out on their bed."

"You just made me so happy, Ari! I love you, baby. Hey, don't forget Mr. Reynolds is coming to take a look at the stables this week. I have a few things I need to take care of, but this guy's visit is going to be big if he agrees to breed with us. Well, shit, it will be huge if it all works out."

I smiled because I knew how much Jeff wanted this. I knew that Jeff was already talking to Gunner about going into a partnership with his ranch. Ellie and I overheard them discussing it right before Gunner and Ellie left on their honeymoon.

"Listen, we better get back out there, so we can eat. I'm sure Ellie is wondering what the hell is wrong with me, and Emma...well, um...she needs that thing from town," I said.

Jeff gave me a funny look and pulled me in for another kiss. I wasn't sure why I did it, but I kissed him back like it was our last kiss. I poured so much love into that kiss that it left me breathless.

"Jesus, Ari....that was some fucking kiss, baby." Jeff said with a laugh.

We walked back out into the kitchen, and I looked at Emma who was giving me a questioning look. I just shook my head to her, and she looked down.

After we ate, we cleaned up and put away everything.

Then, Ellie pulled me into the living room.

"Ari, what the hell is going on? You're pale as a ghost. What's with this we-have-to-run-into-town shit?"

"Can we talk about this when we get into the car, Ellie? Please just go along with me. It's a code blue."

"Alright. Well then, let's get going."

I walked back out into the kitchen and grabbed my purse. Heather was already outside on the porch with everyone else. After she grabbed her purse, Ellie followed right behind me.

"Okay, so come on, Heather. We need to run into town to pick up that thing for Emma," I said as I gave Heather a pleading look. She wasn't catching on, so I mouthed code blue to her.

"Oh! Oh yeah, um…let me grab my purse." Heather jumped up and ran into the house.

I noticed Josh was watching her every move. After she came back out, Josh stood up.

"Do y'all want me to drive? I don't mind taking you in. It's getting kind of late," Josh said.

"No!"

All three of us said at the same time. *Shit.*

Jeff started to laugh along with Gunner.

"Dude, they want their girl time. What do you need to get?" Jeff said. He looked at me first and then back at Emma.

I snapped my head at Emma, and she glanced at me with the most relaxed look on her face. "I need some mason jars for pickling in the morning."

Garrett looked confused. He was about to say something, but then Emma gave him a smile that just made him not even open his mouth.

Fuck, I need to learn how she did that!

Jeff stood up and handed me his truck keys. "At least take my truck. It's dark, and the deer will be out."

I grabbed his keys and kissed him on the cheek.

"I love you, Jeff."

He tilted his head and looked at me funny.

"I love you too, Ari. Be careful, okay?"

***

Once we got in Jeff's truck, I let out the breath I had been holding.

"What the hell is going on, Ari? You're starting to scare me. I could even tell Emma was covering for you. Spill it," Ellie said.

I looked at Ellie, who was sitting next to me, and then I turned to Heather, who was in the back seat.

I started the truck and almost had to laugh when "Truck Yeah" began playing. *Damn it, Jeff.*

Ellie reached over and turned it off. "Shit, I thought Gunner deleted that damn song!"

I pulled out and headed down the long driveway. My hands started to shake, and I felt like I was going to cry again. I glanced over at Ellie as her mouth fell open.

"Why are we going to town, Ari?"

"Um…well." I let out a small laugh as I shook my head. "Emma seems to think that I might be pregnant, and she wants me to get a test…like tonight."

Heather and Ellie let out a gasp at the same time.

"Fuck me!" Heather said in almost a whisper.

With wide eyes, I stared at Heather through the rearview mirror. "Wow, Heather, one road trip with Josh, and you're dropping the F-bomb."

Ellie looked confused. "Wait…what road trip? Oh my god! Are you and Josh?"

"No!" Heather yelled. "It's a long story and one I don't feel like talking about. Okay, so back to you, Ari. You told me you missed a pill last weekend. How can you know that fast?"

I took a deep breath and prepared myself for a really big lecture.

"Well, um I kind of might have missed a pill or two about a month and a half ago."

"*What?*" Ellie and Heather shouted at the same time.

"Ari, how could you be so stupid?" Ellie asked.

I glanced at Ellie. *Why is she being so mean?* I felt my eyes burning from trying to hold back the tears.

"It's not like I did it on purpose, Ellie! What the fuck?"

"Stop it, both of you!" Heather cried out. "Let's just go to the store, buy a test, and find out once and for all. We'll deal with the what-ifs later."

I looked at Ellie, and we both tried to smile at each other.

"Ari, sweets, I'm so sorry. I can't imagine how hard the last week has been on you with this whole Rebecca shit," Ellie said.

I cleared my throat getting ready to pitch my idea. I might as well get it over with.

"Um, yeah…speaking of that…I'm gonna need to call another code blue for Monday. I have a doctor's appointment with my gynecologist. I need y'all to be there with me."

"Of course, we'll be there with you. I don't have anything going on. Shit, I'm supposed to still be on my honeymoon," Ellie said.

Heather added, "I'm free, too. Count me in. Wait…is something wrong? I thought you just went in for your yearly a few months ago."

My hands started to shake again. I told them my original reason for going in, and then I explained my plan.

By the time I pulled up to the small grocery store in town, Ellie and Heather were just sitting there silently staring at me.

"Oh. My. God. You must be pregnant because you've lost your damn mind, Ari!" Ellie finally said as she jumped out of the truck.

"Wait. Why do *I* have to wear a low-cut blouse?" Heather said as she shut the door to the truck.

"Jesus, I'll explain it all later. Let's just get this shit over with." I sighed.

***

After we got back into the truck, I looked at the six tests that I had in the bag. I looked at Ellie and then Heather. We were all just staring at each other.

"So, should I do it now?" I asked.

"Do you want to go back in to the restroom or wait until we get back to the ranch?" Heather asked.

I let out the breath that I didn't even realize I'd been holding in. "Now…we better do it now."

***

I handed Heather the last test and stepped out of the stall. Ellie had lined up all the tests on the little counter.

"I didn't look at any of them, so I don't know." Ellie's voice was shaking.

I stood between Ellie and Heather and grabbed each of their hands.

"Together?" I asked.

They both nodded their heads. We started to walk up to the counter, and then I glanced at both of them.

"Jesus, Mary, and Joseph. Y'all have your damn eyes closed!" I said.

"Oh shit, sorry! I didn't even realize I had closed my eyes," Ellie said with a giggle.

We walked up to the row of tests, and we all looked down at them. My heart just about stopped when every single test read the same result.

"Holy hell." All three of us said at the same time.

Ellie and Heather both slid their arms around my waist. I looked over at Ellie, and she smiled.

"Do you want me to say congratulations or should I start preparing to hold your hair while you puke?" Ellie asked.

I felt a tear slide down my cheek.

"Both."

CHAPTER SIXTEEN

JEFF

Gunner, Josh and I were all sitting on the front porch, waiting on the girls to get back. I was starting to get worried. *What the fuck is taking them so long?*

Just then, I saw the headlights of my truck, and I let out a breath of air.

"It's about damn time. I was starting to get worried," Josh said as he stood up, running his hands through his hair.

Gunner looked at Josh and let out a laugh.

"Is there something I should know about, dude?"

Josh looked at Gunner, confused, and then he realized what Gunner was getting at.

"I wish. I can't figure Heather out for the life of me. One minute, she acts like there might be something between us, and the next, she's trying to get as far away from me as she can. I really don't know whether I'm coming or going."

"Ask her to be your date for the dance here in town this Friday," Gunner suggested.

"Gunner, if I ask her out one more time and she turns me down, I'm really afraid that I won't want to ask her again," Josh admitted.

Gunner stood up as Ari parked the truck. He gave Josh a slap on the back and laughed. "Dude, there's only one way to find out, and I'm afraid that means you'll have to ask her."

Ellie jumped out of the truck and ran over to Gunner before she jumped into his arms. I had to smile at how happy they both were. Gunner kissed the shit out of her, and then he picked her up and swung her around. *Gesh, they act like they haven't seen each other in days instead of just a few hours.*

Heather was walking up with a case of mason jars, which Josh promptly took out of her hands. He turned to take them into the house. Heather gave him the sweetest smile as she followed him.

Ari was still sitting in the truck. *That's weird.*

"Ellie, is Ari feeling okay?" I asked, looking at her.

Ellie's face went from a smile to a panicked look within a second.

"Um…I think she's feeling a bit, um…under the weather."

I walked over to the driver's side of the truck and opened it to find Ari with her head leaned up against the steering wheel.

"Baby, are you alright?" I asked as I reached in to get her out of the truck.

She was completely limp in my arms while she just buried her head into my neck. Normally, her hot breath on my neck would have turned me on, but this time it was actually starting to scare me.

"Take me home, Jeff…please," she whispered.

Home? What the hell?

"Ari, that's a few hours' drive back to Austin, baby. Maybe you should just."

"Not Austin, Jeff…our home. Please just take me to our house," Ari said.

My heart soared when she called the ranch house *our* home.

I kissed her forehead and looked back up at Ellie and Gunner. I walked her around to the passenger side and put her into my truck. She just sat there and stared straight ahead. *What the fuck was going on? She was fine when she left. Oh my god. I hope Rebecca didn't call her.* She'd been trying to call me all evening, and I ignored every call. She never once left a message, so I figured it wasn't important.

"I'm going to go say good night to Gunner and Ellie. Will you be okay until I get back, baby?"

She turned to look at me. "Yeah…I'm fine really. I just feel a little sick. That's all."

I shut the door and walked up to Ellie, who was looking at Ari in the truck. Then she glanced back at me, then back at Ari, and then back at me.

"Ellie, what the hell happened? Rebecca didn't call her, did she?" I asked confused.

Ellie looked at Gunner and then back at me. She was acting really strange.

"Um…well, um….no, Rebecca didn't call her. She just, um…she just got sick and threw up. So, yeah, she's probably just really stressed. You know this whole thing just has her thrown for a loop, Jefferson."

I turned and looked back at Ari. She was still sitting in the truck, just watching us talk. She was staring at Ellie like she wanted to get out of the truck to say something. When I turned back to look at Ellie, she was mouthing something to Ari.

Then she looked at me and smiled.

"I think she just needs some sleep, Jefferson. She'll be fine. I promise."

"Okay…Gunner, will you make sure you tell Garrett and Emma we said thanks for dinner again? I guess I'm heading over to our place. Talk to y'all tomorrow?"

Gunner and Ellie both said good night and watched as I drove the truck around to the gate that was between both ranches.

****

During the whole drive to our house, Ari just stared out the window. It was 11:30 at night, and I was exhausted from moving furniture all day. I just wanted to get home, shower, and go to bed.

I pulled up to the house and jumped out. I ran around to the other side of the truck, but Ari was already getting out. She was staring at nothing as she walked up to the house.

I grabbed her arm and turned her around. Pulling her close to me, I said,

"Ari, this will be the first time we'll stay here in this house as an engaged couple."

I was hoping that would have at least made her smile. Instead, she just pushed back away from me and stared at me. *What the hell is going on?* Her eyes looked so…lost.

Just then, the corners of her mouth started to move up, and she gave me her beautiful smile that always took my breath away. She stepped closer to me, and I leaned down to capture her mouth with mine. She kissed me back with so much passion that my knees just about buckled.

She slowly pulled away from me as she looked at me. She had tears streaming down her face. I reached up my hands to cup her face as I used my thumbs to wipe her tears away.

"Will you please make love to me, Jeff?" Ari whispered.

I never in my life could love this girl more than I did right now. As much as I knew I was hurting her, I was still the one she wanted to help her forget and feel better.

I couldn't even find my voice to speak. I reached down and scooped her up in my arms. She leaned her head into my chest as I made our way into the house.

I thanked God that I'd gone ahead and put fresh sheets on our bed earlier today. Josh had given me hell about it the whole time. The last thing I'd wanted was for Ari to be searching through all the boxes for clean sheets.

As I stepped into our room, still holding Ari in my arms, I heard the moment when she let out a gasp. She wasn't prepared to have our room all set up and ready. I softly laid her down on top of the quilt that Emma had made for us.

As I pushed Ari's beautiful hair back behind her ears, I leaned down to whisper in her ear.

"You're so beautiful, Ari. I love you so much."

She closed her eyes briefly. When she opened them again, I could see the moonlight from the window sparkling in her eyes.

I slowly pulled her up to me as I started to kiss her. The moment she bit down on my lower lip, I let out a moan. She sat up on her knees on the bed and started to take off my shirt. We only broke our kiss long enough for me to get my shirt off. As I removed her shirt, she placed both of her hands on my chest, and then slowly started to push me down onto the bed. Her whole body was shaking, making me wonder if she was nervous or just cold.

I watched her face as she started to unbutton my jeans with that damn smile of hers. I would do anything she asked me to do just to see that smile. I lifted my hips up off the bed as she began to take my pants off.

Her head snapped up at me and she raised her eye brows. "Commando, huh?"

I just laughed as I pulled her down on top of me. I rolled her over and started to slide off her shorts. I sat up and stared at her. *God, her body is amazing.* She was wearing a pair of pink lace thongs with a matching bra. I couldn't take my eyes off of her. I looked up at her perfect chest and moved my eyes down until they landed on her panties. I softly moved my hands up her legs. The moment my hands touched her, she jumped and got goose bumps.

"Ari, are you feeling up to this, baby?"

"Jeff...please don't stop! Please."

I started to pull down her panties when my fucking cell phone rang. *Motherfucker! Are you kidding me?*

I ignored it, and I made a mental note to get my fucking phone number changed. I wasn't even sure if Ari noticed the phone ringing because she didn't move or make a sound. I reached over and turned on my iPod.

I leaned down and started to kiss the inside of her thigh. She let out the most amazing moan I'd ever heard. I wanted to taste her so fucking bad.

I moved up to between her thighs and quickly took her in my mouth. She grabbed my hair and pushed me in closer. The sounds that she was making were driving me crazy. I placed two fingers inside her, and her whole body jerked up. Then, I placed another finger inside, and she started to call out my name.

I stopped kissing her after she seemed like she was coming down from her orgasm. I placed soft kisses all along her hips, moving up to her stomach, until I came face to face with her. The love I saw in her eyes was amazing. She seemed to be glowing. She let a small smile play across her face before she moved quickly, flipping me over. She was now sitting on top of me with a devilish grin on her face.

"It's my turn to be in control, baby," she said as she aimed her hips on top of mine.

The moment she sank down on me, I felt like I was going to lose control. I ran my hands up and down her body. With each motion, she about killed me with her moans of pleasure.

"Jesus, Ari, you feel so good."

She threw her body back, and before I knew it, she was calling out my name again. This time, I lost all control and came right along with her.

She laid her head on my chest, trying to catch her breath.

"I love you, Jeff. You have to know how much I love you." She slowly looked up at me.

Son of a bitch. She was crying again. It felt like someone had just kicked me in the stomach. Just then, Maroon 5's "Wipe Your Eyes" started to play. *Perfect fucking song.* I wiped off the tears from her face as she smiled at me. My heart shattered into a million pieces. She was hurting, and I couldn't fix it. She put her head on my chest.

"I know, baby. I love you just as much…if not more."

Lying there with her in my arms, I listened as her breathing become more and more relaxed as she finally drifted off to sleep. I rolled her over and pulled the sheets up over her. I sat there for a few minutes, just watching her sleep. She seemed so at peace. I wished that she was that way when she was awake.

Then, I heard my phone chirp. I knew that who-ever had called before had left a message because my notification alert kept going off. There was no way I would have told Ari we needed to stop, so I could check my phone. I already knew who had been calling.

I quietly moved off the bed and reached into my jeans pocket to get my phone. Sure enough, there was one missed call and one voice mail message from Rebecca.

I walked through the living room and stepped out onto the front porch. Rebecca had sounded panicked in her voicemail. She'd said she needed to know if I was alright because she had been trying to get a hold of me all day. *No shit.*

I looked at the time. It was close to 1 a.m. I guess I better call her.

"Jeff! Oh my god! I've been worried sick. I've been calling for hours," Rebecca said.

"Well, Rebecca, I'm fine. I told you that I was coming out to Mason and that I didn't get very good cell phone coverage here. If it was important, you could have left a message."

"I remember that now. Gesh, it must be pregnancy mind. I tend to forget things a lot lately. I was wondering what you were doing this weekend. I really need to get the baby's room ready, and I'm afraid that I'm running out of time. Is there any way you can help with painting and setting up the crib and such? I can't get anyone to help me."

"You have until the middle of August. Why are you in such a rush to get the baby's room done this weekend?"

"Jeff, please. You never know. What if something happens and the baby comes early? *Please.* If I have to beg and plead, I will. I really need help. My parents have pretty much disowned me. I have no one."

Motherfucker! Ari's going to be pissed. "Fine. I'll be there sometime tomorrow morning. It'll probably be closer to lunchtime."

"Oh, thank you so much, Jeff! You don't know how relieved I am. I'll plan on making us lunch."

"Okay. I'll be there around eleven."

"See you then Daddy!"

I ended the call and almost felt sick to my stomach. I turned around to see Ari standing in the doorway. *Fuck.*

"So, now, you feel like you have to go outside and talk to your baby mama at 1 a.m."

"Ari, it's not like that. I just didn't."

"I have a doctor's appointment on Monday with Dr. Wyatt."

"Why? Is something wrong?"

"Only the fact that Rebecca and I share the same doctor. No, nothing is wrong. My mother asked me to get tested for Fragile X, so I am."

"Shit, baby. Do you want me to go with you?"

She shook her head. "Sounds like you have a busy weekend planned. You better get to bed,"

Ari turned and walked away from me, leaving the front door open.

Fuck me! Why the hell did she have to wake up and over hear my conversation? I followed her into the bedroom and tried to get her to talk to me.

"Jeff, I'm tired. I don't feel good, and I have a lot on my mind. I'm not really in the mood to talk to you about how you're going to play Daddy and fix up a fucking baby room!" Ari shouted.

"What the hell do you want me to do, Ari? Leave her to fend for herself? She needs help, and her family has abandoned her. You really want me to be that cruel to her?"

Ari glared at me before she grabbed a pillow and a blanket.

"I'm sleeping on the sofa. I might need to get up in the middle of the night. My stomach is feeling sick again."

"Ari, please don't sleep out in the living room. Stay here with me, baby."

Ari turned to look at me, and I could see the tears building in her eyes. *Motherfucker, this sucks.* She gave me a weak smile and then turned and walked out of the bedroom.

I sat down on the bed and pushed my hands through my hair. *Why couldn't it be Ari who was pregnant and not Rebecca? Why do I keep hurting the one person I loved the most?* Laying down, I stared at the ceiling until around 4 a.m. My heart was breaking a little more with each passing minute. I never once heard Ari get up and get sick.

My alarm went off around 7:30. I got up and walked out to the living room to find that Ari was already gone.

Heading back to the bedroom, I grabbed a pair of jeans and put on a t-shirt before I went to my truck.

This day is gonna suck.

CHAPTER SEVENTEEN

GUNNER

Jeff and Ari had left a while ago and I was exhausted mentally and physically. Not to mention, I was pissed that we had to cut our damn honeymoon in half.

Grams and Gramps had been talking about my dad for the last hour. I looked over at Ellie. She was struggling to keep her eyes open. I thought back to the day before yesterday when I'd watched her sleep on the beach. My heart hurt so much from just thinking about how much I loved this girl.

She must have sensed me looking at her; she looked up at me and smiled. Her smile stopped my whole world. I would do anything to see her smile like that. She winked at me and then turned back to Grams.

"Emma, please let me know what I can do to help out with the party. Or maybe you need help getting things ready for when Grace and Jack get here? Whatever I can do to help keep Jack comfortable, please just let me know. I'd love to help out in any way."

"Ellie, darlin', you're a sweetheart. I'm so sorry y'all had to cut your honeymoon in half. Your mother is sick over it, Drew. Drew?"

I couldn't peel my eyes away from Ellie. I swore that\this girl didn't have a mean bone in her body. The minute I told her about my dad having a heart attack, she had started packing up our things. She had never once said a negative thing about giving up our honeymoon. Now, she was offering to help out a man who didn't even bother to show up for our wedding.

"Gunner, maybe we should head to the cabin. You must be exhausted," Ellie said with a sparkle in her eye. I smiled back at her and her smile grew bigger.

"I'm sorry Grams. I couldn't pull my thoughts away from my beautiful bride sitting over there. What did you say?"

Grams let out a laugh, and Gramps stood up and hit my back.

He leaned down toward my ear.

"Go on home, son. We can talk tomorrow. I can see that you're itching to have your bride in your arms."

I laughed as I stood up and shook Gramps' hand. I swore that the bastard grew wiser by the minute.

Ellie stood up and hugged Grams. They talked about getting together tomorrow to cook up a storm. Then, I noticed Grams leaned in as she whispered something to Ellie. Ellie pulled back with a surprised look on her face as she nodded her head. Grams pulled Ellie in for a longer hug as she said something to her. I couldn't even listen to what Gramps was saying to me. The look on Ellie's face was so sad. *What the hell is going on?*

***

The drive to the cabin seemed like it took forever. I held Ellie's hand the entire time as she looked out the window into the darkness.

"Sweetheart, what's wrong? I can tell you're bothered by something."

Ellie turned toward me and let a small smile play across her face.

"I guess I'm just nervous. I'm nervous about being home, helping you with the ranch, and meeting your dad. I'm also worried about what's going on with Ari. I don't know. It's all just so crazy."

I pulled her hand up to my mouth and pressed a soft kiss on it. "Don't be nervous about the ranch Ells. Gramps and Grams will help us. As far as my dad is concerned." I let out a laugh as I shook my head. "I'm not so sure that I can tell you not to be nervous about meeting him. He's a hard ass, and to be honest, he's made me nervous my whole damn life. Don't worry though, sweetheart, he's going to fall in love with you the moment he sees you, just like everyone else has."

I parked the truck as we pulled up to the cabin. It seemed like just yesterday when we had been here and I asked her to marry me. I sat there for a second, trying to get my heart-beat under control.

I jumped out and ran around to open the truck door for her. I reached in and took her hand as I helped her out of the truck.

"Such a gentleman," Ellie said with a giggle.

"I'll get the suitcases in the morning. I don't think you'll need any clothes tonight," I said as I wiggled my eye brows up and down.

Ellie let out a laugh as she jumped into my arms.

"I'm so glad to be home. I loved our honeymoon, and a part of me wishes that we were back there, listening to the ocean, but being home just feels so right."

I reached down, scooping up her legs, and carried her onto the porch. Right when I stepped up on the porch, the locusts starting singing. I had to smile while I thought about that first night on the ranch a year ago when Ellie had gotten scared and ran into my arms after she'd heard the whip-poor-will's.

"Welcome home, Mrs. Mathews." I gently started to slide her down my body. I held her as close to me as I possibly could.

The moment I felt her feet hit the porch, I captured her lips with mine. The small moan she let escape her mouth traveled throughout my body. I wanted nothing more than to make love to her right here and now.

Ellie pulled back just a little as she smiled against my lips. "Listen, they're playing our song," Ellie whispered.

I laughed and took a step back from her.

"Well, it would be rude of us to just ignore such a beautiful song, now wouldn't it?"

I held out my hand for Ellie, inviting her to dance with me. She threw her head back and laughed while she placed her hand in mine. I pulled her close, and we started to dance on the porch of our new little home. I thought that my wedding day had been the best moment of my life, but here was yet another moment with Ellie that just took my breath away.

"I love you, Drew." Ellie said as we slow danced to the Locusts humming in the trees.

"I love you, too, Ellie."

She looked up at me and smiled. "I never want this feeling to end...ever."

I smiled back at her, watching as her eyes turned from love to passion within a matter of seconds.

"What feeling would that be, sweetheart?"

"The feeling of being so incredibly in love with you that I can hardly even breathe. I'm so happy here, Gunner. I'm so very happy here in our little world."

Our little world. I couldn't have said it better even if I tried.

"I feel the same way, Ellie. I couldn't stop staring at you earlier. The only thing I could think of was getting you back to this cabin and making love to you all night long, baby."

Ellie pulled back some as she tilted her head up to me. "Well, what are you waiting for, Mr. Mathews? I'm ready to start christening this cabin."

That was all I needed to hear. I reached down and grabbed her as she let out a giggle. I opened the door, and the moment we walked in, I smelled flowers. I smiled as I thought about making love to Ellie as man and wife for the first time in this cabin.

Ellie reached behind us and turned on the lights. We both let out a gasp as we took in the cabin. Daisies were everywhere. A bottle of wine with two glasses sat next to a large tray of fruit and chocolate-covered strawberries on the kitchen table.

Ellie was staring at me as I looked at her. We both let out a laugh. At the same time, we said, "Jenny!"

"Damn, that girl is good!" I said. I started to put Ellie down…in that oh-so-slow way I knew she loved.

Ellie walked up to the table and leaned down to smell the flowers. She turned back to look at me and smiled that smile that she saves only for me. I instantly felt my dick get harder than a rock.

My knees just about buckled when she lifted up her T-shirt up over her head. Then, she slowly started to unbutton her jean shorts as she gave me the sexiest damn look I'd ever seen. She stood there in a pair of white boy short panties and white lace bra, and she had the cutest damn smile on her face.

"Well, Mr. Mathews, how long are you going to wait before you make mad passionate love to your wife in our new home?"

I'd never moved so fast in my life. She let out a laugh as I picked her up and walked us over to the bed. I tossed her on the bed and started to take off my shirt and shorts. I couldn't tear my eyes away from her. She was now sucking on her finger as she slid her legs up and down against each other. *Motherfucker*…I felt like it was our first time all over again. *The things this girl does to me.*

I slowly crawled onto the bed, lying down next to her. *My god, she is so beautiful.* She rolled onto her side to face me. Lying there, we just stared at each other. I would never get tired of just looking at her. I took the back of my hand and ran it down the side of her face. She closed her eyes as she sucked in a breath of air. When her eyes opened back up, they were on fire.

"You know, I never did thank you properly for that carriage ride," Ellie said as she slowly started to get up.

She slowly pushed me down until I was laying flat on my back. She started to kiss my neck, and then her lips moved down my chest.

"I think my favorite part of your body is your chest, Gunner."

"Oh yeah?"

"Ohh…yeah," Ellie said as she kept kissing all over my chest.

"I could say the same thing about your chest, Ells," I said with a laugh.

I quickly stopped laughing when I felt her take me in her hand. Now, it was my turn to suck in a breath of air.

I thought I just died and gone to fucking heaven. She was kissing further down my body, and with every kiss, my body felt more sensitive. The moment I felt her take me in her mouth, I had to do everything in my power not to lose control.

"Ellie." I groaned.

Good Lord, this girl was going to be my undoing. Then, she moaned, and I felt it move through my whole body. Reaching down, I grabbed her by the shoulders and pulled her up to me.

"What's wrong? Was I doing something wrong?" Ellie asked pouting.

I wanted to laugh at the look she was giving me, but more than anything, I just wanted to be inside her.

"No, baby, you were doing it too well."

I rolled over and crawled on top of her as she opened up her legs for me.

"God, Ellie…I love you so much that it hurts sometimes, baby."

Ellie arched her body toward mine as she ran her hands through my hair. I kissed the side of her neck, and moving up to her ear. It drove her crazy when I sucked on her ear-lobe. I barely slid inside of her before I backed out and made my way down her neck to her chest.

As I started to suck on one nipple, I played with the other one. Ellie let out a moan that about had me come on the spot. I barely slid back in again before I pulled out.

"Oh god, Gunner, please stop teasing me. I want you so bad…*please.*"

I smiled as I looked up at her. I watched her reaction to my every move.

I thought about how someday, I hoped soon, we would be making a baby together.

Ellie's eyes were closed as her head was thrown back slightly. I stopped there for a few seconds, just watching her. I started to enter her again, and I'll be damned if she didn't smile. It took all of my control to move slowly. I just wanted to make her feel good.

"Gunner…oh my…that feels *so good!*"

Ellie looked up at me, and our blue eyes met. I leaned over her and gently bit down on her lower lip. She started to move her hands through my hair faster. Then she grabbed me and pulled me closer to her.

Oh god. I loved the way she moved perfectly with me as we made love. She pulled away from the kiss and started to call out my name. It took everything out of me not to come with her.

When she finally came back to me, I rolled her over so she was now on top of me. I smiled up at her, and I was rewarded with the most beautiful smile ever.

"My turn, baby." I said as I winked at her.

It took every ounce of energy to last five minutes with Ellie riding me. Nothing had ever felt so good as when she was in control. The moment I heard her calling out again, I let go. She collapsed on top of me, and we were both breathing like we had just run a damn marathon.

"How was that?" Ellie said with a giggle.

God, I love her.

"Ellie, sweetheart, I want to have kids right away." I wasn't sure why I said it, but it came out before I could stop myself.

Ellie sat up and just stared at me. Then, I saw her eyes tear up, and I watched as a single tear rolled down her cheek.

Motherfucker, What did I just do?

CHAPTER EIGHTEEN

ELLIE

It took everything out of me not to jump up and down when Gunner said he wanted to have kids right away. I felt the same way, but I didn't know how to talk to him about it. I just thought he'd say we were too young, but I knew I wanted kids right away. I tried not to cry, but I was so happy I couldn't help it.

Gunner sat up and pulled me onto his lap. I placed my head on his chest, and I just lost it. I wasn't really sure why I was crying. *Is it the idea of Gunner wanting to have kids right away? Or maybe it's the fact that I was scared shitless because I'm worried that I'll be a shitty mother?*

Then, I thought about Ari. She had begged me not to tell Jeff about her being pregnant. I knew she thought that Jeff had a lot on his mind with Rebecca's stupid stunt, but I also didn't think she should hide it from him.

"Baby, I'm sorry. I didn't mean to upset you, Ellie. We don't have to start having kids right away if you're not ready. I just thought."

I leaned up to kiss Gunner. He pulled away. He seemed so confused.

"Ellie, baby, please tell me why you're crying," Gunner said as he wiped away the tears from my face.

"I want nothing more than to start having kids with you, Gunner. I would like to start right away, too. I was so afraid to talk to you about it and kept putting it off. I was worried that you would think we were too young or maybe I wouldn't be ready."

"Stop right there, Ellie. Don't ever think that way again, baby, ever. You're going to be an amazing mother." Gunner placed his hand on my stomach and smiled at me.

That damn crooked-ass smile of his gets me every time. I couldn't help but smile back at him as I placed my hand on top of his.

"So, should we? Should I stop taking the pill? Can we do this, Gunner?"

The next thing I knew, I was lying back down as Gunner kissed me so passionately that I could hardly breathe. I could practically feel his love and happiness pouring into me with every kiss. Just his touch was enough to drive me crazy. I loved him more than life itself. The thought of us trying to start a family just about had me wanting to jump up and run around the room.

Then, I thought about Ari again and I tensed up.

Gunner pulled away from me and frowned. "Ellie....what's wrong?"

"Gunner, I have to tell you something, but you have to promise me that you won't say anything to Jefferson. Will you promise me?"

Gunner rolled off of me, and we turned to face each other again. As he pushed a piece of my hair behind my ear, I had to smile.

"Of course, Ells. You know I would never betray your trust. Is everything okay?"

I shook my head. My heart started to ache as I thought back to Ari in the bathroom, throwing up as tears just poured down her face. I don't know who was more shocked, Heather or me. I'd never seen Ari so broken. She should have been happy. She should have been excited to run back to tell Jeff. Instead, she'd sat on a cold bathroom floor, scared shitless as she cried her eyes out.

"No. Tonight, when we went into town to pick up mason jars for Emma well, that's not why we went into town."

Gunner let out a laugh. "I knew that wasn't the reason, Ells."

"You did? How? Why didn't you say anything to me if you knew that wasn't the reason we were going into town?"

"Well, I figured if Grams was backing y'all up, then it must have been something important between you girls. I wasn't about to pry. I figured if you wanted me to know, you'd tell me."

Oh. My. God. I married a fucking saint. My heart was bursting with love for this man. Just when I thought he couldn't get any better, he proved me wrong.

"Gunner, I just want you to know that I love you so much. Thank you so much for trusting me and knowing I would never hide anything from you."

"Ellie, I love you so much, baby," Gunner said before he leaned in to give me a soft, sweet kiss.

"Plus, I know that Grams has like two hundred mason jars in the cellar. The second I heard her hush gramps after she gave that excuse, I knew y'all were up to something."

Laughing, I pushed Gunner's shoulder back.

"Anywho…Gunner something happened tonight with Ari. It's something big, and I'm not so sure that I can help her with it."

Gunner sat up with a sick look on his face.

"Jesus, tell me she's not leaving Jeff. He would be devastated."

"What? No! Oh my gosh, no, she's not leaving him."

"Thank God. I don't think Jeff could take another blow right now. He's really torn up with this whole Rebecca pregnancy thing. I think one more thing just might just push him over the edge."

Oh shit. Now I was starting to feel sick. I'd been so wrapped up in my own happiness that I didn't even talk to Jeff about everything today. *Shit, shit, shit!*

I sat up, pulling the covers over me a bit. Gunner instantly yanked them back down, exposing my breasts. I smiled but quickly frowned as I thought about how Jefferson might be about Ari being pregnant.

"Ellie, what's wrong? You just went white as a ghost."

I just blurted it out. "Oh, Gunner! Ari found out tonight that she's pregnant."

Now, Gunner looked like a ghost.

"What? Holy shit, Ellie. Is she okay? I mean, how did she take it? Is she going to tell Jeff tonight?"

"Um... Well, I don't think she's okay. She had already scheduled a doctor's appointment for Monday, so she could be tested for the Fragile X gene. So, she's worried about that, but I think she's more scared about how Jefferson is going to take it."

"Ellie, you have to know that Jeff is going to be ecstatic about it. He wants nothing more than to have a baby with Ari."

"Well, yeah, I'm sure under normal circumstances he would be overjoyed, but with Rebecca being pregnant, I'm not so sure. Ari said that Jefferson drops everything every time that bitch calls. I think Ari is about at her breaking point. She also thinks that Rebecca is lying. When Jefferson and Rebecca met for lunch on Monday, Ari got a good look at her. She said that Rebecca looks a lot bigger than seven months."

"Shit. This is all so fucked up. I can't even imagine how Ari is feeling right now. Are you going with her to her appointment on Monday?"

Oh Lord. I thought about Ari and her big plan. I just nodded my head and tried to smile.

"Gunner, no matter what, we have to be there for both Jeff and Ari. She's not planning on telling him anytime soon. I think she's making a mistake, but I told her that I would honor her wishes. I just don't want her to take this on all alone. By the way, Emma knows. As a matter of fact, Emma was the one who told Ari that she was probably pregnant. I swear that your grandmother has magical powers!"

Gunner threw his head back and laughed. "Yeah, my cousins and I used to say that when we were little. She always seemed to know when we were up to something. We thought it was pretty cool that she was so smart. Now it just seems kind of creepy how she knows something before you even know it."

"Well, I sure wish she could use her powers to help Ari and Jeff figure this shit out."

"I know, baby. We'll be there for both Jeff and Ari. Don't worry. Let's just get Ari through her appointment on Monday, my dad's arrival Tuesday, Grams and Gramps party on Wednesday. Shit."

I knew Gunner was nervous about his father coming to the ranch. It had been four years since he's even talked to his dad.

I got up on my knees, letting the sheet fall completely off my body. Leaning over, I captured Gunner's mouth with mine as I ran my hands through his beautiful messy hair. I tried to kiss him with as much passion and love as I could. The moan he let out just about gave me an orgasm right there on the spot.

"Drew, make love to me, please."

Gunner gently laid me down, barely putting any weight on me, while he returned my kiss with just as much passion and love.

"Shall we practice making that baby?" Gunner said as he smiled against my lips.

Letting out a giggle, I wrapped my legs around him. The moment he pushed himself inside of me it felt like heaven.

"Yes...and I think we're gonna need a lot of practice."

CHAPTER NINETEEN

ARI

I watched as Jeff pulled up and parked. He looked around as he walked up to Garrett and Emma's house, and then went inside. I was sure that he was looking for me.

I'd gotten up earlier and taken one of the horses out for a ride. *God, I wish I could just ride away from all of this shit.*

I put my hand down on my stomach while I imagined telling Jeff about the baby. *He would be so happy. He would take me in his arms and tell me how much he was going to love both of us, no matter what.*

I closed my eyes and pictured a little one running around the ranch. I would teach her how to ride a horse for the first time, play chase all over the country-side, and swim in the river.

My eyes flew open the moment I thought of Matthew. My sweet, sweet baby brother. I loved him so much. He made our lives so incredibly special. *But am I as strong as my mother? Would I be able to handle a child with Fragile X?*

I heard the screen door open. I pulled Big Roy back behind the tree while I watched Gunner and Jeff talking. I wondered if Ellie had told Gunner about me being pregnant. I knew that Gunner would honor my wishes and never tell Jeff.

I saw Gunner and Jeff shake hands, and then Gunner slapped Jeff while he walked back out to his truck. Running his hand through his hair, he looked so damn sad as he looked around again.

Just then, my cell phone rang, spooking both Big Roy and me. Grabbing it quickly, I answered it without looking to see who was calling.

"Ari! I love you!"

I let out a laugh. "Hey, little buddy! I love you, too, Matthew. What are you doing today, sweets?"

"Can we go to lunch today, Ari? Please? Jeff too. I want to see Jeff, Ari. Where is he today?"

My heart broke.

"Um… well, I can have lunch with you today, buddy, but Jeff can't. He has other plans with someone else. Give me a couple of hours to get home, okay Matt? Can I talk to Mommy?"

"Okay! Here is Mommy. I love you, Ari."

"I love you, too, Matt."

I heard Matt running up to my mother to hand her the phone.

"Ari, sweetheart, how are you doing?"

Oh, fuck a duck. The moment I heard her voice the tears started.

"Um…" I sniffled.

"Ari! Are you crying? What did he do to you, Ari? Your father will kill him."

I had to let out a laugh. *God how I love my parents.*

"Mom, I'm fine. I'm just a bit…emotional. Jeff didn't really do anything other than drop everything this week whenever the bitch called him."

My mother let out a sigh. "Talk to me, Ari. Are you outside? It sounds like wind is blowing into your cell phone."

"Yep, I took Gunner's horse out for a ride this morning. I needed some fresh air and a strong man between my legs to clear my head."

My mother let out a giggle and said something about raising me right.

"Ari, I hear it in your voice. Something's not right, sweetheart. Please talk to me."

There was no way I was telling her about the baby.

"I have a doctor's appointment on Monday mom, I'm getting tested. I guess I'm just scared."

That wasn't a lie. I was scared shitless.

"Do you want me to go with you? Is Jeff going?" she asked.

I sighed as the conversation from last night came rushing back to me full force. I thought about Jeff standing on the porch, talking to Rebecca.

"No, Jeff isn't going. Ellie and Heather are going with me. There's no need to worry Jeff with anymore shit. I'll be fine, Mom. I'll have my girls with me."

"Are you sure, Arianna? I really don't mind going with you. I'm sure you'll have a lot of questions, but Dr. Wyatt is so good. You're in good hands, honey."

"Yeah, Mom I know. Don't worry about me. I'm a strong bitch. What is that Katharine says, Mom? 'Drive on. We'll sweep up the blood later!' That's me."

My mother laughed.

Jesus, Mary, and Joseph. Now I'm quoting Katharine Hepburn. Fuck. If this was what being pregnant was all about, then I was in for a long damn ride.

"So, Matthew wants you to take him to lunch today, honey, but I wasn't sure if you were coming into town or not."

"I would love to have lunch with him. Give me a few hours to get there. I need to put Big Roy up and get him taken care of. I'll grab a quick shower, and then I'll head in. Oh, I didn't tell you! Gunner and Ellie are back early from their honeymoon. Gunner's father had a heart attack. He's okay, but Gunner's mom and dad are coming to stay at the ranch for a few weeks."

"Oh no! That's terrible. I met Grace at the wedding. She seems like a sweet lady. She told me a little bit about Gunner and his father's troubled relationship. I look forward to seeing them at

Garrett and Emma's anniversary party. I hope Gunner and his dad can make peace with each other."

"Yeah, so does Ellie. Alright, Mom, I'm gonna let ya go, so I can get ready to head in."

"Alright, sweetheart, be careful driving, and we'll see you soon."

***

Matthew came running out of the house the moment I pulled up and got out of my Jeep. He ran into my arms, and I picked him up and gave him a big bear hug. I held on to him just a little longer than normal.

"Ari! Put me down now. You will suffocate me with your bear hug!" Matthew said with a laugh.

"Oh my gosh! Do you think I'm that strong, buddy?"

"Where's your horse, Ari?"

"She is at Jeff's ranch back in Mason. She has a new stall, and she loves it. You'll get to see her in a few days when you come out to Garrett and Emma's big party."

"Another party? Is this a wedding, too? Do I get to be in it again?"

I threw my head back and laughed. "Not this time, sweets. Come on. Are you ready to go eat?"

I looked up and smiled when I saw my mother standing on the porch watching. She tilted her head and gave me a funny look. She started to walk down the steps while I was buckling Matt's seat belt.

"Y'all have fun this afternoon okay?"

I turned to look at my mom, I started to answer her when she stopped dead in her tracks.

She looked me up and down and then smiled. "Oh. My. God."

I looked behind me and then all around me. "What? What's wrong? Shit! Do I have a flat tire or something?"

My mother walked up and placed her hands on my shoulders. As she looked at me, she said,

"Arianna Katherine Peterson. How long have you known?"

What the fuck is she talking about?

"Um, Mom...when did you take up drinking in the mornings? What the hell are you talking about?"

My mom shut the door to my Jeep and pulled me a few steps away.

"Smile big, Ari. Let me see your gums?"

"What the hell, Mom? Oh my god, does Dad know you finally snapped? You need a vacation in a bad way."

My mom threw her head back and laughed. Then, proceeded to try and stick her fingers in my mouth to look at my gums.

"Mom!"

"Ari, when did you find out?"

"When did I find out what, Mom? Oh my god, just come out with it. You're starting to scare me."

"That you're pregnant. How long have you known?"

Fuck. A. Duck. What is with these women and their super-natural powers?

"How did you...what made you think...wait..." I couldn't even talk right, I was so shocked that my mother just had to look at me to know I was pregnant.

My mother started to laugh as she pulled me into a hug.

She pushed me out at arm's length, her eyes moving up and down as she examined me. Then, she frowned. "You haven't told Jeff, have you?"

I let out a sigh and turned to check on Matt. He was playing with his Play Station. He looked so content, like he was in heaven.

"Mom I just found out last night. It was really weird because Emma was the one who told me she thought I was pregnant. Mom, you can't tell anyone, not even Dad!"

"What? Why, Ari?"

"Can we talk about it later, Mom? I really just want to spend some time with Matt. We'll talk when I get back, okay?" I kissed my Mom on the cheek before I ran around to the driver's side of the Jeep.

I took one last look at my mom. She was blowing kisses to Matt. Then, she looked up at me with a sad smile. *Shit.* The last thing I wanted was sympathy from anyone.

***

"Ari, I like their chocolate milk shakes here," Matt said.

I laughed because it was the fourth time that Matt had told me he liked the milk shakes at Mighty Fine Burgers.

Just then, I saw Brad Smith come walking in. Our eyes met at the same time and he gave me that bright-ass smile of his. The last time I saw him was when my parents took Ellie, Jeff, and me out to dinner on graduation night.

Brad gave me a wave, and I smiled and waved back.

"Hey, Matt, I'm gonna go order you a chocolate milk shake. Will you sit right here and eat your hamburger and french fries for me?"

"Sure, Ari! Make sure you get chocolate."

I walked up to the counter and stood in line behind Brad. After he finished ordering his food, he moved to the side, waiting for me as I ordered Matt's milkshake.

"Ari, my god, look at how beautiful you look. You're practically glowing!" Brad said.

Jesus, please don't ask me if I'm pregnant.

"Ha! Thanks, Brad. How are you?" I walked up to him and gave him a quick hug.

"I'm doing good thanks. How about you? I heard you and Jeff Johnson are an item now."

I held up my left hand, showing him my engagement ring, and smiled. "Yep."

"Well, I'll be damned. Congratulations, darlin'. He's one lucky bastard."

I let out a laugh as they called my name for Matt's shake.

"Are you eating alone? You want to join my little brother, Matt, and me?"

Brad looked over toward Matt and smiled.

"Sure, if he doesn't mind the extra company, I'd love to join y'all."

***

We sat there for a good fifteen minutes, catching up on things. Brad was going to vet school at Texas A-&-M, and was in town for the summer. Matt asked Brad twenty million questions. At first, Brad had seemed to be frustrated but then he must have remembered that Matt had Fragile X. Brad was trying to be patient, but I could tell it was getting to him. I'd only met one guy who had the patience of a saint when it came to Matt, and that was Jeff.

Brad just finished telling Matt a silly joke. As we all started laughing, I glanced up and saw Jeff and Rebecca walking in. I let out a gasp, which caused Brad to turn around to see what I was looking at. Jeff saw me the moment he walked in the door. His eyes shot from me to Brad to Matthew and then back to me. He looked confused as hell.

Brad turned back and looked at me.

"Um, Ari, why is your fiancé walking in with another girl…a very pregnant girl?"

I couldn't pull my eyes away from them. Rebecca had yet to see me. I was pretty sure that once she did, she'd run out the door screaming.

"Ari? Are you okay?" Brad asked.

I looked back at Brad and tried to smile.

"Ah, it's a really long story, Brad. Jeff hooked up with this girl before we got together, and he just found out last week that she's expecting, um…she's having a,…um."

I turned back to look at Jeff and Rebecca. That bitch was smiling at me. She leaned up and whispered something to Jeff. Then, he glanced at me, frowning. *What the fuck?*

"She's having his baby, Ari. Is that what you're trying to say?" Brad said.

"Jeff is having a baby, Ari?" Matthew asked. Then, he saw Jeff and yelled,

"Jeff!"

Reaching across, I grabbed Matt and pulled him back to me.

"No, buddy, we can't talk to Jeff right now. He's with…he's with a friend right now, Matt. So, can you sit back down like a good boy and finish up your shake? We need to leave, buddy."

I looked at Brad. He looked confused as hell. He kept looking at Jeff and then back at me.

"Ari, is there anything I can do to help out? I mean…shit. If you just need someone to talk to… you know, if you need a friend or something."

"She has all the friends she needs, dude." Jeff interrupted.

I looked up and saw Jeff standing there, giving Brad a go-to-hell look. Matt jumped up and ran toward Jeff. He bent down and gave Matt a big hug.

I felt the tears building in my eyes again, but then I looked over at Rebecca, who was glaring at me. My sadness was quickly replaced with anger. *Bitch.*

"Hey, buddy! I didn't know you were having lunch with Ari today." Jeff looked over at me and tried to smile.

"He called me earlier this morning and asked if we could have lunch today, " I explained.

Jeff stood back up and walked Matt back over to his chair.

"So how'd you meet up with your friend here?"

Jeff asked me as he looked at Brad.

Brad stood up and introduced himself.

"Hi, I think we might have met last year. I'm Brad Smith."

Jeff reached out and shook his hand. "Yeah...I remember you."

"I just happened to run into Ari."

"I asked him if he wanted to join Matt and me for lunch." I looked back to where Rebecca was standing at another table. The look she was giving me made me sick to my stomach.

I swear to God the moment she has the baby I am going to beat the shit out of her.

"Looks like Rebecca's waiting for you, Jeff," I said with a faint smile.

Jeff just looked at me. Without another word, he turned around to walk toward Rebecca.

Fuck! Out of all the places they had to go to lunch, why did they come here?

***

By the time I got back to my parents' house, the last thing I wanted to do was talk to my mom, but she was waiting outside, so I couldn't avoid her. I helped Matt out of the car, and walked up to the house.

"Did you have fun with your sister today, honey?"

"Yep! And we had lunch with Brad. He is Ari's friend, but Jeff didn't like him."

My mother looked up at me, and I gave her a don't ask look.

"Run along inside, Matt. Your daddy is waiting in the living room for you. Ari, I have to talk to you for a few minutes."

I gave Matt a kiss and hug good-bye. Watching him run into the house, I couldn't help but smile. The fact that he picked up on Jeff not liking Brad made me laugh.

I sat down on the porch step and waited for my mom to join me.

"So, I take it you ran into Jeff? And who is Brad?" she asked.

"Brad Smith. We ran into him on graduation night, remember? I dated him for a bit in high school."

"Yes, I do remember him now. And Jeff?"

I let out a gruff laugh. "Oh, yeah. Well, I guess Jeff and his baby mama had a hankering for a burger. I didn't know they were going to be there. Jeff came up to the table, and I guess he wasn't too pleased to see Brad sitting with Matt and me."

"Wait. What was Jeff doing with Rebecca?"

"Oh, well, he was playing the good Daddy, Mom. You know, he's painting the baby room, putting up the crib. Playin' house, and all."

My mother shook her head and looked at me. "Now, Ari, don't be bitter. It's not becoming for a young lady."

I just looked at her. "I'm not bitter, Mom. I'm pissed! I'd bet you my inheritance that she is further along than she says. I'm going to find out, you just watch and see."

"Oh dear Lord, I don't even want to know what you have up your sleeve, Arianna. Just please don't break any laws and embarrass your father."

"Thanks for the vote of confidence there, Mom. I won't break any laws...at least not on purpose!" I said with a wink.

We both laughed, and then my mother took my hand in hers. *Here we go.*

"Ari, don't be scared tomorrow, sweetheart. Let me know the moment you leave if they can tell how far along you are. Get your prescription for your prenatal vitamins filled as soon as you leave. Take them every day. It's all going to be okay, Ari. Even if you are a carrier, there's a chance that you won't pass it along. Chin up, my dear. Now, tell me why you're not telling Jeff that you're pregnant."

I put my head down on my knees, I tried to take a few deep breaths. As I felt my Mom's hands moving up and down my back, I instantly felt calm.

"Mom, I can't tell him... at least not for a few more weeks anyway. He's going with Rebecca to an appointment next week. If she truly lets him go, then I have no doubt in my mind that she's telling the truth about the baby being his. What if he doesn't want the responsibility of having *two* kids mom? He's going to be so overwhelmed. What if...what if her baby is healthy...and mine."

"Arianna Peterson! You did not just start to say that. Look at your brother. He is one of the best things that has ever happened to this family. He is a blessing. You see how much Jeff loves him and how good Jeff is with him. Even if this child does end up with Fragile X, you know it's not the end of the world, Ari. I'm shocked at your thinking."

I looked at my mother with tears filling my eyes. "Mom, I'm not you. I'm not strong like you. What if I can't do this? What if Jeff ends up falling in love with Rebecca's baby? He won't want to live two hours away from him. Did I tell you that she's having a boy mom?" Then, I completely lost it and just started crying.

My mother pulled me into her arms and rocked me back and forth. *Shit.* This whole crying thing was starting to piss me off! We sat there for a good fifteen minutes. We didn't talk as my mom just held me, letting me get it all out. I cried so much that I was sure we were both going to need to change our shirts from my water-works.

Just then, I heard a car coming up the driveway. I felt my mother tense up. I looked up and saw Jeff pulling up. I jumped up and ran into the house, leaving my mother alone to fend for herself.

I went into the bathroom and splashed my face with cold water. Then, I heard a knock on the door. *Shit! Why would she let him come in?* I slowly opened the door and peeked out to see my father looking at me. *Fuck me. I can't handle any more today.*

"You okay, princess? Do I need to kick his ass? I'll do it, baby girl. Just give me the word, and I'll hire a really big guy to kick his ass."

I started laughing uncontrollably. I laughed so hard that I had to lean my hands on my knees as I tried to catch my breath. Just then, Jeff and my mom walked up.

"What did you say to her Mark?" my mom asked.

"Ah...nothing. I um, just offered to, um...take care of something for her. She just lost it."

Jeff started to laugh and then both my parents did.

"Well, whatever you said, thank you. I've been missing that laugh," Jeff said as he smiled at me.

***

After my laughter episode, I said good-bye to Matthew and my parents. Jeff walked out with me to my Jeep. He grabbed my arm and pulled me into a hug.

"Hey, I just wanted to make sure you were okay. I figured you were here, so I took a chance at coming over," he said.

I tried to breathe in the smell of him, but all I could smell was perfume...and not my perfume.

I pushed away from him and covered my mouth. I instantly felt sick.

"Ari, what's wrong? Is your stomach still upset?"

"All I smell is her perfume on you! Why do I smell her perfume on you?"

Jeff looked confused, and then he shook his head. "Um...well um...maybe because she broke down when we finished up painting. She started crying, I just gave her a hug, to um...well I don't know...make her feel better, I guess."

Son of a bitch. "I'm heading back out to the ranch. Are you done?"

"No, I just had to run out and buy a screwdriver, I didn't have the right one in my truck, and Rebecca doesn't have any. I needed it to put the crib together."

I just stood there and looked at him. I didn't even know how I should be feeling right now.

"I have to go."

"Ari, wait! The hug didn't mean a damn thing. How do you think I felt when I walked in to see you having lunch with an old boyfriend?"

I spun around, narrowing my eyes at him.

"What? Are you fucking kidding me, Jeff? I ran into him while I was having lunch with my brother. What's your excuse for your little lunch date with your baby mama? You two looked awfully cozy together. I can see how painful it is for you to be with her. I'm heading back to Mason. I guess I'll see you when you're done playing house."

"Jesus Christ, Ari can we just stop doing this?" Jeff shouted.

I jumped back for a second shocked that he raised his voice so loud.

Without another word, I walked to the driver side of my Jeep and got in.

***

The two-and-a-half hour drive back to Mason was the longest drive of my life. I did nothing but cry, think, and cry some more.

I pulled up to Garrett and Emma's house to see Ellie and Heather sitting on the porch. I smiled at the sight of my two best friends. I was so glad that Ellie was back. She looked so happy with a huge smile on her face. I did my best to act normal, but it was so hard when all I was doing was dying inside.

I took a deep breath and got out of the Jeep. Ellie and Heather both stood up and started to walk toward me. The moment we reached each other, Ellie took me into her arms.

Heather hugged both of us. She whispered into my ear.

"Let it go, Ari. We're here, baby. Just let it go."

CHAPTER TWENTY

JEFF

I sat outside Rebecca's place, trying to decide if I should go in or just head home to Ari. I slammed my hand down on the steering wheel. *God, I'm such a stupid asshole!* I couldn't believe that I'd gotten upset with Ari just because she ran into someone.

I'd almost fallen over when I saw her sitting there with Matt. Then, I noticed that jerk sitting there with her, and I almost lost it. I could have killed Rebecca the second we'd walked in. She'd said she was going to make us lunch. When she suggested going out because she was craving a hamburger, I had thought it would be okay. I'd never fucking dreamed that Ari would be sitting there when we'd walked in.

Taking a deep breath, I grabbed the Home Depot bag and made my way to Rebecca's apartment. I knocked and then opened the door. I walked in to see her standing there with a cold beer in her hand.

"I thought you might like a beer, you know, just to take the edge off or whatever."

Shit, I actually could use one. When I reached for it, she placed her hand on my arm, caressing her fingers up and down. I instantly took a step back away from her, and she gave me a frown.

"Jeff, I'm just trying to be appreciative. There's nothing wrong with that, is there? I really don't know how I would have done this without you. So, we're pretty much done painting the room. Do you like the color?"

I walked into the small bedroom, I looked around at the pale blue walls. Rebecca walked into the room and started talking about all the things she was going to hang up on the walls.

I started to picture Ari, standing where Rebecca was, with a seven month pregnant belly. I bet she would look beautiful pregnant. *Beyond beautiful.* I dreamed of the day when Ari told me she was having our baby. *What would she want? A boy? I bet she would want a girl.* Then, I thought of Ari's appointment on Monday. My smiled faded for a second until I looked at Rebecca.

She was still talking away about decorating the baby's room. I took a good look at her. She had that glow; the kind people say pregnant women get. Her skin really did look beautiful. Her blonde hair had grown longer falling past her shoulders. She was probably an inch or two shorter than Ari. I smiled at how her hands were moving wildly. She was really getting into the description of the letters she wanted to put on the wall. I looked down at her stomach, and a strange feeling came over me. I walked up to her and placed my hands on her belly.

She instantly stopped talking. Just then, I felt the baby move. It felt like he was doing a somersault in her stomach. I smiled, making Rebecca laugh.

The next thing I knew, she was reaching up to pull my face down to hers. She started kissing my lips, and for one brief second, I pictured myself kissing a pregnant Ari. The moment Rebecca let out a moan, I was snapped back to reality.

Pulling back, I placed my hands on Rebecca's shoulders, moving her a step away from me.

"What the fuck, Rebecca? You can't do shit like that to me!"

I glanced down at Rebecca's chest that was moving up down, fast and hard. I looked back up and caught her eyes.

"Jeff, I don't know why you keep fighting this connection we feel for each other. We're having a baby, It's normal to be attracted to each other."

Oh shit. "Rebecca, I was just feeling the baby. It had nothing to do with how I feel for you. Let me remind you again that we are just friends. I love Ari. I'm going to marry Ari."

She let out a laugh and turned to walk out of the bedroom. "Please, Jeff. If Ari is so in love with you, then why is she making this so hard for you? She should be more supportive. She shouldn't be having lunch with some other guy."

"She would be more supportive, Bek, if you dropped the damn restraining order. What's going to happen when he's born? I'm going to want Ari to be in his life whether you like it or not."

Rebecca placed her hands on her stomach and then leaned up against the wall. She almost looked like she was in pain.

"Rebecca, what's wrong? Is something wrong with the baby?" My heart started to race, and I instantly felt sick. *Fuck me.* If I caused this, I would never forgive myself.

I helped her over to the sofa where she sat down and started to take deep breaths.

"Do you need something? A glass of water? Your phone to call the doctor? Just tell me!"

She let out a giggle and looked up at me. "Jeff, calm down. It's okay. I think it's just Braxton Hicks contractions. They're just really uncomfortable."

"Contractions! You're not far along enough to have contractions," I practically shouted.

"They're not true labor contractions, Jeff. Christ, calm down or you'll get me upset again. This is why I can't stress about things. I can't go into labor early. It'll be bad for the baby."

Shit. I ran my hands through my hair as I sat down on the sofa next to her. "I'm sorry, Rebecca. This is just so hard for me. Ari and I waited so long to be together, and now, I feel like we're just drifting apart so damn fast."

Rebecca started rubbing her hand up and down my back.

"Jeff, this is my fault. I'm so sorry that I dropped this pregnancy thing on you like this. I really thought that I'd be able to handle it by myself, but I just felt so guilty not telling you about the baby. The whole restraining order…I'll drop it first thing Monday morning. I guess I was being silly with that."

I turned to look at Rebecca who was giving me a big smile. I reached over and hugged her. "Jesus, Rebecca that would be awesome if you could do that. I'm sure it would put Ari's mind at ease!"

Pulling back, I placed a kiss on the side of her check. I felt like a ton of weights had just been lifted from my shoulders. I jumped up and grabbed the Home Depot bag and took the screwdriver out.

"What do you say we build ourselves a crib?" I said.

Rebecca started laughing as she stood up.

"That sounds great! Let's do this."

***

I heard Ari moving around in the kitchen. *Fuck, why is she up so damn early?* She barely spoke two words to me Saturday night after I got back from Rebecca's. Yesterday, Gunner and I pretty much worked all day in the stables, so I hadn't really talked to her in a couple of days.

Mr. Reynolds was coming tomorrow to check out everything. If I could work out a deal with him to breed our horses with a few of his stallions, then we would have the start we needed.

I heard Ari talking to someone on the phone. I walked into the kitchen and just stood there, watching her.

"Heather, goddamn it, just wear it. I don't have time to argue with you about this. Ellie isn't arguing. She's being a good friend. Just do this for me! Yes! Okay, sweets. See you in a few."

Then, she put her ear plugs back in and started up her iPod. Just barely, I could hear Wil.I.Am's "Scream and Shout." Ari started dancing, and I couldn't help but smile at her. *Damn, this girl can move. I'm a lucky son of a bitch.* Then, she started singing. *How does this girl make my knees weak just by dancing around and singing in a kitchen?*

She was standing at the sink, cutting up vegetables and fruit.

I walked up behind her, putting my arms around her. I started to kiss her neck. *Damn, she feels so good in my arms.*

She spun around and gave me that beautiful smile of hers. She looked breath taking. I couldn't really place it, but she just seemed so different to me lately.

She pulled her earphones out and reached up and gave me a kiss. I pulled her in closer, deepening the kiss. She let out a small moan that went right through my body. I picked her up, so she could wrap her legs around me. I turned her around and set her down on the kitchen island.

She was dressed in baby blue lace panties and a white T-shirt. *Shit.* She wasn't even wearing a bra. Through her shirt, I saw when her nipples instantly got hard. Reaching up, I grabbed some of her hair and pulled her head back, exposing her neck to me. I started to kiss from one side of her neck to the other. I could practically feel her coming apart in my hands. Slowly, I started to lift up her shirt. I broke our kiss only to pull her T-shirt up and over her head.

After another five minutes of just kissing the woman I loved, I started to unbutton my pants. Ari smiled against my lips, and I swore that I could hear my heart beating in my ears.

"Babe, I'm gonna make love to you on our kitchen island," I whispered in her ear.

"I think that's how we should start our day every day!" Ari said with a giggle.

Just then, my fucking cell phone rang. I ignored it. I pulled Ari closer to me. I was just about to enter her when the phone went off again. I closed my eyes, praying that it would stop.

We sat there for a second to see if it would ring again. When it didn't, we both smiled, and Ari wiggled her eye brows up and down.

Then, someone knocked on the door. *Motherfucker!* All I wanted to do was slam my fist into a wall. Ari pushed me back and jumped off the island.

"Who the hell is here so early?" she asked.

"Well, I guess the only way to find out is for you to go answer the door in those sweet-ass panties and white T-shirt."

"Fuck you, Jeff. There's no way I'm going to the door half-naked. I thought we could walk around our home naked if we wanted to. Isn't this the country for fuck's sake?"

Ari stormed off into the bedroom, and I couldn't help but let out a laugh. I loved it when she was spit and fire. I think it turned me on even more.

I pulled open the front door to see Josh standing there. He looked…well, honestly, he looked like shit.

"Dude, what the fuck happened to you?" I asked.

Josh just gave me a smile and pushed his way into the house. He walked over and sat down on the sofa, putting his head down in his hands, he said,

"Jeff, I don't know what to do anymore. I'm at a total loss with Heather. I want to say that I would sit here and wait forever for her, but I'm not sure she's ever going to change her mind about me. I'm not sure if I even want her to."

"What the hell does that mean? If you want her to? I thought you really liked her."

Josh sat back and let out a sigh.

"I do. I mean, I've never felt this way for anyone in my life. A part of me just wants to take her and lock her in a room with me until she talks to me. The other part wants to push her as far away from me as I can. She deserves someone better than a damn man whore."

Shit. I was having a déjà vu big time.

"Listen, Josh, if I can offer one piece of advice, it would be to fight for her. Don't let your past stand in the way of what could be a really great thing. I've seen Heather look at you. I'm pretty damn sure that girl has feelings for you. Maybe it has nothing to do with you and everything to do with her. From what Ellie and Ari have told me, Heather pretty much put up a wall when her mom and dad died. Maybe she's just afraid to let anyone in for fear of losing them. You need to talk to her and let her know your feelings, so she can let you know hers."

Josh turned and looked at me. He was giving me a strange-ass look.

"What the hell has happened to you and Gunner? He said the same damn thing to me yesterday. Fuck, I just need to get screwed."

"Well, there's the Josh we all know and don't love,"Ari said from behind us.

I turned to see her standing there, wearing a pair of capri jean's and a black t-shirt that said *"Dear Math, I'm not a therapist. Solve your own problems."*

"Yeah, hello to you, too, Ari. Are you going to see Heather today by any chance?" Josh asked.

I noticed when Ari tensed up. I knew she was worried about this appointment and it was killing me she wouldn't let me go with her.

"Yep, she's going with me to a doctor's appointment. Do you want me to remind her of how much of an ass-wipe you are or something?" Ari said with a wicked smile on her face.

Josh jumped and turned to face Ari. "Are you telling her that?"

I thought Josh was about to cry. *Pussy.*

Ari let out a laugh and shook her head. "Calm down before you break down and start crying, you big pussy. No, I'm not telling her that shit. I'm not really sure what that girl sees in you, Josh, but I do think she is smitten with you."

Josh let a small smile play across his face. Then he shook his head. "I asked her to be my date to Garrett and Emma's anniversary party, and she said *no*. I don't know what else to do. Every time I ask her out, she just flat turns me down. I don't get it."

Ari walked over and gave Josh a hug. It somewhat surprised me, but I think it shocked the hell out of Josh.

"Let me talk to her, Josh. I really think the issue is more than just your man-whoring ways sweets." Ari let out a laugh before she, turned to walk into the kitchen.

I started to laugh as I slapped Josh on the back. "Don't worry, dude. If it's meant to be, it'll happen."

"Yeah, I guess so. Anyway, Gunner needs help feeding the cows and repairing the fence in the south pasture. You in?"

"Sounds good. Just give me a few minutes, and I'll meet y'all at Garrett's place."

I watched as Josh drove off in his pussy truck. *Damn, why did that boy get a Dodge gas truck?* I turned to walk back in as Ari was heading out.

"Wait. You don't want to finish what we started, baby?" I said.

I grabbed her and pulled her into a kiss. She pulled back and laughed.

"As much as I would love to do that, babe, I really have to go. Ellie and Heather are waiting for me at Emma and Garrett's place."

"Let me grab my hat, and I'll ride with you. I have to meet Gunner and Josh at the house anyway."

***

One the way over to the ranch house, Ari barely spoke two words to me. When she did talk, she was a nervous wreck. I really hated that she wouldn't let me go with her.

I watched as Ari drove off with Ellie and Heather. The moment she saw Ellie, I could see her relax. Emma hugged her and whispered something into her ear while Gunner just stood there and stared at me. I felt like the fucking black sheep of the herd. I was part of it, yet I was also an outcast because I was trying to do the right thing by Rebecca.

The rest of the morning, all I could do was think about Ari. I kept checking my phone to see if I might have missed a call. I silently said a prayer for her tests results that she wasn't a carrier of the Fragile X gene. Ari was so stressed over it. It wasn't that I wouldn't love any child we had together because I would. I adored Matthew with all my heart.

I walked over to the Jeep and pulled out a bottle of water from the ice cooler. I took a long drink, pulled out my cell again and hit dial.

It was time for me to make plans with my little buddy to go fishing. The moment Susan put Matt on the phone, my heart swelled up with love.

Yeah, it really didn't matter. I just wanted kids with Ari, I just wanted our home to be filled with laughter.

CHAPTER TWENTY-ONE

ARI

Sitting on the table in Dr. Wyatt's office, I just stared at all the pictures of pregnant women, babies, and big tummies. The whole bulletin board was covered in pictures. I smiled when I saw a picture of my mother holding Matt from nine years ago. I was standing in the picture next to them, holding up rabbit ears behind my mother.

Dr. Wyatt came and sat down on the stool. He smiled at me, and I smiled back, but I felt like I wanted to throw up.

"Well, Ari, we drew all the blood we needed, and I should get the genetic tests back in two weeks. Your urine test came back positive for pregnancy. The next thing I would like to do is a transvaginal sonogram, so that way we can take a look and maybe see how far along you are. From our earlier conversation and the date of your last period, I'm guessing that you're about nine weeks. That would put us at a due date of January thirtieth."

My head was spinning. *Nine weeks! Oh. My. God. I have a little baby in me…growing inside of me…holy hell.*

"Um, when do you think I'll start showing?" I asked as I pulled at the gown I was wearing.

Dr. Wyatt reached up, taking my hands in his.

"Ari, I know you're scared for a number of reasons. Let's just take this one step at a time, okay? There's nothing we can do about Fragile X until we get the results back. Don't stress yourself out. Now, to answer your question, you'll probably start showing around the first week of October. Keep in mind though that everyone is different though."

I shook my head. Dr. Wyatt asked me to lie back on the table. He stuck his head out and called for a nurse.

As a nurse joined us, Dr. Wyatt said,

"I need you to relax now, Ari."

I kept my eyes on the monitor while I started to take deep breaths. Then, I saw it. It looked like a little peanut. I could hear it's heart beating like crazy. My eyes started to tear up, and I looked away.

"Ari, honey, are you okay?" The nurse asked me.

I looked back at her and smiled.

"He should be here. I should have told him," I said while tears poured down my cheeks.

The nurse took a hold of my hand and gave it a little squeeze.

"Honey, there are tons of women who come in here and get the first sonogram alone. You're not always one-hundred percent sure that you're pregnant. Some women like to wait until they know for sure before they tell the fathers."

I tried to smile at her. When I looked back at my peanut, my smile grew bigger as I saw her little arms moving back and forth.

"She's waving to you," Dr. Wyatt said with a laugh.

"She?" I asked as I looked at him. There's no way they can tell this early.

"Well, I usually call them all *she* until we find out for sure. It's an old habit I picked up years ago," He said with a laugh.

***

After Dr. Wyatt and the nurse left the room, I sat there for a few seconds, looking at the picture I held in my hand of my peanut. I placed my hands on my stomach, I closed my eyes.

"We just need to hold off another month, baby. Once Daddy finds out that the evil witch is not carrying his child, we can tell him about you. There's no fucking way- oh god! Oh. My. God! I just swore at you. Oh, holy shit, I'm gonna make a piss-ass mother. OH! My! GOD! I did it again!"

I jumped down off the table and quickly got dressed.

I wondered how Heather was doing with the use-your-boobs-on-Bruce- to "find-out-any-information-about-Rebecca. I couldn't believe how much she belly ached about wearing a low cut-shirt. I'd simply asked her to flirt with him and then ask about her friend, Rebecca. Somehow I was counting on tit-loving Bruce to spill the beans.

The moment I walked out into the waiting room, I heard Ellie raising her voice. *Who the hell is she talking to that loud?*

"Listen, you don't own this doctor's office, lady. Ari has been coming here for years, so you need to back the fuck off!"

Holy hell. I stopped dead in my tracks.

Rebecca.

Ellie looked up when she saw me. She immediately came over and stood next to me.

"What are you doing here? Your appointment isn't until next week," I said in a stunned voice.

Rebecca just smiled at me and tilted her head.

"So, Jeff shares that information with you, does he? He really is excited about this baby. I wish you could have seen the way he smiled at me when he had his hands on my stomach Saturday. Oh wait…you can't because you're not supposed to be anywhere near me."

"Listen here, bitch," Ellie started to get in Rebecca's face.

As I pulled her back, I said,

"I had a doctor's appointment, Rebecca. How was I supposed to know that you would be here? Wait, where is Jeff? Does he know your appointment is today?"

Rebecca's face fell for just one brief moment. "I tried to call him a few times today to let him know I had to move it."

I looked down at her stomach. *No way. This bitch was about to pop.*

Smiling, I walked up to her.

"I'm on to you, Rebecca. Whatever game you think you're gonna win, you won't. You see, I don't play very nice on the play-ground with other kids I don't like. I win when I choose to, sweetheart, and I don't like to lose. If you think for one minute that I'm to just gonna sit back and let you take Jeff away from me, you have another thing coming. Pregnant or not, bitch, I will take your ass down."

Rebecca's smile faded. She looked over my shoulder at Ellie and then over at Heather who was still standing by Bruce. *Heather really does look like a slut dressed the way she is.*

"Bruce, can you please call the police? She just threatened me, and I actually have a restraining order out against her." Rebecca said.

I looked at Bruce, who looked totally confused. The new girl sitting next to Bruce immediately picked up the phone and started to talk to someone.

I turned back to see Rebecca smiling at me.

"I hope you have fun sitting in jail, Ari."

The next thing I knew, Ellie was pulling me out of the way as she got all up in Rebecca's face.

"You will get what is coming to you. You will *not* get away with this. You're not only messing with my best friend, you whore, you're messing with my brother. Have you ever heard of karma? That bitch is going to come back around and bite you in the fucking ass, you douche-twat whore!"

"Ellie!" Heather said as she tried to pull her away from Rebecca.

"Um, miss I'm going to have to ask you to leave. I can't have you…um, yelling at our patients." Bruce said.

"What?" Ellie yelled at Bruce.

"Can't you see that she's the one who egged it on? She's taunting Ari. She's trying to get an excuse to put her in jail!"

Just then, the door opened and two APD officers walked in.

Fuck me. This wasn't going to turn out good.

***

"I cannot believe they arrested all three of us. I've never even been in detention before for fuck's sake!" Heather said as she paced back and forth.

Ellie and I both glanced at each other and smiled.

"Wow, being in the slammer really has given you a mouth, sweets!" I said with a laugh.

Heather spun around and glared at me. I quickly stopped laughing as I looked down at the floor.

"Heather, it's going to be okay. Ari called her father, and he'll get the charges dropped. Don't worry. You're not going to have a record." Ellie said.

She started to laugh and then I lost it.

"Oh yeah, the two of you just keep laughing. I want to be an elementary school teacher you bitches. What am I going to put on my application? *Oh…well, you see, this one time my crazy-ass friend talked me into dressing like a slut. She told me to flash my tits around at a male reception guy…who by the way…is gay as all get out! Oh, and I was supposed to somehow magically get him to tell me how far along my friend is.* Even though if she was really my friend, I would already fucking know that information! *Then, my other friend went crazy and started threatening a pregnant woman by poking a finger in her chest and calling her a whore.* The best part of all, is that we all got arrested, and now, I'm in jail looking like a goddamn hooker! How in the hell is this not that bad, Ellie?"

Ellie sat there with a stunned look on her face as she stared at Heather. I on the other hand, lost it again and just about died from laughing so hard.

"Jesus, Mary, and Joseph…you swore like seven times just now, Heather!"

When I looked over at Ellie, she glanced at me and let out a giggle. I had tears running down my face. I peeked up at Heather, who was now smiling. She started to laugh, too. *Oh my god, I so needed this.*

I laughed so hard that I was pretty sure I might have pissed in my pants.

Just then, I heard voices. One sounded like my father. I looked up to see my dad standing there with Jeff, Gunner, and Josh.

"I'm glad to see you find the humor in this, Ari," Jeff said with a dead-ass straight face.

I immediately stopped laughing and tried to get Ellie and Heather's attention. I stood up and looked at my father. He didn't look very happy either. *Oh shit.*

After Ellie and Heather got themselves composed, Heather leaned over in my ear and whispered, "Holy hell, your dad called Josh?"

I let a small smile play across my lips. I turned and shook my head.

"I bribed the officer to let me have two phone calls, I called Josh. There was no way in hell that I was going to pass this up. I had to let him see you dressed like that! I just didn't realize that he'd bring Jeff and Gunner with him," I said as I turned back to look at Jeff.

This is going to be one long-ass ride back to Mason.

CHAPTER TWENTY-TWO

JEFF

The moment Josh got the phone call from Ari, I was pissed. I wasn't sure if I was more pissed that she called Josh and not me or that she was in jail for breaking the restraining order against Rebecca. *What the fuck was she thinking?*

During the whole drive into Austin, I never said a word. Gunner was on the phone with his mother. They were coming in a day early and would be in Mason around six tonight. I could tell Gunner was beside himself. Now, he had to deal with getting my damn sister out of jail.

What in the hell were they doing?

Mark called to say he'd just pulled up to the police department and would meet us inside. I could tell from his voice that he was pissed. Then we heard the three of them laughing. I had never felt so damn angry in my entire life.

After the girls got processed and their items were returned to them, we all walked outside.

Before Mark could even say anything, I turned and started in on Ari.

"Of all the stupid-ass things you could do, Ari, why would you break the restraining order? What in the hell were you thinking by threatening Rebecca? Then, you laugh about it like it's some joke. What if you caused her to go into labor early? What if something happened to the baby? What the fuck, Ari?"

Everyone stood there and looked at me, stunned.

Mark stepped between Ari and me. Giving me a dirty look, he asked in a calm voice.

"Where did you get your information from, Jeff?"

"Well, Josh at first, since Ari felt the need to call him to come get them out of jail. Then, Rebecca called and left me a message, saying she wasn't feeling well and was turning her phone off. I called her back and she said Ari threatened her today. She couldn't even talk."

I looked at Ari, who had her hands balled in fists. She looked really pissed.

"Fuck you, Jeff, and your baby mama, too! Daddy, can I please come home with you?" Ari said as the tears started to roll down her face.

"Jeff, you're a prick! Why don't you at least let us explain before you go off attacking Ari? You don't even have the facts straight," Ellie said as she poked her finger in my chest.

"Okay, everyone just calm down. Ellie, honey, just back off your brother for a second, sweetheart. Why don't one of y'all explain to us what happened." Gunner said.

I looked at Ari and she was still crying in her father's arms. Gunner pulled Ellie back away from me and whispered something in her ear. Josh was...well shit...Josh was trying to look at everyone but Heather.

"Fine, I'll explain what happened." Heather said as she also gave me a dirty look.

"We were at Dr. Wyatt's office, waiting for Ari to finish up with her appointment. Rebecca walked in, and the moment she saw us there, she started asking why we were there and if we were following her. Ellie tried to explain to her that Ari had been seeing Dr. Wyatt for years and that she had an appointment. Well, crazy Rebecca started raising her voice to Ellie, and that's when Ari came out. Rebecca was egging Ari on, Jeff. I mean, she was really going after her. She mentioned how you had your hands on her stomach the other day and how happy y'all both were with each other. It actually was Ellie who got in Rebecca's face and started to threaten her."

Heather looked over at Ellie, who was smiling like the Cheshire cat at me.

"Wait a minute. Y'all didn't know that Rebecca would be there?" I asked.

"How the fuck would we know that, dickwad? I had this appointment already set up. Her appointment was supposed to be next week. She said she had tried to call you to tell you that she had to change it to today. Funny though, huh? I bet you never got a phone call from her, did you? Oh, but wait. I'm sure she'll have an excuse. Her call must not have gone through since you were in Mason," Ari said.

My heart started to beat faster. *Shit, I just fucked up big time.*

Ari turned to her dad and said something to him. I didn't even hear what she had said my mind was spinning so fast. *Rebecca changed the appointment day? Why?* She'd told me she was going to drop the restraining order against Ari first thing this morning, but she didn't. I looked back at Ari. She was just glaring at me.

"Ari, I'm so sorry, baby. I guess I didn't realize where you saw Rebecca at and."

"Just stop. I can't do this anymore with you. You need to make a decision, Jeff, and you need to make it soon. I'm not really sure how much more of this I can take."

Ari turned and walked off with her father.

I just stood there. I didn't even know what to think. *What does she mean I need to make a decision?*

"Are you just going to let her walk away, Jeff or are you going to go after her?" Ellie asked me with a confused look on her face.

I started to jog over to Ari and Mark. "Ari, please wait a second. Please!"

Mark stopped walking which forced Ari to stop. She turned and looked at me. The look on her face about gutted me. She looked so unhappy, and it was my fault.

"Ari, baby, please just ride back to Mason with me. I'm sorry I jumped to conclusions. I really am. Please don't walk away from me." I could hear the pleading in my voice.

Mark looked at Ari. "Sweetheart, what do you want to do?"

"Fine, but don't expect me to talk to you for awhile you ass-wipe."

Ari turned and gave her dad a kiss goodbye. "Thank you for your help, Daddy."

"You're lucky that I was able to get this taken care of, Ari. You really need to try and avoid this girl, especially if she's going to go out of her way to get you in trouble." Mark said. Then, he looked at me and gave me a look that should have killed me on the spot.

"I know, but I really didn't expect her to be there, Dad." Ari hugged her dad one more time before she headed over to where everyone else was still standing.

I needed to take care of something, and I needed to do it right away.

As I walked back over, I heard Heather jumping all over Josh.

"I swear, Josh, if you look at my breasts one more time, I'm going to haul off and punch your ass."

Josh started laughing. "Wow, a little time in the slammer and you're all bad ass Heather."

"Push off, Josh." Heather said.

Josh walked up to Heather and leaned in to ask her something. Heather took a step back and walked a few feet away from everyone. Josh followed.

Jesus, this group of friends, I swear.

"I'm starving from my time in the slammer. Can we grab something to eat before we head back?" Ellie asked.

"As long as it's quick, sweetheart. My mom called this morning and said that she and Dad would be in around six tonight."

Ellie clapped her hands and jumped up in the air. "Oh my gosh! They're coming in a day early. Let's just head back to Mason then. I know Heather wants to go home. She plans on coming back out tomorrow and staying until Thursday morning. We can just drop her off on the way home."

Just then, Heather walked up and kissed Ellie on the cheek. "Thanks, Ells, but I'm just going to have Josh drop me off." Heather said.

She walked up to Ari and hugged her good-bye.

"Thanks for the interesting day, Ari. If you need *anything,* you know you can give me a call anytime, right?"

"Thank you Heather. I love you, girl. I think it'll be okay," Ari said.

We said our good-byes, and I watched as Josh and Heather walked away. Ari and I stood there, not saying a word.

"You ready to go, Sweetheart?" Gunner asked Ellie.

Ellie nodded and took Ari's hand. They started to walk on ahead.

We had to stop three times so Ari could use the restroom. *What the hell was wrong with her?* Ellie kept saying it was her nerves.

I took the opportunity to step outside the truck to call Rebecca.

"Jeff! Hey! I tried calling you this morning, but couldn't get through."

"Is that right? What were you calling about?"

"Well, I'm sure you already know the answer to that. I'm guessing you've already been to the police station to bail your crazy girlfriend out of jail."

I instantly got pissed. I didn't want to get Rebecca upset, so I pulled the phone away from me and took a deep breath.

"I just want to know why you didn't drop the restraining order like you said you would. In fact, you did a one-eighty Rebecca. Why were you at the doctor's office today? I thought your appointment was next week."

There was nothing but silence.

"Rebecca? Are you still there?"

"I um… I had to change the appointment because I was having more Braxton Hicks contractions, and I got worried. But Dr. Wyatt said everything was going to be okay. I just need to take it easy. I'm so sorry you couldn't go. I wish I had a better way of trying to get a hold of you besides your cell."

I saw Ari coming out of the store. She was drinking down a bottle of water like she was dying of thirst. *Fuck, I hope she's not getting sick.*

"Listen…I can't talk right now. Yeah, I, for sure, need to be at that next appointment. The next few days are going to be busy for me. Unless you have an emergency, maybe you can lay off the phone calls for a few days okay?"

"Oh yeah, sure. No problem, sweetheart. I'll talk to you in a few days."

"Yep, and Rebecca, let's just stick with Jeff, okay?"

I hung up with Rebecca and opened the door for Ari to get into Gunner's truck. She quickly fell asleep and slept the rest of the way home. I never took my eyes off of her. Something wasn't right, and I needed to find out what the hell was going on. I had the strangest feeling that she was hiding something from me.

CHAPTER TWENTY-THREE

JOSH

I just needed to get Heather back to her apartment and out of that shirt, so I didn't have the urge to keep looking at her damn chest.

"Heather, can I ask you one question?"

She let out a long drawn-out sigh. "Yes."

"Why the hell are you dressed like that? It's so not you!" I said with a laugh.

"Why are you laughing? You don't think I have the body to dress a little sexy? Well Bruce certainly thought I had a nice body. He couldn't keep his eyes off my chest even though I'm pretty sure he's gay."

I looked over at her as I laughed my ass off. *God, I love this girl.*

Whoa...what the hell?

"I'm glad to see I can amuse you, Josh. Really, I am. It's a long story that I would rather not get into if you don't mind. I just want to get home and get my boobs off display."

I glanced at Heather as she looked at me.

"Josh, are you okay? You're white as a ghost. Listen, I'm not mad at you or anything. Ari wanted me to get information on Rebecca's due date. She said this guy was a breast guy and that I had the best breasts out of all of us. I mean, it was such a stupid idea. The only reason why I went along with it is because Ari's pregnant, and I feel bad for her."

Wait...what?

I pulled into a gas station and threw the truck in park. I needed air.

Heather jumped out of the truck and came around to where I was standing with my head ducked down and my hands on my knees. I felt like I couldn't get any air in.

"Oh my gosh, Josh. Are you okay?"

The moment her hand rested my back, I felt it, the electric shock every time this girl touched me. *Oh my god, what the fuck is going on with me? And did she just say Ari is pregnant?!*

It took me a few minutes to get my breathing under control. *Jesus.* This had never happened to me before. I looked up at her, and her eyes caught mine.

I love her.

Holy shit, I love her.

Heather bent down to look at my face. "Josh, you're really starting to scare me. Please tell me what's wrong."

I did everything I possibly could to *not* look at her damn chest.

"I need just a second, Princess. Just give me a second."

Heather stood up and took a few steps back. Then, she threw her hand over her mouth.

"Holy hell. Oh my god...I just told you about Ari. Is that why you're freaking out?"

Umm...no.... "Yeah, I guess it just took me by surprise."

"Josh, you can't tell Jeff! Ari made us promise not to tell anyone."

"Heather, don't you think Jeff has the right to know that Ari is pregnant with his baby? I mean, did Ari not learn anything with Rebecca?"

"Of course, he has the right to know. I don't disagree with you on that one. Ari just doesn't want to stress him out. She's trying to hold off until Rebecca has the baby, so they can find out for sure if it's Jeff's."

I stood up, leaning against the truck. "Holy hell, this is so messed up. I mean, I know that Jeff wants to have kids with Ari so much, and he would be over the moon if he knew she was pregnant, Heather. I don't understand why Ari is waiting to tell him. So what if Rebecca is having a baby and it turns out to be Jeff's? He's a good guy. He'll do right by both of them."

I shook my head. I silently thanked God that I'd never found myself in this situation. I looked back at Heather, and she was just staring at me.

She tilted her head to the side, smiling.

"Okay, spill it. What really happened just now? There's no way you'd have that type of reaction just because you learned that Ari is pregnant. Plus, you were acting funny before I even said she was pregnant."

"To be honest, I'm not really sure what happened, Heather." That was the truth.

"Okay. Well, are you better now? I really want to get home and change out of this shirt and skirt."

I let out a laugh as I got back in the truck.

Heather just rattled on and on the whole way to her apartment. I didn't think I'd ever heard her talk as much as she was talking right now.

I pulled up to her building and parked the truck.

She sat there for a minute, like she was thinking something over.

"Do you want to come in for a glass of sweet tea or something?"

Fuck yeah, I do. "Sure, I'm not in a hurry to get anywhere."

***

We sat together in her apartment for almost two hours, talking about everything and anything. I told Heather about my desire to take over my father's furniture-making business, and she told me about her dreams of becoming an elementary school teacher.

Before I knew it, we had finished two bottles of wine.

While we were laughing about them being in jail, I said,

"I have to admit that I was surprised when Ari called *me* to come and get y'all out of jail. I just figured that my phone was the only one she was able to get through to."

"Well, you know the only reason why she called you was so you could see me dressed like a damn whore," Heather said as she laughed.

She must have thought about what she had just said because her head snapped up to look at me.

Now, why would Ari do that unless she thought Heather had feelings for me? I'm done playing games. It's time to find out.

Heather was leaning up against the counter while as I sitting on one of her bar stools. I got up and walked toward her. Pulling her into my arms, I didn't even give her time to think before I backed her up against the wall.

As I started to kiss her she ran her hands through my hair. The small moan that escaped her lips made me want to rip off her damn clothes. When I lifted her up, she wrapped her legs around my waist. The kiss was quickly turning more passionate by the second.

Son of a bitch. I've wanted to kiss this girl for so long now. She tasted sweeter than anything I could've ever imagined.

She pulled back slightly, trying to catch her breath.

"Josh...I've... I've never been with anyone before and..." Her voice trailed off as she looked down at my lips.

My knees just about buckled out from underneath me. I had to put one hand on the wall to hold myself up. *Holy shit. Heather's a virgin.*

Closing her eyes, she put her head back against the wall. Leaning down, I started to kiss her neck.

Two minutes ago, I'd been ready to ask the way to her bedroom. There was no way in hell that I was going to do that now. Now, all I wanted to do was make her feel cherished.

"Princess, look at me."

As she lifted her head up, her blue eyes captured mine, and all I saw was sadness. My heart broke in two.

"I'd never do anything that you weren't ready to do, Heather. Ever."

"Josh…I really want…" She paused, stopping mid-sentence.

"You really want what?"

The look in her eyes suddenly turned to pure panic. She started to shake her head.

"I need you to put me down!" she practically shouted.

"What?" I asked, confused.

"Put me down, Josh. Now!"

What the hell is happening?

I put her down, and the moment her feet hit the floor, she pushed me away.

"Heather, I don't understand. What's going on? What did I do?"

Turning away from me, she walked into the living room and stopped at the front window, staring outside.

"I really think you need to leave now. This was a bad idea. I was stupid to think that we could ever just be friends. You'll always want more than this."

Motherfucker. My head was spinning.

"Um… I'm sorry, princess, but it sure seemed like you also wanted more a few seconds ago. What changed?"

When she turned around, I almost lost my breath. She was crying.

"Don't ever call me princess again. I don't want anything more than friendship with you. I'll never want anything more than that. I had a moment of weakness. It must have been because of the wine or something. I don't want you, Josh, not in that way. I'm sorry if I led you on. I think it would be best if we just stopped right now."

I didn't know what to say. I had seen the look in her eyes. I knew she had wanted me as much as I'd wanted her. *Why is she pushing me away?*

"Heather...if I walk out this door right now, I'll keep in mind everything that you just said to me. I promise you that I'll never approach you again with anything more than friendship. I just need you to make sure that this is what you really want. I have feelings for you. Honestly, I feel things for you that I've never in my life felt for any other girl, and that scares the shit out of me. I don't want to walk away from you, but if you tell me that you don't have any feelings for me, then I'll leave. I won't ever bring it up again."

I watched her as she just stared at me with tears rolling down her face. I walked up to her and reached out to wipe them away. When she took a step back, I almost dropped to my knees.

She quickly wiped her tears from her eyes. Looking right into my eyes, she said,

"I don't have feelings for you other than friendship. I'm sorry."

My whole world shattered into a million pieces. *How could I be so happy one minute and then feel so incredibly sad the next?*

I had never in my life cried, but at that moment, I felt like I was about to lose it. Quickly backing away from her, I turned to grab my keys off the counter.

"I'm sorry, Heather. I guess I'll see you on Wednesday at Garrett and Emma's party."

I walked to the door, and every ounce of me was praying that she would stop me. I gave up all hope by the time I got to my truck. Once outside, I sat there for a minute, watching her door.

Then, I started my truck and drove away from the one thing that I thought would finally make me feel happy and complete in this world.

CHAPTER TWENTY-FOUR

HEATHER

The moment the front door closed, I fell to the ground and cried. *What did I just do?* I had never in my life felt the way I did when Josh was kissing me. I'd wanted nothing more than to tell him that I needed him, heart and soul.

He must have waited to see if I'd come after him. After a few minutes, I heard him start up his truck before he drove off.

He left.

He just walked away from me and never looked back.

Oh. My. God. Feeling sick to my stomach, I jumped up and ran to the bathroom. Just when I didn't think I could throw up any more, another round of nausea hit me. Sitting down on the bathroom floor, I leaned back against the wall. I touched my fingers up to my lips as I closed my eyes.

Princess, look at me. I'd never do anything that you weren't ready to do, Heather. Ever.

Why did he call me princess?

I thought back to my sixteenth birthday.

***

"Daddy, why can't I see where we're going?"

"Princess, you really need to have more patience. You'll get to see it soon enough."

Daddy was taking me to get my birthday present, but he wouldn't let me see what it was.

"Okay, we're here. Hold on. Let me go around and open your door."

The next thing I knew, Daddy was holding my hand, leading me somewhere. I could hear people talking, but then it got really quiet. I felt warm breath up against my ear.

"Happy birthday, darling," my mother whispered in my ear.

My heart started to pound. *Mom was here?*

"Okay, princess, are you ready for your surprise?"

"Yes, Daddy! I've been ready for like the last hour!"

I heard my mom and dad laugh. Someone took off the blind fold, and then I opened my eyes. We were in the parking lot of my favorite restaurant, The Oasis. I saw Ellie and Ari standing there with huge smiles on their faces. My whole family and a few close friends were all here.

"Oh my gosh, is everyone here for my birthday?" I said, looking at my mom and then my dad.

"Princess, take a good look around."

I turned toward Ellie and Ari, and then I noticed Ari was leaning up against a white Nissan Pathfinder with a huge bow on it.

I spun around and looked at my parents. "You didn't?"

My dad laughed and then smiled at me. "We did."

"Daddy, I don't even have my driver's license yet. I can't drive it. I'm too afraid to drive it! Oh my gosh, who's going to drive it home? Do we have to leave it here?"

Putting his hand on my shoulders, he looked into my eyes. I wasn't even sure why I was panicking.

"Princess, look at me. I'd never make you do anything you weren't ready to do. You can drive the car, baby girl, when you're ready."

***

Putting my head down on my knees, I just cried. The moment when Josh had said almost those exact words to me, memories of my father had instantly flooded into my mind.

I couldn't believe that Josh had also called me princess. He hadn't known that my dad had called me that. At first, I had liked it, but then something had happened. When he'd kissed me, I had fallen even more in love with him.

I couldn't let him get close to me. *What if something happened to him, making him leave me like my parents did?* I just couldn't let that happen to me again. I wouldn't let that happen to me again.

I thought about what Josh had said right before he'd left.

"I have feelings for you. Honestly, I feel things for you I've never in my life felt for any other girl, and that scares the shit out of me. I don't want to walk away from you, but if you tell me that you don't have feelings for me, then I'll leave. I won't ever bring it up again."

Oh. My. God. I'd let him walk away from me. I'd just let him walk right out of my life. The hurt that I had seen in his eyes would haunt me for the rest of my life.

Just then, my cell phone rang.

I slowly got up and made my way into the living room. By the time I got my purse and pulled the phone out, it had stopped ringing. I had secretly hoped that it was Josh, but instead, I saw that I had missed a call from Ellie.

My voice mail notification went off. After I hit the button to retrieve the message, I turned on the speaker phone.

"Holy hell, Heather! What happened with you and Josh? He just called Gunner, and he was so upset that Gunner could hardly understand what he was saying. Josh said something about going to get drunk. Before he hung up, he said he'd see us Wednesday. Please call me back on the land line at Emma and Garrett's."

I hit delete and then tossed my phone on the sofa. I had a sick feeling in my stomach. *What if he went out, got drunk, and slept with some girl?* I'd over-heard Josh telling Jeff that he hadn't had sex in months. I knew he was doing it for me. I threw myself back into the sofa.

Shit! I just made the biggest mistake of my life. I let out the loudest scream I could. *What is wrong with me? What did that stupid therapist say? It was something about me needing to let go of the past to move on with my future.*

Is Josh my future? I could certainly see him in my future. As I closed my eyes, I imagined what it would be like to make love to him. *Would he be sweet and gentle or full of passion and lust?*

I had so wanted to take off his shirt earlier, just to get a good look at his chest. I'd seen him without a shirt plenty of times. He had tattoos going up and down his arms, but the tribal tattoo that he had on his side was my favorite. Ugh!

Sitting up, I grabbed my phone. After I pulled up his number, I just sat there, staring at it for a few minutes. Then, I finally hit dial.

The phone rang and rang. *Damn it Josh, answer the phone.*

I hung up when I got his voice mail.

I waited ten more minutes, and then I called him again. This time, when I got his voice mail, I decided to leave a message.

"Hey, Josh…um, it's me, Heather. Listen, I shouldn't have let you leave like that. I'm sorry for what I said. Is there any way that you could maybe call me back or come back over so we can talk? I'll be home all night."

After I watched two movies, I hit the gym. I came back home, and there was still no word from Josh. I decided to call him one more time. If he didn't answer, then I'd know that he didn't want to talk to me.

The ringing stopped, and then all I heard was lots of voices and music. It sounded like a bar. *Oh shit.*

"Josh? Hey, it's Heather. Can you hear me?"

"Um...this isn't Josh. It's Marie. Josh is dancing right now."

"Okay, why are you answering his phone, Marie?"

"He left it here, sitting on the bar, and I saw your name pop up. He's been talking about you all night long, sweetheart. My girlfriend, Jen, and I are out for a girls' night. We've been trying to keep the vultures away from him."

I was so mad that I was shaking from head to toe. "Is he drunk?"

She started laughing again. "Ah, you could say. Listen, do you want to come get him? I can drive his car back to your place, and Jen can follow me. He seems like he really loves you. I'd hate to have some whore try to hook up with him tonight."

Wow, this is unexpected. "Okay, yeah. Where are y'all?"

"Fado's."

"I'll be there as soon as I can, but I'm not twenty one, so I can't come in."

Marie gave me her cell phone number to call when I got there. I grabbed my purse and headed out the door.

***

By the time Marie and Jen had helped me get a drunker-than-drunk Josh in my apartment and into my bed, we had become close friends. It turns out they had been keeping the girls away from him all night since all Josh did was talk about me.

"Let me just tell you this, Heather. That boy passed out on your bed right there is madly in love with you. He wouldn't stop talking about you all night. I hope y'all can work things out. He seems like a nice guy,"

I stood there, stunned. *Josh was talking about me? To these women?* I looked down to see that they both had on wedding rings.

After Marie and Jen left, I sat down on the bed and watched Josh sleep. He looked so cute passed out on my bed.

I had the sudden urge to just crawl into bed to lie down next to him. *Would he be angry if I did?*

After the things I had said to him earlier, he was probably so pissed at me. Maybe I was just dreaming here. The way Marie had said he'd acted all night could've just been the alcohol talking. He'd probably only wanted in my pants.

Despite my doubts, I leaned over and kissed him on the cheek. He opened his eyes and gave me a crooked-ass smile that just about melted off my panties. *Jesus, now, I understand what Ari and Ellie were talking about.*

"Hey, princess, I must be dreaming right now," Josh mumbled.

When I smiled down at him, he closed his eyes.

Yeah, I better sleep in the spare room or on the sofa. I grabbed a pillow and headed out to the living room. Tomorrow, I would talk to Josh about how I felt. I needed to be honest with him about my feelings. If he was willing to be patient and go slow, I thought I might be able to get used to the idea of letting someone back into my heart.

***

I heard a noise and flew up off the sofa. I must have fallen asleep out here. I looked around and didn't see anyone. My head was pounding. I picked up my phone, and I had three text messages.

The first one was from Ellie. She said that Gunner's mom and dad got in last night. The only word she used to describe it was "*awkward*".

Ari sent a text, asking if I was coming out today and staying the night. She wanted me to stay with her and Jeff. *That might work.* I thought that Josh had mentioned that we was staying there with them.

The third text was from...*Josh?*

Josh: *I'm sorry you had to come out so late last night, but thanks for letting me crash at your place. I'm guessing Jen or Marie asked you to pick me up. Anyway, thanks again. See you either today or tomorrow in Mason.*

Wait...what? I jumped up and ran into my bedroom. The bed was made, and Josh was gone.

I ran back out to the living room and grabbed my cell. I pulled up Josh's number and hit call.

"Hey, Heather." Was all Josh said when he answered the phone. He sounded so sad.

"Hey, Josh. Why did you leave without waking me up? I kind of wanted to talk to you about um...well, about yesterday."

There was a long pause.

"I think you made yourself pretty clear yesterday, Heather. I'm really not in the mood for any more rejection."

His voice was so cold and distant.

"Okay, I guess I deserve that, but do you think we might be able to talk? I mean, I'd kind of like to explain my reaction yesterday."

"I think it was clear what your reaction was."

Oh wow.

"Listen, I'm on my way to Mason in a little bit. Maybe we can talk there. Are you heading out today or early tomorrow?" Josh said.

My hands started to shake. The threat of tears was starting to overwhelm me.

"I'm...ah..." I paused when my voice cracked. I had to clear my throat twice before I could speak again. "I'm heading out today."

"Alright...well, I guess I'll see ya when you get there. I'm sorry, but I need to go, I have another call coming through."

"Oh, okay...sure, yeah. I'll talk to ya later."

I hung up the phone with a sick feeling in the pit of my stomach.

Why did I get the feeling that I probably just lost the best thing that's happened to me since the death of my parent's?

CHAPTER TWENTY-FIVE

JEFF

I couldn't believe it's was Tuesday morning, and Mr. Reynolds was heading out now to look at the place. I had no idea where Ari was. She'd been pissed ever since I'd jumped on her about the whole restraining-order shit.

As I headed out onto the porch, I saw a white F250 pull up.

Motherfucker. He was early, and I had no idea where the hell Ari was. I stepped down off the porch and walked over to his truck. The guy that got out was young.

"Mr. Reynolds, it's a real pleasure to meet your sir."

"How's it going, Jeff? Please, call me Scott." We shook hands and gave each a good once-over. This bastard couldn't have been more than five or six years older than me.

"I can tell by your expression that you're wondering who the hell the young guy is standing in front of you," He said with a laugh.

I smiled back at him. "As a matter of fact I am."

"I'm Scott Reynolds, Jr. My father is good friends with Garrett. I'm actually taking over my father's ranch, so he thought it would be best if I came and met with you, to check out your place."

"Sounds great. So, you probably know Gunner? Were you at the wedding?"

He started to laugh. "Yeah, I know Gunner really well. We used to be buds when we were growing up. I couldn't wait for the summers when I knew he was coming to visit. He's a good guy. I was at the wedding, but I left right after the ceremony. One of my mares foaled, so I had to leave early. It was a beautiful ceremony. Your sister is breathtakingly beautiful."

"Um, thanks. She's pretty special, that's for sure. Anyway, do you want to head down to the barn, check out the stables, and all?"

"I'd loved to. How many broodmares do you have so far?"

"Right now, I have four. Two of them are on the Mathews' place."

"Are any of them pregnant?"

"One."

As we made our way over to my truck, I realized that this guy really knew his shit about horses. He was asking me every goddamn thing under the sun.

"I used to come to this ranch when I was little. I had a friend we called Smitty. He used to come and visit his grandparents here. You've really done an amazing job of getting it fixed up," Scott said.

"Thank you. I appreciate that. We've been putting a lot of blood and sweat into it, that's for sure."

"What made you decide on breeding horses?" Scott asked.

I parked my truck as we pulled up to the barn. I turned and just smiled at him.

"My fiancé. She has a passion for horses. She's really the one who wants to train them for roping and barrel racing."

"Has she ever done either of those?" he asked with a smirk.

"Yes, sir, she has," I said with a smirk of my own.

As we walked up to the barn, I could hear Ari singing. When we rounded the corner, I saw her mucking out the stalls, her back facing us. She was listening to her iPod. The only thing I could see was Ari moving her fucking hips as she danced with a pitch-fork while singing loudly to Christina Aguilera's "WooHoo."

"Did she just say 'you know you wanna put your lips where my hips are'?" Scott asked.

Kill me now. "Ari," I said, trying not to shout at her. "Ari? Ari!" I shouted.

Nope, nothing. She was still dancing and singing. Reaching down, I picked up a horse brush and threw it at her, hitting her right on the ass.

"What the fuck?" Ari said as she whipped around.

She gave me a dirty look, but then she noticed Scott standing there. She immediately ripped the head phones out of her ears and smiled.

"Oh my gosh, I'm so sorry, y'all. What time is it?"

"It's around nine," I said.

Ari looked back over at me. Her cheeks were blushed either from dancing or being embarrassed. She looked so damn cute…and I was pissed as hell at her.

"Ari, this is Scott Reynolds, Mr. Reynolds' son. He's taking over his father's business."

Ari put the pitch-fork up against the stall before she made her way over to us. I looked over at Scott, who couldn't seem to pull his eyes away from Ari. I took another look at her and instantly knew why.

She was wearing a pair of cut-off blue jean shorts, a white tank top, and a pair of pink cowboy boots. She looked fucking hot.

Ari quickly wiped her hands on the ass of her shorts and then reached out to shake Scott's hand.

"It's a pleasure to meet you, Mr. Reynolds. I'm so sorry. I didn't think you would be here until around noon," Ari said with that damn smile of hers.

The fucking bastard let his eyes travel up and down Ari, and I swore that he looked at her damn breasts for a good ten seconds.

"I had an appointment cancel this morning, so I sent Jeff a text, saying that I would be here earlier. And the pleasure is all mine."

I looked at Ari again to see that she was blushing even more.

***

We spent the next few hours talking about the horses, the barn, the broodmares, and the studs. If it had to do with horses, we talked about it. Most of the time, Scott was a little too interested in Ari. He asked her a million questions about her wanting to train the horses for barrel racing and roping.

"Well, Jeff, it seems to me that you have a really nice set-up here. I'm really looking forward to doing business with you. I would love to see a few of your mares take some barrels. Ari, maybe you could demonstrate that for me," he said with a smile on his face.

Ari smiled back, giving him a bring-it-on look.

"You bet I'll demonstrate for you," Ari said as her face flushed again.

What the fuck?

"Well then, how about right now?"

Ari looked stunned, but she agreed. She left to go saddle up a horse she'd been working with the last few months.

***

Scott must have liked the demonstration because he wanted to know how soon he could bring his stud out. The mare Ari rode was obviously in heat. The horse was moody, and I could tell that Ari was working extra hard with her.

While she was taking off the saddle from the mare, I pulled Ari off to the side.

"Ari, why did you ride Rose if you knew she was in heat? She's already a feisty-ass horse?"

Ari just looked at me, and then she glanced over my shoulder and smiled. I turned around to see Scott walking into the barn. I was ready to fucking hit him square in the nose if he kept looking at Ari the way he was.

"So, how about I bring out Samson? Let's say Friday?" Scott said as he looked at me. Then, he watched as Ari took care of Rose.

"Sure, Friday sounds great, Scott." I shook his hand.

Then, he walked up to Ari and shook her hand.

"By the way, I loved the song choice Ari. I'm sure you keep the horses *very* entertained." He winked at Ari and started to laugh.

Fucker.

Ari laughed back and there went that blush across her cheeks. I noticed she kept putting her hand on her stomach. *Is she feeling sick again?*

***

I took Scott back to his truck and made all the arrangements for Friday. Right as he was driving off, Ari came up to the house in her Jeep.

She walked up to me and smiled. "He sure was nice, and he seemed really interested in working with us."

Something inside me snapped. "Oh yeah. Especially after he heard you singing about fucking oral sex, he got really interested in a lot more than the horses."

Ari looked at me, stunned. "What?"

"Ari, I'm not in the mood for your damn games. You knew the guy was attracted to you, and you played it up the best you could. You being jealous of Rebecca and trying to get my attention is starting to get old." I started to walk into the house, fully expecting her to lash out right back at me. Before I went in, I turned around to look at her.

She was just standing there, staring at me. There was no emotion what-so-ever in her eyes. Her hands were resting on her stomach, and she started to shake her head back and forth. She looked down at the ground and then back up at me.

When she started to run up to me, I thought she was going to run into my arms. Instead, she pushed me out of the way and ran into the house.

"Ari...fuck, wait a minute. I didn't mean to say that..." I stopped talking when I saw her run into the bathroom.

She fell to the floor and started throwing up. *Shit!*

I walked up behind her and bent down next to her.

"Baby, I'm sorry. I didn't mean to take out my frustration on you."

"Leave me alone Jeff. I really don't want to see you right now, let alone talk to you."

I stood back up with tears stinging my eyes. *Why do I keep hurting her?*

As I turned to walk out the door, she whispered something I couldn't hear.

"What did you say, Ari?"

"It doesn't even matter anymore. If you can give me about thirty minutes to get cleaned up, I'd like to head up and meet Gunner's parents."

"Um, okay sure." I turned and headed toward the kitchen.

I could have sworn that she'd said something about how stupid she was to even think of telling me. *Telling me what?*

***

The moment she walked out of the bedroom in a beautiful sundress and cowboy boots, I just wanted to take her in my arms and kiss her. When I walked up to her, she took a step back.

"Ari, I'm so sorry, baby. You know I didn't mean what I said. I was frustrated. I think I was looking to pick a fight because that fucker wouldn't stop looking at you and flirting with you. It drove me nuts."

She stood up just a little taller and squared her shoulders off. "It's fine, Jeff. Let's just forget it and move on," she said with absolutely no emotion in her voice.

I took another step toward her, and this time, she took one toward me. Leaning down, I captured her lips with mine.

"I love you, Ari. More than anything in this world, I love you."

She smiled up at me, but her smile didn't touch her eyes.

I was slowly losing her, and it was nobody's fault but my own.

CHAPTER TWENTY-SIX

ARI

I tried really hard to not let what Jeff had said to me back at the house affect me. I knew he was stressed, and Scott was going out of his way to flirt with me right in front of Jeff. I tried to make small talk with him on the way to meet Gunner's parents.

Ellie had sent me a text, saying things were moving slowly with Gunner and his dad. She said they had barely spoken two words to each other since his parents had arrived last night.

Ellie was waiting for me on the porch. She practically came running over to Jeff's truck. As soon as I got out of the truck, she grabbed me and hugged me.

"How are you feeling?" She whispered in my ear.

"Fine."

"Lying bitch. Did you tell him?" Ellie asked as she pulled away to look at me.

I shook my head. I could see the look of disappointment on her face.

"Hey, sis. No love for your big brother?" Jeff said as he walked up.

He took Ellie in a big bear hug and spun her around. She started laughing and then told him to put her down.

"How are things with Gun and his dad?" Jeff asked, looking up to the house.

"Well...um...they really need to spend some time alone together, I think."

Gunner had sent Jeff a text and said that his dad's old best friend, Drake was so happy to see his dad that he pretty much came and took him to the barn for awhile.

"I was hoping maybe you could talk Gunner into heading down there," Ellie asked Jeff.

"Yeah sure, Ells, I can get him to do that. You okay with that, Ari?"

I smiled, trying to act like I really gave a rat's ass what he did. At this point, I was so tired and weak that I probably wouldn't have cared if he said he was going to Rebecca's.

"Yep, no worries. Y'all have fun catching up."

Ellie took me by the arm, and then we started to walk into the house.

The first person I saw was Grace.

She smiled and walked over to give me a hug.

"Congratulations on your engagement, Ari and Jeff. I'm so very happy for both of you."

Jeff and I both said our thanks, and then Jeff was somehow able to talk Gunner into heading down to the barn.

As soon as they left and it was clear they were gone, the attack began.

"Why the hell have you not told him, Ari? You said you were going to tell him this morning!" Ellie yelled.

"Oh, Ari, honey. I have to agree with Ellie. You need to let him know," Emma said as she wiped her hands on her apron. She walked over to give me a hug.

"Wait…what are we talking about?" Grace asked as she looked between the three of us.

"Well, um…" I had to start laughing. *Jesus, everyone was going to know before Jeff.* I needed to tell him tonight.

"I'm pregnant. I haven't actually told Jeff yet, but that's because some bitch he slept with before we became a couple is now saying she's pregnant with his baby. It's really a soap opera that's not worth watching."

Grace got up and walked over to me again. She took me in her arms.

Oh shit, here come the waterworks again.

I pulled back some and smiled. I looked over at Emma and Ellie.

"I was going to tell him this morning. I got up early and headed to the barn to clean out the stalls before Mr. Reynolds came. I needed time to think. Y'all know how the horses calm me down. How was I supposed to know that his son was going to be the one coming? Or that his son was going to catch me listening to "WooHoo" and singing out loud about oral sex? Sorry, Emma and Grace. And how was I supposed to know that he would flirt non-stop with me the whole time? Then, to have Jeff accuse me of purposely flirting back with Scott just to make him mad, that was the topper. I swear that I think Jeff wanted to fight with me. So, by the time all that shit happened, sorry again Emma and Grace, I just wasn't really in the mood to tell Jeff. What would I say? *Hey, guess what, dickwad? I'm pregnant.* He might have accused me of doing it to steal Rebecca's goddamn thunder. Sorry, Emma and Grace."

I looked around at the three women who were just standing there, staring at me. Poor Grace looked even more confused, Emma looked like she was trying to process what I had just spit out, and Ellie, *that bitch,* was trying to hide the fact that she was laughing. *Some best friend she is.*

"Okay, well…wow, Ari, honey. Let's pour some sweet tea and go sit out on the porch. I think we could all use some fresh air right about now," Emma said as she pulled out four mason jars and filled them with ice and sweet tea.

***

When we were outside, I sat down in the rocking chair and just rocked. Closing my eyes, I pictured holding a baby while rocking her to sleep on this porch. I loved it here so much. I loved the country air, the smells, the sounds, and the dead silence. I took a deep breath and opened my eyes. I had three women just staring at me. *What the hell?*

I panicked. "Oh. My. God. Is there a bug on me?" I said.

Standing up, I started jumping around while Ellie laughed her ass off.

"Ari, for Pete's sake, sit down girl. There's no bug on you," Emma said with a laugh.

***

We talked for a good thirty minutes about me, the baby, Jeff and Rebecca. I was emotionally exhausted and tired of talking about me.

Just then, a BMW pulled up. Emma had a huge smile on her face.

"Looks like Jim, Michelle, and Lynda are here." Emma got up and started to walk down to greet them.

I glanced over at Ellie, who had a sour look on her face.

"Heather is going to freak. Have you talked to her?" I said.

Ellie shook her head then looked at me. She clearly didn't want to talk in front of Grace.

Lynda came running up the steps and then hugged Grace. "Aunt Grace! Oh gosh, I'm so happy to see you. Where is Uncle Jack?"

Grace let out a giggle as she returned Lynda's hug. "He's with Drake, Gunner, and Jeff down at the barn sweetheart."

"Is he okay, Aunt Grace?"

Grace smiled and nodded her head. "Excuse me sweetheart. Let me go say hello to your parents."

Lynda turned and smiled Ellie.

"Ellie! How was the honeymoon? I'm sorry you had to cut it short. I hate that Uncle Jack had a heart attack, but I sure hope this pushes him and Gunner to make up."

Ellie and Lynda talked for a few more minutes. I tried desperately to tune them out. There was something about Lynda that I didn't like.

Just then, Josh pulled up in his truck. I tried to see if Heather was with him. He parked and got out alone. *Shit.*

"Holy hotness. That boy has me drippin' in my panties every time I see him," Lynda said as she started to walk toward the steps.

I glanced over at Ellie to see she was staring at me. *Yeah, I really don't like this bitch at all.*

"Um, you know, Lynda, our friends Heather and Josh are kind of…well…."

Lynda spun around and looked at Ellie. "Kind of what? Are they seeing each other?"

Just then, Heather pulled up. *Shit, this is gonna be interesting.*

Josh turned and watched as Heather parked. She got out, looked up at Ellie and me, and waved. Her smile faded for a quick second, and then it was replaced by a totally fake-ass smile. I looked over at Josh. He quickly turned away from Heather and said something to Grace. Then, he started to walk down toward the barn.

Oh shit. Ellie and I glanced at each other again, and I was pretty sure that Ellie's face matched mine. *What the hell was going on with those two?*

"I guess we're about to find out now. Aren't we ladies?" Lynda said with a snarky attitude.

"Hey, y'all! Looks like everyone decided to get here at the same time," Heather said with a laugh.

"Hey there, Heather, it's so good to see you again, especially so soon after the wedding. I'm surprised to see that you didn't come with Josh," Lynda said.

Fucking bitch.

Heather looked at Lynda, confused as all hell. "Why would I ride with Josh?"

"Oh, well, your friends here seem to think that y'all are a couple and all. I just thought if you were then you would have driven out here with him."

Heather actually looked like she was about to throw up. *Huh, she looks like how I feel.* She quickly peeked at me and then Ellie and then back to me again. I just shrugged my shoulders. *Hell if I know what to say to that.* Josh and Heather had been going back and forth for so long. When he took her home the other day, I thought for sure they would have moved on, especially when Heather sent a text to me, saying Josh and her were polishing off a bottle of wine.

Heather's shoulders slumped as she took a deep breath. "No, Lynda, Josh and I are not a couple. We're just friends."

Lynda did a little hop as she made a high-pitch sound. Then she started to make her way down the porch steps.

"Uh, Lynda, where are you going?" Ellie called out after her.

"I'm gonna go say *hi* to a certain cowboy who makes my panties melt. I'll catch up with y'all later!"

I walked up to Heather slapped her on the head.

"Hey! What the hell did you do that for?"

"Oh. My. God. Heather! You just gave her permission to go after Josh. What's wrong with you? The last time we texted it sounded like you and Josh were moving past this whole friendship bullshit."

Heather tried to smile at me as she looked at Ellie and then back at me. The minute I saw the tears, I knew. Grabbing her hand, I pulled her into the house and up the stairs to one of the guest bedrooms. Ellie followed right behind us.

The second the bedroom door shut, Ellie and I both said, "Spill it!"

Heather sat down on the bed and just lost it. I'd never seen her cry like this before. A part of me wondered if it had to do with her parents. She had tried to be so strong, putting up a front for everyone.

Ellie dropped to her knees on the floor in front of Heather while I sat down next to her on the bed.

"Oh, Heather, no. What did that bastard do?" Ellie said rubbing her hand up on Heather's shoulder.

It took Heather a minute or two to calm down.

"Shit, I'm so sorry. I didn't mean to break down like a baby," Heather said as she looked back and forth between us.

"Heather, what did Josh do? He seemed so sad when you pulled up and got out of the car."

"Oh. My. God. Ari! I messed up so bad with him, and I don't think it can ever be fixed."

I looked at Ellie with a confused look on my face.

"Wait...*you* messed up? Josh didn't do anything to you? What in the world could you have possibly done to him?" I asked as I ran my hand up and down her back.

Heather shook her head. She took a deep breath and then slowly let it out.

"The other night, after the whole jail thing, Josh brought me home. It was so wonderful to just spend time together. I mean, we talked, we laughed, and we drank a lot of wine. Then, he just stood up, and grabbed me, pushed me up against the wall, and then kissed the living hell out of me."

Ellie looked up at Heather and smiled.

"And what happened after that?" Ellie asked.

She looked at me and gave me a quick wink.

"I fucked up."

Wow. For Heather to say that, I knew this was not going to be good.

"I'm sure it's not that bad sweets. Tell us what happened," I said as I moved to sit down on the floor next to Ellie, so Heather could look at both of us.

"Well…considering I was totally about to ask him to take me to my bedroom…I felt the need to just blurt out that I'd never been with anyone. I thought it would have scared him off but it did just the opposite. The look in his eyes changed from pure lust to."

"Pure love?" Ellie asked as she wiggled her eye brows up and down.

"No! I don't think it was love. Shit, I don't know what it was. All I can remember is that he called me princess and said he would never do anything I wasn't ready to do. Then I had a flash-back…."

Heather broke off her sentence while she tried not to start crying again.

"It's okay, sweets," Ellie said.

Just take your time," I added.

"So, anyway, I had a flash-back to my father calling me princess on my sixteenth birthday, and I just panicked. I started to push him away, and I yelled for him to put me down and …oh god. He was so confused! I'll never forget the look in his eyes."

"What happened after that? Did he get mad?" Ellie asked.

Heather let out a small laugh. "No…it sure as hell would've been easier if he had. He did just the opposite. He was so sweet and he admitted that he had feelings for me. He said that he had feelings he had never felt for any other girl."

My heart started to pound. Man whore Josh was in love with our Heather, and Heather had just admitted she wanted to have sex with him. *Holy hell. This was good!*

"And…what did you say?" I asked.

"Ari, I messed up so bad. I told him that I didn't feel the same way and that we would only ever be just friends. I wasn't exactly nice in the way I said it either. He told me he was leaving, and that if I let him walk out the door, he would never again ask me out or anything. We would just be friends."

"You let him leave, didn't you?" Ellie said as she looked at me. She had the saddest look on her face.

My heart was breaking for Heather and for Josh.

Heather started to cry again, but this time, she buried her face in her hands.

"Yes! Then, I got your message Ellie. I tried to call Josh a few times, but I kept getting his voice mail. Then I called again later that night and some girl answered his phone. She said he was drunk, and he kept talking about me all night to her and her friend. The girls were super sweet. Both are married, and they were out for a girls' night. They pretty much kept all the skanks away from Josh."

Heather finished telling Ellie and I the whole story, describing how the two girls helped Heather get Josh back to her apartment and then how Josh had left the next morning before Heather had woken.

I called him as soon as I realized he'd left. I told him that I wanted to talk to him, but he said he wasn't in the mood for any more rejection. I thought that maybe after a couple of days out here together, he might let me try to explain, but now…fuck…now that trampy little Lynda is here. I didn't even think about her being here for Emma and Garrett's party."

I stood up and walked over to the window. It looked like everyone had come into the house, but I saw Josh leaning up against his truck, talking to Lynda. He looked nervous while he kept looking back at the house. I bet he was wondering if Heather was watching him talk to Lynda. Lynda was so close to him that she might as well have been straddling his ass.

Little tramp.

I turned to look at Heather and Ellie sitting on the bed. I had the strangest feeling that this was going to be a very long and painful twenty four-hours.

Turning back toward the window, I saw Jeff, Gunner, Drake, and someone else who must have been Jack walking up from the barn. Lynda ran and jumped into Jack's arms. Then, she turned to hug Gunner. Jeff and Josh were talking off to the side. They were both laughing like they didn't have a care in the world.

Fucking men.

CHAPTER TWENTY-SEVEN

GUNNER

The moment my dad had stepped out of the car, I had been a nervous wreck. Ellie had been amazing. She immediately walked up to him and she introduced herself. My father had fallen in love with her in mere seconds.

Last night had been a bit awkward, but today was like a dream. Sitting in the barn with my dad, Gramps, and Drake, I'd never laughed so hard in my life as we spent the day shooting the shit. I saw a side of my father I'd never seen before. He was relaxed and actually enjoying himself. He seemed…normal to me.

He asked a lot of questions about Ellie and our future. When I told him we wanted to start a family right away, he smiled and gave me a wink. I had thought he would have given me a lecture about how we needed to wait.

Gramps leaned over and whispered something in my father's ear. He started laughing and called Gramps a wise old man.

Why couldn't he have been like this my whole life? It sure would have been nice to grow up with a normal father instead of a prick.

As we started to walk back toward the house, Lynda came running toward us before she jumped into my dad's arms. He gave her spin as he told her how grown-up she looked.

As Jeff and Josh stepped aside to talk about something, I looked back at the house, wondering where my Ellie was.

"Oh my gosh! I'm so excited about the party tomorrow, Gramps!" Lynda said as she hugged Gramps.

"Yeah, well, after fifty years of Emma putting up with me, the least I could do was throw her a damn party," Gramps said.

Everyone laughed as Dad, Uncle Jim and Gramps started to walk back up to the house.

Lynda made a bee-line toward Josh, practically throwing herself into his arms. He seemed a little taken aback. Pushing her away slightly, he looked back at the house.

"Hey, um Lynda. Um do you think I could talk to Jeff and Gunner alone for a bit?" Josh said as he gave Lynda that famous panty melting-smile of his.

"Oh, sure, Josh. Yeah no problem, I'll just see y'all inside," Lynda turned to head back into the house.

"What the hell is going on, Josh? I didn't hear from you again last night or this morning. What happened between you and Heather?"

Jeff asked confused as hell as he looked back at Josh and then me.

Josh threw his hands into his hair and let out a sigh.

"I kissed Heather."

"About fucking time, dude. Jesus, it took your ass long enough," Jeff said as he slapped Josh on the back.

I knew there was more though.

"Yeah… well, I didn't get the reaction I was hoping for. I mean, at first, she was *really* into it. Then, all I did was tell her that I would never push her to do anything she wasn't ready for, and she pretty much did a one-eighty on me."

"What do you mean? What did she say?" I asked as I watched Josh kick the dirt with his boot.

"She basically told me to stop touching her. I tried to tell her that I had feelings for her…strong feelings." Josh cut off his sentence as he leaned over, putting his hands on his knees.

In the four years I'd known him, I'd never seen him this affected by a girl.

"Dude, are you okay? What the hell did she say to you?" Jeff asked.

Josh stood up, leaning against the truck.

"Jesus Christ, y'all. I've never felt like this before. This is why I never wanted to get involved with anyone. I just wanted to avoid the same shit my dad went through."

Josh took a deep breath and then looked up at me. *Motherfucker*. I could see the hurt in his eyes.

"She pretty much told me that she didn't feel the same way I did and that we would only ever be friends. I'd never felt so gutted in my life. I was almost one-hundred percent positive that she felt something for me. At least, her kiss sure said she did."

"What happened after that?" I asked.

"I told her that if I walked out the door, I would never ask her out again or bother her about wanting anything more than just friendship. Then, she just let me walk out."

"Damn, Josh. That really sucks, dude," I said.

"Yeah, the worst part was I got trashed later. I ended up spilling my guts to two girls who were out on a girls' night out. I guess Heather called, and one of the girls told her I was drunk. Long story short, I woke up this morning in Heather's bed. She was on the sofa sleeping. She had left a voice-mail the night before, saying she wanted to talk. I wasn't really in the mood for more rejection, so I just left without waking her up."

"Oh hell, Josh, that was a stupid-ass move. Maybe she wanted to explain why she freaked out. I mean, I've known Heather a long time, and I can honestly say that I've only seen her date a few guys at most. Maybe the idea of getting closer to you scared her." Jeff said.

Josh started kicking the dirt again. He looked up at the house when Ellie, Ari and Heather all come out. Heather looked directly at Josh with slight smile. Just then, Lynda walked out the door and walked up in between Heather and Ari. She said something that caused Heather to frown, and then she turned around and headed to the other side of the porch.

"Josh, go talk to Heather," Jeff said, giving him a slight nudge.

"Dude, she doesn't want anything more than friendship."

I was watching Lynda closely. She obviously had a thing for Josh, and if I knew Lynda, she would do whatever it took to get what she wanted.

"I agree with Jeff. Dude, you need to go talk to her."

Looking back to the porch, I smiled at Ellie as she gave me that beautiful smile of hers. I'd never get used to how this girl made me feel.

"Okay, I'll go talk to her, but if she turns me down again, this will be it. I've never in my life begged or chased a girl, and I sure as shit am not about to start now."

Josh started to walk toward where Heather was sitting at the side of the house. Lynda came running down and stopped him. He must have told her that he needed to talk to Heather because her whole body sagged as she turned to head back up to the porch.

Ellie and Ari started to walk toward us, Ellie gave me a strange look. I knew what she was trying to tell me, but I'd already figured out that Ari hadn't told Jeff about the baby yet. He would have said something to me by now.

"So, standing out here guy-talking huh?" Ellie said reaching up on her toes to give me a kiss.

I picked her up and deepened the kiss. It took everything out of me not to let out a moan. *Shit.* The things this girl did to me drove me crazy. I just wanted to load her up in my truck and take her home.

Ellie slightly pulled away from my lips and smiled. "I love you, Drew."

"I love you more, Ells."

"Yep, the whole newlywed thing is starting to get a little sickening, y'all. Take it back to your house if you're going to hang all over each other," Ari said as she gave us a smirk.

"Don't be jealous, baby. That'll be us soon," Jeff said as he put his arms around Ari.

He placed his hand on her stomach, Ari jumped and stiffened. She tried to relax before Jeff noticed, but it was too late. He turned her around, giving her a funny look.

"Ari what's wrong? Are you still feeling sick?"

Just then, Mom called us all to come in so we could talk about the party tomorrow. Ellie told Jeff that Ari was fine, and then she took Ari's arm in hers as they walked up to the house together. Jeff grabbed my arm, holding me back.

Motherfucker. Please don't ask me...please don't ask me.

"Gunner, has Ellie mentioned anything about Ari's appointment yesterday? She won't talk to me about it. I know she had the genetic testing done. She's a nervous wreck. I think she's worried about the results. I just wish she would talk to me," Jeff said as he ran his hand through his hair and down the back of his neck.

"I know Ari was upset about a few things yesterday, the test, the whole Rebecca throwing them all in jail, and then you sticking up for Rebecca. Did you ever find out if she really tried to call you?"

"She said she tried to call. I don't know what to think anymore. She seems to be telling me the truth, but Ari is so damn sure that Rebecca is lying. I just don't know anymore, Gunner. I want to believe Ari, but...fuck I'm so damn confused. I just want to do the right thing for both Ari and this baby. I don't know what to believe anymore."

I just stared at him. "You need to believe the woman you love and who loves you, not some crazy bitch who never thought to call you until after she was seven months pregnant." I turned and walked away from him.

Stupid fucker. Even I thought Rebecca was lying. A part of me wondered if Jeff was hoping this baby was his.

***

We spent the next few hours talking about the party tomorrow. I kept looking from my grandparents to my parents. My mother looked scared. She kept asking my dad if he was okay, and I could tell he was trying to be patient. My dad had changed. I wasn't sure if it was from the heart attack, from being home again, or from maybe realizing what he had lost out on. I mean, it had only been a week since he'd refused to come to my wedding. *What changed?*

After dinner, we sat on the porch for a while. Josh and Heather's talk must not have been a good one because they pretty much avoided each other all afternoon and evening. Lynda took full on advantage and never left Josh's side.

"So, I have the guest rooms all made up. Grace and Jack, you take the room with the queen bed in it. Lynda, you can have the room next to the bathroom. Jim and Michelle, you can take the other bedroom." Grams said. Turning to Heather she asked, "Heather would you like to bunk with Lynda?"

"Actually, Emma, Heather's going to stay with us." Ari said.

I took a quick peek at Lynda. She looked like she was about to have a heart attack herself.

Josh snapped his head over toward Heather. Lynda leaned over and whispered something to Josh. He just smiled at her. Then he glanced back at Heather, and she didn't even try to hide her reaction. She just rolled her eyes as she stood up.

"Thank you everyone for a lovely evening. Ari and Jeff, if y'all don't mind, I think I'm going to turn in. I had a late night."

Everyone said good night to Heather as she made her way to her car. Josh never took his eyes off of her for a second.

Everyone went up inside, and I was left sitting on the porch by myself, waiting on my mom, Grams and Ellie to finish up plans for tomorrow. I heard the screen door shut, and I looked up to see my dad walking toward me.

I sat up a little straighter, force of habit I guess. *Shit, something's never change.*

"Drew, I um, I'd really like to talk to you for a few minutes if you'll let me."

Huh, this was new. He's asking me for permission for once.

"Sure, Dad. Yeah, that's fine."

He sat down next to me and didn't say a word for close to five minutes.

Finally, he let out a sigh. He leaned back and smiled.

"Do you know where my favorite place in the world used to be when I was growing up here?" he asked as he looked over at me.

"I didn't know you had a favorite place here. You always made it seem like you hated it here," I said turning away from him.

He'd never said one good thing about the ranch. He'd only talked about how much he hated it.

"I guess I deserved that one."

"I'm sorry. I wasn't trying to hurt you."

My dad leaned forward, putting his arms on his knees, as he let out a nervous laugh.

"When Garrett called to tell me you were getting married…"

He paused, clearing his throat.

"I, um…I have to admit that it killed me when it wasn't you who called to tell us. I mean, I understood the reasons why it wasn't you, but the look of pain on your mother's face about gutted me because I knew it was my fault. I took something that she loved very much away from her."

I didn't even know how to respond to him. My dad had never opened up to me like this before. I just sat there, stunned.

"Then, Dad told me where on the ranch you would be getting married." Shaking his head, he let out another small laugh.

"Drew, I think it's about time I told you the truth about why I was such a damn hard ass on you your whole life."

"Dad, really, it's alright. I don't want you to get yourself worked up when you're here to relax."

My dad smiled at me, leaning back into the chair again.

"Ever since you were little, I could see you were gonna be just like your grandfather, kind heart but hard-as-hell shell. I remember taking you out to a spot here on the ranch. I sat there with you as we watched the cattle. One of the calves was hurt, and you begged me to do something to help her. You couldn't have been more than five years old. I told you that she'd be fine. I said I'd let Gramps know, so he could make her better. You looked up at me and smiled. I'll never forget what you said to me then."

I tried so hard to remember what he was telling me. Honestly, I couldn't recall my dad ever being at the ranch with me. Every time I came to visit, I remembered coming by myself. Either I'd fly on a plane on my own and Gramps and Grams would pick me up at the airport, or if we were stationed close by, my parents would drop me off and then turn around and leave.

"What did I say, Dad?"

He turned to look at me with tears in his eyes. *Motherfucker.*

"You stood up and put your hands on your hips. You told me flat-out, 'I'm gonna grow up and be just like Gramps. I'm gonna help all the cows, and I'm gonna be a rancher, a really, really good rancher Daddy. I'm even gonna marry me a girl right here on this very spot.'"

I let out a laugh. I remembered telling Gramps millions of times that I was gonna be a better rancher than he was. I stopped saying that when I was old enough for him to slap me on the back side of my head while he told me that no one, except for God, would ever be a better rancher than him.

"Something happened to me in that moment, Drew. I panicked. When I was growing up, I had wanted nothing more than to be just like my father. I wanted to walk in his footsteps and to take over the ranch someday. Jim couldn't have cared less about the ranch. He'd always wanted the big fancy house in the city. I'd wanted the country life. I'd wanted to marry me a girl in the same exact spot you said you did when you were only five years old."

I was so confused that I had to shake my head. "Wait…you always said how much you hated it here. If I ever even talked about the ranch, you used to get pissed at me. It always ended in a fight, and then you'd threaten me with military school. If you wanted to run the ranch, why did you leave?"

My dad stood up, walked over to the edge of the porch, and leaned against the post.

"Drew, I left because I was afraid. I was afraid that I'd never be able to walk in the footprints of my own father. I almost killed your grandfather once. During my senior year of high school, I was helping him bring in the cattle for vaccinations. Dad was yelling at me to do it a certain way, but I thought my way was better. Long story short, his horse reared up, and he fell off. He almost got trampled to death, and it was all my fault. He never once said it, but I knew that it was. I was a stubborn asshole who had to prove that I could do it better than him."

Holy shit. I'd never heard this story before in my life. My dad turned to look at me, and I could see the tears glistening in his eyes.

"I knew at that very moment, I had to leave. I'd only ever wanted to be a rancher, so college was out of the question for me. I went into town the next day and joined the Army. This was my easy out. So, that day, when you were five and you declared your dream to me, I panicked again. I thought the only way to keep you from making the same mistake as me, was to keep you from following that dream."

He shook his head and walked over to me. He slapped me on the back and then sat back down.

"The only thing is…you're a Mathews. It's in your goddamn blood, just like it's still in mine. When I sit here, I smell the country air and hear the noises of this ranch, and it takes every part of me not to go saddle up a damn horse and rope me calf." He laughed again.

"Dad...I don't even know what to say. I'm stunned. I never knew the story of you and Gramps or how you really felt about the ranch. Why didn't you just tell me?"

"Oh shit, Drew. Someday when you and Ellie have kids, you'll see the stupid shit you do, thinking you're doing the right thing for them. I thought I was doing what was best for you, but in my heart, I knew all along that I was keeping you from your dream. I was just too full of pride to admit that I was wrong."

"All those years, Dad...they were just wasted."

He nodded his head. "When Garrett told me where you were getting married... well, I think that was the beginning of my heart attack," He said with a gruff laugh.

"What?" I asked, completely confused.

He turned and looked at me, I saw a tear rolling down his cheek.

"Drew, you got married under the same tree that you and I had sat under when you were five. It was that same tree where you'd declared to me you were gonna become a rancher and then marry you a girl, in that very spot."

I felt a chill run up and down my spine. *No fucking way.*

"When I was growing up, I used to ride my horse out to that big ol' oak tree, I'd just sit there for hours. It was my place to think. I knew you also went there a lot when you were growing up. Your Gramps told me plenty of times when he saw you sitting under that tree."

"Dad...I don't even..." I couldn't even finish my thought.

He stood up.

"I'm so damn proud of you, son. I know that I've never once led you to believe that I was proud of you, but I truly am. You knew what you wanted. You knew what your dreams were, and you went for it, even when your stubborn, stupid old man tried to hold you back from it. And Ellie…you're a lucky son of a bitch…you sure did take after me in that area. You sure as shit know how to pick the right woman, son. I just had to look at the two of you to know how perfect you are for each other. I'm sorry that I wasn't here for your wedding, but, if you'll have me, I'd love to be here to help you with the ranch and to someday…." As his voice cracked, he paused to clear his throat.

"Someday, I'd like nothing more than to sit under that same tree with my grandson and granddaughter and say how proud I am of their daddy and the man he has become."

I stood up, and grabbed my father, and hugged him. I had never in my life felt as complete as I did in this very moment.

It almost felt like a huge weight had just been lifted off my shoulders.

"Dad, please don't ever push me away again."

"Never again, Gunner…never again."

It wasn't lost on me that my father just called me Gunner.

CHAPTER TWENTY-EIGHT

ELLIE

Grace and I started to head out to the front porch. I had seen Jack come out here and knew Gunner was outside. I wondered if they had a chance to talk yet.

I was following Grace out the screen door when I slammed right into her. Before I knew it, her hand was covering my mouth.

What the hell is she doing? I looked at her and then followed her gaze. Gunner and Jack were standing there…hugging?

Fuck a duck.

Oh. My. God. My eyes grew bigger as I glanced back at Grace, who was smiling at me. She motioned her head, silently tell me to go back inside, so I slowly started to back up as she removed her hand from my mouth.

"You don't have to leave, Grace," Jack said with a laugh. We both stopped dead in our tracks as Grace smiled at me.

As we walked out, I saw Gunner quickly wiping his eyes. As soon as Grace went up to Jack, he picked her up and kissed her so passionately that I had to look away. I looked over at Gunner. He was watching his parents with the biggest smile on his face. He reached out, grabbing me, as he pulled me to him.

He whispered into my ear, "Let's go home, and try to make a baby."

Okay!

"Sounds like a wonderful idea."

***

We said good night to everyone and made our way back to the cabin. Gunner told me all about his talk with his father, and my heart was overfilled with love and happiness. I'd never seen Gunner so happy in my life.

When we got back to the cabin, he flew out of the truck, running over to my side. I opened the door, he reached in, picked me up and carried me into the cabin.

My heart was beating a mile a minute. I wondered if we would always be this way, filled with so much passion.

After we made our way over to the bed, Gunner slowly put me back down on the ground. As he started to kiss me, I reached up and ran my hands through his hair. He let out a moan that I swore caused a flood in my panties.

He slowly walked me back to the bed. He never broke our kiss, except to take off my T-shirt. As soon as it was over my head, he captured my lips again and kissed me with so much love that I felt like I was going to explode at any moment.

"Ellie, sweetheart, I'm going to make sweet love to you now."

Oh. My. God. My heart was beating like it was my first time all over again.

He slowly unbuttoned my jean shorts and then slid the zipper down. The moment his hand slipped inside my panties, I let out a gasp.

"So ready for me, Ells. You're always so ready, baby."

"Gunner..." I could hardly think to even compose any words. I pushed my hips into his hand to help ease the ache. *God, I want him so much.*

Then, he started to take off my shorts in that oh-so-slow way of his. After my panties came off, I was left standing there, wearing only my bra, while his hungry eyes traveled up and down my body. He placed his hands on my shoulders and turned me around. The next thing I knew, my bra was off, and he was kissing my neck.

My whole body started to shake.

"I love what my touch does to you, Ellie."

Oh god, me, too.

"Lie down, Ellie."

I crawled onto the bed and turned over to lay on my back. Gunner slowly placed gentle kisses starting on my feet and then moved his lips up my legs, to my stomach, then to my chest… *oh my god.*

By the time his sweet, soft lips landed on mine, I was about ready to beg him to be inside me. He slowly eased himself into me, and with each kiss, he went just a little farther.

After he was all the way inside me, he slowly started to move while he continued to kiss me all over my face, neck, and chest.

"Oh god, Gunner."

"I know, baby. You feel so good."

Before I knew it, I was having one of the most intense orgasms of my life. I swore that it was never going to end. I didn't even remember moving, but the next thing I knew, I was on top. I smiled down at the love on my life as he gave me that crooked smile of his.

I loved him so much that it almost hurt.

As I started to move slowly his hands were on my waist, gripping me harder, while he was trying his best to hold off.

"Ellie, you're so beautiful, sweetheart."

"I love you, Drew, so much."

Leaning up, he put his head on my chest as he wrapped his arms around me. I'd never felt so secure in my life.

I knew the moment I let go, he was going to come with me. This was one of our most amazing moments together. It was then that I knew this man would always make me feel so loved and wanted.

I collapsed on top of him and tried my best to catch my breath.

Gunner let out a laugh and pulled my body closer to him.

"Sweetheart, you need to start running with me."

Sitting up, I laughed and hit him on the chest. *Bastard!* I made a mental note to myself that when Gunner went out for the morning feedings, I would start running. Maybe I could see if Ari wanted to start hiking around the ranch more often. I knew she missed the gym, and now, with her being pregnant, she'd have to make sure she was getting exercise to stay healthy.

I wondered if Gunner and I just made a baby. I stopped taking my pills the moment he asked me to. *Could it happen that fast? It did for Ari, so why couldn't it for us?*

I rolled over, lying next to Gunner, and I put my hands on my stomach. Rolling over onto his side to face me, he placed his hand on mine and smiled at me.

"It'll happen sweetheart, when it's meant to happen. Don't stress about it, okay?"

I tried to smile at him, but I had the strangest feeling come over me. *Why do I think this is not going to be as easy as we both thought it would be?*

"I love you, Drew. I love you so much."

Gunner leaned down and gently kissed me on the nose and then on my lips.

"I love you too Baby, more than you'll ever know."

I didn't think it was possible so soon, but before I knew it, he moved on top of me, and I was lost again in his sweet love making.

CHAPTER TWENTY-NINE

JEFF

Josh had insisted on coming out with me to make the food rounds this morning. I knew it was only because he didn't want to be at the house with Ari and Heather. I tried to get him to talk, but I ended up just letting him sulk for about thirty minutes.

A new stud horse, Romeo, had arrived yesterday. I was mucking out his stall, when I saw Josh walking into the barn. He looked like hell.

"What the fuck, Josh? What happened yesterday when you went to talk to Heather?"

"Fuck if I know. I asked her if she still wanted to talk. At first, I thought she was going to, then Lynda called around the corner, asking if we were still on for heading into town for lunch. I'm not even sure where the hell that came from since I didn't even ask Lynda to lunch. I simply told Lynda that I would talk to her in a minute, and when I turned around, I swear Heather had steam coming from her ears. Then, she accused me of moving on fast. Moving on from *what?* She was the one who said there was no future for us and that we were just friends. I'm so fucking confused right now. I don't know which way is up and which way is down for Christ's sake."

I shook my head and closed Romeo's stall, while he was trying to push his damn way out. *Shit, this horse is a feisty bastard.* Ari had begged me to let her ride him last night. There was no way in hell I was letting her get on this horse.

"Josh, listen to me, dude. Women are...fuck, I don't really know how women are. I just know that at least more than half the time, when they say something, they really mean the opposite. I don't why. God made 'em that way, and I ain't about to question God on it. I really think you need to talk to her and get it out there before Gunner's cousin moves in and tries to eat you alive."

Josh started laughing. "Yeah, Lynda is something else. I like her. I mean, if Heather wasn't in the picture, I could probably see myself dating Lynda. She just moved to Austin to finish school at UT. I don't know. Maybe I just need to move on since Heather only wants to be friends."

"If you think that's what she really wants, then maybe you should," I said, raising my eye-brows at him.

"Well, that's what she keeps repeating to me so, I guess that means I need to move on."

***

By the time we made it back to the house, Josh was in an even worse mood. I was guessing that the idea of walking away from any kind of relationship with Heather just pissed him off. It was either that or it was because Romeo nipped at his hand.

I walked into the kitchen to see Heather and Ari sitting at the kitchen island. Ari looked up at me and gave me that smile that I swore could bring me to my knees every damn time. I smiled back at her and looked down to see she was drinking orange juice and not coffee. *That was two days in a row now.*

"What's wrong with the coffee?" I asked as I walked over to pour myself a cup.

Josh followed and poured some into his mug.

I leaned down to give Ari a kiss. She let out a small moan, and I just about grabbed her and hauled her ass into our bedroom. *Fuck.* She smelled so damn good. I nipped at her bottom lip, and then I pulled away, so I could sit down next to her.

Josh leaned up against the kitchen counter and looked everywhere but at Heather.

Ari just busted out with, "So, what the hell is going on with you two anyway?"

Heather choked on her coffee, and Josh looked like he was about to kill Ari. It took everything out of me not to laugh. Ari never was one to beat around the bush. That was one of the things I loved about her. She was a no-bullshit kind of girl.

"Ari! I can't believe you," Heather said giving Ari a go-to-hell look.

Josh seemed to compose himself, but then I saw a look in his eyes. It was that same look he used to get when he was putting on his game face.

"There's nothing going on but friendship. Ain't that right, Heather?" Josh said.

Oh fuck.

"Um…I um."

"Heather, didn't you want to talk to Josh about something?" Ari said, her eyes pleading with Heather.

"I, um." Heather looked over at Josh.

He actually looked pissed. *What the hell?*

"I think you made your self clear yesterday as well as the other day. Or is there something else you needed to tell me besides to fuck off?"

Ah, shit. This is going south. I looked at Ari, who was staring at Josh in shock. Then, she glanced at Heather, who also had a shocked look on her face. This seemed to be turning into something I was not used to seeing on Heather.

Suddenly, she appeared to be very pissed-off as her hands were balled up in fists. I tried to decide who I was putting my money on.

Getting up from the bar stool, Heather just glared at Josh.

"To think that I even thought."

"You even thought what, Heather? I know it wasn't about a relationship with me. 'The bastard manwhore.' I believe those were your words to me yesterday."

"You had just made plans to go have lunch with Lynda, yet there you were, trying to talk to me! Are you kidding me right now, Josh?"

"Okay, hold on a second here, y'all. Let's just calm down and talk about this," Ari said as she stood up and walked over toward Heather.

"There's nothing to talk about, Ari. Heather made herself pretty fucking clear where she stood with me. Isn't that right, Heather?"

Josh gave Heather a smirk,

Then he glanced over at me. I was completely stunned as to why he was being such a prick.

For a second, it looked like Heather might cry. I watched Josh's whole body sink when he saw the same thing I did.

Josh said, "Heather, I didn't."

"No, Josh you're completely right. I did tell you where I stood, and you told me if you walked out the door, then that was it. So, we're done. There's nothing left to talk about. If you'll excuse me..."

Heather's voice cracked as she started to back out of the kitchen.

"I think I'll get ready and then head up to see if Emma needs any help before the party."

Heather turned, leaving as fast as she could. Ari looked at Josh and just shook her head.

"She pushed you away because she got scared, Josh. She wanted to tell you she didn't mean anything she had said, you fuckwad! You just blew probably the best thing that'll ever happen to you because you had to run into the arms of the first girl you came across."

"Wait...what? First off, how do you know she didn't mean any of it? And what the hell do you mean I ran into the arms of the first girl I came across? I haven't been with anyone in months!" Josh yelled.

"I know because she sat there and cried to Ellie and me about how much she cares about you and how she messed things up with you. But you didn't let her explain that, did you?"

Ari started to walk out of the kitchen, but then she stopped and turned back around.

"Lynda, you stupid ass. You made plans with Lynda, and she made sure to tell us how you said you would only dance with her at the party."Ari turned her back to us as she was leaving the kitchen. "I'm going to see if Heather is okay."

Josh was now leaning over with his hands on his knees.

"Josh…dude, you okay?" I walked over and helped him sit down.

He looked up at me and started to shake his head. "I'm so fucking confused that I can't even think straight. I never asked Lynda out to lunch yesterday. She kept asking me if I was going to dance with her. I never said I was only going to dance with her. They must have misunderstood her. I don't…" Josh paused, standing up. "I'm heading up to Garrett and Emma's place. I know Drake needs help with the tables and shit. I'll talk to you later, dude."

As Josh was leaving, he walked right into Heather who was also heading toward the front door. They both just stood there and stared at each other. Josh was the first to move. He stepped around her and headed out. Heather turned to me and gave me a weak smile before she left.

Holy hell. If this is any indication, this was going to be a very interesting party.

***

Ari walked back into the kitchen a few minutes later. The moment I saw her, I had to catch my breath.

Damn. She was dressed in a white shirt with a pink tank top underneath. She had on a pair of jean shorts and a belt with a buckle that was so damn big and blingy that I just had to smile at her. As I moved my eyes down her body, I noticed the pink cowboy boots. *My cowgirl sure the hell knows how to dress.*

"Baby, those shorts…maybe you should…"

Ari turned and gave me a look that said I should know better than to say anything about what she was wearing.

"I'm just sayin' they're kinda short, baby."

"They are not short, Jeff. These are the longest damn pair of shorts I have that still fit me. I think I'm getting bigger already."

"Already? What do you mean by that? Isn't it supposed to be, we get married, you get happy, and then you start getting bigger because you're so damn happy with me?" I said with a laugh.

Ari looked like as pale as a ghost.

"Ari, I'm just kidding, baby. You look amazing." I walked up to her and pulled her into my arms.

She instantly relaxed and started to run her hands through my hair. She pushed her hips into me, and that was the only sign I needed. I picked her up, and she wrapped her legs around me as I started to walk her into the bedroom.

"Oh god Jeff. I need you so bad."

I let her slide down my body while I took her mouth in mine. She let out a moan, and I couldn't wait anymore. I pulled my mouth away from her to take her shirt off.

Just then, someone knocked at the door.

"Motherfucker!" Ari and I both yelled at the same time.

"Just ignore it, Jeff. Please just ignore it," Ari said nearly begging.

I pulled her shirt over her head and then put my hand up under the tank top. *God, she felt so good.* She slowly started to back up to the bed. When she was lying down, I crawled on top of her and captured her lips with mine again. Reaching my hands down, I started to unbuckle her belt. Then, I thought I heard the front door open.

Ari pulled back and whispered,

"Did someone just come in?"

"Jeff? Ari?" Garrett called out.

We heard him walking down the hall-way. Ari pushed me away and rolled over, landing on the floor next to the bed.

I just leaned over and looked at her.

"What the hell are you doing?" I whispered to her.

"Go talk to him! Shit! I don't want him walking into our room to see me half dressed!"

I was confused because she was still wearing her tank top and shorts. I crawled off the bed, I could hear Garrett in the kitchen.

I adjusted my harder-than-rock-hard dick while I made my way out to see what was going on. I made a mental note to always make sure the front and side doors were locked from this point on.

I walked into the kitchen to see Garrett pouring himself a cup of coffee.

"Hey, Garrett, what's up?" I asked.

"Hey, son. Gunner asked me to come fetch you to help set up the tables and all that shit for the party this afternoon. Your front door was open, so I just helped myself."

I tried really hard to smile as I made another mental note. The next time I had enough beers in me, I was gonna have a talk with Garrett about him just walking into the house. While I was making all these damn mental notes, I better make one to warn Gunner.

Just then, Ari came running in through the front door. *What the hell? How did she...?*

"Hey, Gramps! What's shaking?" Ari said as she bounced up to give him a hug and a kiss.

He grinned and gave her a look that I didn't understand. She shook her head, and he gave her a faint smile back.

"Get it done, kid," he said to her.

Then, he slapped me on the back and told me to get my ass in his truck. Ari started laughing and then grabbed my arm as we headed outside.

I pulled her back for second. "How the hell did you get outside?"

She looked at me like I had just asked her the stupidest question ever. "I climbed out the bedroom window."

"Why?"

"I didn't want Garrett to think we were messing around. If I came out from the bedroom, he would have."

I just stared at her. She made it sound so logical. I leaned down to kiss her as she let out a giggle.

"God, I love you, baby!" I barely pulled my lips away from hers.

"We'll pick up where we left off later," I said as I smacked her ass.

"Sounds good. Um, Jeff, I really need to talk to you about something. It's really important."

As I looked down at her, I ran the back of my hand down the side of her face.

"Do we need to talk now, baby? I can just tell Garrett that I'll be up in a little bit."

"No, they need help, and this is Garrett and Emma's big day. We can talk after the party."

"Okay, baby, if you're sure. Is everything okay, Ari?"

She smiled at me, and the spark that was in her eyes made me smile back at her.

"Yeah, at least, I um…yeah…no, really, it's fine. Come on, let's go."

I took Ari's hand as we made our way outside. Garrett was waiting for us, leaning up against his truck.

"Hey, Garrett, I'll just follow you. That way when it's time to leave, I won't have to ask anyone for a ride." I said as I held open the truck door open for Ari.

He nodded and got in his truck.

***

We spent the morning setting up tables and chairs for the party. Gunner was practically flying high after working with his father. Ellie was so in her environment, and I was glad to see her smiling as much as she was. She adored Emma, and Emma adored her. Grace seemed to be falling right into the role of mother-in-law perfectly. She and Ellie got along so well. And at times, my heart just wanted to burst because I was so happy for Ellie.

Heather seemed to be slipping further into a funk, especially with Lynda following Josh around. Josh just seemed…shit, I don't know how Josh seemed. Fucked-up is the only way I could describe it. It wasn't a good sign that he had already started drinking around lunch-time.

Sitting on one of the hay bales, I tried to listen to Gunner going on about something with the cattle, but I couldn't pull my eyes away from Ari. *My beautiful Ari.* She looked happy, but at the same time, she looked so lost. She had such a beautiful glow about her, I lost my breath just watching her.

She was now arguing with Josh about where he was going to put the washers game. Josh looked like he was about to pull his hair out. *I should really be a better friend and go save him from my beautiful, outspoken future bride.*

I decided it was kind of fun just sitting here, watching the two of them.

Ari put her hands on her hips and tilted her head at him. I watched the whole thing play out. Ari tilted her head and put her hands on her hips. She just looked at him with that look of hers, and the next thing I saw was Josh moving the game.

I smiled, and just then, Ari looked over at me. Her frown turned into that goddamn smile of hers. If I had been standing up, my knees would have buckled.

Gunner nudged me with his shoulder, and I moved my gaze away from Ari to look at him.

"Dude, you do know how lucky you are to have her, right?"

I smiled as I looked back at Ari, who was still looking at me. Her face seemed....concerned. I knew she wanted to talk to me about something, she seemed excited about it but nervous as hell also.

She started to walk toward us, I instantly felt my body react to her. As she reached me, she lowered her head, looking at me through those beautiful long eye lashes of hers. It was almost like she knew how much I wanted her.

I turned back to Gunner and smiled.

"Yeah, dude....I know."

CHAPTER THIRTY

ARI

I watched Emma and Garrett laughing while enjoying the company of all their friends and family. I looked over at Jeff who was talking to my mom and dad. *Someone was going to slip soon about the baby.* I really needed to talk to Jeff soon. I almost died earlier when I'd made the comment about me getting bigger.

Matt came running up to Jeff, calling out Jeff's name. Jeff bent down and picked up the oh-so-happy Matt. I smiled as I watched the two of them. I put my hand to my stomach and instantly felt like I couldn't breathe. When I leaned forward, I felt a hand rubbing my back. I knew in an instant that it was Ellie.

"Breathe, baby girl. Just breathe."

"Jesus, Mary, and Joseph, I can't do this, Ellie! What if this baby has Fragile X? I'm not like my mother. I can't do it. I just can't!" *Holy fuck, I was having a melt-down.*

Worried that Jeff might see me freaking out, I looked over and noticed he was taking Matt down to the barn. *They must be going to look at the horses.*

Ellie reached over and placed her finger under my chin and turned my head towards her.

"Listen to me right now, Arianna. You're going to be fine, and this baby is going to be fine. You aren't even sure if you're a carrier, so stop worrying yourself sick. But, sweets, ya have to tell Jeff. You have to tell him tonight. No more excuses. You can't keep trying to do this on your own. Jeff loves you more than life itself, and he's going to be so damn happy. Please, Ari, go talk to him."

I felt the tears building up in my eyes, and I willed myself to stop them. I smiled at Ellie, I leaned over and kissed her on the cheek.

"Have I told you today that I love you?" I asked, winking at her.

"No. No, you haven't bitch," she said winking back with a smile.

ve stood up and hugged. I held on to her just for a few
ger than needed. *I would be lost without this girl.*

.., . .u gonna go talk to him right now. I've been sitting here
all day waiting for someone to accidentally slip and say something
to him!"

Ellie let out a laugh as I turned and made my way down to the
barn.

As I rounded the corner, I could hear Jeff and Matt talking.

"Where's Ari's horse, Jeff?"

I stopped to listen, peeking into the barn. I was curious to see if
Jeff was going to remember to be specific this time.

"Well, buddy...she's over on our property. I have her out in a
pasture right now. She's not the type of girl who likes to be held
down in a stall for too long. She really loves to be free and run
around with the sun on her."

"Like Ari! Ari likes the sun on her face, too, doesn't she, Jeff?"
Matt said as Jeff had a huge smile on his face.

God, how I love Matt. His heart was pure, and his laughter was
infectious. He was so special to us. There was something about
him that just made people feel so loved when he smiled.

"Yeah, buddy, she does. Ari is just like Stargazer no one can hold
her down. She's probably the most amazing woman I've ever
met."

"Jeff, you're an assmole! Ari is a girl, not a woman!"

Oh shit! I couldn't help it when and I let out a small giggle. I had
to laugh every time Matt said assmole.

"Matt, buddy, trust me Ari is a woman," Jeff said, placing his hand
on Matt's head.

"I'm gonna give you a hug, buddy, okay?" he asked as Matt smiled
up at him. Jeff gently pulled Matt in for a hug.

I felt a single tear run down my face. Just then, my mother walked up next to me, putting her arm around me. Reaching up, I wiped away my tear, trying to get myself back together again.

"It's going to be okay, Ari. You know what you have to do, baby girl."

I shook my head as my mother and I walked into the barn. Jeff looked up and smiled at us.

"Matthew, sweetheart, come on back with me. Emma just bought a new mop," my mom said.

Matt just about screamed because he was so happy.

"I want to mop!"

I watched as my mom and Matt walked out of the barn toward the house. Taking a deep breath, I turned to face Jeff. Taking me by surprise, he grabbed me and kissed me so passionately that my legs almost went out from under me.

"Arianna, I love you so much."

I smiled as I looked up into his beautiful green eyes. "I love you, too, Jefferson…so very much."

As he kissed me again, I almost wanted to talk him into making love to me right here and now, so I could lose myself in his love.

Knowing I had to do this though, I pulled away just a little.

"Um, Jeff, I really need to talk to you," I said, looking up at him.

He smiled as he took my hand and walked me over to a hay bale.

"Alright, baby….talk away."

"Well, um….I'm not even sure how to tell you this, but."

His cell phone rang. He pulled it out of his pocket, looking at the display, he frowned. He shoved it back into his pocket and looked at me.

"Don't stop, Ari. Keep going."

"Okay, well, when I went to the doctor on Monday, I um, I found out."

"You got the results back already? Ari, why didn't you tell me, baby? What did they say? Are you a carrier of the gene?"

Wait...what? Oh god. My head was spinning.

"No, I won't get the results back until after another week or so."

"Shit, Ari, I thought you had been holding this in for the last two days."

I let out a small laugh. "Ah, no, but I did find out something else."

Just then, his phone rang again. *Of all the fuck-ass times, why is he getting a signal now?* He looked at it and then back at me.

"Give me just two seconds."

I sat there, stunned. It had to be Rebecca.

"Hey, Rebecca. I thought I asked you to not....*what?* Are you okay?"

I'm going to hell for the thought that just crossed my mind.

"Yeah, I'll leave right now.

Jeff jumped up and started to walk away from me.

What the fuck?

"Jeff!" I yelled.

He turned around to look at me.

"Oh shit, Ari! I'm sorry, baby. Rebecca is having contractions. They're pretty far apart, but she's freaking out."

"Wait, Jeff, I really need to talk to you. Can she not wait just a few extra minutes for you?" I said, almost pleading with him.

"Ari, baby, is this really that important?"

Tears started to build in my eyes. *Oh my god.* He was picking her over me. I felt like I was going to throw up.

"Ari! I need to go! Is this something that can wait until later tonight or tomorrow?"

"Tomorrow? Are you planning on staying with her tonight?"

"Well, no, of course not. But what if she needs to go to the hospital or something?"

When his phone rang again, he lifted it up to answer it, but I grabbed it from him, sending the call to voice mail.

"Ari, what the fuck? Give me the phone."

Now, I was just plain pissed off.

"No, I have to talk to you about something, and I need to talk to you about it now, Jeff. It's very important, and it involves *our* future. So, no, I won't wait until tonight or tomorrow."

The fucking phone rang again, and Jeff grabbed it out of my hand. *Of all the times for him to have cell coverage, this is the worst!*

"Did you call them? Okay, good. No, its fine. Just calm down. We don't want you going into labor early, Rebecca. I'll be there soon. Yep...bye." Jeff hung up the phone and turned back to me.

"Ari, I promise you that I'll be back tonight. We'll talk then, baby, but I have got to go now."

He leaned down to kiss me, but I stepped back away from him.

"Ari, please don't do this to me."

"It's me or her."

"What?"

"I said...it's me or her. You decide right now, Jeff. If you walk away from me, you are deciding on Rebecca and this baby that you don't even know if it's yours, or you stay here with me and our future."

He just stared at me.

"Ari, you can't do this to me. I love you, but if this baby is mine and I just walked away from him…do you know what you're asking me to do?"

"It's me or her."

"Oh fuck, Ari. I don't have time for this bullshit game. I'll be back tonight, and we'll talk then."

He turned and walked away from me.

The moment he rounded the corner, I fell to my knees and started crying. *Oh. My. God. He left me.*

He left. I put my hand to my stomach and cried so hard that I could hardly breathe.

He left…us.

***

I slowly started to walk out of the barn. Heading back up toward the house, I could see a few people dancing on the dance floor that Gunner, Josh and Jeff had made. Taylor Swift's song, "The Moment I Knew," was playing. *Jesus, Mary, and Joseph, what a perfect song to play right now.*

My head was spinning. *I knew he would pick her over me. I knew it.*

I looked out to the dance floor and saw Josh and Lynda dancing together. I looked over at Heather and I saw a tear run down her face. Oh hell no. She was not going to fall apart in front of him.

Rushing over, I grabbed Heather's hand and pulled her up.

"Fuck no, you don't! You will not cry over that fucker!" I practically shouted at Heather.

Heather took one look at me and sucked in a breath of air. "Oh my god, Ari, you've been crying."

While I led her toward the barn, Heather kept trying to get me to stop walking. By the time we got there, she yanked her hand from mine and came to a dead stop.

"Ari, what the hell is going on?" I looked at her and lost it. She ran over to me and pulled me into her arms.

"It's okay, sweets. It's okay." Heather just kept repeating it over and over again.

"Heather? Ari? What's wrong?"

Ellie's voice just sent me into another fit. *Oh my god.* I felt Heather moving down with me to the ground.

Ellie ran over and fell to her knees. She grabbed my face to look at her.

"What happened?"

"He left."

"Who left?" Heather and Ellie said at the same time.

"Jeff. I was just about to tell him about the baby, and he got a call from Rebecca. When he hung up, he just turned away and started walking out. He wasn't even going to say good-bye until I yelled out his name."

"Wait...I'm confused, Ari. What happened to Rebecca to make Jeff just leave like that?" Ellie said, wiping tears off my face.

"She, um...I don't know. She was having contractions or something like that. I'm telling you that she is further along than she says, and he won't believe me!" I shouted.

Then, I stood up. *I need to ride.*

I walked over and grabbed a saddle and made my way over to Rose's stall.

"Ari, are you going for a ride now?" Ellie asked as she walked over to help me.

"I think I'll go also. I need to get away from the Josh-and-Lynda show," Heather said.

"Oh Jesus, I guess that means I'm going, too. Um, should I go tell Gunner that we're heading out?" Ellie asked as she watched me saddle up Rose.

Rose is still acting feisty as hell.

"If you want," I said.

"Just a quick ride, right? It actually looks like a storm is about to come in. Emma is in a panic, and I don't want to leave her too long." Ellie said while she made her way over to saddle up Big Roy.

After we all got our horses saddled up, the three of us headed out.

Ellie noticed right away that Rose was acting up a bit.

"Ari, are you sure you want to ride Rose? She seems to be spooked about something. Maybe the storm coming in?"

I rolled my eyes at her. "Ells, I've been riding horses long enough to know when I shouldn't be on one."

***

We rode for a good thirty minutes in complete silence.

When we started back, Ellie broke the silence.

"Ari, you have to know that Jeff wasn't thinking clearly. I mean, there is a chance this baby could be his, and he's just trying to do what's best for the baby."

I started to feel the tears building in my eyes again. *Shit, I've never cried so damn much in my life as I have these last few weeks.*

Rose started jumping around a bit. I pulled back on her to get her to settle down.

Ellie turned Big Roy out of the way while I tried to get Rose under control. She seemed to be calming down until a huge bolt of lightning hit close by. It scared the shit out of all the horses. When Rose reared up, it took everything out of me to stay on her. The next thing I knew, she was running off. I heard Ellie yell out for me as we headed toward the creek.

Oh fuck, Rose. Don't jump it.

She jumped it.

All I heard was Ellie and Heather both scream.

Oh shit. I knew I was in trouble the moment I flew off the back of the horse.

CHAPTER THIRTY-ONE

JEFF

I was almost into Austin when my cell phone rang. It was Rebecca. *Shit, I hope nothing happened.*

"Hey, I'm almost to your place. Are you doing okay?"

"Yeah, they've slowed way down, and the doctor said it was just Braxton Hicks again."

"I thought you said they were painful and coming faster?" I asked, clearly frustrated.

"They were, but now, they've settled down."

Shit. This was another time when I rushed away from Ari, except this time, I had a really strange feeling that I fucked-up more than normal.

"Well shit, Rebecca, I drove all this way. Damn it. Have you eaten today?"

"No, I haven't had anything since breakfast. I've been too nervous, I guess."

"Want to go grab something then? That way, you can eat, and we can make sure you weren't feeling the real thing. Then, I have to head back to Mason. I kind of walked out on Ari and a party."

"Oh no! I'm so, so, sorry Jeff. I know you said to call only if it was important, and I really thought it was important."

I could almost hear the smile in her voice. Somehow, I figured that I totally just got played here. I thought it was time to have a heart to heart with Rebecca, regardless of the risk of an early birth or not.

***

After I picked up Rebecca, we headed to the restaurant. Along the way, I tried to call Ari five times. Each time, it went straight to voicemail. *Shit! Why did my cell phone work out there today but Ari's isn't?*

"Thank you so much for rushing in Jeff. I'm pretty sure everything is going to be okay. You really don't have to baby-sit me, you know. Like the doctor said, it's just Braxton Hicks contractions. I think if I just take it easy, I'll be able to make it to term with no problem." Rebecca said with a smile

There was something about her smile that seemed wrong. I was starting to get a strange feeling that maybe this was all just a game with her. As we made our way to the table, I glanced down at her stomach. She really did seem pretty big to have a month and a half left. Then again, what the hell do I know.

Suddenly, the sickest feeling came over me. I reached for my phone and tried to call Ari again. *Nothing.* I tried Ellie's cell and then Gunner's. *Something's wrong.* I could feel it.

Just as the waitress was about to take our drink order, Rebecca grabbed the table. "Oh no."

"What? What is it, Rebecca? What's wrong?" I jumped up and walked around the table to her.

She looked up at me with a panicked look on her face. "Um, nothing, Jeff. It's nothing. I guess the baby just kicked really hard. That's all."

"Are you sure? Do we need to go to the hospital?"

She tried to laugh, but I could see the pain on her face. She was trying to hide it. She shook her head and reached for her phone.

"Who are you calling?"

"I'm gonna call Crysti. I really just want to go and lay down. She can stay with me at my apartment to make sure I'm alright."

While she started to talk to Crysti, my head started spinning. *What the fuck is going on here?*

"Rebecca, don't be crazy. I'll take you home and stay with you until Crysti gets there. Don't you think you should call the doctor again?"

"No! Jeff, listen to me. I just need to go lie down." Rebecca looked away from me, returning to her phone conversation. "Yeah Crysti, I know....I know! It'll all work out. Just trust me on this, *please.* Just come to Maudie's. Yep, the one off of Lake Austin Boulevard."

Rebecca hung up the phone and tried her best to smile at me.

"Rebecca, I don't understand. I drove all the way in because you said you didn't have anyone to be here for you. You said you were having contractions. Now you're fine, and you just want to go home and lie down. You don't want me to take you home even though I just drove a few hours to get here. What the fuck is going on? Clearly something is wrong."

"Jeff, really, I just need to stay calm right now. I sense that you're upset that you had to leave the party and Ari. You've tried calling her a number of times. Really, you should just head back to Mason. I promise I'm okay. Crysti is on her way, so I'll have someone to stay with me. I can't go into labor this early. I'm just nerv-v-v."

She grabbed the table again.

I looked up and noticed the waitress was still standing there. She just kept looking back and forth between us. Then, she took a step back and glanced at Rebecca's feet.

"Um, can you give us a few minutes? Just two waters for now, please," I said smiling up at the waitress.

She looked back at Rebecca.

"Listen, I really think you need to go to a doctor now," the waitress said.

Rebecca gave her a dirty look.

"Um, I really think you need to mind your own goddamn business!" she yelled.

"Rebecca! Holy shit!" Turning to the waitress, I said, "I'm sorry."

"Listen, I've had three kids, sweetheart and I hate to tell you this, but your water just broke."

Rebecca's face turned white as a ghost.

"*No!*....Oh no. Oh god no! This can't be happening!" Rebecca just kept repeating to herself over and over again. She reached for her phone and called Crysti again.

"You need to hurry. My water just broke. Yes Crysti! I know!"

It took a good two minutes for everything to soak in before I jumped up and headed over to Rebecca. I reached down and picked her up in my arms.

"What the hell are you doing, Jeff? Put me down!"

"Jesus Christ, Rebecca. You're in labor. We're going to the hospital now!" I couldn't believe it. *Fuck!* She still had a month and two weeks to go. This was not good.

"Oh god, Jeff. Please...I just need you to leave. Crysti can take me to the hospital. I'm sure it will be fine. They will get the contractions under control. I'll probably just be put on bed rest or something. Really, I just need you to leave!"

When we got to my truck, I gently set Rebecca down while I opened the passenger door.

"What the fuck are you talking about? Your water broke! You're gonna have this baby, Rebecca, regardless if it's time or not. I'm not leaving. I missed the first seven months. Do you really think I'm going to miss the birth of my son?" I held the door open and helped her in. *Poor thing seems like she was scared to death.*

Rebecca was panicked during the entire ride to the hospital. *I thought she was going insane. Motherfucker, is this a normal reaction?*

She just kept saying the same things over and over again. How this can't be happening. This wasn't part of her plan.

"Rebecca, I'm pretty sure Mother Nature's plan outweighs yours. It's going to be okay."

She called the doctor's office, saying that her water broke. Then, she began crying hysterically. *What the fuck?*

***

Twenty minutes later, things were only getting worse. The nurses were telling Rebecca that she needed to calm down. She even tried to tell one of the nurses that I wasn't allowed in the room.

"What the hell? I'm the father! You better bet your ass I'm gonna be in the room!"

The nurse was yelling at me to stop yelling at Rebecca. My phone started ringing, and I looked down to see it was Ellie calling. I went to answer it, and the nurse just glared at me.

"Really? Turn it off and put it away, Mr. Johnson! *Now!*"

Shit! I sent it to voice mail and put it back in my pocket.

Rebecca looked at me and tried to smile.

"Jeff, I really need you to just not talk to anyone if you're gonna stay. Please I just need peace and quiet. What I really need is to be left alone. I'll call you after I have the baby."

When I looked at the nurse, she was staring at Rebecca. Then she pulled me outside of the room.

"Mr. Johnson, clearly Ms. Moore is very upset. I'm not really sure why she keeps asking you to leave. Honestly, it's a bit strange, but over the years, I've learned not to question what women in labor do and say. With that said, we really need her to calm down. Her contractions are coming faster, and Dr. Wyatt is almost here. I need to tell you though that the baby is getting stressed. I cannot stress how important it is that we get her to calm down."

I nodded my head. "I understand what you're saying, but I'm not leaving. I missed the whole pregnancy. I can't miss the birth. I just can't."

Just then, my phone rang again. I pulled it out of my pocket and saw it was Gunner. I hit ignore. A minute later, I got a text. I looked at it quickly and noticed I had one message from Ellie and one from Gunner.

Ellie: *"Jeff, please call me ASAP. It's about Ari. Please call."*

Gunner: *"Jeff, it's really important that you call one of us back right away. It's Ari, dude. Something has happened."*

Shit! Ari was probably so pissed off that I left. *Mother fucker. I can't deal with this shit right now.*

I sent Ellie and Gunner a text back.

Rebecca in labor. At hospital. Will call later.

Just then, a doctor walked out of Rebecca's room. *What the hell?* I didn't even see him go in there.

"Are you Mr. Johnson?"

I held out my hand to shake his. "Yes, Jeff Johnson."

He gave me a once over and shook his head. *What the hell?*

"I'm afraid we are going to have to put Ms. Moore under. She won't calm down, and her blood pressure is way too high. I'm having an OR prepped for a cesarean right now. The baby is stressed. It appears the cord is wrapped around the baby's neck, so we need to move fast. Please go in and try to calm her down. Then, one of the nurses will take you to get ready."

My head was spinning. I wanted to ask him if the baby would be okay since Rebecca went into labor so early, but then my fucking phone went off again. *Ellie.* I sent it to voice mail and turned off my phone. I would deal with Ari later. I needed to think about Rebecca and the baby right now.

"Um…okay. I'll try to get her to calm down, but I think I'm making her more upset for some reason."

"Just try your best. I'll see you in a bit." He walked away with a different nurse following behind him.

When I walked into the room, Rebecca looked up at me with panic in her eyes.

"Hey, honey, please don't worry. It's going to be okay. It will all be okay, Rebecca. I need you to calm down, okay?"

Two more nurses came in and asked for me to go with the one nurse to get ready for the C-section.

All I could hear as I walked out of the room was Rebecca begging them not to put her to sleep. I looked down the hall and saw Crysti. She was white as a ghost and barely smiled at me as I started to make my way to her.

The nurse took my arm and guided me in the other direction. "Mr. Johnson, this way, please. We need to get moving."

I turned back and looked at Crysti who was just watching me walk away.

Something is not right. I had the worst feeling in my stomach, like something terrible was about to happen.

***

The moment I heard the baby cry, I almost started to cry. Thank God he was breathing and healthy. Rebecca would only be out for about thirty more minutes, so I took advantage of holding my son.

I just stared at him. I wanted so badly to love this baby, but I didn't feel a connection. *Is it because I missed out on so much of the pregnancy? Why am I not feeling anything?*

I felt sick in the pit of my stomach, almost like I had lost something. I was confused though because I hadn't lost anything. I had just gained something.

Dr. Wyatt came up and patted me on the back as he smiled at me.

"Dr. Wyatt, is he going to be okay? I mean, he looks strong and healthy. He's so big for being born a month and a half early. Will he be okay?"

Dr. Wyatt just gave me a strange look.

"Rebecca was due in two weeks, Jeff. Her due date was July seventeenth, not August. The baby's going to be just fine."

If I hadn't been holding the baby in my arms, I was pretty sure my legs would have gone out from under me.

"*What?*"

"You thought she was due in August?"

"She told me she was due in August. She told me she was..."

Then, everything that had happened hit me – her wanting Crysti to pick her up, her panicking when I stayed. It hit me like a ton of bricks. This was her plan all along. She never had any intentions of me being at the birth because I would find out that she was further along than she'd said. *Motherfucker.* Everyone was right. *Ari was right.*

***

I sat in the chair next to Rebecca's bed. When I heard her starting to wake up, I sat up, putting my arms on my legs. She looked over at me and smiled.

"Where's the baby?" she asked as she started to look around.

"He's fine. He's in the nursery. They're just waiting for you to wake up."

"Is he beautiful, Jeff?"

I just nodded.

"Why…why isn't he in here? Why are you not with him?"

"Why would I be, Rebecca?"

She looked confused, and then it hit her. As she looked away, I saw a tear run down her face.

"You weren't really due in August, were you?" I asked.

"No." she whispered.

"You thought Ari and I were getting married, so you tried one last-ditch attempt at getting me back? You didn't think I'd be getting a paternity test done, Rebecca?"

"I thought I could make you love us...love the baby...so you would want to stay. Then you wouldn't want to be with Ari...you'd want to be with me and your son."

"He's not my son."

"But he can be. We can be happy together Jeff if you just give us a chance!"

Holy shit! Is this girl serious?

"Rebecca, I love Ari. I only want to be with Ari. I only want to have children with Ari. I'm sorry, but I don't have those feelings for you. I never have, and I never will."

Tears were streaming down her face as she looked away from me.

"Who is the father, Rebecca?"

She wiped the tears away from her eyes before she turned to look at me again.

"Jason Reed."

My stomach dropped. *What the hell is she saying?*

"Jason? Jason was dating Ari at that time you got pregnant...wait." Motherfucker, this girl was more evil than I could've ever imagined.

"You knew Ari was with Jason, didn't you? You did this on purpose! From the very beginning, you had every intention of hurting Ari, didn't you?"

I stood up and walked over to her side of the bed.

Rebecca started crying again. She looked up at me, shaking her head.

"I just wanted to get back at her for taking you away from me, Jeff. I didn't think I would end up pregnant. Then she broke up with Jason days after we slept together. I told him about the baby, and he said he wanted nothing to do with it. When Crysti told me that she heard you and Ari were getting married, I panicked. I had to come up with something to get you back, and I thought...."

"You thought you could lie to me and tell me I was the father of the baby. How exactly were going to pull it off, Rebecca?"

Turning away from me she whispered, "Does it even matter anymore, Jeff?"

"Yes."

"Fine...I was trying as much as I could to pull you away from Ari. I figured she would get sick of it and make you choose between us. I was banking on you taking the side of the baby because I knew about your father. I thought it would work out perfectly. I was planning to just call you after I had the baby, so you couldn't be here for the birth. I was going to use the excuse that I couldn't get through to you because of you were so far out in the country."

I felt sick to my stomach. I thought back to a few hours ago when Ari did exactly what Rebecca wanted. And I did just what Rebecca hoped I would do.

"You didn't think I would ask for a paternity test?" I asked, taking a few steps away from her.

I needed to get out here, away from this nut case, and back to Ari.

Ari. I had the worst feeling come over me. Something was wrong.

Rebecca was now looking at me, "I figured you would fall in love with him and then not even care about the test."

"I need to leave. Don't *ever* contact me again, Rebecca. Do you understand me? If you so much as look at Ari or me ever again, I'll make sure you regret it."

I took my phone out of my pocket and turned it on. I needed to talk to Ari. I had sixteen missed calls and five text messages.

I started to walk out of the room, as I called Ellie.

"Jeff, wait! Please don't leave me alone," Rebecca said, before she started to cry again.

I turned around to look at her when Ellie answered her cell.

"You motherfucker!"

I stopped dead in my tracks. *What the hell?*

"Ellie?"

"I never thought I could be as angry with you, Jefferson as I am right now. I hate you!"

Holy shit. What the hell is going on?

"Jeff?"

"Gunner? What the hell is wrong with Ellie?"

"Did Rebecca have her baby?"

"Um, yeah, but turns out."

"Okay, do you think maybe now you could come to Hill Country Memorial Hospital in Fredericksburg? Your fiancée needs you."

Oh my god. Ari.

"What's going on, Gunner? Is Ari okay?"

"She was upset after you walked out on her. She took Rose out for a ride. Rose got spooked by a bolt of lightning and then took off running. She jumped a small creek and Ari fell off. She has a few bruised ribs and some other issues."

I turned around and glared at Rebecca. This was her fault. I hated her more than I ever thought I could. I turned back toward the door and left before I did or said something I would regret.

"What other issues Gunner? Is she okay?" I started to jog down to the elevator. After I stepped in, I lost my cell signal.

"Mother fucking son of a bitch!" I yelled as I slammed my hand into the wall.

***

Once I got out of the hospital, I called Gunner back while I ran to my truck.

"Gunner, talk to me. What's wrong with her? Is she awake? What else did she hurt?"

"Jeff, calm down. She hit her head, but they said she just has a mild concussion. And."

"And *what, Gunner!*"

"She wants to be the one to tell you herself."

What the fuck? "What? Okay, I'm on my way. I'm leaving Austin and heading to Fredericksburg now." I threw the phone down in the passenger seat and took off.

***

By the time I got to the hospital in Fredericksburg, I was shocked I didn't end up with at least five speeding tickets. I rushed in to the ER and was told Ari was in her own room. When I got to her floor, walking off the elevator, I had the worst feeling. This was twice today, that I had the feeling that I had just lost something important to me.

I looked up to see Gunner, Ellie, Mark, Sue, Emma and Garrett all sitting in the waiting room. *Shit!*

Ellie jumped up and started to walk over to me, but then Gunner got up and grabbed her. She looked pissed.

"Um, how long have y'all been here?" I asked, looking at everyone.

"Did she have the baby?" Ellie asked.

"Yeah, um, she did. It, ah…turns out she was lying to me the whole time. She was actually further along than she said. I only found out because I asked the doctor if the baby would be okay since he was born so early, and then he told me that Rebecca's due was in two weeks."

Ellie's whole body started shaking.

"You left her! She told you that bitch was lying, and you just walked away from Ari. We all told you! You walked away, this is all your fault!" Ellie screamed.

As Gunner tried to pull her away from me. My heart started beating faster.

"Ellie, stop!" Gunner yelled, turning her around to face him. "Sweetheart, calm down, please."

Emma walked up and took me by the arm. When I glanced over at Sue and Mark, I saw that Sue was crying.

"Emma, please just tell me what happened to Ari," I practically begged as we started walking toward Ari's room.

Emma looked at me and gave me a weak smile. "She should be awake. She asked to be alone until you got here."

When I opened the door and saw her, I almost fell to my knees. My beautiful, strong Ari was lying in the bed. She was broken, alone and crying.

I'd never felt such heartache in my life.

CHAPTER THIRTY-TWO

ARI

My heart started beating faster the moment I heard Ellie talking to Jeff. I tried so hard not to start crying, but then I heard Jeff and Emma outside my room. As the door opened, I could feel the moment he walked into the room. I was looking out the window while the tears slid down my face.

I turned to him, and he looked like he was about to throw up. *Good that motherfucker.*

"So did you have your baby?" I asked with as much sarcasm as I could manage.

A tear rolled down his face as he looked me up and down. I was sure that I looked awful. My head was pounding, my chest was throbbing, and I even had a black eye. I wasn't sure how I managed that one. *I still say my ribs are broken. Stupid country doctors.* I couldn't even cry without everything on my body hurting.

"Oh god, Ari. I'll never forgive myself for this, baby."

Jeff came over and started to reach down to kiss me. I turned my head away from him.

"Ari, please...please don't do this. What else was I supposed to do?"

"Did. She. Have. Your. Baby?"

"Yes, she had the baby, but he isn't mine."

I snapped my head back toward him. I wasn't sure if I should be relieved or angry.

"What?"

"It turns out that she faked the whole contraction story to get me away from you. She had this whole plan, Ari. She was trying to pull us apart. Then her water broke, and she started freaking out that I was there. They put her under for a C section. When I asked the doctor if the baby would be okay since he was born early, he told me…"

Jeff just stopped and stared at me.

I knew it! I knew that bitch was lying the whole time. She was the reason this happened to me. I hated her more than ever.

"He told you what, Jeff?"

"He, um, he told me Rebecca's due date was in two weeks. I confronted her when she woke up, and she told me the truth about everything. She's so fucking twisted, Ari. It's unreal. Baby, I don't want to talk about her. The baby's not mine, so we can put this whole thing behind us now. It can just be you and me, baby."

He reached for my hand, and even though I didn't want to touch him, I didn't have the strength to pull it away.

"No, it's not that easy Jeff. You left us. You picked Rebecca and that baby over us. I'll *never* forgive you for this. Ever."

Jeff looked confused as the tears started to slide down his face.

"Ari, no. Please don't say that, baby. I didn't pick her over you. I didn't know what else to do, Ari! I was worried about the baby and."

I shook my head. "Please just stop! Stop talking about that baby." I looked back at him. "You left us, Jeff."

"Ari, I'm here, baby, I'm here now. I promise you that I'll never leave you again. I promise baby, never again."

I just stared at him.

"Do you want to know what I was going to tell you before you left?"

"Of course I do, Ari."

"I was going to tell you that *we* were having a baby, that *our* future was growing in my stomach. I wanted to tell you how scared I've been for the last week, how scared I was that you were going to be upset because I missed my pills and got pregnant, how scared I was that you would pick Rebecca's baby over ours, and how scared I was that our baby might have Fragile X. I was going to tell you all of this, but you left. You left to go be with Rebecca and a child who you didn't even know was yours when I knew for a fact that you were the father of my baby."

Jeff's face turned white as a ghost. "Ari...we're gonna have a baby?"

When I saw the smile slowly spread across his face, I died inside all over again.

I turned my head away and started to cry. *Why didn't I tell him sooner? Why am I blaming him when it was entirely my fault?* If I had just told him, he might not have walked away from us.

"Ari, baby, I could never, ever be upset with you. When I held that baby in my arms, I felt nothing, and in that moment, I knew he wasn't mine. I only want to have kids with you...only you."

He reached over and turned my face back toward him.

This was tearing me up inside. I needed to tell him even though I knew I was about to devastate him.

"I lost the baby when I fell off Rose."

He stood up straight and started to shake his head. "No... oh God... no."

He slowly started to lower himself to his knees. When his knees hit the floor he put his head on the side of the bed and started to cry.

"Oh god...Ari. I'm so sorry, baby...oh god...this is all my fault."

I wanted so badly to comfort him, but at the same time, I wanted him to hurt just as much as I did.

"I need you to leave, Jeff. I need to be alone."

He looked up at me, eyes filled with tears. "I'm not leaving you again, Ari. I'm never leaving you again."

"I don't want you here!" I shouted at him. I winced in pain from my bruised ribs and pounding headache. *Motherfucker!* Jesus, Mary, and Joseph, that fucking hurt.

"I'm *not* leaving you baby. You can shout and scream all you want, Ari. I'm never going to leave your side again. It doesn't matter if you want me here or not."

Ellie walked into the room. "Is everything okay, Ari?"

When Ellie looked at Jeff on the floor, she saw that he was crying. Walking over, she dropped to her knees next to him.

"Jefferson."

He turned and hugged her, and then he started crying even more.

Of all the times I've fallen off a horse, why do I now get ribs that hurt so damn bad I can't move? I just wanted to be the one to hold and comfort him.

Shit! I'm losing my goddamn mind. I just told him to leave, and now, I'm jealous of Ellie hugging him.

"It's all my fault, Ellie. It's all my fault."

Ellie kept telling Jeff it was okay.

No, it wasn't okay.

"No, it's not okay!" I yelled.

Ellie and Jeff both looked at me with concern.

Jeff stood up, took my hand, and kissed it.

"No, baby, it's not okay. I'm so sorry I did this to you, Ari. Please don't ask me to leave you. I just need to be with you."

Ellie stood up and walked over to the other side of the bed. The two most important people in my life were on either side of me, so why did I feel like I was so alone?

"I…you didn't do this to me, Jeff. It just wasn't meant to be," I struggled to keep the tears from falling again.

Jeff shook his head. I knew he was beating himself up inside right now. I was feeling so many things that I couldn't keep them straight. I was tired. I hurt everywhere. I was angry, sad, and devastated. All of this rolled up into one. My urge to comfort Jeff was pissing me the fuck off also. I just wanted to be angry with him.

"Ari, I love you more than life itself. I'll do anything for you. I will do *anything* for you, baby."

I smiled at him because I knew he meant every word he was saying.

"Can you go push Rebecca down an empty mineshaft?"

Ellie let out a giggle.

Jeff smiled. "Baby, if you really want me to, I'd do it in a heartbeat."

"As much as I really want to say yes…no, I don't want that."

I turned to Ellie and she gave me the sweetest smile.

"Ellie, please tell everyone they can leave. My parents need to get back to Matt. If Josh and Heather haven't killed each other by now, I'm sure they're ready to go insane with my baby brother. I have Jeff now. I'm gonna be fine." I smiled at the love of my life.

The most overwhelming feeling of comfort came over me. Just having him smile at me and tell me how much he loved me brought such a peace.

My heart was breaking inside, but somehow, I knew it was all going to be okay.

Ellie kissed me gently good bye and walked out of the room.

Jeff leaned down to softly kiss my lips.

"I love you, Arianna."

"I love you, too, Jeff."

"It's all going to be okay. Please tell me you believe me."

"I believe you."

Too bad my heart didn't agree with what I just said.

CHAPTER THIRTY-THREE

JOSH

I stood there at the kitchen entrance, watching Heather play with Matt. She was amazing with him. It was no wonder she wanted to be a teacher. She had a gift. I couldn't believe how patient she was with him, it was clear that he loved her.

They were both mopping Jeff and Ari's kitchen floor…again.

"Heather, do you like mopping with me?" Matt asked.

He had the cutest damn smile I'd ever seen. *Little guy is moving in on my girl.*

My girl…I wish.

She had barely spoken two words to me since everyone had left. I had finally talked Lynda into heading back up to Emma and Garrett's house after an hour of her rolling her fucking eyes at Matt and Heather.

As I started to walk into the kitchen, Matt held up his hand to stop me.

"Oh no, Josh. Don't walk on the wet floor. You'll fall!"

"Gotcha, buddy. I wouldn't dream of walking on this beautiful clean floor, especially not after the wonderful job you and Heather did cleaning it." I smiled at Heather. I was shocked that she smiled back at me. My heart dropped to my stomach.

"Matt, how about I take the mops and bucket outside and then Josh can take you to go see Stargazer? Would you like that?" Heather asked as she gave me a wink.

I swore that I would do anything this girl asked me to do.

Matt jumped up and down and then ran over to me.

"I'm gonna take that as yes. So, let's go see Stargazer buddy."

When Matt smiled at me, my heart melted. Then, I thought about Jeff. Sue and Mark called to say they were on their way back to pick up Matt. That must've meant Jeff was with Ari. If I knew Jeff, he was falling apart inside, blaming himself.

I thought Gunner and Jeff were nuts for wanting to have kids so soon. I thought they needed to enjoy life for a bit before they got tied down with kids.

Heather walked by and gave Matt a kiss on the top of his head before she headed outside to dump out the bucket and clean the mops. She looked up at me and smiled again. There went my heart dropping to my stomach.

Maybe Gunner and Jeff weren't so nuts.

***

Matt and I were just about to take Stargazer out for a walk on her lead when Sue and Mark pulled up. Matt started to run over to Sue, but then he quickly turned back and ran up to me.

"Josh, can I give you a hug good-bye, you assmole?"

I tried not to laugh, but I had to. I got down on my knees, and Matt gave me a big bear hug. Then, he did something I wasn't expecting.

"I love you, Josh. Bye!" He spun around and ran off.

Sue called out her thanks as I waved good-bye to them.

I couldn't stand up, so I sat down on the ground as I watched them walk off. Sue stopped to talk to Heather. I watched as Heather threw her head back and laughed.

I wanted what Gunner and Jeff had. It hit me like a ton of bricks the moment Matt said he loved me. I wanted it, and I wanted it with Heather. When she looked over at me, she stopped laughing. She turned back to Sue, and it looked like they were saying their good-byes.

After she gave Sue a hug, she started to walk toward me. Then, she stopped dead in her tracks. I heard someone come up behind me. I felt a kiss on my cheek, and I turned around to see Lynda standing above me.

"Hey, handsome. What are you doing down here on the ground? Did Matt wear your ass out?" Lynda laughed and then sat down next to me.

When I looked back at Heather, I saw that she was now walking back toward Jeff and Ari's house.

Fuck me.

"Hey, Lynda. I thought you were going to wait for Emma and Garrett to get back."

"Oh, they're home now. I heard them mention to Gunner's folks that Sue and Mark were on their way to pick up Matt, so I thought I would come and see if you'd like to go out tonight. Maybe we could hit the honky-tonk in town and do some dancing?"

"Well, yeah… maybe. Let me talk to Gunner and see how Ari and Jeff are doing first."

Lynda's smile faded. "I'm really so sorry to hear about Ari losing her baby. I mean, I didn't even know she was pregnant, but still, I hate to see that happen to anyone. She seems like a really nice girl."

I smiled at Lynda. I knew she was just trying to be nice, but I was pissed that she caused Heather to turn and walk away.

"Did you drive over here?" I asked standing up.

"Um, yeah. I thought you might like to come back with me, and then we could head out tonight. I mean, if you feel like it."

I looked back over to where Heather had walked back to the house.

"You know what? I am in the mood to go out and grab a few beers. How about I get ready and meet you back at your grandparents, place?"

Lynda gave me a smile before she hugged me. "Oh, you won't regret it, Josh! A night out is just what you need."

I watched as Lynda drove off in the Jeep toward Emma and Garrett's place. I started to head back to the house when Gunner sent me a text.

Gunner: *I need some fucking drinks and loud music. You up for going out tonight.*

I sent him a text back: *Fuck yeah. How's Ari? Where the hell was Jeff?*

Gunner: *Shit, dude. I'll tell you all about it over a beer.*

I replied: *Okay, I'm going to jump in the shower and then head over.*

I walked into the house and heard the shower going in Jeff and Ari's bathroom. *Why is she taking a shower in their bathroom?* I wondered if Heather was going to go out tonight also.

I walked into the kitchen and made a mental note to have the place cleaned up before Ari got home. The last thing she needed to do was worry about cleaning. I reached into the fridge, pulling out a beer. I practically downed it right there. *Shit, I need to just get drunk tonight.* I needed to get Heather out of my mind, and I only knew one way to do that. It had been too damn long since I'd fucked someone.

I slammed the rest of my beer and threw the bottle in the trash.

When my phone beeped, I pulled it out to see Lynda had texted me with a picture of what she was wearing tonight.

Motherfucker. The picture she sent me was hot. I knew just the person to get Heather off of my mind.

I was sending Lynda a text back when I ran right into Heather coming out of Ari and Jeff's bedroom.

We hit dead-on and she dropped all her bathroom stuff as I dropped my phone. We both started to lean down to pick up everything. As I stood back up to let her go first, my head hit her in the chin.

"Motherfucker!" Heather grabbed her chin and stumbled backwards.

She looked like she was about to fall, so I reached out, grabbing her other hand, as I pulled her toward me.

"Holy shit Heather! I'm so sorry! Are you okay, princess?" I placed my hands on either side of her face while I moved her head back and forth looking at her chin.

Watching her poor eyes water up, I knew she was trying to hold back the tears. When she reached out her hands and put them on my forearms, I saw the first tear slide down her cheek.

Oh. My. God. I wiped the tear away. I felt like such a douche for hurting her even though it was an accident.

"Oh shit, Heather, I'm so sorry, princess. I didn't mean to hurt you."

She tried to smile at me. "S'okay Josh. I should've been looking where I was going. Ouch, I think I bit my damn tongue!" she let out a small laugh.

Her hands were still on my arms, and I let my eyes look down her body.

Holy motherfucking shit! The blue robe she was wearing was open, and of course, she was naked underneath. My legs wobbled just a bit, and she grabbed my arms tighter.

"Oh my god, Josh are you okay? I didn't think my chin was that hard! Do you need to sit down?"

I looked back up to her, and she must have caught on to what I had been looking at. I slowly moved my hands down her face to her shoulders and pushed the robe off of her.

She just stood there, staring at me. I thought for sure she would reach for her robe, but instead, she licked her lips. I almost had to grab the wall to stand up straight.

I grabbed her neck, pulling her to me, and then I started to kiss her.

Her hands immediately went to my hair, and she let out the sweetest, softest moan I'd ever heard. I pushed her back against the wall as I started to move my other hand down her body. I lifted up her leg, hooking it over my hip.

"Heather," I whispered against her lips.

I was waiting for her to come to her senses, but then she pushed her hips against mine. I went for it. Moving my hand all over her body, I caressed up her side to her chest. When I cupped one of her breasts in my hand and I let out a moan. She fit perfect in my hand.

Then, I moved my hand down to between her legs and touched her clit. She bucked her hips into me while she grabbed a handful of my hair. As she pulled me closer to her lips, I put one finger inside of her and then another.

"Oh god," I moaned. *She's so fucking wet.*

"Josh, please don't stop."

I put two more fingers inside her, she was so tight. I started to move my hand faster while she pushed harder against me. The next thing I knew, I was capturing her screams in my mouth.

Fuck me. Am I dreaming? Is this really happening?

She pulled away from my lips to catch her breath. When she started to move her leg away, I grabbed it and picked her up.

"Wrap your legs around me, princess."

She did just what I asked and didn't even hesitate. Shit…It had been so long since I was with someone and all I wanted to do was be with Heather and only Heather. I pushed her back against the wall again and kissed her with as much passion as I could.

She pulled back away from my lips just some.

"Josh," she whispered so softly. "I want you so badly."

Holy fuck. What was she saying?

"Heather, I want you, too, but."

"Please, Josh, I need this so much."

I moved my lips back to kiss hers. I loved her so much, and I didn't want to rush making love to her. It had to be special.

With her legs wrapped around me, I slowly walked us up the stairs and into the room where I was staying. I stopped right at the edge of the bed. She removed her legs from around me, and she gently slid down my body to sit on the bed. She started to move back, I crawled over her, just barely kept my body weight on top of her.

Then, she smiled at me, and my heart melted on the spot. *I would do anything for this girl. I'd give up my own life for her.*

"Heather, I don't want your first time to be like this. It needs to be special, a night you'll always remember with a smile and without any regret princess."

Her smile faded. "Do you not want me?"

Wait…what?

"Holy shit, Heather. I'm using every goddamn ounce of energy I have not to make love to you right now."

Leaning up her head, she captured my lips. She tasted like honey. She was so sweet and delicate. I needed more. I started to move my hand along her body.

"Wait, Josh. Was that the front door opening?" Heather whispered.

I stayed completely still and listened.

"Josh? Heather?"

"Garrett!" We both said at the same time.

I immediately flew off of her. I grabbed the comforter and threw it over Heather. I ran to the door and looked down the stairs to the hall. I could hear Garrett in the kitchen, so I ran downstairs to get Heather's robe. I took it back to the room and started to help her put it on. She kept hitting my hands away.

"Jesus H. Christ, Josh. I can put it on myself. Go distract him so I can get dressed!"

"I've never heard you swear so much, Heather…it's kind of a turn on." I said as I gave her a quick kiss on the cheek. She smiled back at me and told me to go.

I ran down the stairs and jumped over the mess that was on the floor in the hallway and made my way to the kitchen. I was gonna have to tell Jeff that he needed to make sure his damn doors were locked if Garrett was just going to help himself inside.

"Hey, Garrett, what's going on?"

"I called for ya," Garrett said as he held up the empty coffee pot.

"Damn, where do I have to go to get a cup of coffee? I had to get away from all the clean-up from the party. Gunner said y'all are going to head into the honky-tonk in town, huh?"

"Um, yes, sir, we are. I'm just waiting to hear back from Jeff about how Ari is doing. I still can't believe she lost the baby."

Garrett shook his head and sat down on the bar stool at the kitchen island. *Motherfucker*. Less than five minutes ago, I was in heaven with the girl of my dreams, naked, and now I was standing across from Gunner's grandfather, wondering what the hell he was doing here.

"Did you need something other than coffee, Garrett? Anything that I can help you with? I asked.

I could hear Heather picking up everything she'd dropped in the hallway. I reached for my phone in my back pocket but it wasn't there.

Shit! I dropped it when I ran into Heather.

"Nah, I just needed to get away from the house for a bit."

Garrett and I talked for about another ten minutes before Heather came into the kitchen. She was dressed in a white shirt, jeans, and cowboy boots. I smiled at her, but she just glared at me.

What the hell? It wasn't my fault that Garrett had shown up.

"Garrett, do you think I could catch a ride up to the house with you? I'm going to meet Ellie and Gunner there," Heather said.

"Are you going out, too? That's good, honey. You need to cut a rug once in a while. Sure, let's head on up." Garrett stood up and started to make his way to the front door.

I just stood there, staring at Heather. *Why does she want to leave with Garrett?*

I stepped in front of her and held her back.

"Why are you leaving with Garrett, princess?"

Heather looked up at me with tears building in her eyes. My heart stopped, and I had the worst feeling in my chest.

"Heather, what's wrong?" I asked as I reached for the side of her face.

She backed away from me as one single tear rolled down her cheek.

"I've never been made to feel so foolish in my entire life," she said, her voice cracking.

"What are you talking about? We just shared."

"Stop! Don't even talk about it."

She tossed my phone at me, and I just barely caught it.

"Your fuck buddy is waiting for you." Heather walked around me and left out the door.

When I hit the home button on my phone, I saw the text message I had sent to Lynda.

Damn, girl… ur looking hot…looks like I might be getting lucky tonight with this.

Motherfucker. I had forgotten that I'd sent this message.

It took me a few seconds to get my wits about me before I ran out after Heather. I caught up to her at the Jeep. Garrett was waiting in the driver's seat.

"Wait! Heather, please wait. You have to let me explain." I was ready to fall to my knees and beg for just five minutes.

She turned and looked at me. Her eyes were filled with such sadness.

"To think that I almost…I wanted to..." She started to move her head back and forth, like she was trying to clear her mind.

"How could I ever be so stupid to think that you would only want me? Enjoy your night with Lynda." She jumped in the Jeep.

Garrett looked at Heather and then at me.

"Heather, darling, are you sure you don't want to stay here and talk with Josh?"

"I have nothing left to say to him, Garrett, but thank you. I'm just ready to go."

Garrett started the Jeep and gave me one last look. It was almost like he was trying to tell me something.

"Heather, please don't…please don't do this."

I reached for her hand and she pulled it away.

"Garrett, please leave," Heather said as she wiped away tears rolling down her cheeks.

I stood there, watching as the Jeep got farther and farther out of sight.

The moment I could no longer see it, I fell to the ground and buried my head in my hands.

I was pretty sure that I just lost the only thing I ever loved and wanted.

CHAPTER THIRTY-FOUR

HEATHER

One the way back to Garrett and Emma's place, I tried desperately to keep my hands from shaking. I could tell that Garrett was trying to give me some space. I kept replaying what had happened between Josh and me only thirty minutes ago.

"Heather, I don't want your first time to be like this. It needs to be special, a night you'll always remember with as smile...and without any regret, princess."

He didn't want to make love to me because he was planning on fucking Lynda tonight. *I should have known. He'll never change. Ever.*

Just then Garrett pulled me from my thoughts.

"Heather, are ya gonna let the boy explain?"

I spun my head toward Garrett and just stared at him.

"What?"

"Are you going to at least let him explain? He looked pretty torn up."

Oh. My. God.

"No! Not to be rude, Garrett, but you have no idea what happened between us back there. Josh is a womanizer. He will never change, and I was crazy to think that I might be the one he would change for."

I started to think about my father telling me how someday my prince would come for me. I felt the tears welling up in my eyes again.

I missed my mother and father. Why did they have to leave me all alone?

***

We drove up to the house just as Gunner and Ellie were pulling up. I flew out of the Jeep and started to make my way over to Ellie. The moment she saw, me she knew something was wrong.

"Ari?" Ellie asked in a panicked voice.

Oh shit. How could I forget about Ari? What kind of friend am I?

I shook my head and tried to smile. I needed to pull it together. Ellie didn't need to hear me bellyache about Josh.

Fucker that he is.

"What's wrong, Heather?"

"I guess I'm just thinking about Ari. Have you heard from her since you left?"

Ellie's eyes filled with tears.

"No, but I did talk to Jeff. He's not doing so well. He's blaming himself. He was crying so hard on the phone that I could hardly understand him."

"What happened with the whole Rebecca thing?"

"Oh god, I'll fill you in on the ride over to the club."

Gunner let out a laugh. "Ells, it's not a club. It's a honkytonk."

Ellie shrugged her shoulders. "Whatever."

As we walked up to the house, I heard someone pulling up the driveway. I turned around to see Josh's truck. I started to walk faster, taking the steps of the porch two at a time, only to run right into Lynda.

"Jesus, watch where you're going, Heather."

I took one look at her and wanted to puke. She was dressed in a low-cut, very low-cut light blue shirt. I could see her bra through the shirt, and her shorter-than-short skirt was damn near up to her crotch. Her black cowboy boots rounded out the whole hooker-looking outfit. I ran my eyes up and down her.

"You think Josh will like what he sees?" She asked, giving me a wink.

I had an incredible urge to knock the crap out of this girl. I was just about to say something back to her when I heard Josh behind me.

"Heather, I really need to talk to you. Please." His voice was practically begging me.

I turned around to face at him. *Damn.* He looked good in his white button-down shirt, jeans, and boots. I had the most intense feeling between my legs, I actually felt myself pushing my legs together.

What the hell is wrong with me?

"Heather, please don't walk away from me after what happened between us. You have to let me explain."

I glanced over at Ellie and Gunner. They both looked very confused and looked at me and then at Josh.

"Wait…what do you mean what happened between y'all?" Lynda asked glaring at me.

I didn't want to air my dirty little secrets in front of everyone, especially the tramp standing next to me. I started to walk toward the barn and Josh followed me.

Lynda tried to stop him. "Josh, wait, I thought we."

"Lynda, please, I just need to talk to Heather for a few minutes. Just give me a couple of minutes."

I walked as fast as I could down to the main barn. Before I could turn around, Josh grabbed me and pushed me up against the side of the barn.

He kissed me with so much passion that I almost lost myself in him. Finally pulling my lips away from his, I tried to push him away.

"Stop, Josh! Just stop right now! How dare you even think of kissing me after what you did to me! How could you?"

Josh went to say something, but I cut him off.

"You never had any intention of sleeping with me because you already made plans to fuck Lynda tonight!" I screamed at him.

Josh closed his eyes. When he opened them, I swore it looked like he had tears in his eyes.

"Heather, I don't know how to explain this to you. I was trying to do something the only way I've ever known how to do it. I wanted you so much, but you just kept pushing me away, and."

"So, you're saying this is my fault? I tried to explain myself the other day, but you wouldn't let me. You just acted like a stubborn ass, and then you started hanging all over Lynda like the man whore that you are."

The moment I said it, I regretted it. The look on his face just about killed me.

"Okay. So, that's what I'm always going to be to you, isn't it?"

I just couldn't stop. I needed to push him away before he hurt me anymore.

"I guess so…at least according to your text message. So, tell me, Josh. What was it you were trying to do? Forget about me by sleeping with Lynda?"

The look he gave me caused me to gasp.

"Oh. My. God. That's it, isn't it? You were going to sleep with her just to..."

I couldn't even finish my sentence. *He was going to sleep with Lynda to forget about me.*

"No…I mean, yes…no, wait. I might have sent her that text, but I wouldn't have done it. Princess, I haven't been with anyone in months. I love you. I only want to be with you."

I felt like I couldn't breathe. No…he doesn't love me. I can't breathe.

I took a few steps away from him. I leaned over, placing my hands on my knees. I needed my parents. *Oh my god. Why did they leave me all alone?*

"Heather…baby, are you okay?"

Josh started to reach for me, and I jumped back.

"No, you couldn't possibly love me. Why would you even think about sleeping with someone else to forget about someone you loved? That doesn't even make any sense!" I started to laugh.

Josh stared at me with a strange look.

"Heather, can we please just go back to Jeff and Ari's place? Just to talk about this, please. I don't want to lose you."

I looked up into his eyes, and my heart broke in two. I was about to do the only thing I knew to keep my heart from being broken anymore.

"You can't lose something you never had."

Josh took a step back away from me. He started to shake his head.

"Don't do this again, Heather. Don't push me away. If you push me away this time, I swear to God… I'm done with all of this."

My heart starting beating so fast, and my legs felt like they were about to give out on me.

"I believe your date for the night is waiting for you."

Josh grabbed the side of the barn, like he was trying to hold himself up. I instantly wanted to run into his arms and beg him to take me back to Jeff and Ari's house. I started to take a step toward him when he looked at me. His eyes were different. The look from earlier was replaced with anger. I stopped dead in my tracks.

"I'm sorry that I made you feel that way, princ, um Heather. I guess we're clear on where we stand with each other so…."

I just stood there and stared at him. *Am I really going to just let him walk away from me?*

"Yeah, I guess we're clear. Excuse me, I'd like to find out how Ari is doing and what happened with Jeff and Rebecca today," I said.

I started to walk past him. When he took me by the arm, I stopped and looked up into his beautiful green eyes. I'd give anything to see him smile, giving me that dimple he had on his right cheek.

"No matter if you believe me or not, I'll always love you," he whispered.

I sucked in a breath of air. I couldn't move.

Josh leaned down and kissed me on the cheek.

"Please come back to Jeff and Ari's tonight. I promise that I won't bother you."

With that, he turned and headed back up to the house. The moment he left, I leaned back against the barn and started to cry. I cried so hard that I felt like I couldn't breathe. *What is wrong with me? Why did I just push away the only man, besides my father, that I've ever loved, ever needed?*

I tried to calm myself down. I was sure Ellie would come looking for me if I didn't come back right after Josh.

Sure enough, I heard her call out my name.

I looked up at her with tears streaming down my face.

"Oh my god, Heather! What did he do to you?"

I let out a laugh.

"He didn't do anything I didn't ask him to do."

"Heather, this is insane. What the hell is going on between you two? Josh just walked up and grabbed Lynda. He told Gunner that they would meet us at the bar. I thought you two were working it out."

It took me another minute or so to stop crying and start breathing normally again.

"Shit, Ellie, I think I just made the biggest mistake of my life, but I'm not sure. My heart is telling me one thing, and my head is telling me another."

"Take some deep breaths and just start at the beginning," Ellie said as she walked me over to two chairs.

I told Ellie all about how great Josh had been with Matt all day and then about what had happened between us before Garrett had shown up.

"By the way, y'all better keep your doors locked. Garrett just walked right into Jeff and Ari's place without even knocking. I was naked for Christ's sake!"

Ellie was laughing her ass off, which was just pissing me off even more. "What the hell is so funny?"

"I'm so sorry. I don't know if I'm in shock from what happened between you and Josh or the fact that Garrett did the same damn thing to Jeff and Ari the other day!"

I told Ellie about Josh's text message to Lynda and then Josh's explanation about it.

How he kept trying to say he wouldn't have done it. Then, how he told me he loved me and would always love me.

"Holy hell, Heather. Josh told you he loved you?"

I nodded my head as I felt another tear roll down my face.

"Heather, did you ever think that maybe Josh is telling you the truth? I mean, I've heard Jeff and Gunner talk about how they've never seen Josh go this long without hooking up with a girl. I'm not trying to say he was right, thinking about sleeping with Lynda to forget about you, but...he is a man. Their thinking is pretty fucked-up to say the least."

I let out a small laugh. My heart was screaming for me to go to Josh and beg him to be with me, but my head was telling me something all together different.

"Ells, do you honestly believe that a guy like Josh is really interested in a girl like me?"

"What the hell does that mean, Heather? A girl like you? You're beautiful, funny, and smart as hell. Yes! I do believe a guy like Josh would be lucky as hell to have a girl like you."

"My heart wants him so badly, but my head tells me that he'll never be true to me. He'll never be happy with just me."

"I don't believe that for one minute. Just because he was a player in college doesn't mean that he can't find a girl to love and be with just her. Deep down inside, Josh is a sweetheart. Did you know that he's a Big Brother? He meets with his little brother at least once a week and pays for all of his sports at school because his single mom can't afford it. He's also helped build three Habitat for Humanity houses, and he's helped his dad make all the pews for their church. He told Gunner and me that his dream is to make custom furniture and take over his dad's business someday. He has a straight head on his shoulders, Heather. He just needs to find that right girl to round it all out."

I sat there in a state of shock. I didn't know any of that. Josh had never once mentioned any of those things. My heart was hurting even more.

"I just wish my mother and father were here. They would tell me what to do."

Ellie looked at me, and then stood up and grabbed my hand pulling me into a hug.

"Oh god, Heather. I know how much you miss your parents, baby, but I promise you that they would've told you this has to be your decision. Only you know your heart, Heather. I know how much you depended on your dad and how much of a rock he was for you. But, baby, you need to know that you can do this on your own. You can't be afraid to let someone else into your heart because you're afraid of losing them."

I pulled back and smiled at my best friend. Then, I thought about Ari.

"How's Ari?"

"Come on, we'll talk on the way to the bar…or as Gunner keeps calling it, the honky-tonk."

Hooking our arms together, we started back toward the house.

Gunner was leaning up against his truck, talking on his cell phone. He didn't look very happy.

This whole damn day just sucked.

As we got closer, Gunner hung up and looked at Ellie.

"What's wrong?" Ellie asked Gunner.

He pushed his hands through his hair.

"That was Jeff. He just needed to talk to someone. I guess Ari's been crying nonstop, and Jeff is doing nothing but blaming himself. I'd really like to go into Austin and give Rebecca a goddamn kick in the ass."

"Maybe we shouldn't go out. I mean, with Ari in the hospital and Jeff so upset…Gunner, maybe we should go back to the hospital."

"I asked him if he wanted us to and he said no. He and Ari really need to be alone. Come on, let's get going. I've got two beautiful women I need to take dancing tonight."

Gunner held open the doors for Ellie and me to get into his truck. Leaning in, he helped Ellie buckle her seat belt, and then kissed her and told her he loved her.

My heart swelled at the love these two had for each other.

Will I ever find that kind of love?

A part of me knew I already found it…

And then let it go.

CHAPTER THIRTY-FIVE

GUNNER

On the way into town, Ellie filled Heather in on everything that had happened with Ari and Jeff. I still couldn't believe how crazy Rebecca was. Thank God Jeff found out now before he got attached to the baby.

"I knew she was lying. I knew it! What the hell? Did she really think that Jeff wouldn't ask for a paternity test?" Heather asked.

"I know, Heather. Believe me, I've been thinking about it ever since Jeff told me. A part of me wants to just drive to Austin and beat the shit out of her."

I had to let out a laugh. I could picture Ellie walking right into the hospital room and knocking the shit out of Rebecca.

"So, let me see if I got this straight. Rebecca slept with Jason, while he was still dating Ari. Rebecca got pregnant, but she slept with Jeff one night when they ran into each other at Rebels. Then, Crysti overheard someone talking about the wedding, but she thought Jeff and Ari were getting married."

"Yep, she called Rebecca, and Rebecca panicked. Her last-ditch attempt to get Jeff back was to tell him the baby was his. I guess she told Jeff that she had thought she would just be able to have the baby and then call him afterward. Her little act of fake contractions today though did her in. She practically tried to have him removed from the hospital."

"Wow…what a nutcase. I feel so sorry for that baby."

By the time we got into town, heading into the bar, Heather had filled Ellie in on what happened with Josh. My head was spinning from how fast the two of them had talked. Snippets of what they had talked about were replaying in my head.

"Oh no, he didn't text her that!"

"Oh my god! He told you that?"

I need a fucking beer. I just wanted to forget this day ever happened. My heart was aching for Jeff and Ari. I wanted to kick Josh's ass for what he did to Heather. I was worried about my father. *Shit.*

I walked up to the bar and ordered three beers. By the time I walked back to the table and set them down, I knew something was very wrong. I looked at Ellie and Heather. They were both just staring out at the dance floor. Heather looked like she was about to start crying.

"Cookie Jar" by Gym Class Heroes was playing, and I was having a déjà vu moment. *Do I want to turn around and look?*

No…but I did. I immediately saw Josh and Lynda dancing. *Oh fuck.* They were all over each other while Josh was kissing her. *I'm going to fucking kill him.* He already had a beer in one hand, on his way to getting drunk. The way he was grinding into Lynda was enough to piss me off.

I turned back around and saw Ellie looking at me. She mouthed *do something* to me. *What the hell am I supposed to do?* Lynda was an adult, and Josh and Heather weren't together. *So, what does Ellie want me to do?*

Heather was still staring at Josh and Lynda. Then, she looked over at Ellie and started laughing.

"What in the world could you possibly find funny about this, Heather?" Ellie asked.

Heather shook her head and shrugged her shoulders. "I was just thinking that this is the perfect song for that asshole. It's pretty clear to me that he has moved on, so maybe I need to do the same thing." Then, she picked up her beer and started to down it.

I looked at Ellie as I sat down.

"Aren't they going to want to card Heather and me when they see us drinking these beers?"

"I've been coming here for years. They don't even ask for my ID anymore. Country-living, Ellie."

"Huh, I'm gonna have to remember that when we have kids," Ellie said as she took a sip of her beer.

I threw my head back and laughed. Then, I leaned over and gave her a kiss. *I love this damn girl.*

***

As the night went on, Heather and Josh were both trying to drink each other out of their minds. The two of them were getting wasted and not giving a shit about it. Heather was dancing with every guy who asked, and Josh and Lynda looked like they needed to get a fucking room.

"Gunner, I'm worried about Heather. She's really getting drunk, and you know she doesn't drink this much very often. Maybe we should leave now," Ellie said, watching Heather talk to the DJ.

"Yeah, I'm thinking it's about time to go as well. I think you're going to have to drive my truck, sweetheart, since you only drank one beer. There's no way I'm letting Josh drive with as much as he has had to drink."

I watched as Heather walked up to the guy she had been dancing with for the last thirty minutes. She reached out her hand, and then they both started to walk toward the dance floor. She led him right next to Josh and Lynda.

Britney Spears' "Womanizer" started to play, and I knew that this wasn't going to end well. I looked at Ellie, who was just staring at Heather with her mouth hanging open. I glanced back out to the dance floor to see Heather and this guy all over each other. I was about to tell Ellie to go get Heather.

Then, she said, "Oh, holy fuck."

I looked back and Heather and the guy were kissing, and his hands were all over her. Then, he moved his hands up her shirt. I looked over at Josh and saw the look in his eyes. I jumped up and started to walk out toward them when Ellie grabbed my arm.

"Gunner, wait. Stop. Don't get involved, please."

Just then, I saw Josh grab this guy from behind and spin him around. *Motherfucker.* He's going to punch him.

Sure enough, Josh swung and knocked the shit out of the guy. I pushed Ellie's hand off of my arm and ran over to Josh. I grabbed him before he went after the guy again.

"What the fuck is your problem, you asshole?" The guy shouted at Josh.

"That's my girl you're kissing, you motherfucker."

Heather had her hand over her mouth in shock. Josh was trying to get out of my grip, but he was so drunk he could hardly stand up. When Josh yelled out that she was his girl, Heather started to laugh.

She walked up to Josh, and he instantly stopped struggling against me.

"*My girl?* Are you kidding me? You practically fucked *her* on the dance floor all night long, and then you have the nerve to hit a guy for kissing me! You really are a jerk, do you know that?" Heather said as she poked her finger over and over again in Josh's chest.

"He had his hand up your shirt, Heather. You're not that kind of girl," Josh said as he tried to pull out of my grip.

"Josh, if I let you go, will you settle down?" I let up some on my hold.

"Fine, Gunner, just let my ass go. If this is what she wants, then so be it." Josh started to walk away.

"Fuck you, Josh!" Heather shouted.

He slowly turned around and smiled at her.

"You already had your chance. It's someone else's turn now."

Ah shit. Ellie walked between Josh and Heather just as Heather was about to go after Josh.

"Heather, stop this right now and let's just go. Lynda, are you riding with Gunner or me?"

"She's going with Gunner. I'm sure her and Josh haven't finished what they started."

Heather pushed past Ellie and Lynda and then followed Josh out of the bar.

Jesus, what a crazy-ass group of friends I have.

I took Ellie by the arm and led her out of the bar. When we got to the side of the building, I pushed her up against the wall and kissed her. Her hands immediately went up to my head, as she pulled at my hair. She let out a moan that traveled throughout my whole body.

I pulled slightly away from her and smiled.

"Wow. What the heck was that for?" Ellie asked, pushing her body into me.

My dick instantly got hard, and I wanted nothing more than to get her home.

"For marrying me and loving me," I said, pushing a piece of hair behind her ear.

She smiled up at me. Leaning in, she was about to kiss me when we heard Josh and Heather going at it again.

"Holy shit, it's like Ari and Jeff all over again!" I said.

I took Ellie's hand and led her to the parking lot as she let out a laugh.

CHAPTER THIRTY-SIX

JEFF

Ari had finally cried herself to sleep thirty minutes ago. I just sat there and watched her sleep as I thought about how I'd walked away from her earlier.

Fuck. If only she had just told me once she'd found out about the baby, I would have handled things so differently.

I put my head down in my hands and felt the tears coming again. This was entirely my fault. Just like Ellie had said, I'd left them both to run to some nutcase whose only goal was to tear me away from the only person I'd ever love.

Our baby is gone. I never even got to place my hand on her stomach to talk to the baby. I never had one second to just enjoy the idea of being a parent with Ari.

God, I can't imagine how scared she must have been this last week. I knew something was different about her. I haven't even gotten a chance to just hold her. I just wanted to comfort her.

I stood up and pulled out my cell phone. It was about to die, there was no way I was going to my truck to get the charger. With my luck, Ari would wake up and find me gone.

The nurse had come in earlier and said that Ari would be able to leave tomorrow morning. I walked over to the side of her bed. She'd managed to roll over on her side even though I knew she was in pain from her ribs. I had to smile when she kept cussing out the doctor, insisting her ribs had to be broken because she was in so much pain.

I love this girl so damn much.

I needed to hold her. I crawled onto the bed and tried to very gently to lie down next to her. I didn't want to touch her for fear of waking her up or, worse yet, hurting her.

"It's about fucking time you got in bed with me."

I smiled and then let out a laugh. *There's my girl.*

"I want to hold you, Ari, but I'm afraid I'll hurt you, baby."

"Please, Jeff. Please just hold me. I need to feel you."

That was all I needed. Moving closer to her, I gently put my arm around her. I felt her relax instantly.

I was just about to fall asleep when she started to talk to me.

"I'm so scared, Jeff."

"Why are you scared, baby?"

"What if I can't have kids?"

"What? Ari, why would you even think that? Women have miscarriages and then have other kids all the time."

"Do you think I'll be a good mother? I mean, like my mom? If we do have a child with Fragile X, can I."

I leaned over and kissed the back of her head. I wanted nothing more than to just take her away from all of this. If only I could turn the hands of the clock back to this morning, I would have never walked away from her.

"Ari, I have no doubt in my mind, baby, that you're going to be a wonderful mother. I see you with Matt. I see the love and patience you have with him. I'm in awe when I watch you. I love you, Ari, and I'm so sorry I did this to you."

She didn't say anything for a few minutes, and I could tell she was crying.

Then, for the hundredth time tonight, the guilt hit me like a brick wall. All I wanted to do was call Rebecca and tell her how much I hated her. What good would that do though?

"Jeff?"

I cleared my throat and attempted to talk.

"Yeah, baby?"

"I really started to love the idea of having our baby. I feel like I took that away from you. Just because we lost her doesn't mean that you shouldn't have been able to feel the same joy I felt. But now…now, I just feel like a huge part of me is missing, like I just lost the most precious gift ever, and I never even gave you the chance to feel it also. What type of person does that make me?"

My heart was hurting so bad in my chest that I couldn't breathe. I had to get up. I started to sit up carefully, so I didn't move the bed too much. I didn't want to hurt Ari.

Ari slowly turned, trying to sit herself up.

I felt like I was going to be sick. I knew there was something wrong the moment I had Rebecca's baby in my arms. Instead of being happy, I'd felt sad, like I had just lost something. I knew in that moment, the baby wasn't mine, but what I didn't know was that I was truly losing my own child.

"Ari, what time did you fall off of the horse?"

"What difference does it make?"

"I just want to know."

"I don't know. It was probably an hour, maybe an hour and a half after you left. Why?"

I leaned over and started taking deep breaths. This was my fault. If I hadn't left her, she would have never gone riding. She would've told me about the baby, and we would be home right now, making love…celebrating…and hoping Garrett didn't walk in on us.

I had taken that gift from her. I tried with all my might not to do it, but I started to cry. I fell to my knees and just lost it. *I took our child away from her.*

The next thing I knew, Ari was on the floor next to me, holding me while I just cried.

"I'm so sorry, Ari. I'm so very sorry I left y'all. Oh god…please forgive me."

"It wasn't your fault, Jeff. I'm to blame, and so is Rebecca. If she'd never tried to deceive you or if I had just told you the moment I found out about the baby... none of this would've happened. Please don't blame yourself. Please, baby, don't. We're going to get through this… you and me together. Just promise me one thing."

"God, I would promise you the world, Ari."

"Please don't ever let me feel like I felt when you left me today. I never want to feel like that again."

I gently moved her onto my lap and kissed her. The kiss soon turned passionate, and Ari let a soft moan escape her mouth. I just wanted to lose myself in her.

"Make love to me, Jeff."

I had to start laughing. "Um, did you forget where we are, baby?"

Ari looked around the hospital room and made a face.

"Fuck a duck."

Just then the nurse walked and immediately stopped, staring at us.

"What happened? Why are y'all on the floor? Ms. Peterson, why are you on the floor?"

"I'm not on the floor. I'm on my fiancé's lap."

"Why are you on his lap on the floor?"

"Can I go home now? Please," Ari said as she looked at the nurse and gave her a pouty face.

The nurse shook her head as she walked over to us and looked down. I felt like I was in middle school, and we just got caught making out.

"Mr.?"

"Johnson, Jeff Johnson." I smiled up at the nurse.

She gave me a stern look in return. Yep, this felt just like middle school, especially knowing I didn't want Ari to get up just yet because of my hard-on. Ari must have been thinking the same thing I was because she took it a step further as she rubbed her ass on me. Turning to face me, she gave me a Cheshire Cat grin. *Damn, could I love her anymore?*

I leaned over and kissed her. Pulling slightly away from her lips, I smiled.

"I love you."

Ari giggled. "I love you, too."

"Alright, let's go. Let me help you up, Ms. Peterson. Now, take it nice and slow. Once we get you in bed, I will give you your pain pill."

After we got Ari back into bed, she slid over and patted the bed for me to get in. I started to climb on until I felt a hand on my shoulder pulling me back.

"I don't think so, Jeff Johnson. If you want your own bed to lie down in, I can probably arrange that for you since I'm starting to lose my patience."

"Wow, where did you go to nursing school? School of hard knocks?"

"Do you want to stay in here or in the waiting room?" the nurse asked with a straight face.

Jesus, this nurse was in a mood. Smiling at her, I put my hands up in defeat as I walked over to the small-ass sofa to sit down.

"That's better. Now, Ms. Peterson, is there anything else I can get you besides some pain medicine?"

Ari smiled and shook her head. The nurse gave Ari her medicine, and she swallowed the pill. I watched the nurse help adjust Ari, and then she glanced up at me giving me a dirty look.

"Good night…" I looked at her name tag. "Nurse Maggie Jones. Hey, Jay-Z has a song you might like. It's called "Hard Knock….""

"Jeff! Let's allow Ms. Jones to get back to work now. I'm sure she doesn't care about any songs." Ari then turned to the nurse. "Thank you so much for your help. I promise, cross my heart." Ari said, her index finger crossing over her heart, "that I will not get out of bed. She flashed that beautiful smile of hers at Maggie.

Maggie smiled at Ari and then turned and walked over to me. *Why does this woman make me feel like I'm about to be sent to the principal's office?*

"I've got my eye on you. She needs her rest, and she isn't going to get it with you making her get on the floor and sit on your lap."

"Wait a minute, I didn't."

"Shhh! I will make you sit in the waiting room all night if you don't allow her some rest. Do I make myself clear, Mr. Jeff Johnson?"

I looked up at her. "Did you just shush me?"

Ari let out a small laugh before she moaned. Jumping up, I was at her side so fast that Maggie didn't know what had happened.

"Ari, are you okay?" I stroked the side of her face as I leaned down to kiss her.

"Maggie, please, Jeff is fine. What I'd really like is for us to be left in private, please."

After another look that surly should have dropped me dead on the spot, Maggie warned me that she would be back in two hours to take Ari's vitals and I better not be in Ari's bed.

After she'd left the room, I walked around the bed and crawled in next to Ari.

***

We talked for the next hour about so many things: our future, the horses, more kids. Ari cried a few times, and I tried my best to hold back the tears.

Right before she drifted off into sleep, I whispered in her ear, "I love you, Ari, so much."

"Just promise me that everything is gonna be okay, Jeff. Please just tell me that it's all going to be okay."

"I promise, baby. Everything is going to be better than okay."

I held Ari in my arms while she slept. I wanted nothing more than to protect her from ever hurting like this again. Tears rolled down my face as I thought about how I was the one who had hurt her, causing her pain yet again. I made a promise to myself right then, that I would never hurt her again. I'd die before I'd ever cause her any more pain.

Sleep slowly started to take over my body until a part of me panicked about Maggie walking in.

I finally gave in and closed my eyes.

CHAPTER THIRTY-SEVEN

ARI

I could feel the pain before anything else. Slowly opening my eyes, the first thing I saw was the morning sun shining in through the window. Then, I looked up to see Maggie standing above me.

"Good morning, Ms. Peterson."

"Ari. Please call me Ari. Ms. Peterson is my mother."

Maggie laughed and helped me to sit up some.

"I'm about to leave, Ari, but I wanted to give you your breakfast if you thought you could eat something."

I hadn't even thought about food until that second. I was starving.

Smiling at her, I was just about to say yes when Jeff came walking in the door with a handful of bags.

"Good morning, baby! I went and bought you some of your favorites," Jeff started to set it all out on the small table under the TV.

"I got you a cinnamon twist, a chocolate cream-filled donut, an apple fritter…well, I got two of those 'cause I wanted one, too! Let's see…I got a ham and cheese croissant sandwich, two sausage kolaches…oh and two cream cheese-filled koloches because I know you love those."

I loved over at Maggie. She was just staring at Jeff now as he put all the food on the table. I tried not to let out a giggle for fear of my ribs hurting. When Jeff looked up at me and then at Maggie and back at me, the look on his face was priceless. I let out a laugh and did my best not to show how much pain I was in.

Jeff gave me a goofy smile. While he took a bite out of an apple fritter, he winked at Maggie.

"Do me a favor, Jeff Johnson; please don't ever come back to this hospital again. Please," Maggie said.

Jeff started to laugh. He walked over to Maggie and gave her a hug.

"Oh, come on, Nurse Hard Knock. You know you love me. You let me sleep in the bed with the love of my life all night." Then, he shoved the apple fritter in her face.

"You want a bite, Maggie?"

Maggie started to laugh as she pushed his hand away. "No, I do not want a bite of your half-eaten apple fritter." She pushed Jeff off to the side and smiled at me.

"Good luck with this one, honey. The doctor will be in soon to talk to you, Ari. The next nurse on duty is already starting your discharge papers, so we should have you out of here in no time."

"Thank you for everything, Maggie." I said with a smile.

Jeff said good-bye to Maggie and walked with her out into the hall. That bastard left all the goods on the table out of my reach, and I was starving. *Damn it.* I started to slowly get out of bed. When I stood up, I felt a terrible pain in my stomach. I bent over too fast, which caused my ribs to hurt. I cried out in pain. Just at that moment, Jeff came walking back into the room.

He was over by my side so fast that I swore it was just like that scene in *Twilight* when Edward saves Bella from being crushed by a swerving van. I had to start laughing, which caused me to cry out again. *Jesus, if this is what bruised ribs feel like, I pray I never break them.*

"Baby, what are you doing? Do you need to use the bathroom or something?"

"No! I need something to eat, and you walked out with Maggie and left me hanging."

Jeff helped me back onto the bed and then walked over to the table. He reached into the bag and pulled out an orange juice for me. He brought it over with the other apple fritter and a koloche. Then he just sat there, smiling at me.

"What the hell are you smiling at?"

"Were you hungry, baby?"

"Yes, yes, I was. I haven't had anything to eat since yesterday before the...the um...accident."

I felt the blood literally drain from my face. I had forgotten about it for a whole two minutes. Now, the memories were back, and it felt like someone was sitting on my chest. I couldn't breathe.

Jeff walked over to help me stand up. He gently took me in his arms. "I love you so much."

Then, the doctor walked in.

"Ms. Peterson, how are you feeling today?"

"Like shit. I still say my ribs are broken," I said, as I looked over at Jeff.

Dr. Ross glanced over at Jeff.

"Jeff Johnson, Ari's fiancé," Jeff said as they shook hands.

"Ari, we're going to let you head on home. I need you to take it easy for the next twenty four hours. Get lots of rest and be sure to watch for a fever."

"You are going to go through a range of emotions. Anger, sadness, and grief. You need to allow yourself time to grieve the loss of your child, both of you." Dr. Ross glanced back over toward Jeff and gave him a slight smile.

He also told us he would like for us to wait two months before we tried for another baby. Jeff squeezed my hand and I felt the tears building in my eyes.

Do. Not. Cry.

Standing up to leave, Dr. Ross shook Jeff's hand again.

"Please let me know if there's anything else I can do for y'all. If for any reason you start feeling worse, my personal cell phone number will be on your discharge papers. Or if you just need to talk to someone, I've been where you both are. I know what you're feeling. It will get better."

I was fighting the tears like there was no tomorrow. Jeff was squeezing my hand so hard that I was pretty sure he was going to break it. I looked down at my hand and back up at him, and he must have noticed it because he immediately loosened his hold.

My whole body started shaking and Jeff moved in closer to me. After the doctor walked out of the room, I lost it. I didn't think I'd ever cried so hard in my life, and I couldn't seem to stop. I turned and put my head on Jeff's chest. My side was killing me, but I didn't even care.

"I lost our baby, Jeff. Oh my god...I couldn't even take care of her. I lost our baby...I'm so sorry."

Jeff held me and just kept repeating over and over, "It's not your fault, baby. It's not your fault."

I continued to cry on his chest.

"Ari, I love you so much. This isn't your fault, baby, so please don't cry. We can try in a couple of months to have another baby."

I pulled back and looked up at him. I started to shake my head. *There's no way I can do this again. What if I lose the next baby? What if I'm not meant to have kids?*

"Stop. Stop this right now, Ari. I know what you're thinking. This was an accident, and that's all. It was not your fault or my fault. It just wasn't meant to be yet, baby."

I put my head back on his chest and tried to calm myself down. *We'll get through this together. We can make it through this.*

***

The moment I got into Jeff's truck, I smelled her perfume, and I almost threw up. I knew he brought her to the hospital, I knew he stayed with her while the baby was born, and I knew the baby wasn't his. *So why am I so pissed off at him all of a sudden?*

He jumped in the front seat and must have noticed it, too. He rolled the back windows down. "Do you want to stop anywhere to eat before we head back to Mason?"

I just wanted to get home I shook my head. "No, let's just go home."

Jeff handed me his cell phone and said that Ellie wanted me to call her.

"Hey, Ells, how did last night go? Did y'all have fun?"

"Fuck no, I didn't have fun. Heather got trashed, Josh got trashed, and they were both hanging all over other people on the dance floor. It was a mess. I ended up having to drive Josh's truck back to y'all's place. Lynda begged Josh to let her stay with him, but thankfully he wasn't that drunk. I'm pretty sure Heather would have killed him if he did that."

"Um, I'm pretty sure I would have killed him if he did that in my house! What the hell is going on with Josh and Heather?"

I looked over at Jeff. He rolled his eyes. I had to smile because those two reminded me of Jeff and me once upon a time.

Ellie filled me in on everything that went down between Josh and Heather. *Good lord. What was wrong with those two?* I was going to have to have a long talk with Heather in a few days. I wasn't sure why she was pushing Josh away when everyone knew she cared for him.

***

Jeff and I drove in silence for most of the way before I started to fall asleep. I finally stopped fighting my weariness as I drifted off to sleep.

I had a dream that Jeff and I were walking along the river. Holding hands, we were swinging a little boy between us. We were laughing, but then I stopped laughing when I saw a little girl standing in front of me. She looked so sad, and I asked her what was wrong.

"You let me go."

She turned and started to walk away from me. I yelled for her over and over again to stop. I started to run, but then I fell. I was holding onto my stomach. *Oh my god...the pain is unbearable.*

Then I heard Jeff.

"Ari, baby, wake up. Ari...wake up."

My eyes flew open, and I felt like I couldn't breathe. I looked around; we were stopped and parked outside of our house. I needed out of the truck now.

"I have to get out. I can't breathe, Jeff!"

The next thing I knew, the door to the truck was open, and Jeff was carrying me out, heading up the stairs to the porch. He opened the door to find Josh and Heather standing there, looking at us. I took one look at Heather and could tell she was very upset.

"Heather, what's wrong? " I asked.

Jeff carried me right by the two of them. As we headed into our room, I turned around to see her following us.

"Heather, can you pull the covers down for me?" Jeff asked as he walked me around to the other side of the bed.

"Really, Jeff, I'm fine. You can put me down, baby. I'm fine."

Jeff slowly started to set me down on the bed. My ribs were killing me and I tried so hard to not show how badly I was hurting.

"Ari, do you want me to make you some tea?" Heather asked, looking from me back up to Jeff.

"Oh, thank you, Heather. Then, will you please sit with me for a bit so we can talk?" I looked at Jeff and tried to let him know that I wanted to be alone with Heather for a bit.

"If you got this, Heather, I think I'll go check on the horses," Jeff said. Leaning down, he kissed me and then moved his mouth over to my ear. "I love you so much. Rest, baby. Don't get upset okay?" he whispered.

I nodded. "I love you, too."

I heard Heather in the kitchen. She was talking to someone, but I couldn't tell who it was. I slowly started to get up to make my way to the bathroom. I stopped by my dresser and grabbed a pair of sweats and a Longhorn T-shirt. Ugh, I felt like shit. I decided a shower was just what I needed.

***

When I stepped out of the shower, I saw Grace standing there, waiting for me. She gave me the sweetest smile and my heart melted. I was so happy that Ellie had Grace in her life now. She needed a mother figure, and Gunner's mom just seemed to love Ellie.

Heather was sitting on the bed, looking at me. I could tell she'd been crying. *She looked like shit.*

"Um, I just decided that I needed a shower," I said.

Grace walked up and took my arm and guided me back over to the bed. Passing by the sink, she grabbed my hair brush.

"Come on, baby girl. Let's get you off your feet. You need to not push yourself too much for the first few days. The more you relax, the better it will be. It will get easier, Ari. The pain will go away…well, not all the way, but it will dull."

I looked over at Grace and gave her a weak smile. I didn't want to be cold-hearted, but I just wanted to tell her that she had no idea how I was feeling.

"You can say it, Arianna."

I looked at her, shocked. "Say what?"

"I know you want to ask me how I know that the pain will go away or maybe how I even have the right to tell you that it will get easier."

I glanced over at Heather, who was looking at Grace with the same shocked look on her face that I was sure I had.

I had to clear my throat to get the question out. "You've lost a baby before?"

Grace lowered her head and then looked back up at me. "Yes."

"Oh, Grace, I'm so sorry." Heather and I both said at the same time.

Grace let out a little laugh and then reached for Heather's hand, pulling her over to sit down next to us.

"I was twenty-one and four months pregnant. Drew's dad was out in the field for a few weeks. I woke up with a terrible pain in my stomach. I didn't have anyone to call. My mother and father disowned me after I went off and married Drew's dad. I tried to just push on for most of the day. Gunner was just barely over one at the time. But when I saw the blood..."

Oh. My. God. I couldn't imagine carrying your child for four months, and then...

"Grace, I'm so sorry. That must have been terrible for you," I said.

Grace let out a sigh and wiped the tears from her face. "Ari, it doesn't matter if you're a few weeks pregnant or a few months pregnant; the loss is still the same. You have every right to grieve and miss that child. You will never forget her, and your mind will wonder and think about what might have been. But you will move on, and you will find that joy again. I promise you, sweetheart. You will find that joy again."

Grace leaned over and kissed me on the check. Then, she turned to look at Heather. Heather smiled at her, and Grace placed her hand on the side of Heather's cheek.

"I could *never* replace your mother, Heather, but I'll always be here for you. If you ever need to talk or to cry or to just ask why men are such assholes at times, I'm your girl."

Heather and I both laughed. I loved Grace already. I knew Ellie didn't want Grace to leave, and now, neither did I. Leaning over, Heather hugged Grace and whispered something in her ear.

"I'll leave you two girls alone now to chat. Ari, I made up some chicken and dumplings for y'all. I wasn't sure, Heather, how long you and Josh were staying, so I made plenty for all of y'all. Ellie told me to tell you she'll be over in a few hours. She's helping Gunner and his dad with the cows today. I love how that girl is not afraid to get down and dirty with the boys."

I smiled at Grace and agreed. I wanted to see Ellie so damn bad. I needed to see her. Just the sound of her voice calmed me down and helped me to relax.

After Grace was gone, I looked over at Heather. She attempted to give me a pitiful-ass smile. She moved to the other side of the bed to give me more room to sit back and put my legs out.

"Do you need anything, sweets? Want me to make you something to eat?"

I shook my head. "What happened?"

"What do you mean? What happened with what?" Heather almost had a panicked look on her face.

"You...Josh...something happened. I can see it on both of your faces. I could tell that Jeff and I walked in on something." I gave her a knowing look.

"Ari, it doesn't matter. What happened is over. I can't do anything about it now, so there's no use in talking about it. Really, I'm just ready to move on."

"Really? Because the look in your eyes says you are far from ready to move on, Heather. Please tell me. It will take my mind off of the baby." I stopped myself, looking away before I started to cry again.

"Oh, Ari. Sweets, maybe we should talk about the baby."

"No! I don't want to talk about it right now. Just tell me what the fuck happened between you and Josh."

Heather let out a sigh and sat down on the bed.

***

By the time she got me up to speed, I was sitting there in shock.

"Wait, let me get this straight. You almost slept with Josh?"

"I wanted to, yes, but he wasn't having any of it. Then, Garrett just came barging into your house, and all hopes of anything happening went right out the door. Y'all really need to keep your doors locked...like all the time."

I laughed, holding onto my side. *Shit!* "So last night, he went after the guy who started to kiss you? Sounds to me like Josh is not so ready to move on, Heather. I don't think you are either."

"Well, I am. It's pretty clear to me, Ari, that he's not ever going to change. I mean, he was making out with me when he'd just sent Lynda a message about hooking up with her! What does that say about him?

"Maybe he was frustrated, trying to move on, but he did it in all the wrong ways."

"Are you taking his side?"

"No! I'm not taking anyone's side, Heather. I'm just saying that he's a guy. They don't think with their heads; they think with their dicks. I don't doubt that Josh cares about you. I've seen the way he looks at you. He would do anything for you, you know that right?"

Heather's eyes started to tear up. "I can't trust him, Ari. As much as I try, I just can't trust him. What is it about me that would make him settle for just one girl? I mean, look at him!"

"What? Heather, oh my god, girl, look in a damn mirror. You are beautiful. You have a rocking body, tits I would kill for, an ass that Ellie wants more than anything, and your personality is beyond amazing. Josh would be lucky to have you, and he knows that. Why are you selling yourself short?"

"I just can't. I can't open up my heart up to have him leave me. I can't be left again, Ari. I can't and I won't allow that to happen." Heather's whole body started to shake.

Oh my god, she is so not over her parents' death. She's nowhere near it.

"Heather, what makes you think he's going to leave you, baby?"

"Everyone leaves me. My parents left me. I needed them more than anything, and they just left me alone. I can't do that again. He's going to leave me, Ari. He won't be faithful."

Heather lost it and started crying. I'd never seen her cry so hard. I tried to get up and hug her, but the pain that shot through my side just about made me fall.

Then, I heard Ellie let out a gasp.

"Ari, don't move! Heather, oh my god, sweets. What's wrong?"

Ellie came rushing over to my side and helped me back into a sitting position on the bed. I couldn't take my eyes off of Heather. It was like she was having a breakdown. *Finally, she's letting out the pain and hurt from her parents' death.*

"Just go help Heather, Ells, I'm fine."

Ellie walked over and dropped to her knees in front of Heather and hugged her. I didn't think it was possible, but Heather cried even harder. My heart was breaking. She was so afraid of being left again that, she wouldn't open her heart to the one man who loved her.

Ellie rubbed her back. "It's okay, baby. Just let it out, Heather. It's okay."

"I can't do this, Ellie! I can't do this alone anymore. They left me. Oh my god, they left me alone."

Ellie looked over at me and I could see the tears rolling down her face. I tried to fight the tears, but I felt them stinging my eyes. Heather had been trying to be so brave for so long. It broke my heart to realize that she'd been feeling like this for over a year.

I looked up and saw Jeff and Josh standing in the bedroom doorway.

Heather just kept repeating to herself over and over again. "They left me. They left me alone."

Josh looked like he was about to get sick. He started to walk toward her, but Jeff grabbed his arm, pulling him away.

"Princess, what's wrong?"

Oh shit. The moment Josh called her princess, Ellie and I glanced at each other. Heather looked up at him. I thought she was going to lash out at him. Instead, she broke down, crying again, as she got up and ran into Josh's arms.

What the hell?

Josh looked just as confused as the rest of us. He held on to her. "What's wrong?" He kept asking.

She pulled away from him and took a few steps back.

"I'll always love you, Josh, but...I just can't do this."

She brushed past him as she went out the door. Josh just stood there for a few seconds before he finally snapped out of it. He turned and ran after her.

Ellie got up and walked over to my side. She leaned down and kissed me on the cheek.

"You okay, baby? Do you need to talk?"

If one more person asks me that, I'm going to throw something big and heavy at his or her ass.

"Really, I'm fine. I think I just need to take a nap." I looked over at Jeff and smiled.

Ellie gently hugged me good-bye. "Okay. Um, Grace said she made some stuff for dinner. I guess I'll go see if Heather is okay. I love you, Ari. Call me if you need anything okay?"

She walked over to Jeff.

"Are you okay, Jefferson?"

I couldn't pull my eyes away from his. He didn't even look at Ellie when he shook his head. My heart broke. I could see the tears building in his eyes, and I knew he was blaming himself. A part of me blamed his as well, but I was trying so hard to push it down.

Jeff smiled at me and then turned to Ellie. "Ellie, can I talk to you for a minute?" Then, he followed Ellie out of the room.

I closed my eyes as the tears rolled down my face. I slowly moved onto my side and grabbed a pillow to hug.

You left us. You left us, sweet baby.

CHAPTER THIRTY-EIGHT

JOSH

My heart felt like someone had just reached in and ripped it out. *Why is Heather so upset?* We had been arguing right before Jeff and Ari had shown up, but she had seemed to be more pissed-off than upset.

I followed her to the room she was staying in. She pulled out her bag and started to pack up her stuff.

"I thought you were planning on staying? What about Ari?"

Heather looked up at me, and it felt like someone just kicked me in the stomach. Tears were just rolling down her face. *Holy shit.*

I took a few steps toward her until she held up her hand.

"Stop. Please don't come any closer to me. I don't think I have the strength to push you away right now."

"Then, don't. Heather I don't understand this. One minute, you say you want me, and the next, you push me away. You tell me you love me, but then you push me away again. Why are you doing this?"

"I can't do this right now. I just need to... I just need to get away from here... from you."

"What the fuck did I do? I can't fix it, Heather, if you don't tell me what I did."

Heather stopped packing and looked up at me. "That's the problem, Josh. You can't fix it. I think it's best if we both just move on. There can never be anything between us. You can never be with just one girl, let alone me. Come on, we both know that's true."

"You won't even give me a chance to prove to you how much I love you and how much I just want to be with you. Heather, I don't want any other girl. You're the only girl...woman... I've ever wanted, and the only woman I'll ever want. Princess, please just let me."

"Oh my god, please stop! No! It'll never work, so we need to just stop this now. I don't want to be with you. I said I love you, and I do, but...I don't think you are."

"You don't think I'm what?"

Heather took a deep breath and turned away from me.

"I don't think you're the one."

I just stood there, rejected again. *How many times am I going to do this to myself? How many times is she going to hurt me?*

Just then, my phone beeped. I took it out and looked at it. There were three text messages from Lynda.

"Fine, Heather. I'm done being turned down and pushed away by you. If you want me to leave you alone, you got it."

I turned and started to walk out the door as I hit Lynda's number.

"Josh, please can we still be friends?"

I turned back and looked at her. My heart was hurting so bad that I couldn't even talk to her. I just stood there with my phone up to my ear. I knew the moment Lynda answered, I was about to break Heather's heart, but maybe this was what I needed to do. She wanted us both to move on.

"Hello, handsome!" Lynda answered in a chipper voice.

"Hey, Lynda, how about dinner tonight with me? Are you in the mood?" I said. Then I turned and walked away from the only woman I would ever truly love.

***

I hardly heard a word Lynda was saying. We were sitting in a small restaurant in Fredericksburg that she had wanted to try. I'd told her earlier that I was heading to the restroom, but what I really did was call Jeff to ask if Heather had left yet. She'd left almost as soon as I'd left. Now, all I could think about was what had gotten her so upset and why she'd told me she loved me only to leave me.

"Josh? Are you even listening to me?"

"Um, yeah. I'm sorry, Lynda. I guess I'm just thinking about Jeff and Ari."

"Well, it was nice of you to let them have the house to themselves this evening. I can't even imagine how they both feel. I have to say that I'm relieved that Jeff is not the father of Rebecca's baby. I'm sure he and Ari feel the same way."

I couldn't even think straight. I just stared at Lynda until she finally smiled at me.

"Are you okay?" she asked.

I laughed. "I'm fine."

"The last two days have just been emotionally draining. That's all, Lynda. I'm actually thinking about heading back to Austin tonight. I think Jeff and Ari need to be alone with each other."

Sitting up straighter, Lynda raised her eyebrow at me. I knew what she was thinking. *Do I want to go there?* It had been months since I'd been with a girl. I only wanted Heather, but that wasn't gonna happen.

I reached up my hand and called our waitress over. She had been flirting with me all night, but Lynda didn't seem to care one ounce. As long as I was walking out the door with her, I don't think she would care who flirted with me.

***

As we walked back to my truck, I pulled my phone out to see if maybe Heather had called. *Nothing.* I sent her a quick text message to see if she'd made it to Austin yet.

I wasn't even in my seat when I got a reply back from her.

Heather: *In Austin...out with a friend.*

What the fuck does that mean? I knew her *friend* wasn't Ellie or Ari. *So who the fuck is she with?* I looked over at Lynda. She was staring at me…again.

"I um…I need to step outside and make a phone call that's kind of personal. Do you mind?"

"No, Josh, not at all. Take your time."

I walked a few feet away from the truck and dialed Heather's number. I didn't think she would answer, but she did.

"Is everything okay with Ari?" Heather asked in a panicked voice.

"What? Oh yeah…ah, she's fine."

"Okay. Well then, what did you need?"

"I just wanted to make sure you were okay, Heather. You were so upset when you left, and you never did tell me why you were crying. I, um…I just wanted to make sure you were okay. That's all."

"Thank you, I appreciate that. I'm fine."

"Who are you with?"

"I don't think it's any of your business, do you?"

"Heather, listen, I know you aren't with Ellie or Ari. I just wanted to make sure you weren't alone and that you're okay."

"I happen to be perfectly fine. I'm on a date. Then, her voice sounded farther away. "I'll be right there, Jerry, in just one second."

Jerry? Who the fuck is Jerry?

"You're really out on a date? You move fast, Heather." I was so pissed off that I couldn't even think straight.

"Me? How are you enjoying your dinner with Lynda?"

"We're about to move onto dessert." *Fuck.* The second that came out, I regretted it.

"You're an asshole."

I went to apologize, but then I realized she had already hung up. I wanted to scream and just throw my fucking phone. My hands were shaking, and I couldn't stop seeing Heather dancing with that guy from last night. I turned back to my truck and got in. I looked over at Lynda sitting there, smiling at me.

"Do you want to go back to Austin with me tonight?"

"I thought you would never ask."

***

I dropped Lynda off, so she could pack up her stuff. I told her I would be back as soon as I could.

When I walked into Jeff and Ari's place, Jeff was sitting at the kitchen island. He looked like shit.

"Hey, dude, how is Ari feeling?"

"I think she's feeling better."

Fuck. "Jeff you need to talk?"

"It's my fault this happened, Josh. It's my fucking fault. I walked away from her…the one person I vowed to never walk away from. I just left her while I ran after some damn lying bitch. If I had just given her a few minutes of my time, I don't think I would have left. I would have stayed, and."

"Jeff, stop doing this to yourself. You can't change what happened. It all happened for a reason. I know you want to place the blame on yourself, but, dude, you can't. You didn't know Ari was going to tell you she was pregnant, and you didn't know Rebecca was playing you for a fool."

Jeff snapped his head up. *Oh shit, I should really choose my words more carefully.*

"A fool? Is that what everyone thinks I am?"

Motherfucker. I didn't need this. "No, Jeff, that's not what I meant. You were torn, and I get it. I would have probably done the same thing, Jeff. How were you supposed to know that she was plotting against you? It's all going to work out. I know it will. You and Ari are meant for each other, Jeff. Y'all will find a way to fix this shit. I promise."

Jeff put his head in his hands and let out a sigh. *Man, this guy needs to just catch a break.*

"Hey, um…I was going to head back to Austin tonight. I figured y'all need your privacy, and with Heather leaving…"

"What the hell is going on with you and Heather, Josh? I feel like I'm looking at an earlier version of Ari and me, dude. Just get it the fuck over with and tell her you love her."

I started to laugh. "I already told her that I loved her. She seems to think that I'll never be able to stay true to her. I guess I can't blame her, but fuck…what does a guy have to do to prove he can change?"

Just then, my cell phone went off with a text. Lynda had texted me with a picture of her in a fucking blue lace bra and matching panties. *Fuck me.*

"Actually change, Josh."

"What?" I looked back up at Jeff.

"You want to prove to her that you've changed? Then you've got to actually change, dude. I've seen that look on your face before. You're gonna hook up with someone tonight, aren't you?"

"I don't need a lecture from you, Jeff. Heather's made it very damn clear that she doesn't want to be with me. Shit, she's on a date tonight for Christ's sake! What I am supposed to do? Just sit around and wait for her? Fuck that. I've waited long enough for something I'll never have."

"Wait. How do you know she's on a date? She just left a few hours ago."

"I called her. I wanted to make sure she got to Austin okay, and she told me she was on a date. I even heard her talk to the guy."

"You don't think she might have just been saying that to get you fired up?"

"Why the hell would she do that? Listen, she's moved on, and now, I am, too. I gotta go, Jeff. Lynda is waiting for me."

"Oh fuck, dude. You're gonna sleep with Gunner's cousin? The man code, bro."

"It's his cousin, not his damn sister. Fuck the man code."

***

I packed up my shit and headed back into the kitchen. Ari was sitting at the table while Jeff was pouring her some tea. I walked over and kissed her on the head.

"How are you doing, babe?"

"Fine, thank you. Why are you leaving? You don't have to leave, Josh. Please know that."

"I know, hon. I need to get back to Austin. My dad is making some office furniture for a lawyer's office, and I really want to help him with it. I can't waste my whole summer away. Time to get a real job, ya know?"

"Okay, come back this weekend if you want."

"Thanks, y'all. Take it easy and let me know if you need anything."

***

By the time I picked up Lynda and we headed into Austin, my head was pounding, and my heart was racing. Lynda was talking away like a nervous Nellie. She didn't even hesitate when I asked if she wanted to go back to my place.

The sooner I fucked her, the better I would be.....

And the faster I would get over Heather.

CHAPTER THIRTY-NINE

HEATHER

Jerry just kept talking and talking until he finally asked if I was even listening to him.

"Oh yeah, I'm so sorry, Jer. One of my best friends lost her baby yesterday, and I guess I just have her on my mind. I kind of walked out and left her. Not the best thing for a friend to do, but."

"No worries at all, Heather. You've seemed a little upset since you took that call. Was that her?"

The moment I ran into Jerry at Starbucks, and he asked if I wanted to grab a late dinner, I knew I was doing the wrong thing. I needed to get Josh out of my head though. Then he called, and I'd just blurted out that I was on a date. I guess having dinner with your cousin's best friend wasn't really a date, but Josh didn't need to know that.

"No, it wasn't her. It was a guy. A friend who just wanted to make sure I got back to Austin okay."

"Do you call all your guy friends assholes, Heather?" Jerry asked with a smile.

I let out a laugh and shook my head. Jerry went back to eating his burger while I took a good look at him. He had blond hair and green eyes. They were nothing like Josh's eyes though. His height was about five-eleven and he was built. He played baseball for UT, and he was dressed in a UT t-shirt and shorts. He was wearing his UT baseball cap backwards. If Ari were here, she would probably say he looked very fuckable. She loved it when guys wore their caps backward. I hated to admit it, but I loved it, too, especially when Josh did it which was damn near all the time.

I let my eyes travel up and down Jerry. He sure was attractive, and he had a killer smile that made my stomach drop.

Jerry wasn't as good-looking as Josh, but he was damn near close to it.

We talked for a few hours about nothing and everything. It was nice having a simple conversation. I also didn't have to worry about if he was going to check out the waitress or if she was going to slip him her number. Josh had never done that though. At least, I'd never noticed it.

Josh. I wondered if he was with Lynda. I decided I needed to check up on Ari. I looked at the time, and it was almost ten.

I sent her a text message: *How are you?*

Ari: *I'm reading. Jeff is passed out with his head on my lap.*

I had to smile to myself. Thank God Jeff was not the father in that whole Rebecca-baby drama. I sent her another text and asked if I could give her a quick call. I excused myself as I walked outside of Mighty Fine Burgers to call Ari.

"Hey, girl. How was the trip back to Austin?" Ari said.

"It was fine. I ran into an old friend. Do you remember Jerry Ross? He's my cousin David's best friend. Plays baseball for UT."

"Oh yeah, the one who always wears his damn baseball cap backward. Yeah, I remember him!" Ari said with a small giggle.

I was sure she was trying not to hurt her side or wake up Jeff.

"I'm having a late dinner…well, burgers with him."

"Really? Huh," Ari said.

I heard her tell Jeff to go back to sleep.

"What do you mean, huh? I'm not allowed to have dinner with anyone?" I knew I sounded like a bitch. *What is with the attitude from her?*

"I don't mean anything by it, Heather. Jesus, Mary, and Joseph, between you and Josh, I swear."

"What about Josh? Is he there or still out to dinner with Lynda?"

When Ari didn't say anything, my heart started to pound.

"Is he there Ari?"

"Um, no. He actually left a few hours ago to head back to Austin."

"Really? Did he go back to Austin alone?" Why I even cared was beyond me. I did this to myself. I pushed him away one too many times, and now, I had a feeling I was about to pay for it.

"I'm not really one hundred percent sure on that."

"I can always tell when you're not being honest, you know."

"I overheard Josh telling Jeff that Lynda was going back to Austin with him."

Oh. My. God. I put my hand up to mouth when I almost threw up. *He's coming back to Austin with Lynda.*

"Heather, baby, are you okay?"

"I have to go."

"Heather, wait! Talk to me. I'm so damn confused with what's going on between you two. You told him to move on. Baby, did you mean it? If not, Heather, call him. Call him right now before he does something I know you're both going to regret."

"No, you're right. I told him to move on, and clearly, that is what he's doing. I can't blame him for that. Listen, sweets, I just wanted to check up on you and see how you're feeling. Take it easy and give Jeff a hug and kiss for me, will you? I've got to run. Jerry is waiting on me."

"Heather, please call me if you need to talk, and please call Josh, baby."

"There's no reason for me to call Josh. I'll talk to you later."

As I leaned up against the building, the tears were building in my eyes. I felt so sick to my stomach, and all I wanted to do was scream. *Am I really going to just let him go that easily?* Looking down at my phone, I found Josh's number. I looked back into the restaurant, and Jerry was cleaning off our table while talking to the girl who had been working behind the counter. It looked like she was handing him something. I was sure the place was fixin' to close any second now.

I looked back down at my phone and hit dial.

Then, she answered.

"Hey, Heather! Is everything okay? This is Lynda."

I was so stunned that I couldn't even think of any words to form in my mouth.

"Um..."

"Heather, are you okay?"

I could hear the satisfaction in her voice, knowing she had caught me off-guard.

"Yes, I am. I must have dialed Josh's number by mistake. I was trying to…trying to call Ari to see how she's doing."

"Oh, okay. Well we literally just walked into Josh's apartment, and he's taking a shower. So should I let him know you called?"

What a fucking bitch. I hate her. "Ah, no. Like I said, I meant to call Ari, so no, that's fine. Thanks, Lynda. Enjoy yourself."

"Oh, believe me, we intend to have fun tonight…if you know what I mean."

I just hung up. I leaned over, and the next thing I knew, I felt Jerry's hands on my back.

"Heather! Oh my gosh, are you going to get sick?"

I couldn't breathe. *He's going to sleep with her? Oh god.* I pushed him away, and now, he was going to sleep with her. *I. Can't. Breathe.*

I looked up at Jerry. His face was filled with concern. He truly seemed to be worried about me. *Maybe he's the one?* I didn't think I'd ever have to worry about him leaving me. He didn't seem like the type of guy who would play around.

"Jerry, I don't think I can drive. Can you please take me home?"

Jerry smiled at me and leaned down to pick me up. As he carried me to his BMW, he whispered in my ear, "I'll do anything for you, baby."

***

The light shining through the window was killing my head. I pulled the pillow over my face and let out a moan. *Oh god.* I hadn't felt this bad in months. *Holy hell, how much did I have to drink?* I started to play back the evening in my head. Jerry had stopped and picked up some beer and the fixing's to make Italian Margaritas. I remembered drinking…a lot…laughing…kissing and.

I sat up in bed so fast that I thought I was going to puke. I looked down to see that I was naked.

Oh. My. God. No!

Slowly looking to my left, I almost jumped when I saw Jerry sleeping next to me. *No. Oh god no.* I very carefully tried to get out of bed, and then it hit me. I was sore…down there. When I pulled the sheets back, I saw blood.

I got up and ran into the bathroom. I barely made it in time to throw up. After ten minutes of getting sick while Jerry asked if I wanted a warm washcloth, I sat back against the wall and cried my eyes out. I lost my virginity to a guy I wasn't even dating…when I was drunk… and I don't even remember it.

I closed my eyes and pictured Josh telling me my first time had to be special. I'd wanted my first time to be with someone I loved. I wanted it to be with Josh. I had not wanted to be drunk and sick the next morning with no memory of even having had sex in the first place.

I leaned back over the toilet and started throwing up again.

"Jesus, Heather. You're not much of a drinker, are you?" Jerry said with a small laugh.

Does he even know? How could he not know that I was a virgin?

"I just need a few more minutes. I'm so sorry." I said.

He looked down at me with pity. "Should I make you some eggs, babe?"

Ugh, he called me babe. "Sure." It was not lost on me that I was sitting, naked, on my damn bathroom floor. I closed my eyes and felt the tears again.

Josh…it was supposed to be Josh.

I felt something soft land on my shoulders, and I realized he was putting my bathrobe over me.

"Thank you."

"Heather, if I had known ahead of time, I would never have..."

Oh great…just great. Now, he's sorry for having sex with me. I looked up at him as I felt the tear roll down my face.

"Baby, please don't cry. I feel like shit as it is. I wish I could go back and change it all."

Wow….good-looking and caring…but he's still not Josh.

***

After a few more minutes of me sitting on the bathroom floor, rocking back and forth while I tried to remember anything from last night, I got up and made my way into the living room. Then, I remembered I was butt-ass naked, so I started to turn back to the bedroom when my door bell rang. I looked at the clock on the wall. *Who the hell would be here at seven in the morning?*

Pulling my robe closer to me, I tied it tightly and opened the door. My jaw just about hit the floor when I saw Josh standing there. He looked awful, like he hadn't slept in days.

"Josh? What…what are you doing here? I thought you were with Lynda."

Josh looked confused. "What? How did you know I was with Lynda last night?"

"When I called you she answered and told me you were in the shower. She said y'all were planning on having an enjoyable evening." *Holy shit, I spit that all out so fast.*

"Wait, what time did you call?" Josh asked, looking confused as hell. He pulled out his phone and scrolled through his call log.

Oh no. I felt like I was going to throw up again. "Um, around ten."

"That's weird. I saw her on my phone, and she said it was the wrong number. The last call on my log is when I called you."

Oh my god. She set me up. "Did you sleep with her last night?" I blurted out. *God, please say yes.*

"Heather, can I at least come in?"

"Did you sleep with her last night, Josh?" I almost shouted.

"I almost did, but I couldn't do that to you, Heather. I love you. I only want to be with you."

I felt my legs going out from under me, and then Josh reached over and grabbed me.

"Shit, Heather."

Josh grabbed me and started to bring me into the living room. When I looked up, I saw Jerry standing there, watching us. He looked confused as hell, wearing only his boxers.

The moment Josh noticed him, I felt it. His hold on me tightened, and he sucked in a breath of air. He helped me to the sofa where I sat down. I looked between Josh and Jerry. *Wow, both their names begin with the letter J.* I shook my head. *What the hell, Heather? Really?*

"Um, hey, I'm Jerry."

Jerry reached out his hand out to shake Josh's, but Josh took a step backward. Then, Josh looked at me. I knew the moment when he realized what had happened.

"You slept with him?" Josh whispered.

"Josh…" I tried to talk, but I lost my voice.

Josh glared at Jerry.

Jerry glanced at me, shook his head, and then looked back at Josh.

"Dude, I had no idea y'all were together." He held up his hands in defense.

When Josh looked at me again, I could see the tears in his eyes.

Without even looking away from me, he answered Jerry.

"We're not together."

Then, I lost it and started crying.

"Josh, I don't even remember anything." I went to stand up and walk closer to him.

He took a step back with the strangest look on his face.

"What?" It looked like his legs were about to give out, and he grabbed onto a chair. "How could you do this, Heather? I thought you were different. I didn't sleep with Lynda because I love you. I was coming over here to tell you that I'd wait for you forever if I had to. Then, I find out that you…."

"Josh, please no... don't say it," I said between sobs. I felt like I couldn't breathe. The hurt in his eyes was killing me.

Josh turned to Jerry. "Did you at least know she was a virgin?"

Jerry shook his head, "Not until after. I would never have done that if I'd known. Listen, we both got really drunk last night, and."

Josh held up his hand to stop Jerry from talking.

"You wanted to push me away, Heather… well, I think you finally did it." Josh turned and started to walk toward the door.

My heart was racing and my head was pounding, but I went after him.

"Josh, please. You have to understand that I never intended for anything like this to happen. I was upset when Lynda said y'all were about to have a good time, and I just wanted to forget it all. I wanted it to be you! You have to believe me! I wanted it to be you!" I grabbed his arm.

He stopped and turned to look at me. With his thumb, he wiped away the tears that were rolling down my face.

Josh closed his eyes for a few seconds and then opened them. The moment I saw a tear slide down his face, I died inside.

"You know what's funny, Heather? You were so worried that I was the one who wouldn't be faithful. I would have given up everything for you. There's nothing I wouldn't have done to make it so damn special for you and to make you happy for the rest of your life."

"Oh god, please, Josh... *please.*" I started to shake my head.

He took a few steps away from me.

"I guess you got what you wanted, princess. You've lost me for good."

I cried harder as I reached out for him, but he turned and walked out the door. I called out after him, but he just kept walking. I slowly started to sink down to the floor.

"You've lost me for good."

No! Oh god, he left...just like my parents did.

I just sat there, rocking back and forth, as I kept calling out his name over and over again. Jerry walked up behind me and placed his hands on my arms to help me up. When I turned around, I fell into his arms, telling him how sorry I was.

"Come on, babe. Let's get you dressed and put something in your stomach. It's going to be okay, Heather. It's going to be okay."

I wanted to believe him, but I had a feeling nothing would ever be the same.

It would never be okay because I lost him.

The only man I would ever love... I lost him.

CHAPTER FORTY

JEFF

I was walking up from the barn when I saw Ari sitting on the porch.

The last three months had been hell for both of us. Although her parents had disapproved, Ari had decided not to go back to Austin for school this semester. Instead, she was taking a few online classes with Ellie.

I had only talked to Rebecca once, and she begged for forgiveness. She had called a few more times, but each time, I'd ignore it. On more than one occasion, Ari had just about wanted to drive to Austin just to kick her ass.

I heard the thunder rumbling in the distance, and I smiled, remembering how much Ari loved thunder-storms.

If only I could get that Ari back...

Last night, I'd called Ellie, and I'd told her that I thought Ari could really use a girls' trip into Austin today. She agreed.

As I walked closer to Ari, I could tell she'd been crying. *Fuck.*

"Hey, baby, have you been up for very long?" I asked as I stepped up onto the porch.

She didn't even look up at me. She was growing more distant as the days went on. It had been three months since she'd lost the baby, and now, she wouldn't even let me touch her.

I sat down next to her while it started to rain. She put her head back on the swing and let out a sigh.

"Ari, we really need to talk, baby. I can't keep going on like nothing is wrong. You're drifting further and further away from me. I need you back."

She lifted her head and glared at me. "Maybe you should have thought of that before you walked out on me."

I felt like I was going to be sick. "I don't know how many times I have to tell you that I'm sorry, Ari. I'm sorry for making the biggest mistake of my life. If I could take it back, I would. You don't think I beat myself up every morning and every night? If I could go back and redo it, I would. I'd do anything to make you happy."

She stood up and walked over to the railing. "I want to be alone for a while."

"No."

She spun around and stared at me. "What?"

"I said no, Ari. I'm tired of you pushing me away and not talking to me. I don't even remember the last time you let me hold you or just touch you."

"I don't want to talk about it with you."

"Bullshit. You won't talk to anyone about it, not even your mother, Grace, or even Ellie. Everyone is so worried about you. This has to stop, Ari. We got the go ahead last month, if you want to try for another baby...."

"No! Just please stop talking." Ari stepped off the porch into the rain.

"Where the hell are you going?" I said walking after her.

"I want to be alone, Jeff. That means without you! Please just go back to the house. I'm going to the barn."

I followed her toward the barn.

She turned and looked at me.

"You're such a fucking dickwad! Why can't you just leave me alone? I don't want to be near you, I don't want you to touch me, and I don't want you to make love to me. I don't want you. Holy hell, how many times do I have to say it?"

It was now pouring rain, and I was shaking from head to toe. I knew she didn't mean what she was saying; the counselor we had gone to had told me that this might happen. I'd kept doing what the counselor said. I'd given Ari the space and time she'd needed, but now, I was done with this bullshit. I wanted my girl back. I wanted the life we were supposed to have - *fuck, the life we deserved to have*- back.

When I started to walk toward her, she turned away from me to run toward the barn. I took off after her and grabbed her. She started to scream for me to let her go while she fought me with every ounce of energy she had. I wouldn't let her go. I just held on to her while she hit me with as much force as she could.

Then, she started to cry.

"I hate you! Don't touch me, Jeff. You can't touch me. Please just leave me alone."

She was crying so hard that I could hardly understand her. I just held on to her. She slowly started to sink to the ground, and I went down with her. The pouring rain and loud thunder surrounding us was unreal, but there was no way I was letting her go.

"I lost the baby, Jeff. I lost our baby. Oh my god... I just want to forget it. Why can't I just forget it?"

For the first time in weeks, she turned and held on to me so tightly that I thought I was going to burst with happiness and sadness at the same time.

"Baby, you didn't do anything wrong. It just wasn't meant to be. She's up in heaven, looking down on us, and she'll always be a part of us... always, Ari. There will never be a day that goes by that she won't be with us. She's our angel watching over us, baby."

Ari buried her face in my chest. She was crying so hard. I would do anything to take away her pain. As she slowly pulled away from me, the rain mixed with her tears, both just pouring off her face.

She stared into my eyes and said, "Make love to me, Jeff. Please make love to me."

Oh dear God. I wanted her so much. It had been so long that I just wanted to just rip off her clothes right there in the rain. I picked her up and walked her into the barn to an empty stall. I gradually slid her down my body as I looked into her beautiful eyes. Those eyes were slowly getting life back into them.

Reaching over, I grabbed Stargazer's blanket. I bent down and laid out the blanket while Ari just watched my every move. As I started to take off her sneaker, she put her hands on my shoulders while she lifted one leg at a time.

Standing up, I captured her mouth with mine. The moan she let out moved through my whole body.

We hadn't been together in three months. I didn't want to rush this. I wanted to show her how much I needed her. I wanted to make her forget for just a little bit.

I started to kiss her neck and then slowly moved up to her ear. "Take off your clothes, Ari," I whispered as I stood back to look at her.

For the first time in months, I saw a fire in my girl's eyes. Ari stepped back and started to peel off the T-shirt that was plastered to her body. Slowly, she began taking off her white lace bra. My dick was getting harder by the second.

She dropped her bra on top of her shirt, and then she gave me the smile that I'd do anything for. I let my eyes move up and down her beautiful body.

Stepping forward, I hooked my finger on the belt loops of her jean shorts and pulled her to me.

"Take off all your clothes."

She unbuttoned her shorts and slid them down her wet body. I didn't think I'd ever been as turned on as I was in this very moment. Just the sight of her had me going insane. *I love this girl more than anything.*

She stepped back and raised her eyebrows at me. "Do you really think it's romantic to make love on my horse's blanket?"

I couldn't pull my eyes away from her lips. "Yes, I think making love to you anywhere would be romantic as long as we are together."

With a smile, Ari walked up to me and pulled me closer to her. "It's your turn to strip, you bastard, if you know what's good for you," she said with a wink.

I didn't think that I'd ever taken off soaking wet clothes that fast before in my life. The moment her hands touched my body, I sucked in a breath of air. *Fuck, I've missed her touch.* I was trying so hard to think of anything other than her touch that was driving me crazy.

She started to kiss my chest from one side to the other. Then, she dropped to her knees and took me in her mouth. I swore that I almost came on the spot.

"Ari, baby, I don't think I can hold off if you keep doing that."

She let out a small moan that just made me combust.

I reached down and pulled her up to me.

"I want to be inside you. Now!"

"Well, who am I to deny that command, Mr. Johnson?"

Ari slowly lowered herself down onto the blanket. I moved over her and started to kiss her face, then her neck and moved down to her chest where I gave each nipple equal attention.

Ari let out moan after moan.

"Oh god, Jeff. I've miss you so much."

"Baby, you don't know how much I've missed you."

I continued kissing down her stomach to her hips. She grabbed my hair and pulled me back up to her to capture my mouth with hers. The second she bit down on my lip, I knew I couldn't wait any longer. Inch by inch, I slowly started to enter her body. All the while, I never once stopped showering kisses on her.

I gently moved in and out of her warm body. "Are you okay, baby? Am I hurting you at all?"

"Please don't stop, Jeff. You feel so good. I'm so sorry that I've been pushing you away. Please just love me."

I brushed my lips against hers, and then I kissed her deeply. I pulled away to look into her beautiful green eyes. "I love you so much, Arianna. I hope you know how much I love you."

"Jeff..."

I rolled us over, letting her take control. She'd never felt so good like she did at this very moment. I never wanted this to end. Ari smiled at me, and the next thing I knew, she took us both to heaven and back.

***

I wasn't sure how long we lay there in that stall, listening to the rain, before one of us spoke.

"I'm sorry that I've been so out of sorts, Jeff. It's just."

"Baby, you don't have to explain anything to me. I love you, Ari. I'll never leave you...ever."

Turning on her side to look at me, Ari smiled. "I'm gonna hold your ass to that. I want to get married."

"I'm pretty sure I already asked you that, and you said yes." I lifted up her hand and kissed her ring.

Ari laughed and hit me in the stomach. "No, I mean, I want to get married now, like right away. Let's just go somewhere and get married. We don't need a big production. You and me, babe. How does that sound?"

"Considering your father has already told me that he wants his baby girl to have the wedding of her dreams, I'm going to have to take his side on this one, baby."

Sitting up, Ari pulled her legs to her chest and gave me that wicked smile of hers.

"You talked to my father about the wedding? When?"

"About three weeks ago. When they came out to visit, he came down to the barn and we had what he called… 'a nice little chat about making my little girl happy forever or you will pay dearly for the rest of your life'."

"I love it! Okay, so deep down, I knew we wouldn't be able to get away with running off and getting hitched. So when do you want to get married?"

I had to laugh. *I love this girl.* "As soon as possible," I said. Leaning up, I grabbed her by the back of the neck and pulled her toward me. When I nipped her lower lip, she let out a soft moan that brought my dick back to attention.

"December? Can you wait until December to get married?" Ari asked, moving to sit on me. She raised her eyebrows and smiled at me as she started to impatiently circle her hips on top of me.

"Well, I see there's one thing you can't wait for."

***

We spent the rest of the morning making love and just talking in that stall. For the first time in months, I actually felt like we were on the right road to happiness. Ari was smiling, laughing, and talking about our future together, and I had never in my life felt so fucking happy as I did with her in that barn. I was getting my girl back.

Before we started to make our way back out into the rain to head up to the house, I found another blanket and wrapped it around Ari. Ellie was sure to be heading over to get Ari soon.

Ari stopped and reached out for my arm. I turned and looked at her. Her eyes were holding back tears. *Fuck me.*

"Can I ask you something?" she asked.

"Of course you can, baby always."

"Can we try for another baby? I mean, I haven't been taking my pills, and we just...well, I mean what just happened was so wonderful."

I placed my hand on the side of her face and smiled at her. She was breathtaking; the sight of her standing in the rain, asking me if we could try for another baby, had me just about falling on my knees.

"I want nothing more than to have children with you, Ari. I'm ready, baby, whenever you are."

She gave me that smile, and my heart dropped to my stomach.

"Do you want a boy or a girl?" she asked me with a wink.

"I want a healthy baby, but I won't argue if that healthy baby happens to be a boy," I said with a small laugh.

"I don't care if we have a boy or a girl. I'm thankful that I'm not a carrier of the Fragile X gene, but I'll love whatever God decides to give us. Earlier, Jeff, when you were talking about the baby, you said *she'll* always be with us. Do you think it was a girl?"

"I don't know. The moment I found out you were carrying our baby, even just for those few seconds, I that I was so happy. Something told me it was a girl. It's stupid, I know. I guess I've just always thought of the baby as a girl."

Ari smiled slightly and reached up to kiss me. When she pulled away, her smile grew.

"The second I found out I was pregnant, I knew it was a girl. I felt it."

"Well, here's hoping we both feel the next one is a boy. I seriously want him to kick ass on the football field."

Ari laughed as we started to make our way to the house. When she turned and stared at me with that look, I knew what she was about to do.

She winked at me and started to run toward the house.

"Last one there has to muck out the stalls tomorrow!"

I smiled and took off after her while she laughed the whole way back to the house.

CHAPTER FORTY-ONE

ARI

I'd never felt so alive as I did right at this moment. Jeff's touch alone seemed to snap me out of the funk I had been in for the last few months. After we were back in the house, we got into the shower, and he made love to me again. This was probably one of the best mornings of my life.

***

Looking at myself in the mirror, I put my hand on my stomach. I smiled at the thought of Jeff referring to the baby as a girl. Our little girl was in heaven, and she would always be looking over us. She was our very own special angel. I knew that with all my heart.

"I will never forget you, baby girl…ever."

I heard Jeff walk into the house, arguing with Ellie. *Those two…I swear.* Rolling my eyes, I reached for my sweater since there was a cold front moving in. I knew my ass would be buying one if I didn't bring one.

I walked into the kitchen, and Ellie and Jeff were in such a deep conversation that they didn't even see me standing there.

"She's in rehab and asking to see us both. What was I supposed to say, Jefferson? Grace and Jack were standing right there when I got the call."

"You should have told them to tell our mother to go to hell."

"Believe me, I wanted nothing more than to say that, but instead, I said that I would talk to you about it."

"I don't care that she's in rehab, Ells, or that part of her recovery process is to say she is sorry to us. She can fuck off for all I care."

I cleared my throat so that they both knew I was there.

When Ellie turned to face me, the smile that played across her face spoke volumes. *Well, holy hell, I must have a just-got-laid look on my face.* She glanced back at Jeff and smiled even bigger at him.

"Do you still want to do a girls' day? I packed my gym stuff, so we could hit Lifetime Fitness; I just want one good workout in a real gym!" Ellie said.

"Fuck yeah, I still want a girls' day! I have my stuff packed, and I'm ready to go."

I looked over at Jeff and gave him a wink. I was so happy to see that smile on his face. I knew he'd been so unhappy the last few months, and it was now going to be my goal to make him happy every damn day.

***

It had been so long since I'd laughed as much as I did on the drive into Austin. *God, this feels good.*

Ellie picked Magnolia Café for lunch. She talked me into getting a chicken salad sandwich on some wheat-ass looking bread. *Ugh, healthy shit.*

The waitress brought out our food and put my sandwich down in front of me.

I looked up at Ellie.

"Really? All I wanted was some mac and cheese today, Ellie."

"Stop bitching. We're going to the gym, and if you really want to get married in December, it's time to start eating healthy."

"What the fuck is this green shit in here?"

Ellie raised her eyebrow. "It's spinach."

"I can't eat this shit." I picked it off the sandwich and set it to the side.

"After this, we're going to get ice cream." I said before I took a bite of my sandwich.

"No way. No, I'm putting my foot down."

"Stop being such a bitch to me, Ells. If I want ice cream on my girls' day, I'm getting ice cream, damn it."

***

After lunch, we got back into the car. Ellie looked at me and smiled. She reached over to hit play on her car stereo, and Christina Aguilera's "Vanity" started.

We both looked at each other, and at the same time, we said, "Hells yeah!"

The moment Ellie pulled into Baskin-Robins I wanted to reach over and kiss her ass! *Oh god.* I wanted ice cream so damn bad. I practically jumped out of the car and ran into the place.

"Shit, Ari, it's just ice cream. You act like you've never had it before."

"Listen, bitch, I haven't felt this good in months. If you're draggin' my ass to the gym, I'm gonna at least have something to celebrate that shit."

Ellie hung up from talking to Gunner and raised her eyebrows at me.

"Holy hell, Ari, that's the biggest sundae I've ever seen. You're going to get sick."

I just grinned at her and took a giant bite. I looked up and watched a girl walk in. She was covered in tattoos. I looked back at Ellie with a smile.

"Oh no! There's no fucking way, Ari, I'm going to let you…or me…get a tattoo! No. Way."

"Come on, Ells! I've been through hell the last few months. You know I've always wanted one. *Please!*"

"I'm not getting one. I'd get a nose piercing before I got a tattoo."

I jumped up and walked over to the trash can.

"Come on, let's get a fast workout in, and then let's get some ink and get pierced!"

Ellie just looked at me. "Have you lost your damn mind?"

"Come on, Ells. You have the perfect nose for it." Reaching for her hand, I pulled her and lead her out of Baskin-Robbins. "Think about what you want for a tattoo while you're working out. I already know what I want."

***

The whole time I was on the elliptical, I kept thinking about my morning with Jeff. I closed my eyes and could almost feel his lips on mine.

December. I was going to marry him in three months. My eyes flew open, and I looked over at Ellie.

Oh. My. God. I'm going to get married in three months, and I haven't started to plan a damn thing. Nothing! I needed to call my mom. *Where should we get married? Austin? At the ranch?*

On a beach... far, far away from everyone and everything. That would be the perfect wedding. It was too bad my mother would say hell no and then throw a damn Katharine Hepburn quote at my ass.

I hit Ellie on the arm.

She looked over and pulled her head phones out. Britney Spear's "Toxic" was playing from her earbuds.

"What? We've only been going for thirty minutes."

"I'm freaking out!"

"I would think so. Do you know how much shit you ate in the last few hours?"

I rolled my eyes. "Not about what I ate. It's about the wedding. Jesus, Mary, and Joseph, I'm getting married in three months, Ells. One. Two. Three. Three months and I've done *nothing.*"

Ellie threw her head back and laughed. "Don't worry. We have a secret weapon called Jenny. Ari, it will be fine. We got this thing. I mean we can."

Ellie stopped mid-sentence and stared past me. The look on her face was not good.

I was almost afraid to turn around to see who or what she was looking at.

"Um, how about we call it a day and go get those tattoos?" Ellie stopped the elliptical and jumped off.

Now, I knew it was bad. I hit stop, got off, and turned just in time to see Rebecca standing there, talking to...Jason?

"Ari, let's just go."

Oh fuck no. I'd been dreaming about what I was going to say to her when I saw her again. She had been the reason why I'd lost the baby. It'd been her and her alone. I wanted to pound my fist in her face.

"It's okay, Ells. I got this under control. Honest."

"The hell you do! I can practically see the steam coming from your ears, Ari."

What is Rebecca talking to Jason about? They sure seemed deep in conversation.

When I started to walk toward her, Ellie grabbed my arm.

"Ari, I really think this is a bad idea. There's something Jeff didn't tell you, and I really think you need to just walk away."

I turned and looked at her. "What? What didn't he tell me?"

"Aw shit, Ari! You don't really need to know. It doesn't matter anymore, so please, let's just go, *please.*"

"You can't say that to me and then just expect me to walk away. Tell me now or I will vagina punch your ass right here in the middle of the gym."

Ellie looked over my shoulder toward the bitch.

"Fuck me. Jason's the father of Rebecca's baby."

"Wait…what? He can't be. He was with me when..." Then, it hit me.

"Are you fucking kidding me?" I pushed Ellie's hand off my arm and turned around to head over to the devil's spawn herself.

It didn't take her long to notice me walking up to her. She straightened her body and stood a little closer to Jason. *He's not going to save you, bitch! After I take his ass down, I'm coming after you.*

"Ari."

"Ells, please. I need to do this."

Ellie took a deep breath and gave me a knowing nod.

Right before I got there, Jason turned to see me coming.

"Oh, hey there, Ari and, Ellie. How have y'all been?"

"Fuck off, Jason."

"Listen, Ari, I don't want any trouble. I tried to call Jeff, but he won't take my calls," Rebecca said.

"And you should probably take that as a sign that he's never going to take your calls...ever again."

"Fine. You know what Ari, I don't have time to stand here and listen to you."

I reached out and grabbed her arm.

"Oh, I think you do, and you will make time for me, bitch."

"Don't call me a bitch!" Rebecca said. She looked at Jason as he wisely took a few steps away.

"Oh, I'm sorry I offended you when I called you a bitch, Rebecca, I honestly thought you knew you were one."

"Fuck off, Ari."

I tightened my grip on her arm and pulled her closer to me. Her eyes widened in surprise.

"Because of you, I lost something very precious to me."

She slowly let a smile play across her face.

The fact that she smiled was enough to make me want to hurt her even more.

"What's wrong, Ari, you couldn't keep Jeff around?"

"Oh, don't you wish. Actually, we're getting married in a few months. Don't hold your breath for an invite."

"Let go of my arm."

"Listen to me, and listen very closely, Rebecca. If you so much as ever *think* of getting in contact with Jeff again, I'll make sure you pay for everything you've ever done to me. You so much as look my way ever again, and I'll kick your ass from here to kingdom come and not think twice about it."

Rebecca looked at me and then over to Ellie.

"By the way, Bek, you look like shit. I thought motherhood made you more beautiful. Huh, it must not work for lying, scheming bitches." I let go of her arm and gave her a small push.

I looked over at Jason and smiled. He took another step backward.

"Don't worry, dickwad, you're not even worth my time or energy." I held up my middle finger and smiled at him as I started to walk away.

Smiling, Ellie came up next to me and bumped my shoulder.

"Really, I would've been okay if you kicked the shit out of her."

I reached my arm around and pulled her closer. "Holy hell, girl, I'm so glad you're my best friend."

When we walked out of that gym, I'd never felt better.

***

By the time we walked out of the tattoo parlor, I was flying high. I ended up getting angel wings on my right shoulder in honor of our little girl. I couldn't wait to show Jeff. The belly-button piercing was perfect. I looked over at Ellie and let out a giggle. She still looked like she was about to throw up.

She asked, "What the fuck did we just do?"

Ellie ended up getting a phoenix tattoo on the right side of her back, and I was damn happy she did. If anyone had been reborn, it was this girl.

Now, the nose piercing, yeah, I'm pretty sure that I was not going to let Ells live that one down. I'd never heard Ellie say fuck so many times or use the names she'd called the poor guy who had pierced her nose. I let out another giggle.

"What the hell do you find so funny, Ari? You barely flinched when he pierced your stomach. I thought I was going to die when he put that damn needle through my nose. *My nose, Ari.* I just pierced my nose and got a tattoo on my back. Gunner is going to freak."

"No, he's not. Shit, he has two tattoos himself. He's gonna think it's sexy as hell, and you know it."

Ellie shook her head as she got into her car. "I sure as hell hope this thing doesn't get infected." Ellie looked in the rearview mirror. "Oh. My. God."

When she looked back at me with her smile, I grinned right back at her because I knew what was coming.

"It looks so damn cute!" she said.

I laughed and agreed. "Let's head home. I want to get me some Jeff."

"Oh god, Ari. Come on, I don't need that visual. He's my brother for shit's sake."

***

The drive back to Mason was filled with laughter and tears.

Ellie was starting to get down because she hadn't gotten pregnant yet, and she was getting worried.

"What if I can't have kids, Ari? What if I'm never meant to be a mother? I know how much Gunner wants kids. What if."

"Just stop. First off, you have plenty of time to have a baby, and you will have a baby, Ells. Maybe you're just so worried about trying that you're too stressed to get pregnant. You know, my mom and dad didn't think they were ever going to have kids. They ended up going on vacation, and nine months later, I made my grand entrance in the world."

"Yeah, I know. I've already talked to Gunner about maybe not trying so hard for now. I mean, if it's meant to happen, it will happen. Right?"

"Right!"

"Ari, are you really okay, sweets?"

I looked out the window and felt the tears building for the first time since this morning. Taking a deep breath in, I thought about Jeff with his arms wrapped around me so tightly, his whispers of love in my ear, and the way he just made me feel so safe.

I smiled and turned back to Ellie.

"Yeah, I'm really okay, Ells. For once, I truly feel like Jeff and I are finally on the road we are meant to travel on. I don't think you can get to where you're truly meant to go until you travel that one road…the one that's filled with sharp turns, steep hills, and nothing but pot-holes that you have to try and get around. After you make it off that road, you find the one that is straight, smooth, and filled with nothing but happiness."

Ellie pulled over on the side of the road and stared at me.

"What's wrong? Why the hell did you pull over?"

She reached over and put the back of her hand on my forehead. I just looked at her.

"What the fuck are you doing?"

"I'm just making sure you're not getting a fever or something from that piercing and tattoo. Holy hell, that was some serious shit."

I let out a laugh and pushed away her hand.

"I love you, bitch," I said, hitting her in the shoulder.

"I love you, too. Let's get home and show our guys what we got today!"

CHAPTER FORTY-TWO

JEFF

With Ari's birthday tomorrow and the wedding in four weeks, my head was spinning in every direction.

Ari had been flying high the last two months, which was a relief. I knew things were definitely getting better when she'd gotten back up on Rose. Our ride yesterday morning had been amazing. We'd made a small pit stop to make love under her favorite oak tree.

I smiled when I thought about how fucking sexy that girl was. I had to shake my head when I thought back to a couple of months ago when she and Ellie both came home with tattoos and piercings. With the way Gunner had looked at my sister when she'd showed him the tattoo, that fucker had been lucky as hell that he was married to her. I could practically read his damn mind. *Bastard.*

I heard a truck coming down the driveway before I even saw it. Scott was coming today to pick up the horses he'd left for breeding. I still didn't like this guy. He flirted way too much with Ari for my liking.

Scott pulled up next to my truck and got out with that stupid-ass grin on his face. Walking up to him, I smiled and reached out to shake his hand.

"How's it going, Scott?" I said in the nicest way I could. I couldn't help but notice him looking around for what I was pretty sure was Ari.

"Hey, bud, how's it going? How'd those horses do?"

"Good. We left them out in the back pasture for about a week."

Scott was looking over toward the barn.

Fucker. Okay, let's just make this short and sweet.

"So, let's get your boys loaded up in your trailer."

Scott looked back over at me and nodded. "Sure, let's do it."

"They're in the barn." I turned around and led the way.

***

After we got Scott's two studs loaded up, we were about to shake hands when he broke down.

"So, where's Ari today? Is she feeling better?"

I just smiled at him. "She's doing wonderful. She and my sister are in Austin today, looking for a wedding dress." *Chew on that, prick.*

"A wedding dress, huh? Y'all getting married soon?"

"Four weeks."

Scott smiled and shook his head. "Well, I don't have to tell you that you're one lucky son of a bitch, I'm sure."

"No. No, you don't."

He stuck his hand out to shake mine. From the look on his face, I might have gripped his hand a little bit too hard, but at this point, I couldn't have cared less.

Ari was due back at any minute and all I wanted to do was get him the hell out of here.

I watched as he drove off, and then made my way back into the barn. I set my iPod on the docking station and turned on my song while I started to clean out the stalls. There was nothing like a little Kid Rock's "Cowboy" to get me going.

I started to think about Ari's birthday tomorrow. I smiled as I thought about marrying the girl of my dreams. I was going to do everything in my power to make sure she was happy for the rest of our lives. It was hard to believe a year ago I'd almost lost her to Jason.

Just then, I felt something hit my back. I turned around to see the love of my life leaning up against a stall. I walked over and turned off the music.

"You know, I never thought I would say this, but I actually would prefer for you to listen to 'Truck Yeah' again."

Walking up to her, I grabbed her around her waist and pulled her to me.

"Oh yeah? You don't like my 'Cowboy' song, baby?"

"Um…no. You play it all the damn time, Jeff. I think Ellie is about ready to take away your iPod."

"I love my sister, but her taste in music sucks. Speaking of my sister, how was the dress shopping?"

Ari smiled so big it caused me to smile.

"I found it."

I picked her up and spun her around. *Fucking finally.* I was so tired of hearing Ellie and Ari talk about dresses, looking at dresses, and shopping for dresses. I was just about ready to take her to a beach somewhere and marry her in the nude.

"That's great, baby. I'm so happy you finally found it. Was your mom with y'all?"

Ari smiled. "Yes, and that made it all the more special. Amanda and Heather were there, too. Hey, can I ask you something?"

"Always baby."

"Have you talked to Josh lately? Is he still dating Lynda?"

"I talked to him earlier as a matter of fact. He's coming to your party tomorrow, and yes, he's still with Lynda."

"Huh."

"Why? What's going on? Were you ever able to find out what happened with Heather? I asked Josh, and he's was very vague. All I know is that what ever happened fucked him up for a few months."

"Nope, she hasn't said anything to Ellie, Amanda or me. She's changed though, Jeff. She just seems so…lost. It breaks my heart. I know she loved, or loves, Josh, but this crazy idea of him leaving her or whatever bullshit she's afraid of is just stupid. I mean, he did leave her…at her request. Anyway, she asked about him today. She wanted to know if he was still with Lynda. I told her that I wasn't sure, since we hadn't seen him in a few weeks. I guess she's still dating Jerry. I don't trust that guy one bit. Heather seems to think he would never do anything to hurt her. I just have a bad, bad feeling about him."

I agreed with Ari. I'd already seen the asshole slip a waitress his number. *Dickwad.*

"You want to know what else I did today?" Ari asked.

"Of course I do. I always want to know what my beautiful girl is up to twenty-four seven."

"I went to an appointment with my mom before we met back up with Ellie."

"Really? About the wedding?"

"Nope, not about the wedding at all."

I raised my eyebrows at the cute-ass little smirk on her face.

"Do I have to guess, baby, or do I need to get it out of you another way?"

Ari smiled at me with an unbelievable light in her eyes. I just wanted to take her in arms and make love to her. During the last few weeks, she had such a glow about her even though I knew she was stressed about the wedding. Thank God for Jenny and Ellie.

"I went to see Dr. Wyatt today."

My heart started to pound. *Please God...*

"Yeah?"

"Yep!" Turning, she walked over to Rose's stall and leaned against it.

"Ari, you're killing me. Why did you go see him? Is everything okay?"

She threw her head back and laughed. Then, the look she gave me made my heart drop into my stomach. *God I love this girl with every ounce of my being.*

"Everything is more than okay, Jeff. You're gonna be a Daddy in about seven months."

Holy shit. It felt like my knees were about to give out. I just stood there for a few seconds and stared at her smiling face.

She's two months pregnant...two months ago...the day in the barn. It was the day in the barn!

I walked over to her and put my hands on the sides of her face. Leaning down, I kissed her lightly at first, nipping at her bottom lip, and then I kissed her with as much passion as I could.

After what seemed like forever, I pulled my lips from hers, both of us were breathing hard. When she smiled at me, I almost dropped to ground.

"I love you, Arianna. I love you so damn much."

"I love you more." She giggled.

I put my right hand on her stomach and looked down at it. *I'm going to be a father.* I smiled at the thought of Ari having my baby.

"When I'd asked you to marry me and you'd said yes, I thought that was the best moment of my life…" I looked into her eyes that were filling with tears.

"But I was wrong. This is the best moment of my life."

"So far," Ari said with a wink and a smile.

I laughed and kissed her again. "Yeah, baby, so far."

CHAPTER FORTY-THREE

ARI

I woke up and instantly smiled.

Last night had been perfect…beyond perfect. It had been amazing. I didn't think Jeff had ever made love to me so sweetly and passionately as last night. I touched my still swollen lips, remembering his kisses, and smiled.

I could still feel his hands all over my body, touching me so tenderly. The way he'd kissed my stomach and talked to the baby just about had me melting right there on the spot. I held up my hand and looked at my engagement ring. I still couldn't believe that I was marrying this man. This man who I'd been in love with the moment my young eyes saw him.

I thought back to yesterday when I'd sat, waiting, in Dr. Wyatt's office. When he'd walked in the door with a smile on his face, it only confirmed what I'd already known. This time, I hadn't taken any pregnancy tests. I'd just known. Somehow, I'd known the day when Ellie and I were running all over Austin, threatening Rebecca, getting tattoos, and just being silly and carefree. Earlier that morning on the same day, I'd somehow known that Jeff and I did something amazing together. We'd had sex plenty of times since that morning, but I truly believed that's when I got pregnant. My little angel was watching over us.

***

When I told my mother, the first thing she did was quote the great Katharine Hepburn.

"Always remember, Arianna, 'Children need boundaries, so they can know how far they have to go to get beyond them.'

I had to laugh. "Really, Mom? No congratulations, Ari'? Just another Katharine Hepburn quote?"

"Hey, I'm so beyond excited right now, baby girl. That quote was the first one that came to my mind."

"I'll take it, Mom."

She hooked her arm around mine as we walked to her car.

"Mom, I didn't tell Ellie why I had her drop me off at your house this morning."

"Okay, why didn't you tell her, Ari? You know that she's going to be beyond thrilled."

"She's been trying to get pregnant ever since this summer, and it's not happening. I'm so worried, Mom. What if she can't have kids? Gunner has all but stopped talking about it with her. She thinks he's upset, but Jeff said Gunner just doesn't want to pressure her."

"Has she talked to Grace?"

"Yeah, and Grace pretty much told Ellie the same thing I did. She needs to take a break from trying to get pregnant and just enjoy her time with Gunner. Gunner's learning about the cattle business, so Garrett and Emma can retire for good and he's designing their house. Besides Jeff, I've never in my life seen a man who would do anything for the woman he loves. He absolutely adores the ground Ellie walks on. It's so incredibly sweet, Mom."

"He is a sweetheart, no doubt. I would have to say you and Ellie are two very lucky bitches."

"Oh my god, Mom! Jesus, Mary, and Joseph! And people wonder where I get it from."

"Come on, let's go meet Ellie and find you a dress."

***

I was snapped out of my thoughts by Jeff's voice.

"Good morning, babies."

I had to smile. I sat up in bed and watched him carry over a tray full of food, setting it down over my lap.

"Oh my gosh, what's all this?" I looked at a bowl of fresh fruit sitting next to a plate full of scrambled eggs, two pieces of whole wheat toast, and blueberry muffins along with a glass of orange juice.

"It's breakfast for my two favorite people."

"Two, huh?"

"Yep, you and the boy," Jeff said with the cutest damn smile on his face.

"The boy, huh? What makes you so sure it's gonna be a boy?"

"I'm not sure at all. I figured I'd just take turns each day. Today, the baby is a boy, and tomorrow, a girl. That way, it's equal time for both."

I threw my head back and laughed. "I love that idea. Now, about all this food, Jeff. I can't eat all of this even if I am eating for two."

"Just eat what you can, babe, I'll eat the rest. By the way, happy birthday, Ari. I got you just a little something to start off your day." He reached into his pocket and pulled out a jewelry box.

My stomach had butterflies in it. *How does he do this to me?*

As soon as he handed it to me, I started to take off the wrapping paper, and then I opened the box. When I saw what was inside, I let out a gasp as I looked up at him. He was smiling with tears in his eyes. As I looked back down, everything started to blur. I reached up and wiped away my tears.

"Jeff, it's...I don't even know what to say. It's absolutely perfect."

"Do you like it?" He started to take the diamond angel-wing pendant necklace from my hands to put it on.

Leaning forward, I lifted up my hair. When his hands brushed against my neck, I became covered in goose bumps.

"Like it? Jeff, I love it. Beyond words, I love it."

He leaned over and kissed me so gently on the lips that I let out a moan.

"Shit, Ari, don't make noises like that, or you won't be eating breakfast anytime soon."

I smiled against his lips and then let out another low sexy moan.

The next thing I knew, the tray of food was gone, and Jeff was on top of me, kissing me. What started out with very slow gentle kisses quickly turned into something more heated and passionate.

After I was able to catch my breath, I smiled at him. "I think that was the best birthday present *ever!*"

"I'm so glad to hear that, baby. Come on, I have another surprise for you at Garrett and Emma's house."

"Jeff, wait. Before we go up there, I need to tell you something."

"Is everything okay?" Jeff looked panicked.

"Yes, I mean, it is with me, but this is about Ellie."

"What about her? Is everything okay with her?"

I let out a small laugh. "Would you just let me finish? I didn't tell Ellie about the baby. She's been so upset with the fact that she has not gotten pregnant yet, and I feel like if I told her then I'd be rubbing it in her face."

Sitting down on the bed, Jeff rubbed his hands down his face.

"Fuck. I didn't even think about how this was going to be for Ellie and Gunner." He looked over at me and reached for my hand. "They're going to be happy for us, baby. You know that right?"

"Yeah, I know that, it's just... I'm so early on in the pregnancy, so I was thinking of waiting to tell everyone until after the wedding. Maybe we could even wait until after New Years? Just... well you know, just in case."

"Ari, listen to me. Everything is going to be okay. Please don't worry about losing the baby. We're going to do everything we can to make sure this baby is born healthy and happy. You can't live in a glass box, baby. You've gotta live life. As far as telling people, I think you're right. We need to wait until at least after Christmas."

"I love you so much."

"I love you, too, baby. Now, eat your breakfast, so we can head up to the ranch house. Gunner is probably pissed that I backed out on helping him and his dad mend a fence this morning."

Jeff got up and made his way back out to the kitchen. I could hear him cleaning up as I tried to eat all the food he put on my plate.

When my cell phone went off, I reached over to grab it and then saw a text from Ellie.

Ellie: *Happy birthday, bitch! I love you more than life itself. See you soon ☺"*

Then, I saw Heather and Amanda's messages. *Hmm, I must of missed those earlier.* I read both of them and sent off my thank-you's to each.

Then, I sent another one to Heather: *Are you going to be at the party tonight?*

Heather: Yes *of course! I wouldn't miss it for the world. Studying my ass off...ugh. Love you.*

I finished eating what I could, and then I got up to get dressed. When I walked into the kitchen, Jeff was walking around on his cell phone.

"Can you hear me now? Fucking cell coverage!"

His words reminded me of that day we got stranded when the Jeep wouldn't start. I had to laugh at the thought. *Ah, the memories.*

Jeff looked over at me and smiled. "It's alright, dude. The birthday girl just walked in so I can't talk anymore. I'll catch up with you when I get into Austin."

"Oh, that was just plain mean,

Jeff." Jeff looked me up and down, and the lust in eyes almost made me lose my breath.

"Again, Mr. Johnson?"

"Holy hell, Ari. You look amazing, baby. I wish I could, but we need to get up to the house."

I looked down at what I had on: a white T-shirt tucked into my jeans with my brown belt and cowboy boots.

"What's so special about this?"

"You look beautiful. Come on!" He reached down and scooped me up.

I let out a scream.

"I can walk to the truck, you know."

"Oh, I know, but this way, I get to keep you close to my body," Jeff said with a wink.

***

By the time we pulled up to Emma and Garrett's place, Ellie, Gunner, and his parents were all sitting on the front porch. *Oh god.* Ellie was holding a glass of sweet tea. For some reason, I needed a glass, like right now. *What the hell?*

"I'm so glad that Grace and Jack moved back here after Jack retired from the Army," Jeff said.

"Yeah, me too. Shit, I want some sweet tea!" I practically yelled.

Jeff laughed and reached over for my hand right before I was about to jump out of the truck.

"Ari, wait."

I turned to look at him. "Yeah?"

"I just wanted to tell you what a lucky son of a bitch I am to have you love me. I'm so happy right now, baby, but I'm so afraid at the same time."

Oh. My. God. The butterflies were taking flight in my stomach.

"Jeff..." It was all I could say.

I love him so much, I've always loved him, and I will always love him.

"Come on, baby. Let's go get you some sweet tea."

"And apple pie…oh man, I hope Emma has some damn apple pie."

CHAPTER FORTY-FOUR

GUNNER

Ellie and I showed up at 219 West before anyone else did. We went up to the rooftop lounge to get a few tables. Jack was DJing tonight, so I walked over to say hello to him. I felt my phone going off in my pocket, so I pulled it out to see that Jeff had sent a text saying they were parking. I leaned over to tell Ellie where Jeff and Ari were.

Ellie was on the phone, frowning, but then she said good-bye. She tried her best to smile at me.

What's up?" I asked.

"It's Heather. Gunner, I'm so worried about her. She just hasn't been the same since last July. Whatever happened between her and Josh must have been huge. Did Josh happen to mention if they…if they…you know?"

"Slept together?"

Rolling her eyes, Ellie nodded.

"No, the only thing he told me was that he showed up to her house one morning, and she'd made it perfectly clear to him that he was not who she wanted. He said he left and has not seen her since."

Ellie let out a sigh. "I haven't been able to get shit out of her, but I have a feeling something major has happened to her. She ended up taking online courses and has doubled-up on classes this semester. She's probably going to be graduating next December if she keeps up this load."

"Ellie, sweetheart, please don't worry about Heather. If she wants to talk to you, she will. Stop pressuring her into it. Was that her on the phone?"

"Yeah, and the first thing she asked was if Josh was going to be here. I told him he was and that Lynda was most definitely going to be with him."

Just then Ari and Jeff came walking up. Ari was glowing. It was nice to see her so happy after the funk she fell into after losing the baby. Jeff walked up and shook my hand.

"I'm still pissed at you, you bastard," I said.

Jeff gave me a smile.

"What for, dude? You don't own the monopoly on puppies."

"At least Gus will have a play-mate now," I said as I looked over at Ellie, who was laughing at something Ari had said.

Jeff threw his head back and laughed. Jeff had surprised Ari with a puppy for her birthday earlier today. Gramps and Grams hid her for two days at their place, and my father was about ready to kill her.

**

The moment Ari saw the little bloodhound puppy, she let out a scream and ran over to it. Ari picked it up and started to kiss it all over. Ellie laughed and held Gus back while Ari got acquainted with the new addition.

"Ellie, let Gus go, and let's see what they do." Ari said with a smile.

"I'll tell ya what they'll do. They'll chase each other nonstop and shit everywhere," my dad said as he gave Jeff a look.

Jeff shrugged his shoulders. "I know, I owe you one."

"Damn right, you owe me one. This dog is nuts. She's not all there."

Ari looked up at my dad and frowned while she covered the pup's ears.

"Jack! Don't say that about Abby! Oh my god! Abby! That's her name. It just came to me," Ari said as she looked up at Ellie.

They both laughed.

***

"You look lost in thought, baby." Ellie said as she placed her hand on my chest and pushed her body into mine.

"You want something to drink?" Jeff asked me.

"I'll take a Dos Equis."

Jeff looked at me and smiled. "Dude, why didn't you say that in your most interesting man voice?"

Ellie and Ari both started laughing while I just shook my head at him. *Fucker.*

Jeff turned to the waitress and asked for two Dos Equis beers and two sweet teas. The waitress looked at Ellie and Ari and then back at Jeff, who gave her a wink.

"Ari, we have our fake ID's. Why don't you use it to enjoy a beer on your birthday?" Ellie said to Ari.

"No, I only want sweet tea."

Ellie stared at Ari in disbelief while she glanced out at the dance floor. Ari looked like she was itching to dance.

"You don't even want one drink on your birthday? What's wrong? Are you not feeling good or something?" Ellie asked.

Ari looked back and forth between Jeff and Ellie. She seemed to be at a loss for words. Jeff looked at me and gave me a look.

Motherfucker. "Hey, Ells, you want to dance, babe?"

Ellie smiled and moved closer to me. "Yes, I would love to dance with you."

"Give me one second, sweetheart." I walked over to Jack and asked him to play a certain song next.

I headed back over to Ellie, and by the time we walked out to the dance floor, Jack was playing the song I'd asked for. I took Ellie in my arms and started dancing to Christina Aguilera's "All I Need."

Ellie put her head on my chest while we danced in silence.

The moment Jeff had looked at me, I'd put two and two together. Ari was pregnant, and they didn't want to tell Ellie. My heart was breaking for my beautiful girl. All she wanted was a baby, and we'd been trying for months. I didn't tell her, but I booked a trip to New Orleans in March. Ellie had mentioned once how she'd always wanted to go there, so I thought a long weekend was just the thing she needed to relax.

"Drew?"

"Yes, baby?"

"I know what you're doing."

I let out a small laugh. "What is it exactly I'm doing, Ells?"

Ellie pulled back and looked at me.

"You're trying to protect me from something, but you don't have to. I knew something was up a few days ago. I could see the difference in Ari, and when she asked me to drop her off at her mom's for a few hours, I figured she was going to the doctor. Then, when I met her at the bridal store I could see how happy she was even though she tried so hard to hide it."

I brought her in closer to me, tightening my hold on her. I kissed her on the head. "Ells, I love you so much."

"I love you, too. It's really okay, Gunner. I mean, maybe it's just not meant to be right now. I think I'm just going to concentrate on finishing up my online classes and mastering Emma's cooking and gardening skills."

The song came to a stop, and Flo Rida's "Club Can't Handle Me" started. I saw Ari and Jeff on the dance floor.

I asked Ellie if she wanted to sit down and she said no. She was in the mood to dance and just have fun.

I loved to dance with this girl. The way she moved her body was enough to make me want to take her back to The Driskill Hotel and make love to her again, just like on our wedding night.

After dancing to a few more songs, Ellie and I headed back to the table.

Just as we got there, I saw Josh and Lynda walking up. He looked so fucking unhappy. Why he stayed with my cousin was beyond me. I'd told him she was high maintenance and a snob. He'd been drunk the other night and had told me that he'd only slept with her twice. That, had shocked the shit out of me.

Lynda came bouncing over and gave Ellie and me a hug. Then she told *not asked*, told Josh to go get her a drink. When he turned around to head over to the bar, he ran right smack into Heather.

This should be good since neither one of them have seen each other since July. That douche-twat Jerry was standing behind Heather. I'd already told Ellie how I felt about him, and no matter how many times we all had tried to tell Heather he was cheating on her, she would not listen to us.

"Shit, I'm sorry, Heather. I didn't see you there." Josh looked Heather up and down, and then he noticed Jerry standing behind her.

I hadn't seen Josh tense up like that since our football days when he was ready to kick someone's ass. I started to slowly make my way over when Lynda piped in.

"Josh! Please! I'm dying here of thirst."

Josh looked back at Heather and smiled. "You look really good, Heather."

"Thank you Josh, so do you."

Josh nodded and looked up at Jerry.

"Josh, so good to see you again." Jerry held out his hand to shake Josh's.

Josh just glared at him. He moved around Heather and made his way to the bar.

Well, hell, this should be an interesting night. I looked out at Jeff and Ari, and they were happily dancing with each other. As long as those two are happy and Ells is happy, I decided not to worry too much about Josh and Heather and their fucked-up feelings for each other.

As I watched the night go on, it seemed like the only person drinking was Josh. I was having another damn déjà vu.

Ellie, Ari and Heather were all on the dance floor dancing to Christina Aguilera's "My Girls." I was getting pissed as I watched the numerous guys trying to dance with them. Ellie looked over once and smiled at me. I was giving her thirty minutes, and then I was taking her to the hotel. I glanced over at Jeff. He couldn't pull his eyes away from Ari.

He looked over at me, and I just smiled and winked at him.

Jeff's smile faded.

"You fucking bastard. You made reservations at The Driskill didn't you? You mother-fucking-son-of-a- bitchin'-romantic-ass-bastard."

I started to laugh. "Holy hell, Jeff, you've been hanging around Ari way too long. Her cursing has worn off on you."

"I'm taking Ari to Paris."

I sat up, narrowing my eyes at him. "You can't do that! I was going to take Ellie."

"I'm thinking Paris for a honeymoon. Sounds pretty romantic, don't you think?"

"To think I called you my best friend and agreed to be your best man."

Jeff threw his head back and laughed. Just then, Ari came walking up and straddled Jeff, giving him a long kiss.

"Oh god, that's my brother, Ari. Yuck!" Ellie yelled.

While Lynda was out on the dance floor with Josh, I looked over at Heather. She was watching them and couldn't seem to pull her eyes away from them.

When Pink's "There You Go" started to play, Jerry nudged Heather. "Hey, do you want to dance?"

Never taking her eyes away from Josh and Lynda, Heather simply said. "No."

That was when it happened. Heather looked over at me, and I could see the tears building in her eyes. I got up and took Ellie's hand.

"Hey Jeff and Ari, I think we need to get Heather home."

Jeff and Ari both looked over at Heather.

"Sure, that's fine. I'm exhausted anyway," Ari said as she gave Ellie and me a hug good-bye. "We have a long way back home."

"No, we don't, babe, I booked us a room at The Driskill Hotel." Jeff said as he winked at me.

Bastard. I was still pissed about the whole Paris thing.

I smiled at him and shook my head. "I have taught you well, my friend."

Ellie and Ari both looked at us, confused. I grabbed Ellie's hand and walked over to Heather. I reached down and took Heather's hand.

As we started to head toward the stairs, Jerry came after us, and I stopped the girls and looked at him.

"Listen, asshole. I can't tell you how many times I've seen you slip your fucking phone number to random girls. We're taking Heather home; she's upset and ready to leave. I also suggest you don't call her anymore."

Jerry looked over at Heather, who was staring at me, stunned.

She turned back to face Jerry.

"Jerry, is that true?"

"You know what? Fuck this. We slept together once, Heather, and ever since then, you've been nothing but distant and pining over some jerk. So, yeah, I've been with other girls since we started dating. You certainly weren't putting out so."

"Shut the fuck up now, or I'll shut you up," I said as I took a step toward him.

Jerry took a few steps back, lifting both hands.

"Fine, I'm done here anyway. Enjoy your life as an elementary school teacher, Heather. It fits you perfectly."

I turned to find Ellie holding Heather. Poor girl looked like she was about to throw up.

"Come on, sweetheart. We have a hotel room right down the street."

Ellie snapped up her head and looked at me with a small smile. I just winked back at her. The thought was there even if we wouldn't be able to use it tonight the way I'd wanted to.

After we got to the truck, Heather asked to just be taken home. Ellie was in the backseat with Heather. I turned on the music so they could have some privacy, but I could still hear Heather crying.

I was shocked as shit to hear that she had slept with that asshole. *What the hell was she thinking?* I pulled my cell phone out of my pocket because it kept going off. I had four text messages and two missed calls.

Fuck. Josh was one of them. I hit voice mail and listened to his message.

"Gunner, what the hell happened? I saw you walking off with Heather, and then I saw Jerry come back alone. Is she okay?"

***

We pulled up to Heather's apartment, and Ellie asked me to give her a few minutes with Heather.

"Baby, take your time. I'm in no rush." If I'd been standing, her smile would have dropped me to my knees. *Damn the things this girl does to me.*

I pulled up the text messages: two from Jeff and two from Josh.

Jeff: *Hey, Ari is worried about why y'all took off with Heather and why Jerry-the-jackass came back alone and pissed off. Have Ells text Ari.*

Jeff: *Never mind dude. These girls have weird mind powers. Ells just texted Ari and told her what's going on. Why the fuck would Heather sleep with that douche bag?*

Josh: *Gunner, I tried 2 call u. Is Heather ok?*

Josh: *Never mind, Talked 2 Jeff & Ari. I'll call u 2morrow, dude. Taking Lynda home.*

Holy hell, our circle of friends is a crazy bunch. I looked up to see my girl walking toward the truck. She jumped in, leaned over, and kissed the shit out of me.

"What was that for?" I asked, nearly breathless.

"That was for booking a room at The Driskill Hotel, for loving me, for never giving up on me when I was so stupid, and for being patient with this whole baby thing."

"I love you, sweetheart. Now, what the hell is going on with Heather?"

Ellie sat back in her seat and sighed. "Fuck a duck. Where do I begin?"

CHAPTER FORTY-FIVE

ELLIE

By the time we pulled up to The Driskill Hotel, I was emotionally exhausted. This had been such a crazy night. Earlier at the club, I corned Ari in the bathroom, and I'd told her I wouldn't let her leave until she explained what was going on. I was overjoyed when she told me she was pregnant. I'd truly felt happy for her and Jeff, but at the same time, my heart had broken in two. *Why am I not getting pregnant?* I'd already made an appointment with Dr Wyatt, Ari's doctor, and was planning on talking to him about it.

Maybe everyone was right. I just needed to push this from my head and not worry about it. *If it's meant to be, it's meant to be. But what if I'll never be a mother?* Maybe God thought I would make a terrible mother since I had no example of a real mom growing up.

I felt the tears building in my eyes. *No, I'm not going to go there.* I looked over at Gunner as he parked the truck in front of the valet. He jumped out and gave his normal this-is-my-girl speech to the poor kid who just kept looking at the truck and me.

Wait for it...

"Sir, you're talking about the truck, right?"

Gunner looked over at me and winked. "Both."

***

When we got up to the room, Gunner opened the door, and lifted me up and carried me in. Then, he oh so gently laid me down on the bed. He leaned down and softly kissed my lips. Before he pulled away, he grabbed my lower lip with his teeth and let out a moan.

"I'm going to go run you a hot bath, Baby."

I smiled as the thoughts started running through my head. I would never get tired of making love to Gunner in a bed, on the floor, in a bathtub, on a beach. I let out a sigh. Each and every time, he'd made me feel so special.

My smile grew as I thought about the last time we were in this hotel and how he made me feel on our wedding night.

"I hope you're smiling because you're thinking of me," Gunner said in a low Southern drawl.

I felt my body reacting to his voice instantly.

"Yes sir, it most certainly is."

I sat up and pulled my knees to my chest. Just the sight of him standing in the doorway with nothing but a towel wrapped around his waist was enough to drive me insane.

I lifted my eyebrows at him as he gave me that damn panty-melting smile of his. His dimple still gives me butterflies in my stomach. *I love him so much.*

"Drew…"

"Yeah, baby?"

"I'm gonna need you to take that towel off."

Gunner let out a small laugh and raised his eyebrows up at me. "Is that so? What are your intentions once I remove the towel, Mrs. Mathews?"

God, I can't believe how much I want him. I was about to explode. I'd never imagined that loving and wanting someone so much could be this magical and special.

"That, Mr. Mathews, is something for me to know and you to find out," I said with a wink.

Gunner had been playing with Matthew the other day, every time Gunner had asked Matt a question, every response Matt had given was, "That's for me to know and you to find out, Gunner." Gunner absolutely adored Matt and laughed every time Matt had said it to him.

Gunner threw his head back and laughed. Then, he slowly walked over to me. He reached out his hand, and I took it as he helped me stand up. My heart was beating a mile a minute and I felt like I could hardly breathe. He reached over to the iPod deck next to the bed and hit play. When I looked down, I saw his iPod in the deck. *When did he put that in there?*

Faith Hill's "It Will Be Me" started to play, and I looked back up and smiled at him. My true romancer.

"Dance with me, baby," he said.

"Always."

As Gunner took me into his arms, he started to sing along with Faith. It felt like my knees were going to give out, and I could feel his arms tighten around me. I loved this man so much that it hurt my heart in such a good way. I closed my eyes and just listened to his sweet voice sing to me as he moved against my body so closely. We didn't even have to be making love for it to feel like we were one.

After the song was over, I didn't even pay attention to what song came on next as Gunner started to lift my shirt over my head. I'd had no idea that he'd planned on staying here, so I was secretly thanking my lucky stars that I'd worn my new beige-and-black lace bra and panties that Ari and I had bought yesterday while shopping for her wedding dress.

He slowly started to take off my shorts, moving them down my body. As he bent over he placed soft kisses along my stomach, then from one hip to the other, and then on my upper thigh. My whole body trembled with his touch.

He stood up, and his eyes traveled up and down my body. Every time he looked at me, it was like he was seeing me for the first time. The passion in his eyes caused me to tremble again.

"God, Ells, you're perfect. You're so beautiful and so perfect. I love the way your body reacts to my touch. I could stand here, staring at you for hours, and still never get enough of you."

Oh my.

He took my hand, leading me into the bathroom.

"Your bath is getting cold."

Gunner led me into the bathroom and turned me around so that I was facing the mirror. He stood behind me while he unclasped my bra and slowly took it off. He placed kisses all over my back while I watched him in the mirror. Then, his hands moved down my body to remove my panties.

I already felt so close to having an orgasm. *How does he make me feel this way when he's hardly touched me?* I closed my eyes as he moved his hands softly back up my body. Then, I felt his body pressed up against mine, and my eyes flew open. My blue eyes captured his in the mirror. We just stared at one another.

"I love you, Ellie, more than life itself."

"I love you, too, Drew, more than you'll ever know."

He turned me around and kissed me with so much passion that every ounce of doubt and worry about a baby just melted away. It was just him and me…together. All we needed was each other, and if we were blessed to have a baby someday, it would just be a bonus.

As Gunner led me over to the bath-tub, he got in first, and then I followed. Just lying there, with my body up against his in the hot water, was the most relaxed I'd been in months.

The way he stroked his hands all over my body just about had me begging him for relief. He slowly moved his hand down between my legs. *Holy hell,* His finger tips were like magic. He spread open my legs even more as his fingers entered by body. I threw my head back against his chest and let myself go.

I finally came back down from one of the most intense orgasms ever.

Gunner whispered in my ear,

"I'm going to make love to you now, Ellie."

"Okay." *Jesus.* After that one word came out of my mouth, I wanted to die, but it was the only word my brain could think to say.

Gunner helped me out of the bathtub. While he dried me off, he continued laying kisses all over my body. He picked me up and carried me to the bed where we spent one of the most amazing nights of my life making love to each other. I wasn't sure how he was able to do it, but he gave me two more orgasms. He made love to me so slowly and so beautifully that I found myself praying to God that this night would never end.

***

I woke up to the sun shining on my face. I grabbed a pillow and pulled it over my head. *No!* I just wanted to sleep in for once. I moaned as I rolled over and reached out for Gunner.

Nothing.

I sat up and looked around as I called out his name. I saw his clothes were gone, so he must have gotten up earlier. I stretched out and could feel every muscle I had used last night. I smiled at how I was a little bit sore. I'd never been on top as much as I was last night...or when Gunner woke me up at 4 a.m for another round.

Just then, I heard a key slide to unlock the door. I pulled up the covers over my chest as I watched the door open.

Gunner walked in, and he smiled as soon as he saw me. "Good morning, baby. How did you sleep?"

Sitting up straight, I purposely let the covers fall away from my chest. The look on his face caused me to let out a small laugh.

"I slept very well, thank you. Better than I have in ages!"

"Good. You're gonna need your energy for today."

When I raised my eyebrows at him, he laughed.

"Not for that, but I'm more than ready if you want to skip this yummy breakfast I just bought for you."

Laughing I reached over and grabbed my shirt, and I slipped it over my head. Gunner sat down next to me and pulled out a bowl full of fresh fruit, a strawberry-banana yogurt, and an orange juice. This was my favorite breakfast as of late.

***

I was shocked at how fast I ate everything. I must have been starving.

"So, what's the plan for today? I see you thought this through" I nodded my head toward the overnight bag he'd brought in and set down on the chair.

"I thought a trip out to Enchanted Rock sounded like fun. Are you up for some hiking and climbing today, babe?"

"Yes! Oh my gosh, I love Enchanted Rock." I reached over and gave him a hug.

"I already called Jeff and Ari, and they're down for it as well. At first, I thought it would just be you and me, but since that bastard brother of yours stole my idea, and they're here as well, it might be fun having them go with us."

"Sounds perfect. One thing though, can I ask Heather if she'd like to come? I feel so bad for her, Gunner. She's been through so much, and I'd never seen her cry so much as she did last night. I hate that she keeps calling herself a whore. God, it just tears me up. I knew something was wrong. I just knew it."

"Of course, ask her. My heart hurts for her. She deserved to have her first time with someone she truly loved."

"Yeah...and she doesn't even remember it, Gunner. That's what makes me so sad. Then Josh came and found out the next day. He must have been so heartbroken. Do you think things will ever be the same between them?"

"I'm not sure, baby. He and Lynda seem to be getting closer and closer. Although, I don't know how he puts up with her ass. She might be my cousin, but holy shit, she's demanding and treats him like shit. I never thought Josh would end up with someone like that."

I shook my head as I looked at Gunner. *Shit, I'm so lucky he never gave up on me.*

Reaching down into my purse, he pulled out my cell and handed it to me. "Call her, Ells. She needs her friends right now. Then, get dressed. Jeff and Ari are meeting us in the lobby in fifteen minutes."

After ten minutes of convincing Heather that she needed this, she finally agreed. I hung up and smiled. Being around friends who loved her would be good for her. Hopefully, we can take her mind off of Josh and Jerry-the-asshole.

***

When we pulled into the state park, Gunner saw Jeff's truck and parked next to it. Ari and Jeff were leaning up against it, and Ari looked so happy. I smiled, knowing that she was going to be a mom soon. June fifteenth was her due date, so it looked like we would be spending our one-year anniversary with our niece or nephew.

When Gunner opened the door, I jumped out of the truck, walked up to Ari and hugged her.

Just then, I heard another voice. *Josh? Fuck a duck. Are you kidding me?* I pulled away from Ari to see Jeff slapping Josh on the back. I glanced at Gunner to see him staring at me with a panicked look on his face.

Turning around, I grabbed Ari and walked her away from the group.

"What the fuck, Ells. What's wrong?"

"Oh my god, what is Josh doing here?" I started to look around the parking lot.

Heather would be here any minute; she was only ten minutes behind us the last time I'd talked to her.

"Jeff invited him. Why?"

"I invited Heather to come along. She's going to freak!"

"Oh Jesus, Mary, and Joseph. Ellie, is she okay? I mean, I called her last night, and she told me everything. My heart is breaking for her. I can't believe she had sex with Jerry-the-fuckwad."

"Never mind that right now. Is Lynda here?"

"No, she couldn't make it."

Just then, I saw Heather pulling up. Ari and I stepped out of the way, so she could park.

"She's gonna be so pissed at you!" Ari said as she raised her eyebrows up at me.

"Me? Why me? Why not you? Y'all invited Josh."

"You invited her, and I'm sure she asked if he was going to be here."

Oh my god. I wanted to kill my BFF so badly at this very moment. "I swear, Ari if you weren't pregnant, I would."

Ari let out a laugh. "Oh, come on, bitch, I can take you, pregnant or not!"

Heather got out of the car and smiled at both of us. Her smile quickly faded when she looked between the two of us.

"What's wrong?"

I looked at Ari and she looked at me. Then, I heard Josh laugh, and Heather looked behind us.

"I'm pregnant!" Ari shouted out.

I just stared at her a what-the-hell look. She glanced at me and shrugged her shoulders.

"What? I panicked, okay?" Ari said with a smile.

Heather seemed confused for a moment.

"Wait...what? You're pregnant, Ari? Oh my god!" She let out a scream and hugged her.

Ari looked at me over Heather's shoulder and made a face that made me laugh out loud. *Only Ari.*

Just then, Josh, Jeff and Gunner walked up. Gunner looked like he was about to puke, Jeff was shocked that Ari had just screamed out to the world that she was pregnant, and Josh couldn't tear his eyes from Heather.

Heather pulled back away from Ari and smiled at her. "How far along are you?"

"Oh. um, two months."

"Wow...early on into it."

"Yeah, well, I wasn't going to say anything to anyone until after the wedding, but y'all are different. I just got too excited, and I couldn't hold it in." Ari shrugged her shoulders and looked at Jeff.

He had a huge smile on his face. My stomach did butterflies, thinking about my brother becoming a daddy. I smiled at him as he grinned and winked back at me.

Heather turned and saw Josh standing there, looking at her. I could tell she was somewhat shocked and mad as hell. She turned to glare at me. I just smiled and shrugged my shoulders.

"So, who wants to hike up a giant ass granite rock?" Gunner said with a smile.

As we all started to head up the trail, Heather grabbed my arm and pulled me back.

"What's he doing here?" Heather said through gritted teeth.

"I didn't know! Jeff and Ari invited him."

"I don't want to see him, Ellie."

"Listen, Heather, I know it upsets you to see him just as I'm sure it upsets him to see you, but we're all friends. You're going to see him when we all get together sooner or later."

Heather let out a sigh and looked down the trail. "Where is the bitch girlfriend of his?"

I shrugged my shoulders.

"Fine. I'm only doing this because I need the fresh air and exercise, but I have no intentions of talking to him."

Heather pushed past me and started to walk up the trail. Gunner stopped and waited for me. By the time I caught up to him, I was fuming mad.

"Sweetheart, what's wrong?"

"Heather. She's what's wrong. She is so messed up in her stupid-ass thinking that she's pushing away the one and *only* person she is ever going to love. She's pissed because he is here, and she won't talk to him. I mean, I love Heather like a sister, Gunner. Does she even realize that she is the one who keeps hurting him?"

Gunner looked at our friends walking down the trail. Jeff and Josh were in the lead, and Ari and Heather were behind them talking.

"Don't worry, Ells. Things have a funny way of working themselves out," Gunner said with a wink.

"I sure as shit hope you're right."

CHAPTER FORTY-SIX

JEFF

I opened the truck door and helped Ari into the truck. After I gave her a kiss, she smiled at me and then looked past my shoulder. When I turned around, Josh was standing at Heather's car, talking to her.

Jesus, those two. I thought Ari and I had acted like idiots, but these two were making us look like love at first sight. I looked back at Ari and leaned into the truck.

"Don't worry, baby. They'll be okay."

Ari gave me a funny look and nodded her head. I shut the door and started to walk around to the driver's side of my truck.

Gunner and Ellie had already left to head back to the ranch. We'd decided we were all going to go to a barn dance tonight. The couple who were hosting the dance were good friends with Garrett. I was surprised that Heather decided to crash at our house since she'd found out that Josh was staying there also.

The drive back home was dead quiet. My princess had fallen fast asleep with her hands on her stomach. Each time I looked over at her, my heart swelled more and more. For some reason, knowing that our child was growing in her body just turned me the fuck on. When I saw a small gravel dirt road coming up, I smiled. I turned down the road and drove a few miles until I found an open field. While my truck drove over the bumpy field, Ari woke up.

"Holy hell, where the fuck are you going? See, I knew it. I knew if I fell asleep, you'd get lost. I just knew it."

I started to laugh as I looked over at the love of my life, who was now carrying the next love of my life. I pulled up under a large Oak tree, turned off the truck and looked at her.

She glanced around and then turned back to me. The smile that spread across her face would have dropped me to my knees if I had been standing up.

"You horny-ass bastard," she said with a wink. "How far from home are we?"

"Not far, but Josh and Heather will be there, and I want you...now."

"Oh yeah? How bad do you want me?"

"Pretty fucking bad…enough to turn down a damn gravel road, trespass on someone's property, and risk getting caught making love to my future wife."

The next thing I knew, Ari jumped out of the truck and looked at me with a smile that had my stomach knotting up. She lifted up her finger and motioned for me to come toward her.

So, she wants to play, huh? I opened the door, slowly got out, and started to stretch.

"Oh man, this place is perfect for cows or horses. I wonder how many acres it is. Hmm, why the hell isn't it fenced?"

Ari looked around and then she started to walk over to me. It was everything I could do to act like I was checking out this ranch. When she stopped right before she got to me, I turned to face her.

"Oh damn, you're good," she said before she spun around and took off running into the open field.

It didn't take long for me to catch up to her. I grabbed her and picked her up while she yelled for me to put her down.

As I put her down, she slowly turned around to face me.

"Be careful, babe. I don't want anything to happen to you or the baby."

She stared up into my eyes and smiled.

"Take me under that giant-ass tree before we both want some food again!"

I laughed when she jumped up and wrapped her legs around me. I brought her back over toward the truck, showering her with kisses the whole way.

After I slowly let her down, I reached into the backseat of my truck to pull out the quilt that Emma had insisted I keep in the truck at all times. I was beginning to think that she and Garrett were masters of fooling around in other places besides their bed.

Ari threw her head back and laughed. "Damn, I love Emma and Garrett. I bet those two were hot and heavy in their day."

I laughed and laid the blanket out on the flattest, softest area of grass I could find. I sat down and leaned up against the tree. Ari gave me a crooked smile and came over to sit down on my lap.

"Hmm…this feels familiar," She said with a wink.

I looked around and then back at her. "It's a good thing there are no horses around this time. I'd kick your ass in another race."

The way she laughed caused my dick to get even harder. I gently rolled her off my lap, slowly laying her down on the blanket.

"Ari, I'm gonna make love to you now."

When she bit down on her lip, I let out a small moan. *Son of a bitch, the things this girl does to me.*

I took her mouth with mine and never stopped kissing her the whole time we made love.

***

We wrapped ourselves up in the quilt and stayed there for a bit talking. We talked about the wedding, the baby, the wedding some more, and horses. I loved my life so much, and in that moment I thanked God for giving me such a blessing.

Then, I thought about how I was going to tell Ellie that our mother had called again, saying that she wanted us to come visit her so she could apologize. Quickly, I pushed that last thought out of mind.

I kissed Ari's head and gave her a hug.

"We better go. I'm sure Josh and Heather are probably going out of their fucking minds, wondering why we dared to leave them alone."

***

We got dressed, jumped back into the truck, and got back on the road. Ari talked nonstop, and I just smiled the whole way. My baby was happy, and that made me happy as hell. Now, I just had to get her to stop talking about going riding. I was scared to death that she would have another accident.

"I'm gonna ride, Jeff, I can't live my life scared to move, and you shouldn't want me to."

"I don't want you to, baby. It's just, god Ari, if anything ever happened to you or the baby, I would never forgive myself. If I could, I'd put your ass in a bubble and lock you away for the next seven months."

"Ha-ha, very funny. It's going to be fine. I promise to stick to the older mares or Big Roy."

"Big Roy, just stick with him."

Ari laughed and grabbed my hand.

"Okay, babe, I'll only ride Big Roy."

***

When we pulled up to the house, Heather and Josh were talking, sitting next to each other on the steps. *That has to be a good sign.* Heather stood up and gave us a total go-to-hell look. *Okay...maybe that isn't such a good sign.*

"Where the hell have you two been?" Heather asked.

Ari walked up to her and smiled.

"Sorry, y'all. Jeff had to make a quick pit stop."

"Yeah, I'm sure he did," Josh said as he punched Jeff in the arm. "Horny bastard."

"Oh my god, Josh. Really?" Heather said as she started to follow Ari into the house.

"Dude, am I right?"

I smiled and winked at him.

"See, I know you. It's about damn time you got here though. I was running out of stuff to talk to Heather about."

Heather turned around and gave Josh the finger before she walked inside.

"Still nothing?" I asked.

"No, to be honest, I'm not really trying anymore. I mean, I'm with Lynda now, and I'm just trying to get back to being friends with her. That's all. It doesn't have to be awkward for any of us, like it was earlier today."

"Josh, hold on a second." I grabbed his arm, pulling him aside.

"You have to know that Heather is absolutely devastated about what happened. From what Ari told me, she only slept with Jerry that one time. She has this crazy fucked-up thinking about letting you in and then you leaving her like her parents left her."

Josh looked down at the ground and then back up to me. His eyes glazed over, and I knew he was fighting back tears.

"I can't do it, Jeff. When I walked in and saw that guy there, what happened between them hit me hard. I knew in that moment that I couldn't do it anymore. She's so worried about me leaving her, but it's her who left me, Jeff. I need someone in my life that's going to trust me and not worry all the time if I'm going to cheat or leave her or whatever other fears she might have. I can't do it. I'm doing most of the business at my dad's now, and I really think I could make this business grow even more. I need to concentrate on that, and Heather needs to work on finishing school. I think we are on the paths we are meant to be on."

I looked at him and shook my head. "Do you really believe that load of shit you just spit out, dude?"

Josh sighed and turned to walk into the house. "I have to, Jeff. It's the only way I can get up every day and move on."

Ari and Heather were in the kitchen, laughing, and of course, talking about what to wear to tonight's barn dance. I smiled when I saw Ari leaning up against the counter. She looked beautiful. Her skin looked like it was glowing, and her smile lit up the whole room. I was going to have to keep her pregnant often because she was even more beautiful carrying my child.

Josh and I sat in the living room and talked about the wedding. When I looked up, my breath was taken away. Ari was standing there, wearing a Longhorn T-shirt, blue jean shorts, and a pair of Longhorn cowboy boots. I let my eyes travel up and down her body.

Fuck me. She's so damn beautiful.

"Those shorts are too short, Ari." I tried to hide my smile when she raised her eyebrows at me.

"Um, no, they're not. Sorry, I'm gonna wear the shit out of this stuff until I can't fit into it anymore." She gave me a wink and came over to sit on my lap.

I looked into the kitchen and saw Heather getting out a Diet Coke from the fridge. Then, I glanced over at Josh, who must have seen her the same time I did.

I almost felt like I should walk over and shut his mouth for him. Heather had on a white tank top, blue jean shorts, and a pair of pink cowboy boots. How two girls can wear just simple shirts and shorts and look so good was beyond me.

"Close your mouth, Josh, unless you want to catch flies," Ari said.

Josh snapped his head over to Ari and looked dazed for a moment or two. Just then, his cell phone went off. *Ah, the bitch must have some kind of radar, she sensed him looking at Heather.*

Josh pulled out his phone and looked at it, frowning

There was no way in hell he was happy with Lynda. I could tell just by his reaction to her call. She was fucking nuts, jealous as hell, and I had a funny feeling she was playing around behind Josh's back.

He got up and walked outside before he answered it. I looked at Ari who, was also frowning. She stood up when Heather walked into the living room.

"Y'all ready to go?" I am *so* in the mood to go to a barn dance," Heather said as she smiled at Ari and me.

"Well then, let's go. I talked to Gunner a little bit ago, and he and Ellie will just meet us there."

***

By the time we got to the barn dance, Heather and Josh seemed to be getting along as friends. I even heard them laugh a few times. Ari looked over at me and smiled. I knew what she was thinking, and I was a little less optimistic.

As we walked toward the barn, I saw Garrett and Jack were talking to a couple of older guys, and Emma and Grace were laughing with a group of women. Gunner came walking out of the barn with three beers in his hand while Ellie carried two. Gunner handed me one first and then gave one to Josh. Ellie tried to hand one to Heather.

"No, thanks. I'm only drinking Diet Coke tonight," Heather said.

Ari let out a laugh and looked at Heather.

"You're such a good friend to only drink soda because I can't drink!"

Heather smiled just a little. "Not really, sweets. I stopped drinking last summer."

Josh's head snapped up to look at Heather, who was now looking down at the ground.

Garrett walked up and slapped Gunner on the back. "I can tell you that if I had all these beautiful women standing around me, I sure as shit wouldn't be standing out here, all just staring at each other."

"You heard the man. Take me in there and swing me around that dance floor, Jeff, before I find me another cowboy to do it," Ari said with a wink.

"Yes, ma'am," I said as I took Ari's hand and led her into the barn.

Just as we walked in, Jason Aldean's "When She Says Baby" started up. I spun Ari around before we took off two-steppin'. I'd never been with a girl who could dance to every kind of music out there. *Girl sure as hell knows how to two-step.*

I looked over to see Gunner and Ellie laughing as they danced right by us. Gunner gave me a wink and then he leaned down and kissed the shit out of my baby sister. *Bastard.*

Then, I saw Jack and Grace. I smiled when I thought about how happy Gunner was to have his parents living on the ranch. The plan was for Gunner and Ellie to finish building their house, and then Jack and Grace were going to move into the cabin. Jack seemed so happy and at peace, and I knew he loved working with Gunner on the ranch.

"Do you see Garrett and Emma dancing?" Ari shouted.

I shook my head and looked around. Just as I spotted them, Garrett was spinning Emma around. They looked so damn happy. I glanced down at Ari, and she smiled. I knew she was thinking the same thing I was.

"Do you think they still keep a quilt in their truck?" Ari asked before she started to laugh.

I threw my head back and laughed along with her. "I bet they do, baby. I bet they do!"

***

After two hours of dancing, drinking, and laughing my ass off listening to Garrett and a few other old timers talking, Josh, Gunner, and I were sitting at a table looking out on the dance floor.

Ari, Ells, and Heather were all dancing to Chris Cagle's "Let There Be Cowgirls." *Damn.* My dick was getting hard just watching Ari. I loved the way she threw her head back every time she laughed or the way her damn body moved to the beat of the song. I had to adjust myself and look away. I glanced over at Gunner and had to smile. It was a good thing that bastard was married to my sister, or I'd be kicking his ass right now because of the way he was looking at her.

I looked over at Josh. Poor stupid bastard was just staring at Heather out on the dance floor. I really felt bad for him, but I didn't really know what to do for those two.

"How are the wedding plans coming along?" Gunner shouted in my ear.

I rolled my eyes and shook my head. *Holy hell, the wedding plans.* I cringed, just thinking about it.

"Fine."

Gunner and Josh both started laughing.

"Just fine? Come on, dude. You can give us more than that," Gunner said.

I let out a sigh and looked around. Ari's parents weren't there, but I swore I wouldn't put it past her dad to have spies follow my ass around.

Josh got up and moved to the other side of me. "What the fuck are you looking around for?" Josh said as he looked around. "Is it top-secret shit?"

"I'm just putting this out there; I wouldn't put anything past Ari's dad. I can't tell you how many times that man has threatened my life. He refuses to let us pay for any part of the wedding because according to him, 'His baby girl will get the wedding of her dreams.' I'm responsible for the honeymoon though. If I don't make it special, he has threatened to cut off my dick."

Josh and Gunner both laughed again.

"It's not funny. Fucker scares the shit out of me."

Josh took a long drink of his beer. "As he should. I swear if I ever have a girl, I'm gonna threaten any man who comes in contact with her until I'm too old to know any better."

"I gotta agree with Josh. I'd be the same damn way if it came to my girl," Gunner said.

I shrugged my shoulders. "I guess. Anyway, the plans are going good. I think they're pretty much done with it all. Jenny is amazing, and she's really done another fabulous job with everything."

Gunner said, "I tell ya what. Ari couldn't have picked a better place. When I took Ells to the Mansion at Judges' Hill for her birthday last year, it was breathtaking."

"Breathtaking? Dude...marriage has turned you into a pussy," Josh said with a laugh.

"Fuck you, Josh."

I glanced back out onto the dance floor and sat up a little. It looked like some asshole was trying to pull Ellie away from Ari and Heather. Ari looked over at me, and before I could even react, I heard Gunner.

"Motherfucker."

Gunner jumped up and started to make his way out to the middle of the barn.

Jack must have noticed it, too, because he stepped in front of Gunner, giving me enough time to get around them to get to Ellie and the asshole.

"Dude, I suggest you take your hands off my sister now," I said.

The drunk pecker-head let go of Ellie's arm and looked me up and down.

"You about to do something about it?"

I let out a laugh. "I think you'd rather deal with me than her husband, asshole."

"Yeah, well, I think I'll take my chances." He started to reach for Ellie again as she took a step back.

I saw Gunner coming up on my right side.

"Gunner, don't do it."

It was too late. Before I could even stop him, Gunner turned the guy around and punched him square in the face. The poor bastard took two steps back and fell on his ass.

Gunner walked up to him and bent down.

"If you ever so much as look at my wife again, I'll make sure you hurt for months."

Ellie walked over and grabbed Gunner by the arm, pulling him away. The douchebag looked up at me.

I just shrugged my shoulders.

"I told you, dude."

CHAPTER FORTY-SEVEN

ARI

"What fun am I going to have, Ells? I can't even drink. How fun is a bachelorette party when the damn bride can't even drink?"

Ellie rolled her eyes and looked over at Heather. "Heather isn't drinking either, and I already told you I won't."

"Amanda will. You know that red-headed bitch will drink enough for all four of us plus some."

Heather laughed, and Ellie sat down on the sofa, letting out a long sigh.

We were staying at the cottage on my parents' property and the guys were at my parents' place on the lake. I was dying to know what they had in store for Jeff's bachelor party.

I reached over and grabbed my cell phone only to have Ellie snag it out of my hand.

"No! You're not calling him, Ari. You have called him three times in the last hour."

"Don't you want to know what they're up to tonight? What if girls are there?"

Amanda piped in, "Oh, Jesus H. Christ, Ari, stop worrying so much. It's like Ellie's bachelorette party all over again. Now, I haven't been out in months, Brad's mother is driving me fucking crazy, and all I want to do is drink myself under a table and dance with a good-looking guy, who I'm hoping will at least grab my ass once while we dance."

I just sat there and stared at Amanda. I glanced over at Ellie and Heather, and they were pretty much looking at Amanda in the same way.

"Holy hell, Mandy, married life sure is treating you well," Ellie said.

Heather let out a giggle.

Amanda sighed and sat down in the chair across from me.

"I think I got married too soon."

"What?" Ellie, Heather, and I all said at the same time. "Amanda, are you and Brad having troubles?"

Amanda shook her head, fighting back tears. "No, Ari, we aren't having any troubles. Things have never been better."

"Then, why the hell would you say you got married too soon?"

"Because if I wasn't married yet, Brad's bitch of a douche-twat mother wouldn't be bugging me to have a baby. She wouldn't be taking me to lunch once a week and giving me advice on how to get pregnant. She acts like I don't fucking know how to get pregnant."

We all started laughing, and Amanda ended up joining in on the laughter.

"Come on, Ari, let's go. I promise the evening is not going to be filled with naked men or anything that will make your pregnant ass, or Jeff's ass for that matter, have to worry."

"Fine, let's go." I said.

Amanda jumped up and started clapping. Heather rolled her eyes, and Ellie walked over and reached out her hand to help me up. As Amanda and Heather walked out the door first, Ellie held me back.

"Are you okay, Ari? You feeling okay, sweets?"

I let out a sigh and felt the tears building in my eyes.

"Were you scared, Ells?"

"To get married? Yeah, Ari, I was scared to death."

"This is all I've ever wanted, Ellie. I've only ever wanted to be with him, to wake up next to him every morning, and to go to sleep next to him every night. I want to have babies, have fights, make up, and kiss in the rain with him. He is the only one I want to do those things with. So why am I so damn scared? I mean, I'm having his baby in six months. This should be nothing!"

Ellie smiled that smile only she can give me, and I was calmed within seconds.

"Baby, you're getting married in two days to the love of your life, and you're carrying his baby. Smile, baby girl. You're going to be the most beautiful bride ever. You won't even need makeup because that pregnancy glow fits you perfectly."

I slammed my body into Ellie and hugged the shit out of her. "I love you, Ellie Mathews. I love you so much."

"I love you, too, Ari. Come on, let's go have some fun. By the way, I sent Gunner a text a little bit ago. They're staying at the lake house and playing poker. He promised that there will be no women, so don't worry. They'll probably behave better than us."

***

We headed out to dinner first, and I never laughed so hard in my life. It was so nice to be with my three very best friends.

"Oh god, I love Maudie's so damn much. I could eat here every day." Amanda said as she leaned back and put her hands on her stomach.

I smiled at her because she truly looked happy. As much as she had bitched about her monster-in-law she was so incredibly happy with Brad.

I thought back to the night of her wedding. It was the first time Jeff and I had made love. The memories flooded my brain, causing me to drift away from everyone.

Setting my hands on my stomach, I closed my eyes. I was getting married in two days, and I was fifteen weeks pregnant. Although I was barely showing a bump, my wedding dress had to be altered just a little.

I looked up at Ellie, and she smiled at me. My heart was breaking for her because I knew how much she wanted to have a baby. She was such a damn good friend because she never showed how sad she was.

Just then, I felt a flutter in my stomach. *Butterflies?* There it went again. Could it be?

"Holy fuck!" I shouted out.

Ellie stood up quickly spilling her water all over Heather. Heather jumped and hit the table, her tea spilt everywhere. Amanda pushed back her chair, as she laughed her ass off, and I just sat there.

"Fuck a duck, Ari, what the hell is wrong with you?" Ellie said. She was trying to wipe water off of her while staying out of the way of the poor waitress cleaning up the rest of the spilled water and tea.

"I think I just felt the baby!" I said. I just sat there with my hands on my stomach.

"*What?*" All three of my friends, and our waitress shouted out at once.

"But you're only fifteen weeks pregnant. I thought that didn't happen until after sixteen weeks." The ever-accurate Heather pointed out.

I just stared at her.

Ellie came running over and got down on her knees.

"Oh my god...oh my god...oh my god. Move your hand, I want to feel my niece...or nephew!"

Amanda started laughing. Brad's mother was an OB, and Amanda had started working for her part time, helping out on days she didn't have classes.

"Ells, I hate to tell you this, but you're not going to be able to feel the baby yet. Only Ari can at this early stage."

Ellie shot Amanda a look that should have brought Amanda to her knees. "Well, shit, I want to feel it. What does it feel like?"

"It felt like fluttering or bubbles in my stomach. You know like when you have gas moving through your stomach."

"Oh Christ, how romantic, Ari," Amanda said as she rolled her eyes.

"It's the only way I know how to describe it." I reached for my phone and hit Jeff's number.

"I'll be right back," I said as I got up and headed outside.

"Hey, baby, you having fun?" Jeff asked.

"I miss you," I said in as much of a seductive voice as I could.

"Hold on a second."

I heard Jeff say he was going outside for a second, and I had to smile.

"Jesus, Ari, only you can make me go hard in an instant. Want to sneak away and meet somewhere?"

"Yes!"

"Where are you?"

"Maudie's on Lake Austin Boulevard."

"Give me fifteen minutes, baby, and I'll be there."

"Okay, hurry, but be careful driving."

I walked back into the restaurant. The spilled drink mess had been cleaned up, and the girls were all eating from a giant piece of chocolate cake.

When I sat down, all three of them looked at me.

"He's coming to get you, isn't he?" Heather said with a wink.

Damn, these girls know me too well. I just smiled and took a sip of my water.

"Ugh, you horny-ass bitch. If pregnancy does this to you, sign me the fuck up," Amanda said as she smiled at me.

"Are y'all mad?" I asked.

Amanda let out a sigh and sat back. "I'm actually kind of relieved. I know I was all wanting a guy to grab my ass while I danced the night away. Honestly though, with Brad being at his parents' lake house, there's a really good book I want to read, and I would so love the peace and quiet in the house."

"I really am so exhausted from finishing up this semester. All I really want to do is go home and soak in a hot bath," Heather said as she winked at me.

Ellie was staring at her cell phone with a huge-ass grin on her face. When she looked up, we were all staring at her.

"What does that overly romantic-bastard husband of yours have planned?"

Ellie smiled. "He said he's right behind Jeff, and he wants to take me on a carriage ride downtown."

"Good god, where did this man come from? I mean really, he needs to teach a damn class on this shit," Amanda said as she fanned herself.

Ellie and Amanda laughed.

Amanda looked down at her phone and grinned. Heather, you feel like dropping me off at the lake house? Looks like Brad's feeling a little lonely."

Heather giggled as she dug out her keys. "No problem." Has everyone left him all alone?"

"I guess so. He said Gunner and Jeff just left, and Josh was outside on the deck, probably making plans to leave as well."

Heather's smile faded for one brief second before it she smiled again.

"Okay. Well then, let's head out, and I'll drop you off. Are you girls okay with us leaving you until your men get here?" Heather asked.

She and Amanda both stood up and started to hug and kiss Ellie and me.

"We'll be fine. They're only a few minutes away, and we can talk wedding stuff," Ellie said as she looked over at me and winked.

***

After Heather and Amanda left, I looked over at Ellie, who was smiling at me like a damn fool.

"What has you so full of glee, except for the fact that your hubby is taking you on a carriage ride?"

"You. I'm so glad to see you and Jeff finally happy."

I let out a small laugh. "It sure has been a long bumpy-ass road."

"Yep."

I sighed as a wedding detail crossed my mind.

"Oh shit! I forgot to call Jenny about the bouquets." Panicking, I reached for my cell phone.

Ellie reached over and grabbed my hand.

"She called me earlier. I took care of it. That's what the maid of honor does, you know. Don't worry. It's all taken care of, and they're going to look beautiful."

"You know I would be lost without you, don't you?"

Ellie smiled at me and squeezed my hand. "I would be lost without you, too. I love you, baby."

"I love you, too. In case I haven't told you in a while, that nose piercing is really adorable on you!"

Ellie threw her head back and laughed. Then, she stopped laughing and looked at me.

"Oh my god, you're piercing!"

"Yeah, I know. Dr. Wyatt said I need to have it out no later than twenty weeks, but I already took it out. I actually thought Jeff was going to cry when I told him I was taking it out."

Ellie let out a giggle and rolled her eyes. "He really liked it, huh?"

"Oh yeah, he loved it." I said, moving my eyebrows up and down.

"Eww. Okay, I don't need the visual in my head, thank you very much."

I looked up and saw Jeff and Gunner walking toward us. I smiled, and Ellie turned around.

Jeff came up to me, leaned down, and kissed me. Then took my hand, pulled me up and just turned, leading me out.

He turned back around and looked at Gunner.

"You got the bill, right, bro?"

Gunner just laughed. "Y'all have fun!"

CHAPTER FORTY-EIGHT

JEFF

The Wedding Day......

Gunner and I walked around, following Jenny. Everything was set up and ready to go and I was in awe at how beautiful everything was. The Mansion at Judges' Hill really was the perfect choice for the wedding.

We had the rehearsal dinner here last night, and Ari had never stopped smiling. Her dad had even pulled me to the side and finally told me how happy he was we were getting married. Of course, he had to end it with a threat, saying that not only did I have to make Ari the happiest woman on earth, but I also better be the best damn father to his grandchild.

No pressure.

The reception room looked amazing. Ari and Jenny did an amazing job. I looked around and almost felt like I couldn't breathe. In two hours, I was going to marry the girl of my dreams.

Gunner slapped me on the back, bringing me out of my thoughts. "Dude, I'm gonna assume by the smile on your face you're thinking about your future bride."

My smile grew as I looked at Gunner and Jenny. Jenny smiled back and then looked at her watch.

Immediately, she picked up her cell phone and made a call. "Those flowers were supposed to be here by 9 a.m. Yeah, you better be on your way." She hit end and then looked back up at me.

"No worries. It's for the reception. Susan wanted fresh, as in same day fresh flowers for the tables."

I rolled my eyes and shook my head. We walked out to the courtyard. It looked perfect.

"Okay, so if everything looks good to you, Jeff, I need to go and check on the bride. I actually just saw her peeking out the window up-stairs."

I hadn't seen her since yesterday morning when Ellie and Heather got to the cottage and practically dragged Ari away, kicking and screaming. They stayed here last night because Sue was worried that Ari wouldn't be here on time.

I scanned the windows until my eyes captured hers. She smiled and waved at me, and I waved back. Her hair was pulled up, but I couldn't really see how it was styled. No matter what, she looked beautiful. Then, I saw Ellie as she shot me a dirty look and pulled Ari away from the window.

Gunner laughed as he slapped me yet again on the back.

"Damn, dude, you're one lucky son of a bitch. She looks beautiful."

I turned and looked at Gunner as we started to walk back inside. Josh and Brad were talking to Sue and Mark while Matt was climbing all over Josh. I smiled, knowing my little buddy was so happy today.

We had told him last night that Ari had a baby growing in her stomach, and he was full of questions. *I love that kid so damn much.* As soon as Matt saw me, he came running up to me. So I bent down so he could run into my arms.

"Jeff! Are you going to marry Ari today?" Matt asked with a huge smile on his face.

Gunner reached over and rubbed his hand on top of Matt's head. Matt looked up at Gunner and smiled the biggest smile ever.

"I'm gonna stand next to you, Gunner, and help you be the bestest man!" Matt said as he jumped up and down in my arms.

"I know you are, buddy. I couldn't do it without you, you know that, right?"

"Yeah, I know. That's what Ari said, too. She said you would mess it up alone. Gunner, I'll help you to not mess it up, so you're not an assmole like Jeff."

I had to give Gunner credit for not laughing. Matt had quickly learned that we all laughed when he said assmole, so he said it all the time now. Unfortunately, when he said it, he was usually saying I was the assmole. That seemed to please Mark...a lot.

"Ari said that huh?" Gunner asked.

Matt nodded with a huge smile on his face.

Sue walked up to us, reaching out of Matt. "Matt, come on babe, we need to let the boys finish getting dressed and ready, and you need to get into your new clothes that we bought just for today."

Matt turned back at me, smiling as he hugged me. "I'm so glad you're going to be my brother. I love you, Jeff."

With that, he ran over to Josh and hugged his leg. Josh leaned down and returned the hug as he glanced at me. Josh had really taken to Matt. Ari had told me that Josh had even started stopping by the house, so he could play video games with Matt because I had not been able to since we moved.

Gunner let out a sigh and looked at me. I took one last look around the giant ballroom that had been turned into a winter wonderland. I sucked in a deep breath.

Holy fuck, I'm getting married.

"Gun, were you scared?"

Gunner smiled at me.

"Let's go for a walk outside."

Once we got outside, I felt like I could breathe again. The day was beautiful, and I was so thankful. With an outdoor wedding, we had all feared having bad weather. *Ya never know what the weather in Austin is going to be like in December.*

Gunner and I sat down on two chairs and didn't talk for about five minutes.

"How much do you love Ari, Jeff?"

I snapped my head over at him and just stared at him. *What the fuck kind of question is that?*

"I love her more than life itself. I wouldn't be able to breathe without her. I wouldn't *want* to breathe without her. It amazes me that she can just look at me from across a room, and I have to catch my breath. The sound of her voice just about brings me to my knees. Her smile... damn, her smile....makes me want to keep her happy every second of the day just so I can see that smile."

Gunner let out a gruff laugh. "That pretty much sums up how I feel about your sister."

Then, he slapped me on the back again and stood up. "You ready to marry the love of your life?"

I looked up at him and smiled. The sense of calm that swept over my body was unreal. I loved Gunner like a brother. The fact that he just eased my panic without even saying a damn word just showed me how lucky I was to have him in my life... and in my sister's life.

I stood up and slapped the living shit out of his back. "Let's do this thing!"

"Fuck! Why the hell did you hit me so hard, you bastard?"

"Because you've been doing it to me for days now. Payback, bro."

Jenny came walking up to us. I could tell by the look on her face that we were about to be told to go get ready.

"Alright, guys, show-time in less than two hours. Let's go. Ari wants to take a walk around before she gets dressed. So help me, Jeff, if you look out a window and see her, I'll break both your legs."

"Wow, does Aaron know you have this side to you, Jen?" I asked.

"Yes, yes, he does. Now, let's go."

I looked up one more time before I walked in, and there Ari was, smiling down at me. I waved to her, and she waved back.

In less than two hours, she would be forever mine.

CHAPTER FORTY-NINE

ARI

I had walked up to the window to see Jeff and Gunner sitting down in the courtyard. For a few minutes, it looked like they weren't talking. *Is Jeff nervous? Maybe he was having second thoughts. Oh shit.*

Just then, I felt that fluttery feeling again. I put my hand to my stomach and smiled. It was the three of us now. For some reason, thoughts of Rebecca popped into my head. Things could have turned out so differently if that baby had been Jeff's.

"He loves you so much. You know that, right?" Ellie said from behind me.

I smiled as I watched Jeff and Gunner together. They both loved each other just like Ellie and I loved each other. I turned to look at my best friend. She was also smiling while she looked down at Gunner and Jeff.

"Thank you, Ellie."

Ellie glanced over at me, still smiling. "For what?"

"Just being you."

Ellie turned and brought me in for a hug. "It's about fucking time this is happening. Now, we just need to work on dysfunctional couple number three."

We both laughed as I hugged her tighter. She pulled away and gave me a smile that melted my heart.

I turned back to the window and saw Jenny talking to Jeff. He looked up at me. We both waved at each other, and my heart started pounding. I put my hands to my stomach and closed my eyes.

I wasn't sure how long I had been standing at the window. When I felt a hand on my shoulder, I turned around only to have my mother take me into her arms as she hugged the living shit out of me.

"Oh my goodness, my baby girl is getting married. I just can't believe it, Arianna. It seems like it was just yesterday when you were ten years old, and you came back from your first bike ride in the new neighborhood. You walked into the kitchen, and your father and I were unpacking dishes, so we could make dinner. You hopped up on the kitchen counter and made an announcement that almost had your father heading to the hospital."

"I don't remember this. What did I say?"

"You looked at us both, and as serious as all get out, you said, 'I found the boy I'm gonna marry someday. So Daddy, you better start saving 'cause I want a big wedding when I marry Ellie's brother.'"

Oh my god, I totally forgotten all about that. I let out a laugh. "Mom, I so remember that now! Daddy told me to dream on, and then he asked what Ellie's brother's name was because he was going to start having him watched." We both busted out laughing.

"Mom, Jeff swears that Daddy has someone following him."

My mother winked at me, and for one brief second, I thought it might actually be true.

"Alright, since you wouldn't put any quotes from the great Katharine Hepburn in your wedding vows, I'm going to give you one before we go and take a look at everything."

"Mom, really, you've been told this obsession with KH is not healthy, right? I mean, I've told you, and I know Daddy has. And our marathon Katharine Hepburn movie night last night…was that really necessary? I've never seen Heather fall asleep so fast in my life."

"Psssh, that girl is exhausted from too much school. At any rate, do you want to hear the quote or not?"

"Fine, I'm sure I've heard it before though."

"Maybe, but you're going to hear it again. 'Love has nothing to do with what you are expecting to get, only with what you are expecting to give which is everything.' Always love each other with everything you've got, Arianna. And never, ever, go to bed mad because I swear you wake up even more pissed off than you were when you went to sleep."

"Mom, that is beautiful…the quote, I mean. I already know about the whole going-to-bed mad and don't worry. Jeff and I have great make-up se..."

"Oh, for the love of all things good in this world, child, stop your mouth right there!"

***

I was in total awe as Ells, Heather, Amanda and I walked around the courtyard. The decorations were kept very simple out here. White chairs were all I wanted. Each row had a simple silver bow tied onto the end chair. Beautiful branch trees that Jeff, Josh, Brad, and Gunner spray-painted with white glitter paint were placed in buckets and covered up with decorative snow. Somehow, Jenny had placed lights at the base of the trees, and the way the lights shined through the trees were breath-taking. The arbor was simply covered in white lights, and it looked amazing. I smiled, thinking about how I would be under that thing in just a few hours.

"What time is it?" I asked.

"We have an hour and a half. Let's keep moving," Jenny said.

When we made our way into the ballroom, I let out a gasp.

"Holy hell Jen. It's…it's..."

"Magical!" Heather, Amanda, and Ellie all said at once.

I turned, looking at them all, and smiled.

"Oh. My. God. That's what I was going to say!" I said as I jumped up and down.

Ellie gave me a wink as she walked farther in. I saw the center piece decorations and smiled. The square glass candle holders were perfect. We had filled them up with fake snow and placed small branches in them. Cotton branches with the cotton still on the branch surrounded each center piece, and I absolutely loved that Josh had come up with the idea to place them on the tables. His uncle had a cotton farm, and he'd sent us a ton of them to use. The glowing votive candles that were lit added just the right touch. It was perfect.

My mother had insisted we use glass china. The white plates with the sliver-edged lining looked stunning on the table. I was so glad that I let her win that battle. The silver napkins even looked amazing.

The tables had white linen on them, but a beautiful silver lace fabric that Ellie had picked out was laid over it. The chairs were all covered in white fabric with silver sashes tied on them, and all I could think about was how long it would take before some drunken idiot spilled something on them.

The wedding party table was unreal. They had placed bigger birch trees in the middle and surrounded the base with white roses and stargazers. I could smell the flowers. I looked up and saw clear ornaments hanging from the trees. They were catching all the light from the candles and chandeliers.

"I can't believe how incredibly beautiful this all looks, y'all. I'm beyond words right now," I said as I started to feel the tears well up in my eyes.

"Don't cry, we'll have to touch up your makeup even more," Amanda said as she took my hand and led me over to the dance floor.

Gunner's dad was talking to the DJ as he handed him a list. I'd left all that up to Jeff. I didn't care what we had as far as music went. My dad had wanted a band, and Jeff had wanted a DJ. I saw that Jeff won that fight.

Then, I saw the table with the cakes. I smiled when I saw Jeff's cake. It was a chocolate cake with a Ford truck on it. As I got closer, I really started laughing. I looked at Ellie, who was frowning.

"Are you kidding me? You let him put that on his cake?" Ellie said as she placed her hands on her hips.

Amanda and Heather busted out laughing.

"I did, Ellie, it's his cake. He wanted a truck on it with the words 'Truck Yeah.' Who am I to say no?" I said while trying to hold back my laughter.

Ellie turned to face at me. "You're all crazy. I hope you know that."

I gave her a wink and walked over to the bride's cake. It was breath-taking. It was a four- tiered white cake with silver accents along the edge and a few crystal snowflakes carefully placed around it. I loved it.

"Ari, are you happy with everything?" Jen asked as she put her arm around me.

"Oh my gosh, Jen, I'm beyond happy. You've really outdone yourself this time. I mean, this is like a fairy-tale wedding."

"Good," Jen said, smiling.

I turned around to see my dad leaning up against the wall. I smiled at how handsome he looked and how happy he seemed to be.

"Oh, Daddy." I ran into his arms and held him tight. "You've made all my dreams come true with this wedding. It must have cost you a small fortune!"

"You, my baby girl, are worth every single dime. After all, you gave me a pretty good advanced notice when you announced your marriage to your mother and me at the age of ten."

I let out a giggle. "Mom brought that up to me a little bit ago."

"He's a good man, Ari, and he loves you very much."

Oh shit. I was going to cry. I was so going to cry.

"Daddy…."

As my voice cracked, he held out his arms. I walked into his arms, and he held me so tight.

"Always know this, Arianna. No man will *ever* love you like I love you. He will never worry about you like I'll worry about you. He will never be able to hurt anyone who hurts you like I will."

I threw my head back and laughed. "Thank you, Daddy. Thank you so much for everything. I know you like Jeff, Daddy. So why do you give him such a hard time?"

"The same reason why he'll do it to some poor sap when he wants to marry your daughter."

"Fair enough, but can I ask you something?"

"Anything."

"You've never had Jeff followed, have you?"

Daddy gave me his Cheshire Cat smile, winked at me, and then turned and walked away.

Oh shit.

"Ari, we really need to get you back up-stairs, so you can get ready." Jenny said.

She practically pulled me away from my stance as I watched my father retreating and laughing.

***

Missy, who was Jenny's new makeup girl, touched up my makeup. She was a quiet little thing. I guessed my threat of any pink anywhere on my face might have scared her just a bit.

Ellie curled a few strands of hair that had lost their curl and then sprayed the shit out of them with hair spray.

"Jesus, Mary, and Joseph, can you please stop, Ellie? I seem to remember you bitching about the hair spray on your wedding day."

"That is true. I was upset about it, but hey, my hair looked beautiful all night, even after my passionate love making on my wedding night."

I turned and looked at her. "Really? You had to go there? I'd be more than happy to tell you about the night before last with your big brother in the living room of the cottage, then in the hallway, then in the shower."

Ellie held up her hands to ears and started to stomp her feet. "Stop! Okay, I'm sorry….eww….don't talk about Jefferson that way. I think I just threw up in my mouth some, you bitch."

"Ari, it's time to put on your dress," Heather said as she stood next to my wedding gown.

I took off the robe I was wearing and looked in the mirror. I was wearing a beautiful vintage silver corset that Ellie and Heather had bought for me. The matching garter belt was a gift from Amanda.

I sat down in the chair, and Ellie helped me put on the blue garter that my mother had worn in her wedding from her mother, that had worn it in hers.

Then I slipped on the silver Manolo Blahnik shoes my mother had insisted I buy.

Finally, I looked in the mirror and smiled. Jeff was going to faint when he saw me in this.

Ellie bumped my shoulder.

"I don't even want to know what you're thinking about right now."

I let out a laugh. "No, you don't.

"Ugh, gesh, Ari." Ellie rolled her eyes.

When we walked over to the wedding dress, I stopped and stared at it. It was intoxicating, and I knew Jeff was going to love it. Designed by Matthew Christopher, it was a strapless A-line dress with a sweetheart neckline and fitted corset that descended into a flared, full chapel-length train. Two different kinds of lace were appliquéd over the silk shantung.

"Are you ready, Ari?" Jenny asked.

As she took down the dress, Ellie grabbed my hands and turned me toward her.

"You're beautiful, and by far, you are the strongest person I know. You're the only person I can say 'fuck you' to, and you laugh. You've got this, baby."

I smiled at her as I nodded my head.

After listening to all four of them yell at each other for two long-ass minutes about watching out for my hair and makeup, the dress was finally on.

I turned and looked into the mirror as Ellie and Heather put on my veil. *Oh my god, I was getting married.*

"Do you think the baby will ask about us getting married after I got pregnant?"

Ellie looked at me. "Umm, that's random as hell, Ari, but no. Even if she does, it doesn't matter. Y'all loved each other when she was made."

I turned to face Ellie. "She?"

"Or he. It doesn't matter as long as she is healthy," Ellie said with a smile.

I turned around and looked at my three best friends. They were all so beautiful. Amanda had her spit-and-fire attitude and that red hair of hers. Sweet Heather, was blessed with her caring heart and soul, beautiful blonde hair and blue eyes, and those boobs. *Lucky bitch.* Then there was Ellie….my soul sister…my other half. With her beautiful blue eyes and brown hair, she was just breath-taking.

They were each dressed in a fitted strapless silver taffeta dress that flared just at the bottom. The beading on the bodice was amazing, and I loved the corset back. The light from all the candles would reflect off their dresses, and I knew it was going to be so damn pretty.

We all just stared at each other.

My mother had brought Matt in to see me before the wedding.

"Ari, you are most beautiful!" Matt said as he smiled up at me.

"I love you, buddy."

Then, I heard a knock on the door. Jenny opened it and then slammed it shut.

"Holy fuck!"

I turned around to see she was white as a ghost.

"What? What's wrong?" I asked.

"Holy fuck!"

We all turned and looked at Matt. *Oh great, at least he won't be saying assmole anymore.*

"I wanna be a mudder-fucking cowboy, just like in Jeff's song."

I had to grab onto the wall, or I would have went straight to the floor.

"I'm going to kill Jefferson for listening to that song around him," Ellie said.

She walked up to the door and opened it.

Then, she immediately slammed it shut.

"Oh, um…shit."

"Would someone please tell me why y'all keep slamming the door shut?" I asked.

"It's Jeff," Ellie and Jenny said at the same time.

"Wait... what?"

Ellie said, "I'll see what he wants. Everyone just needs to keep getting ready. Jen, the flowers?"

Jenny seemed shocked as hell and out of it for a good minute or so. "Yes…right the flowers."

I watched as Ellie opened the door and went out into the hall. I just stared at the door.

What does he want? Did he change his mind? Oh god, what if Rebecca is here? Wait…why would she be here?

The door opened, and Ellie walked in.

"Um, can everyone leave the room for just a few minutes? The groom would like to talk to his bride."

Ellie looked over at me, smiling as she winked.

After everyone was out, including Matt who kept saying he wanted to be a mudder-fucking cowboy, then Jeff walked in the door. He stopped dead in his tracks and just stared at me.

I sucked in a breath of air when I saw him. I'd left what the guys were going to wear up to him, so he'd said he would surprise me. He was dressed in his black tuxedo pants with a platinum herringbone vest and matching platinum tie. He looked breathtakingly handsome.

"Is everything okay, baby?" I asked.

He rushed over to me and took me in his arms. He kissed me like he was never going to kiss me again.

When he finally pulled his lips away from mine, he held me tighter in his arms.

"Jeff, what's wrong?" I asked as I leaned back to look at him.

His eyes were filled with tears.

"I just needed to make sure this wasn't a dream, Ari. I needed to see you. I needed to touch you. I needed to kiss you and tell you how lucky I am to have you in my life. Thank you so much for not giving up on me when I gave you so many reasons to just walk away. I was so lost when you weren't in my life, baby. You literally saved me, Arianna."

I stood there and just stared at him. I was fighting back the tears. I would be so pissed if I started crying right now.

"Jeff, I love you more than life itself. I never thought this day would come. To be standing here in front of you, pregnant with our baby, knowing I get to wake up to you every morning for the rest of my life, I'm so overwhelmed by happiness I can't even think straight. The only thing I can think about is if Matt's going to walk down the aisle, singing about being a mudder-fucking cowboy."

Jeff threw his head back and laughed. He took a step away and looked me up and down.

"You're breath-taking. Do you know that, baby?"

I smiled and let my eyes move up and down his body.

"You look pretty handsome yourself."

Just then, there was a knock on the door. Jeff walked over and opened it.

"What the hell are you doing in here?" my mother asked.

"I'm leaving right now. I just needed to see my beautiful bride and tell her how much I love her." Jeff turned to look at me.

I smiled at him, and my heart just melted with the smile he gave back. *Good Lord, that boy is handsome as hell. Jesus, Mary, and Joseph, how am I going to look at him and say those vows when all I'm thinking about is getting his ass naked?*

My mom and dad walked in as Jeff left the room. My mother let out a gasp when she saw me, and my father had a grin from ear to ear.

"Tu es belle Arianna."

I loved it when my father spoke to me in French.

"Merci, papa, pour dire que je suis beau."

"Oh Arianna, you literally took my breath away when I saw you," my mother said as she walked up and hugged me.

Jenny walked in and smiled.

"So, Matt and Lauren are ready to go. Lauren is beyond thrilled that she gets to be yet another flower girl. She informed me that she knows what to do, so I can leave it up to her."

I let out a laugh. Lauren my little cousin, looked like a princess and acted like it, too. I let her pick out her own dress. *Damn, that girl has good taste. I've taught her well.* It was an elegant silver satin dress with a pin pick-up in the front and a satin bow. The bodice was embroidered with rosettes. It looked perfect on her.

"Ari, it's about that time. Do you need a minute or two with your mom and dad?" Jen asked.

Daddy looked at me and winked. "Hell no, I paid for some good food, and I'm starving. The faster I get her down the aisle, the faster I can sit down and eat."

I just smiled at my father. He didn't want any time alone with me because his ass was afraid he would cry.

"Allez-vous à pleurer papa?" I asked with a wink.

"No, I'm not going to cry. Now, let's walk you down that aisle baby girl."

As everyone came back into the room, bouquets of flowers were passed out. Heather, Amanda, and Ellie had white and silver roses in their bouquets. I still had no idea how they got the roses to be silver, and I didn't care. They were beautiful.

My bouquet was full of stargazer lilies. I smiled when Jenny handed them to me. She winked at me because I was sure she knew I was thinking back to the night Jeff asked me to marry him.

When I started to hear the music play, I walked over to the window.

Holy fuck. There were a ton of people out there. I moved my eyes up until I saw Jeff standing there with Gunner and Matthew. *Holy hell, is it normal for me to be thinking about nothing but having sex with him right now? It must be the whole pregnancy thing....nope, I think this is just me.*

"Ari, are you ready?" Jenny asked.

As I moved down the stairs, I felt like I couldn't breathe. I needed to stop and catch my breath. I must have squeezed my father's arm because he slowed down a bit and looked at me.

"Baby girl, breathe in your nose and out your mouth. Think about nothing but the love you feel for Jeff and that baby growing inside you right now. Never mind all the people; it's just the three of you."

Oh my god. I'm going to cry before I even make it outside.

I bit down on my cheek as hard as I could, but all that did was make my eyes water. *Motherfucker.*

Ellie turned and gave me one last look before she walked outside. The moment she smiled at me, I calmed down. *I got this.*

When my father and I walked out the door, I looked up. The first thing I saw was Jeff. Our eyes met at the same time, and we both smiled. I didn't take my eyes off of him the whole way down the aisle. I heard oh's and ah's, but I held my gaze on his eyes only.

When my father placed my hand in Jeff's, he leaned over, so only Jeff and I could hear him.

"You ever hurt her, and I'll kill you."

Jeff's face went white, and I let out a giggle.

We walked up to the preacher, and Jeff looked over at me.

He leaned down and put his lips to my ear.

"Gunner told me to whisper something romantic to you, but honestly, your dad just scared the shit out of me. I've got nothing right now."

I laughed, and I swore I almost peed my pants.

I knew there was nothing more that this man could ever do to make me happier than I was this very moment.

"Want to know where we're going on our honeymoon?"

"Now, Jeff? You're going to tell me now?"

I looked at Pastor Rob and smiled. Jeff wouldn't tell me where we were going until after the wedding, so why he was telling me now had me baffled.

Jeff looked over at Gunner and gave him a shit-eating grin. Then looked back at me.

"We're going to Paris, baby."

Oh. My. God. Wait... what?

"You bastard!" Gunner said. Then, he looked at Pastor Rob. "Oh sorry, Pastor."

Jeff let out a laugh and looked down at Matt. *Oh no.*

Matt started singing, "I wanna be..."

Gunner bent down really quick and whispered something into Matt's ear. Matt laughed and nodded his head. Gunner stood up and raised his eyebrows at us.

"Um, are y'all ready now?" Pastor Rob asked.

Jeff and I both looked at each other and smiled. At the same time, we both said, "Yes."

CHAPTER FIFTY

JEFF

I sat back and drank my beer while I watched Ari move from person to person, making sure to talk to each guest. I gave up an hour ago and decided my place to be was right here with a beer in my hand, enjoying the view of my beautiful bride.

During the toast earlier, Ari had taken two sips from a small glass of red wine. We planned on telling everyone about the pregnancy when we came back from our honeymoon.

I felt a hard slap on my back and rolled my eyes. *Damn Gunner.* I looked and sat up straighter. It was Mark.

He pulled up a chair next to me and sat down.

He raised his beer toward mine.

"You did it, son."

Son?

"What did I do?"

"You made my little girl the happiest I've ever seen her, and that makes me happy."

"Well, sir, I'm glad to hear that."

"Jeff, don't call me sir. It makes my ass feel old. Call me Mark."

"Mark, it is. She makes me very happy as well, more than she'll ever know."

Mark smiled and glanced to where Ari was talking to Heather. "I still can't believe I'm going to be a grandfather," Mark said as he kept his eyes on his daughter.

I finished off my beer and set it down on the table. "Mark, can I talk to you about something?"

"Of course, Jeff. Please always know that I'm here to talk."

"My father left when Ellie and I were both pretty young. I remember him more than Ellie does, but, I never had an example and of a father figure, and…well, I'm afraid that…." I stopped because I couldn't even form the next words out of my mouth.

Mark looked over at me and put his hand on my shoulder.

"Jeff, I might give you hell all the time, but do you honestly believe that I would ever allow my daughter to marry a man who I didn't think was going to be the best husband for her and father for her kids? I see something in you, son. You have a drive to be the best you can be and a passion for the work that you do. I see the way you look at Arianna, and I have no doubt in my mind that you love that girl with every ounce of your being. You're going to be one hell of a husband and a wonderful father to my grandkids. If you don't, I'll kill you."

I felt the tears building in my eyes…at least, right up to the point when he threatened my life again.

"You do know you've threatened to kill me at least twice today."

Smiling at me, Mark stood up, finished his beer, and set it on the table.

"And I'll probably do it at least two more times before this party is over."

He walked off laughing and slapped some poor lawyer friend of his on the back.

I shook my head. *That man scares the shit out of me.* I wouldn't be surprised if he knew someone who knew someone who could get rid of a body with no questions asked.

Gunner walked up and sat down where Mark had been sitting. He let out a sigh and leaned his head back.

"Taking her to Paris, you prick."

I let a small smile play across my face. "Yeah, I know."

"Now, when Ellie tells me she's pregnant, you know that I'm going to have to outdo Paris."

I looked over at him and saw him trying not to smile.

"Dude, really? You're gonna try to outdo my honeymoon? That's fucked up."

"You took Paris away from me, Jeff. Paris was mine. I laid claim to it."

"You're going to be a big baby about this, aren't you? Just because I'm going to Paris first? Dude, it was my fucking idea in the first place!"

"I wanted Paris, you bastard."

"Ari speaks French for fuck's sake."

"Doesn't matter, I'm sure you broke some sort of man code."

"Man code? I broke the man code? You bastard, it was my idea…you're the one who broke the man code trying to steal it from me."

"What the fuck are you two talking about?" Josh said from behind me.

"Gunner's pissed because I'm taking Ari to Paris before he takes Ellie. He's being a baby."

"Well, he did lay claim to it, dude," Josh said.

"Thank you!" Gunner shouted out and high-fived Josh.

Traitor bastard is never staying at my house again. He could bunk with Garrett and Emma from now on.

"Go to hell, Josh."

Josh and Gunner both let out a laugh.

"Oh fuck," Josh said as he stepped behind me.

He looked like he was hiding from Lynda.

"Dude, are you hiding from your girlfriend?" I asked.

"Yes! She's fucking driving me crazy. Sorry, Gun, I know she's your cousin, but fuck, she's already pressuring me with marriage. We've only been dating for five months! If she keeps this up, I think I'm gonna need a break from her."

"Dude just tell her she's putting too much pressure on you and to back off," I said.

"I've tried. Every time I do, she says I don't want to get married because I really want Heather. She's driving me mad as hell."

"Why do you stay with her then?" Gunner asked.

"Honestly?"

"Yeah, honestly," Gunner said as he looked at his cousin walking up.

"I'm lonely, and she's not too bad in bed."

Gunner turned and looked at Josh.

Josh held up his arms. "Dude, you asked, and I answered."

"Fucker," Gunner said.

"Hey, boys, whatcha up to? It looks like a deep conversation over here," Lynda said.

She walked up and gave Josh a kiss. He barely smiled at her.

"We were just talking about Jeff and Ari's honeymoon," Josh said.

Lynda jumped up and down, clapping her hands. "Where are y'all going? Does she know?"

Gunner let out a sigh. "I'm going to get another beer."

"Paris, and yes, she knows," I said.

"Oh, how romantic. I hope you're taking notes, Josh," Lynda said as she gave him a wink.

I saw Jenny walking up to us. Ari was right behind her along with Ellie and Heather. As soon as Heather saw Lynda, she moved to the other side of the table, standing as far away from Lynda as possible.

"Jeff, it's time for the first dance. Jack already gave the DJ the song you requested for the first dance," Ari said.

I had asked Ari if I could pick out our song, and she had said yes. Thank God she hadn't been a control freak while planning this whole wedding.

"Would you please do me the honor of dancing with me, Mrs. Johnson?" I said as I stood up and reached for her hand.

"I would be more than happy to, Mr. Johnson."

Jenny walked up to the DJ and nodded her head at him.

"Ladies and gentlemen, Mr. and Mrs. Johnson are now going to have their first dance as man and wife."

Ari looked up at me, smiling, and then put her hand on her stomach. I pulled her to me and put my lips right up to her ear.

"What? Are you nervous about dancing with your old man?"

She leaned back a little and gave me that damn beautiful smile of hers, and I swore I felt my knees wobble.

"No, I just felt the baby move, I think." she said.

I smiled as I pulled her closer to me.

"Everything that I've wanted to say to you is in this song, baby. I love you so much, Ari, and I wouldn't be able to last a day without you in my life. I'll always love you."

Kenny Chesney's "You Save Me" started to play. I took her in my arms and started to two-step with her. She looked up at me with tears rolling down her face.

I will never, ever hurt this girl again.

"I promise you, baby, that I'll always make you happy. Never in my life will I ever hurt you or cause you pain again. I promise you. Thank you so much, Ari, for saving me."

Ari tried to talk but couldn't. She put her head down on my chest, and grabbed my vest, and squeezed it tight. She finally looked up at me and smiled.

"You have that wrong, Jeff. You saved me."

We finished the rest of the dance in silence. When the song ended, we kissed, and I'd never felt so much love pour through my body like I did during that kiss.

"I can't wait until I can feel him moving," I said in her ear.

I started to kiss down her neck and she giggled.

"I have to warn you, Jeff. I'm horny as fuck, so you might want to stop doing that, or I'll take you right here on the dance floor."

Oh god, I love this girl. I reached down, picked her up and started to walk off the dance floor.

Gunner was standing there, smiling.

"We need to leave," I said.

"Now?" Gunner asked in a shocked voice.

"Yes, now. Come up with something. You're my best man dude. You owe me this. My wife is horny, and I need to take care of it now if I'm to start out my husbandly duties right."

"Oh, Jesus H. Christ, I didn't need to over-hear that," Ellie said rolling her eyes.

Gunner let out a laugh as he grabbed Ellie and kissed her. "You're next!"

"Yeah, I didn't need to hear that. That's my sister, you prick,"

"She's my wife."

"Can y'all just come up with a reason for us to leave? I just want a goddamn cheeseburger from McDonald's." Ari shouted.

I set Ari down, and we all just stared at her.

"What? I want a cheeseburger. What's so wrong with that?"

"Nothing, baby. You want a cheeseburger so I'll get you a cheeseburger." I looked over at Gunner. "Gunner, go get Ari a cheeseburger."

"What the fuck? You just said you wanted to leave. Now you're telling me to go get a cheeseburger! I don't remember that in my list of best man duties."

"Who wants a cheeseburger?" Heather said as she walked up from the dance floor.

"Ari does, but they also want to leave," Gunner said.

"Then, just leave."

We all turned and looked at Heather.

"They can't leave yet. They have to stay for at least another hour," Ellie said.

"Fuck a duck. I *need* a cheeseburger." Ari said.

"McDonald's?" Heather asked.

Ari nodded her head, and Heather laughed.

"Well, since my date seems to have decided that he likes dancing with none other than Lynda, I'm more than happy to go get you one."

'Oh god, Heather, I love you! Don't tell my mom though. She'll be pissed if she knew I sent you for a burger."

Heather laughed and headed back up to the room the girls got dressed in to grab her purse and car keys.

I can't believe she's really going to McDonald's for Ari. Damn that's a good friend.

Josh walked over from the bar, carrying a beer in his hand. "Where is Heather going?"

"Well, since your girlfriend won't stop dancing with Heather's date, bitch move by the way, she offered to go and get me a McDonald's cheeseburger. You should go with her. I'm sure she could use the company and I don't want her walking in the dark all alone." Ari said.

Josh set his beer down and looked out to Lynda on the dance floor. "Okay, if Lynda asks where I am."

"Don't worry. I'll take care of it," Ellie said as she pushed Josh toward the door where Heather would be leaving.

Josh took off and never looked back.

"You sneaky little thing you," Gunner said as he looked at Ari.

"What? I don't want Heather walking all alone," Ari said, shrugging her shoulders.

"Come, Ells, dance with my pregnant ass." She grabbed Ellie's hand and off they went. Ari walked up to the DJ and must have asked him to play a song.

"Ah shit, it ain't good when your wife requests a song. She has a history," Gunner said.

I had to laugh. I loved how he called her my wife.

Just then, the DJ stopped the song that was playing. "When the bride asks for a song, it gets played right away," he announced.

Christina Aguilera's "Desnudate" started to play, and Ellie and Ari began dancing.

Damn, the way that girl moves kills me. I just stood there for a few seconds, watching her dance. *My girl sure as shit loves her Christina.* I smiled while I watched her seduce me from the dance floor.

"Heather needs to hurry the fuck up," I said.

Gunner laughed.

"Dude, I never thought I would say this, but when Ellie gets pregnant, be ready. It's like they're horny all the time," I said.

"I'll remember that. Get out there and dance with your bride. Hey, I called the hotel, and you're all set."

I turned to Gunner and smiled. "You really are like a brother to me. Thank you for taking care of that."

Gunner and I gave each other a quick bro hug before I headed out to the dance floor.

It didn't take long for Gunner to join Ellie.

I ended up taking Ari by the hand, and leading her back to the main house to go up to the room the girls had booked.

"Jeff, really, we can't just disappear from our own reception!" Ari said, laughing the whole time I dragged her away.

"The fuck we can't."

CHAPTER FIFTY-ONE

JOSH

When Heather came walking down the steps with her purse and keys in hand, I jumped up from the chair I'd been sitting on.

"Hey."

Heather jumped and let out a small scream.

"Jesus, Josh, you scared the shit out of me."

"I'm sorry. I didn't mean to. I was going to tag along with you to McDonald's."

"Why?"

"I need a cheeseburger."

"What, are you pregnant, too?"

I laughed as Heather just started walking toward the door. We got to her car, and as we got in, I took a deep breath. *Shit, it smells like Heather.* I wanted to let out a curse word because I realized I was in a damn rented tux, so I wouldn't be able to keep her smell on my clothes. I put my head back and closed my eyes. *Motherfucker. I wanted to cry. Maybe I am pregnant. Emotional stupid ass.*

"Josh, are you feeling okay? Are you sick?"

I almost said no but then I decided to see where this would take me.

"You know, I am feeling a little bit sick. I think the fresh air and ride will do me good."

"Are you sure? I mean, maybe you shouldn't eat a cheeseburger if you're feeling sick."

Shit, that went south. "Nah, really, I'm fine."

We drove in silence for a few minutes before she started to talk.

"So, how have you been?"

"Good. I'm pretty much taking over my dad's business. I just made this really cool desk for Ari's dad's home office."

"Really? I bet he'll love it."

"I hope so. If he does and recommends me, that could be huge for the business. I even have a client in Fredericksburg who ordered a few things."

Heather looked over at me and gave me that drop dead gorgeous smile of hers. My heart broke all over again as I thought back that morning at her apartment. Her blue eyes captured mine, and then she looked away.

"Lynda, I'm sure, must be very proud of you."

I let out a small laugh. "Hardly. She hates that I make furniture for a living. She wants me to go back to school."

"For what?"

"Law."

"Oh no, don't do that, Josh. Don't give up your dream because that's what she wants. You have to do what makes you happy."

I nodded my head and looked out the window. I knew Lynda would never make me happy. *Only Heather would.*

"So, how's school? Ellie told me that you're going to graduate this summer. Wow, you must have doubled up on classes," I said.

"Well, I didn't really have anything else to do with Ellie and Ari living in Mason now. So I took more classes at UT and on-line. I have an interview with the Mason Independent School District next week."

I snapped my head up and looked at her.

"For teaching?" I asked.

Heather smiled. "Yeah, I just have to finish some classes this summer and take the state test, but they're looking for three elementary teachers for next year. That's why I doubled up on the classes. It's killing me, but it's worth it."

"Wow, Heather I'm really impressed. I always thought you would make a wonderful teacher, prin...umm, yeah. I always could see you doing that."

She smiled but didn't say anything else. *Fuck, I almost called her princess.*

She pulled up to the drive-through and ordered ten cheeseburgers.

"Ten? I said I only wanted one, Heather."

She threw her head back and laughed.

"I know, but as soon as I hand one to Ari, Jeff and Gunner will wish they had one, too."

I let out a laugh. "Smart and beautiful."

She smiled as she drove up to the window to pay. I handed her a twenty, and she pushed my hand away.

"I've got it Josh."

"Please, I insist." She took the twenty and paid while killing the rude girl in the drive-through with kindness. Only Heather would be extra nice to some rude bitch.

***

By the time we got back to the wedding reception, Heather and I were laughing so hard that we both had tears rolling down our faces. When I told her about Garrett walking in on Jeff and Ari one too many, she laughed even more.

Heather parked the car and was laughing so hard she had to take a couple minutes to settle down before getting out.

"Only Ari would suggest walking out naked to scare Garrett from ever doing it again," Heather said.

"I know, right?"

We sat there for a few seconds, and neither one of us moving or speaking.

"Well, I guess we better get Ari her cheeseburger," she said.

"Yeah, I guess so."

I got out of the car and started to walk next to Heather. Right before we got to the door, I took her arm and stopped her. She turned around and looked me right in the eye.

"Heather, I'm me utterly and completely."

"There you are!"

I wanted to cringe when I heard Lynda's voice. *Fuck me.*

Heather closed her eyes for two seconds before they snapped back open to look right into mine.

"Thanks for keeping me company. I need to get these to Ari. Excuse me, Lynda."

Lynda turned and watched Heather walk inside. I wanted to shout to the top of my lungs right now. Instead, I looked at Lynda and tried to give her my best smile.

"So, you went to McDonald's with Heather, huh? Why didn't you tell me you were leaving?"

"You were a little busy dancing with Heather's date. Since you were both occupied with each other, I decided to get some fresh air, and Ari didn't want Heather walking out here alone."

"Really? Well next time, do a girl a favor and let me know. I was freaking out, and I had to ask Ellie. She said she had no idea where you were. Finally, Ari just told me."

I almost wanted to laugh, thinking about those two devils playing with Lynda like that.

"I'm sorry. I didn't mean to worry you, Lynda. Really, I wasn't even gone twenty minutes."

Lynda turned and started to walk back into the building. I rolled my eyes and then followed behind her.

For the first time since I'd started dating her, I felt sick to my stomach at the idea of having to go home with her.

We got back into the reception hall, and I saw Jeff and Gunner both eating cheeseburgers. When I let out a laugh, Lynda turned around.

"What's so funny?"

"Nothing. I'm gonna walk over and talk to Jeff and Gunner for a bit."

"Okay, well, I'm going to run to the ladies room. Be back in a few minutes."

I nodded my head and walked away.

If I'm lucky she'll get lost.

CHAPTER FIFTY-TWO

HEATHER

I splashed some cold water on my face and forced myself not to cry. *Fucking Lynda. What was Josh about to say? Damn it.* I needed to find a way to talk to him, and I needed to do it without that bitch seeing. *Maybe I could have Brian keep her occupied.* I was doing him a favor by letting him escort me to the wedding. His father worked with Ari's and kept getting on him about not having a date for the wedding. Little did his dad know, Brian wanted to keep his real relationship a secret.

I looked up at myself in the mirror and let out a long, loud sigh. *Christ, I look like shit.*

Just then, I heard someone come into the bathroom. When I turned to grab some towels, I came face to face with Lynda.

"Well, fancy seeing you again so soon!" Lynda said in her chipper fake-ass voice.

Ugh. I dislike this girl very much.

"Hey Lynda, I was just freshening up. I've got to get back to Brian. I'll talk to you soon."

"Oh yeah, sure. Hey, did Josh tell you our good news?"

I stopped dead in my tracks and turned to look at her.

"Um, no, I guess he didn't."

"Oh well, we really haven't told anyone. We've been talking about marriage."

I felt sick to my stomach. All I wanted to do was run into a stall and throw up.

"He asked you to marry him?" I said, a little too shocked.

"Yes…well not officially with the ring and all, but yeah, we pretty much have started talking and planning it. I'm beyond the moon."

"Don't you think y'all should date a little longer before you talk about something like marriage?"

Lynda just laughed. "Gesh, Heather, you sound like my parents. Don't get all elementary school teacher on me. Josh and I are great together, and the sex is pretty fucking awesome."

Oh god.

"I need to go, Lynda. I'm sure Ari and Jeff are planning on leaving soon. It was a pleasure talking to you."

I turned and walked out of the bathroom. I headed back over to where Ellie and Ari were talking to Jeff, Gunner, and Josh. Josh looked up at me, and his smile faded. I was sure I looked awful and I felt even worse.

Ellie took one look at me and stopped talking.

"Heather, are you okay?"

"Actually, I'm not doing so well. I think I'm going to head home. Ari and Jeff, congratulations, y'all, I love you both, and I hope you have a wonderful honeymoon."

I hugged Ari and Jeff, and then Gunner and Ellie. I looked at Josh, who looked confused as hell. I saw him look behind me, and I guessed the troll bitch was walking up.

"Hey baby, miss me?" she said as she walked past me up to Josh.

She went to kiss him, but he turned his head to the side, so she kissed his cheek instead. He never took his eyes off of me. I was so confused. He was looking at me like he wanted to tell me something, but he held Lynda in his arms.

"Okay, well, I'm going to go find Brian and get him to walk me out."

"I can walk you out," Josh said.

"No, Josh, it's best if you let her date walk her out. Don't you agree, Heather?"

I couldn't even answer her. I turned around and walked away.

My heart was beating a mile a minute by the time I found Brian. I asked him to walk me to my car. By the time I got in, he was a little concerned, but I assured him I was okay. I drove about two blocks before I pulled over and cried my eyes out.

He's going to marry her? I almost couldn't believe it. The way he was looking at me tonight was the exact same way he had looked at me the day I begged him to make love to me at Ari and Jeff's house. His eyes looked like they were filled with.

No, I'm dreaming again. It was so obvious that Josh had moved on.

"You lost me…"

The moment I'd slept with Jerry I'd ruined any chance with Josh. *I lost him.*

Just then, my cell phone rang. I pulled it out of my purse and looked at the caller ID.

Josh.

My hands started shaking. *Should I answer it?* I hit ignore and threw my phone back in my purse. As I put my head on the steering wheel, I started to cry even harder.

He's getting married.

CHAPTER FIFTY-THREE

ARI

Thank God it was time to go. If I had to talk to another person and say thank you, I was going to go off on someone.

I looked over at Jeff while he shook someone else's hand, giving him his fake-ass smile. I let out a little laugh. I looked over to my right and saw Emma and Grace walking up. I started to head toward them when Lynda stepped in front of me.

"Before ya say goodnight to Grams, I was wondering if you could do me a favor?"

No, bitch.

"I can try."

"Can you apologize to Heather for me?"

I felt the heat rushing into my face. *I'll kill this girl if she hurt Heather.*

"For what?"

"Well, I'm not sure what happened, but I think Josh must have upset her. When they came back from McDonald's, she was clearly hurt when they were walking in. Then, when I ran into her in the bathroom, she was crying. I know Josh can be a bit of an ass at times, and I know they've had a different kind of friendship."

"Um, okay. Well I'm sure Heather will be fine. Thanks for your concern. I'll let her know what you said the next time I talk to her."

Just then, Emma and Grace walked up. Emma hugged Lynda and talked to her while Grace gave me her congratulations.

I kept looking over at Lynda. There was something about the bitch I didn't trust. Heather seemed fine when she brought me my cheeseburger, but was clearly upset after running in to Lynda in the bathroom. *I don't trust that bitch as far as I can throw her skinny ass.*

Jeff and I said good-bye to, I swore all 150 people at the wedding.

We made our way out to his truck, and after my mother and Grace helped me to get my dress inside the truck we took off.

"So, where are we going, Mr. Johnson?" I asked as I wiggled my eyebrows up and down.

"The W."

"Oh wow, the W *and* Paris? I do believe you are going to start off this marriage by spoiling me."

"That is my every intention, Mrs. Johnson." Jeff said with a smile.

***

After we got to the hotel and checked in, we were standing outside our room. Jeff had told the bellhop to just leave the bags, and he would bring them in later.

Standing at the door of our room, Jeff turned toward me and cupped my face with his hands.

"I will always do whatever I can to make you and our baby happy. Do you believe me, Ari?"

My heart was in my throat. *How can he say something so simple and make me all crazy?*

"Yes, I believe you, Jeff."

Reaching down, he scooped me up into his arms as he tried to open the door and hold on to me. I started to laugh when I felt he was losing his grip on me.

"Shit! This dress is making you slip."

"The dress, huh? You haven't been working out that much lately. Maybe you're losing your brute strength," I said with a giggle.

"Oh yeah?" He set me down for a second, and then picked me up again, throwing me over his shoulder. I let out a small scream.

"Baby, you need to be quiet, or they'll kick us out!"

He smacked me on the ass, which caused me to yell out again.

Once he got the door open, he reached down, grabbed the two suitcases, and carried us all into the room.

He dropped the bags and then slowly, oh so slowly, helped me down. I instantly felt his hard-on and all I wanted to do was rip off his clothes.

"Show off," I said with a smile.

"All for you, baby, all for you."

I turned and looked at our room.

"Holy hell." It was breath-taking. With its totally modern look, it was so different from the Driskill. All I saw were windows with a view of downtown Austin.

"Oh my gosh, the view from up here is amazing." I continued looking around the room, and the next thing I saw was the large curved sofa and the LCD TV.

"That TV is huge!"

Jeff laughed.

"Well, I don't plan on turning it on...at all."

I smiled at him.

"Me either...well until I wear your ass out, and then I'll watch HGTV while you sleep."

Jeff threw his head back and laughed. "That's not going to happen. Come here, let me show you the bathroom."

When we walked into the bathroom, I swore it was like I was walking into a spa. The walls were all gray, and everything else was white. It had modern white sinks and a large bath-tub. *Oh my god, the bathtub.* I just wanted to soak in it. It was tucked near the corner and looked out over the river. It was beautiful.

"I want in that tub."

Jeff came around to stand in front of me. Placing his finger under my chin, he lifted my head up to him. His soft lush lips captured mine, and he kissed me so tenderly that I thought for sure I would melt on the spot.

He pulled away slightly. "How careful do I need to be with taking off this dress?"

I smiled at him and raised an eyebrow. "This is a very expensive dress, Mr. Johnson. What if our daughter wants to wear it someday when she gets married? How am I going to tell her that her daddy put the rip in it because he wanted mommy naked so he could have his wicked ways with her?"

Jeff smiled, and my knees about gave out. *Holy shit, this man is beautiful.* I looked him up and down. His beautiful light brown hair was a tad bit messy, and those emerald green eyes were just sparkling. When he smiled big like he was now, I could see the dimple on his right cheek, and for some reason, that turned me on even more.

"I'll tell ya what, if I rip it, I promise to buy our daughter the most expensive wedding gown that she wants. I just want her momma out of this one."

I turned around and looked over my shoulder as Jeff slowly started to unzip the dress. I heard him suck in his breath when he saw the back of my corset.

"Jesus, Ari…if this is what the back looks like, I can't wait to see the front." He leaned in and kissed me from one shoulder to the other.

My body shuddered.

Then, he placed his hands on my shoulders and slowly pushed off the dress.

"So damn beautiful."

I stepped out of the dress, moving to the side of it. I heard Jeff pick up the dress, and I looked over my shoulder to watch him lay it over the white ottoman. He was handling it with so much care that I had to smile to myself.

I love him so damn much.

"Turn around, Arianna."

Oh. My. God. The sound of his voice ran through my body like a bolt of lightning. *What the hell?* My heart starting pounding and I looked down at my shaking hands. I balled my hands into fists, and then I placed them both on my stomach. *Is it butterflies or am feeling the baby?*

I slowly turned around to face him. Jeff sucked in a breath of air as he looked up and down my body. He took two steps back, hit the ottoman, lost his balance, and then landed right on his ass.

I started to laugh as he jumped back up.

"Wow, if I had known that I looked that good, I would have taken that damn dress off hours ago," I said as I laughed my ass off.

Oh shit! I started to jump up and down. I had to pee. *Oh my god!* If I pissed myself, I was blaming him. I pushed past Jeff and ran over to the toilet. Now, it was Jeff's turn to laugh.

Jesus, Mary, and Joseph…so much for romance.

"That was classic, Ari. Damn, I love you," Jeff said as he walked over to the bath to run the water.

I finished, washed my hands, and took one look at myself in the mirror. I did have a glow. I wondered if it was the pregnancy or just because I was so unbelievably happy?

Jeff walked up behind me and wrapped his arms around my stomach. He gave me a small hug and then turned me around.

"You take my breath away in all this silver, baby, but I'm afraid I need to take it off as well."

Jeff slowly got down on his knees as he picked up my left foot and removed my shoe. Then, he removed my other shoe. He slowly slid his hands up my right leg and unclipped my stockings from the garter belt. He rolled it off my leg and set it to the side and then repeated the same moves on my left leg. Then, he reached up and unhooked the garter belt. I could feel the rush of moisture hit my platinum-colored panties.

Shit, I've never wanted him as much as I do right this very second.

He hooked his fingers on my panties and so very slowly pulled them down. As he did, he placed gentle kisses down my leg. I stepped out of my panties, and he tossed them to the side.

When he looked right at my stomach, I felt it doing flips like never before. *Oh god.*

He placed his forehead and then one of his hands on my stomach.

"Hey, baby boy or girl, it's Daddy."

Mother of all things good. Fucking take me now!

"I love you, little baby of mine. Thank you so much for letting Mommy have a sick-free day today little bit."

Oh. My. God.

"Jeff..."

He kissed my stomach and stood up. Turning me around, he slowly started to take off the corset. Once it was untied he let it drop to the floor.

I turned around and saw the lust in his eyes as his gaze traveled up and down my body. Then, his stare landed back on the small round bump at my stomach.

"Ari, you're so damn sexy. I can't wait to see your stomach grow bigger with our child."

He's trying to kill me. He has to be.

"Jeff, please make love to me…after you turn off the tub because it's fixin' to spill over."

"Shit!" Jeff ran over to the tub and turned off the water.

I let out a giggle as Jeff walked back over to me. He lifted me up and moved me over to the lower counter next to the sink.

"The water will get cold," I said with a smile.

"Then, I'll drain it and fill it up again. Right now, I'm going to make love to you."

My heart dropped to my stomach. No matter how many times he's said that to me, it still caused me to get butterflies in my stomach.

"Okay."

And make love, he did. We started out in the bathroom, and then lifted me up and moved me to the bedroom where he gave every square inch of my body attention. I'd already had two orgasms, and I thought I was going to die if I had another one.

He rolled us over, so I was on top.

Sweet mother of Jesus, he feels so good. I didn't want to stop, but I felt the familiar feeling building up inside of me. Just as I started to come, Jeff sat up and wrapped his arms around me, and came with me.

We sat there for a few minutes, just holding each other while we caught our breath. Then, I felt the baby move. I knew it was the baby because that feeling was getting stronger. I was pretty sure it was a boy, only Jeff could produce a son who could make me feel him move around earlier than he should.

"I love you, Jeff."

"I love you so much more, baby. Let's go sit in a hot bath."

He let go of me, and I collapsed onto the bed.

"I'll just wait here while you take your fine naked ass in there to draw me a bath."

"You got it, babe."

***

The moment I slid down into the hot water, I let out a sigh and closed my eyes. Thank God this day is over. I loved our wedding, and it was more than I could've ever dreamed of. *But fuck, I just want to go to Paris.*

I felt Jeff get into the tub with me, so I moved up so he could slide in behind me.

I leaned back onto his chest, and now it was his turn to relax.

"So, Paris, huh?"

He let out a chuckle. "Yep, we leave tomorrow afternoon. Ellie did me a huge favor by making sure your passport was up to date."

"Well, she wasn't very sneaky about it. She just came out and asked."

Jeff started laughing. "Damn that girl. I really wish she would get pregnant soon," Jeff said, his voice turning sad sounding.

I put my hands to my stomach, silently thanking God for our blessing.

"She will, baby. She just needs to relax and stop worrying about it. Let's get back to Paris. What made you pick Paris? Est-ce parce que je parle si bien le Francais?"

I knew Jeff had no idea what I'd just said, so I let out a giggle.

"Yes," Jeff said with a laugh.

I turned around and looked at him. "Do you know what I just asked?"

He smiled that big ol' smile of his and nodded his head.

"Alright, smart ass, what did I say?"

"You asked if it was because you spoke French so well."

"Je pense que le bébé est un garçon."

Jeff sat up really quick. "How do you know it's a boy?"

Oh my god! "I don't! I said that I think it's a boy. When did you learn French?"

Jeff leaned back and took me with him. I could feel his chest moving up and down, so he must have been laughing.

"The day Gunner and Ellie got married, I was giving him hell about being so damn romantic. I said something about taking Ellie to Paris when she got pregnant. I liked the idea of taking you to Paris because I remembered you and your parents talking about when you went to France before and how much you loved it there. When y'all started speaking in French at dinner, I wanted to know what you were saying, I bought Rosetta Stone for French that night, and I've been trying to learn the language since then."

I sat up, turned around in the bathtub, and looked at him.

"Vous imbécile romantique."

"I think you just called me romantic," Jeff said with a wink.

"Close. I said your romantic fool! Je t'aime, Jeff."

"Je t'aime, Ari."

Turning to face him, I wrapped my legs around him in the bathtub and smiled.

"I'm ready, baby, if you think you can handle me," Jeff said with a wink.

"Bring it on, Mr. Johnson, 'cause Mrs. Johnson is one horny pregnant woman."

"Fuck yeah!"

***

Jeff and I collapsed on the bed around 4 a.m. I couldn't move, and I was starving. I rolled over and cuddled up next to him. He was already asleep, and the motion of his chest going up and down was relaxing me even more.

I thought back to our wedding day yesterday and the night that followed. I didn't think I'd ever be as happy as I was right now.

Then I smiled when I thought about the baby.

That statement wasn't true. This was just the beginning of many more happy moments.

Just the beginning.

CHAPTER FIFTY-FOUR

GUNNER

Late May

I walked around on the slab and took notes. Ellie hadn't been feeling good for the last two weeks, so she took a trip into Austin with Ari for a change of scenery and some shopping. The house was coming along nicely. Now, we just needed it to stop raining so damn much, so the framing could get going.

I looked up and saw Josh driving up in the Jeep. *What the hell? This is a nice surprise.*

He jumped out of the Jeep and came walking up to me, reaching to shake hands.

"Dude, what a nice surprise."

Josh smiled and slapped me on the back. "You couldn't have picked a better spot on the ranch to build y'all's house. Nicely done, bro."

I smiled as I looked around. Our tree, the same tree where it'd all started, was going to be in the back yard of our new house.

"Yeah, I wouldn't want it to be anywhere else. My dad is pushing the hell out of me to get this house done. He's tired of living with Gramps and Grams. To be honest, I think that's why they are traveling so much." I said with a laugh.

"Where are they now?"

"Las Vegas!" I said with a chuckle.

My drill instructor father had turned into a carefree wild and crazy man ever since his heart attack last year.

"What brings you out here?" I asked.

"Jeff, needed some help taking care of some things, and I think a few of those mares are ready to pop. With Ari so close to the due date, he just wanted an extra hand around. I knew about a month ago, so I stopped taking in new orders, and my dad is covering for me. I sure needed the break from work."

I laughed and shook my head. "You know Jeff is going to work your ass to the bone, and I might call on you as well."

"Bring it, dude. The more work the better. You know I love it out here, and this shit is relaxing for me. Besides, I needed out of the city. If it wasn't for Lynda, I think I would move out this way. I love Fredericksburg. I really think I could easily move the business out there and still be close enough to Austin to do work there."

"Damn, dude, that would be awesome to have you closer."

"Yeah, if only Lynda wanted the same thing I wanted, I'd be set."

"How are things with y'all?"

Josh shrugged his shoulders.

"Have you seen Heather since Ari and Jeff's wedding?" I asked.

"No, I heard some shit though that bothered me."

Fuck. I knew where he was going with this. Ellie and Ari had tried to talk to Heather, but they couldn't seem to get through to her. Heather had turned to going out and partying all the time, so much that even Amanda was worried about it.

"What did you hear?"

"Just that she's been partying a lot. Do you remember Smitty from UT?"

"Yeah, I remember Smitty."

"He said she goes out every weekend. Do you know if any of that's true?"

"I hate to say this, but yeah, Ellie and Ari have been really worried about her. She seems to go after her school shit hard all week, and then every Friday and Saturday night, she goes out and drinks with a few friends from school. When Ellie tried to talk to her about it, she said it's the only way she could forget for a while."

"Forget what?"

"Dude, that's the million dollar question."

Just then, I heard my truck driving up. I smiled when I saw Ellie jump out.

She ran over and hugged Josh. "It's so great to see you."

"Ellie, you look beautiful. Country air seems to agree with you rather well," Josh said as I spun Ellie around.

"Josh, you can't stay away for so long like that."

"Josh is talking about moving out toward Fredericksburg maybe."

"No kidding. Heather just interviewed with the elementary school out there. Did you know that?"

Josh looked surprised as shit.

"Um, no, I had no idea. I haven't talked to or seen her since the wedding. Last I knew, she was going to interview with Mason."

"Yep, she did, but she hasn't heard back from them yet. She'll be graduating this summer, so we plan on having a big party for her. You'll come, right?"

"Of course, you can count on me being there. Alright, y'all, I'm gonna let ya go. I'm gonna head on back up to the house and say good-bye to Garrett and Emma. I'm sure Jeff has a laundry list of shit for me to do. Maybe we can all head out to dinner tonight?"

"Sounds good bud, I'll give you or Jeff a ring later on."

Ellie and I watched as Josh got back in the Jeep and headed back up the ranch house. I looked over at Ellie, who had a shit-eating grin on her face.

"What's with the grin?"

She turned to look at me and winked. "Oh, nothing, it's just that Josh is in for a little surprise when he gets to Jeff and Ari's."

"Oh yeah? What kind of surprise, Ellie Mathews?"

"Ari and I talked Heather into coming out and staying for a few weeks until summer classes start. She agreed and said she needed to get out of Austin to get away from the partying."

"You little devils. Did Ari know Josh was coming out?"

Ellie looked at me like I was stupid. "Of course, she did, and she also knew that Lynda was going to Costa Rica with her parents for a few weeks."

I let out a laugh.

"You know what else I found out from Heather that explains why she's been acting the way she has?"

"What?"

"Lynda told her at the wedding that Josh asked her to marry him, but they just hadn't made it public yet."

"What the fuck? Are you kidding me?"

"Nope." Ellie said, popping her p. "I hate to say this, Gunner, because Lynda is your cousin, but I don't trust her one bit. She is jealous of Heather, and I think she'll do or say anything to keep them apart. When Heather told us what Lynda said, all Ari had to do was look at me, and I knew what she was thinking. The Push-Josh-and-Heather-Together Plan has officially started," Ellie said as she turned around and looked back in the direction where Josh had just left.

I pulled her into me and hugged her. "Be careful, Ells. Don't push them too hard baby. Just let them find their way back to each other."

Ellie turned and looked at me. "They are both so unhappy. Why can't they see that Gunner?"

"It's the same reason why Jeff and Ari couldn't see it…or at least, Jeff couldn't see it. Come on, enough about them. I want to give you a tour of our house."

We jumped up onto the slab, and I started pointing out where the kitchen, living room, and master bedroom would be.

"Did you keep the small little study, the one that's in the master room, in the plans?"

"Yeah. Why? I thought you said it would make a great reading room. It's too late to change it now, babe the slab is already poured."

Ellie started walking over to the area in the master bedroom that would eventually be the little study. Facing out toward our tree, it would be all solid windows.

"No, of course, I don't want to change it." She reached into her back pocket and pulled out a piece of paper. While unfolding it, she said,

"It'll make a beautiful reading room and a great little nursery for the first few months after the baby comes home in December."

"Yeah, it would make a great…wait, what?"

Ellie turned around holding up the piece of paper. I walked closer to her. The closer I got the slower I walked. That's a picture of...

I looked up at her. "Is that a sonogram, Ellie?"

She turned the picture around and looked at it. When she looked back up at me, she smiled.

"Yes, it is, Drew. Say hello to our baby."

I was standing in front of her, and then I slowly started to sink down to the cement floor until I landed on my ass.

"Baby, you're pregnant?" I asked.

She sat down on the slab next to me and handed me the picture.

"Yep, looks like your little vacation in March to New Orleans did the trick. I'm due December ninth."

"How far along are you?" My voice cracked.

"About ten weeks. When I missed my period last month, I didn't want to get my hopes up. Then, I missed it this month, and I'd been feeling so sick. I asked Ari to go with me, just in case it came back negative. I didn't want you to be disappointed. I didn't even take a home pregnancy test. I'm sorry you weren't there for the first sonogram, but Dr. Wyatt wanted to check out the baby as soon as the test came back positive."

I looked up at her with tears building in my eyes. *We're going to have a baby.*

"Ellie, I'm not upset about that. I mean, if it's okay, I want to go to all your appointments with you from now on."

"Of course, it's okay! Are you happy?"

I looked up at her and saw the tears in her eyes. I took the back of my hand and ran it along the side of her face.

"I've never felt so happy in my life, Ells. I love you so damn much."

Ellie smiled and those beautiful blue eyes lit up as a single tear rolled down her face. I wiped it away and then stood up. I helped my beautiful girl up to her feet before I grabbed her and kissed her. The small moan she let escape ran through my body.

I pulled away and smiled. Then, I turned and started walking us back to my truck. Later, I'd have Ellie drive me back over here to the pick up the ranch truck, right now I just needed to get her home.

"Wait, where are we going?" Ellie asked.

I was practically dragging her along the way.

"Home. I need to make love to you right now."

She let out a giggle and ran up next to me.

"Well, who am I to argue with such a romantic gesture?"

I reached down and picked her up as she let out a little scream.

"Be ready, baby. I'm gonna rock your pregnant world."

Ellie laughed as she pushed up off my back.

"Bring it on, Gunner. Bring it on."

CHAPTER FIFTY-FIVE

JEFF

I walked down to the barn to check on Josh. He'd been staying with us the last two weeks, along with Heather. I still had to chuckle when I thought of the look on their faces when they both saw each other, then when they found out they were both staying with us. It was priceless. I would have paid a million bucks to have that shit recorded.

Ari told me that they went for a ride together this morning, so at least they were making progress.

When, I walked into the barn, Josh was brushing Sweet Pea, the new mare I bought last week.

"You know, country life agrees with you, Josh. Gunner and I sure could use your help out here, especially with Drake moving to Austin and Aaron helping Jenny more and more with her event-planning business."

Josh turned and smiled at me.

"I would move out here in a heartbeat if I thought I could. My business is growing pretty fast in Austin though."

"Dude, you can make furniture anywhere. All this damn fresh air might also inspire you."

Josh took in a deep breath. "All I smell is horse shit, dude."

I let out a laugh.

"How was your ride this morning with Heather?"

"Good. She still seems distant though, almost like she's doing something wrong by spending time with me."

"I think I know why."

Josh stopped brushing and looked at me.

"Alright, asshole, you're planning on sharing it with me, right?"

"Do you remember when Heather came back from the bathroom so upset on the night of my wedding?"

"Of course I do."

"Well, first off, I need you to know that Heather just told Ari and Ellie this a couple of weeks ago."

"What? What did she tell them, Jeff?"

"In the bathroom that night, Lynda told Heather that you asked her to marry you, but y'all had decided to wait on telling anyone."

Josh dropped the brush to the ground.

"Wait…what? I haven't asked Lynda to marry me. She keeps pushing me, but I've never even mentioned marriage to her."

Josh put his hands on his knees. I walked up to him and put my hand on his back.

"Motherfucker. Is that why she started partying and everything? She thought I was getting married?" Josh asked.

"I guess so. Every time we ever asked her to come along and do something with us, as soon as she found out that you and Lynda were going to be there, she'd change her mind. Josh, do you love Lynda?"

Josh stood up and looked at me.

"I care about her, but do I love her enough to marry her? No, not at all."

"Do you love Heather?" I asked.

Josh looked at me with tears in his eyes. "Yes, I love her more than anything."

"Do you want to spend the rest of your life with her and only her?"

"Yes."

"Then, go the fuck after her. She took Rose, and is down at the river reading."

"Yeah, I know, I helped saddle her up."

"Sweet Pea could use some exercise." I said, raising my eyebrows.

Josh grabbed a bridle and put it on Sweet Pea, and then jumped up on her.

"You're riding bareback, dude?"

Josh smiled and took off toward the river.

"Do you know where she's at along the river?"

"Ari just said Heather went for a ride to the river to read."

"Wish me luck!"

"You got this, Josh. Just be honest with her. Wait!"

Josh stopped Sweet pea while I ran over to my truck and opened the door to the backseat. I smiled when I found the folded-up quilt. I ran over to Josh and handed it to him.

"What the fuck do I need a quilt for?"

I just looked at him.

"Oh, um, right. Thanks, dude!"

I watched Josh gallop off on Sweet Pea. I was hoping for two things: the first, that he made it to Heather in one piece and didn't fall the fuck off the horse, and second, that those two got their shit together once and for all.

By the time I got back to the house, I walked in to see my very pregnant, very sexy wife standing at the kitchen sink. She was listening to her iPod, and those hips were just moving to the beat of the song. I walked up closer to see if I could hear what she was listening to. I could hear Kenny Chesney's "She Thinks My Tractor's Sexy." Then she started to sing, or rather scream the words. The last thing I wanted to do was scare her, but when I came up behind her and put my hands on her hips, she jumped and yelled.

She pulled her earbuds out as she turned around. "Jesus, Mary, and Joseph, you asswipe. You scared the shit out of me!"

I put my hand on her round belly.

"How are you and little bit doing this afternoon?"

She smiled and moved my hand to the right side of her stomach. Right then, the baby kicked…hard.

I smiled as I looked at Ari.

She smiled back at me. "I would say he's doing well. Me on the other hand…I'm so ready for this baby to be out of my stomach. I'm so glad Dr. Wyatt is inducing me in two days. I don't think I could carry him around another day."

I still couldn't believe it. In two days, we would be having a baby at the hospital in Austin.

"Jeff, we really need to decide on a name."

I rolled my eyes and sat down on the bar stool. *Ugh…baby names kill me.* Even after we found out we were having a boy, we still couldn't agree on a name.

"You still set on Luke, Ari?"

"Yep. Are you still set on Hunter?"

"Yep."

"Okay, how about we wait until we see his face, and then we decide. Fair enough?"

Ari smiled and walked up to me. She kissed me so sweetly and softly that I think I would have settled on Luke if she asked again.

"Fair enough, but I'm pretty sure he'll be walking out of the hospital with the name Luke Drew Johnson."

"I'm pretty sure you're right baby."

"Is Josh still down at the barn?"

"Nope, he took off bareback on Sweet Pea when I explained what Lynda said about them getting married."

Ari dropped the knife she'd been using to cut up apples in the sink.

"You told him? I promised Heather that I wouldn't say anything, Jeff. I told her they weren't engaged, and she believed me. Why would you tell Josh?"

"Because he needed to know why Heather pushed him away again. He has a right to know."

Ari smiled and leaned against the sink. "So, he went right after her, did he?"

"Yep, and I even gave him our lucky quilt to take."

Ari smiled and raised her eyebrows.

"That means…they could be down at the river for a while."

I stood up and took her into my arms. "You double lock the backdoor, and I'll double lock the front door."

"I'm on it."

I'd never seen my nine months pregnant wife move so fast. When I looked down the hallway, she was already taking off her shirt. I smiled and headed to the front door. *Shit, I might have to keep her pregnant all the time.* This girl was hornier than a frat boy in a house full of virgins.

"Jeff! Hurry! Let's do this before they come back," Ari yelled out from our room.

I walked down the hallway and headed into our bedroom. She was already undressed and trying to get up on the bed.

She turned and looked at me.

"Be creative! I can hardly move!"

I let out a laugh as I pulled my shirt over my head, and then I started to take off my pants.

"Oh, don't worry, baby. You won't be disappointed."

CHAPTER FIFTY-SIX

JOSH

Shit. I should have asked Jeff if Heather had stayed on his property or if she had ridden over onto the Mathews' place.

Then, I saw her. With a blanket already laid out on the ground, she was lying on her stomach, reading a book. I jumped off Sweet Pea and decided to just let her roam. She would probably make her way over to where Rose was tied up and eating.

As I walked toward Heather, she didn't look up. The sound of the river must have been blocking out my steps.

"Hey, Heather," I called out.

When she looked up, I was hoping that she wasn't going to seem disappointed to see me.

She let a huge smile play across her face, and I felt my own smile spreading across mine.

I love her. I only want her.

She sat up and pulled her knees to her chest. She looked beautiful, sitting there under the blue sky. I could practically see her blue eyes from here.

"Hey, what are you doing out here?" she called out as I was walking closer to her.

By the time I got to her, she had stood up.

I didn't know what to say or how I should even start it. So, I did the only thing I'd wanted to do since I saw her walk into Jeff and Ari's house two weeks ago. I inched closer to her, took her face in my hands, and kissed her.

The moan that escaped from her mouth drove me mad, and my dick was hard within seconds. It had nothing to do with the fact that I had not slept with Lynda in months. It was because I was kissing Heather. I craved her kiss and her touch more than anything else in my life.

I pulled away from her mouth, so we could catch our breath. When she closed her eyes, a tear rolled down her face.

I took my thumb and wiped it away.

"I love you, Heather. I've only ever loved you."

Her beautiful blue eyes opened, and it was like she was staring into my soul.

"I'm so sorry. I never meant for what happened with Jerry to happen. I can't get it out of my head. I've tried to do everything I could think of to just forget it, but I can't. That was supposed to be you. I wanted that to be you so badly, Josh."

She started crying even harder.

I pulled her into me and held on to her.

"I wanted it to be you more than anything."

"It's okay princess. Please don't cry. It doesn't matter anymore. All that matters is you and me, Heather."

She pulled away, looking at me.

"I know what people think about me, and they're wrong. I haven't been with anyone since that night with Jerry. I couldn't be with anyone else but you."

I leaned down and took her mouth with mine. I kissed her with as much passion as I possibly could. I needed to show her how much I loved and wanted her.

Heather pulled away again.

"Josh, I know you're with Lynda, and I wouldn't want you to be unfaithful to her."

I closed my eyes and let out a sigh.

"Heather, I have no intentions of staying with Lynda. The minute she gets back from Costa Rica, I'm going to tell her it's over. She knows that I don't love her. We haven't even slept together in months."

"Really?" Heather asked, her voice a little too excited.

I smiled at her.

"Yes, really. I've never loved anyone but you. I only want to be with you."

Heather slowly lowered herself onto the blanket. When she was lying back all I could see was her chest moving up and down. I knew she was scared to death.

I got down on the blanket and put my hand on her stomach. I felt her whole body tremble under my touch. I was nervous as hell. I hadn't felt this way since the day we were in Jeff and Ari's hallway. I leaned down and captured her lips with mine. Her hands immediately went in my hair, pulling me closer. She was driving me crazy.

Slow, Josh. It needs to be special. This is her real first time.

I slowly moved my lips away from hers.

"Princess, sit up for me."

She looked confused for a second, but sat up anyway. I got on my knees and kissed her forehead, then her nose, and then down the side of her face to her neck.

"Oh god." she said.

I started to kiss her gently on her lips as I moved my hands to her T-shirt. I only broke the kiss to bring the shirt over her head.

"Lie back down, baby." I felt her body trembling as I helped her lie back. I wanted to do everything I could to make her feel loved and wanted.

I took my finger and pushed a piece of her blonde hair behind her ear. Then, I traced down her jaw to her neck and then lower to her chest. When I ran my finger along the edge of her bra, she sucked in a breath. I leaned down and kissed the top of her chest.

I whispered against her skin,

"Breathe, princess...just breathe."

Heather took a deep breath in and then slowly let it out.

Fuck me. Her bra clasp was in the front. I unclasped it and then helped her take it off.

"So fucking perfect."

I leaned down and took one of her nipples into my mouth.

She arched her back and let out a moan that moved through my whole body like a lightning bolt. I'd never felt like this with anyone.

I slowly moved my hand down and started to unbutton her jean shorts.

"Josh..." she said as she tried to catch her breath.

The only thing I could hear was her heart beating.

She lifted her hips as I took her shorts and thong panties off all at once. My heart was fucking pounding in my chest as I looked up and down her body.

"Touch me...please touch me," she practically begged.

I sat up, gazing at her perfect body. There was absolutely nothing I would change about this girl. She was the most beautiful woman I'd ever laid eyes on. When I moved my hand to touch her ankle, she jumped, and I couldn't help but smile. I slowly moved my hand up her leg to her stomach, chest, and then neck.

"I want you to come with me inside you, Heather."

Her eyes flew open, and all I could see was fear. I knew she didn't remember anything about that night with Jerry, and a part of me was so glad. I wanted her first time to be with me.

"I love you, Josh."

I felt the tears building in my eyes.

"I love you, Heather."

I moved on top of her and started to kiss her. I slid my hand down between her legs and slowly opened them to me. I put one finger inside her, and I almost came on the spot.

"You're so damn wet, Heather."

"I want you Josh, I want you so bad."

I moved my finger in and out as she moaned into my mouth. I put another finger in and then another as I moved my hand faster. I could feel her getting tighter around my fingers, so I pulled them out. She let out a moan of frustration.

"Oh god, Josh, please..."

I slowly started to enter her body. *Jesus, she's so tight.* I said a silent pray, hoping that I would last at least five minutes.

"Talk to me, Heather."

"Don't ...know...what...to say..."

"Does it hurt, princess?"

"No...feels good...please don't stop."

I moved in, inch by inch, as I kissed her. I saw the pain in her face, and I pulled back out some. She grabbed my back and pulled me closer to her, causing me to go deeper inside her. She let out a gasp.

"Heather..."

"I'm fine. Oh god, Josh, I feel like you're melting into me. Please don't stop. Please."

I put my forehead onto hers and quickly pushed myself all the way into her.

Pure heaven. I didn't even want to move. I wanted to just stay like this while I listened to her breathing.

I slowly started to move in and out of her.

Then, I remembered.

Fuck. I stopped moving and looked at her. I never fucking forgot…ever.

"Heather, I'm not wearing a condom."

"S'okay. I'm on birth control pills."

"But I've never..."

She looked at me and smiled. I melted on the spot. I smiled back at her as I captured her lips with mine. I started to move again, faster and harder. When I pulled on her bottom lip and bit down on it, she started to call out my name.

Mother fucker. It felt incredible to be inside of her with nothing separating us. I tried to hold off as long as I could, but it felt so damn good. The moment she started to come back to me, I called out her name. There was something about me coming in her that felt so right. *She's mine.* She would always be mine, and I would do anything for her.

I stayed on top of her until our breathing was under control. I leaned down and kissed her. I'd never in my life experienced such an amazing moment. As I rolled onto my side, she rolled over to face me.

I looked into those beautiful blue eyes.

"Heather, I've never in my life experienced anything like what I just experienced with you. Making love to you was…it was magical."

I saw the tear slide down her face, and I caught it before it went into her ear. Leaning forward, I kissed her.

When I pulled back, she smiled.

"Can I ask you something, Josh?"

"You can ask me anything you want, baby."

"Well, it's kind of two things."

I laughed and kissed her nose.

"Go for it."

"Okay…well, um…next time…um, can I be on top? And…how long until you can, um…do that again?"

Fuck me. She's perfection all around.

I smiled at her and pushed a piece of her hair away from her eyes and tucked it behind her ear.

"I think I'll only need a few more minutes, and as far as you being on top…baby, you never need to ask permission for that."

She laughed and pushed my shoulder, causing me to fall back. I grabbed her and pulled her on top of me and she sat up straight. She barely moved and then looked back down at me. She lifted her eyebrow and smiled.

"A few minutes, huh?"

"Looks like I underestimated him."

Heather laughed and then sat up some. Leaning down, she kissed me from my neck up to my ear.

"Will it feel different with me on top?"

She was barely letting my dick touch her, and it was driving me crazy.

"Yeah…" was all I could get out.

"Like how different?"

"Like…I don't know…fuller, I think. Shit, Heather…you're driving me mad."

With a smile, she bit down on my lower lip right as she sat down, letting me enter her body all the way.

We both let out a gasp as she sat back up, putting her hands on my chest.

"Oh god… it feels so good, Josh."

With the way she was moving, there was no way I was going to last long. She looked down at me, and her blonde hair fell forward, partially covering her beautiful breasts.

"Faster, Heather…move faster."

When she did, I could tell she was getting close. Sitting up, I grabbed her and I buried my face into her chest.

Before I knew it, we were both calling out each other's names.

She moved her legs to wrap around me, straddling me. I wasn't even sure how long we sat like that before she said something.

"I never want to leave. I just want to stay right here with you forever."

I closed my eyes and held her tightly.

"I feel the same way, princess. I love you so much."

"I love you, too."

When I slowly laid her down next to me, she put her head on my chest. The next thing I knew, she was sleeping. All I could hear were the sounds of the Llano River and the slow and steady breaths coming from the girl of my dreams.

CHAPTER FIFTY-SEVEN

ARI

Oh. My.God. I was lying there on the bed, panting. *Jesus, how does Jeff do that to me?* I smiled as I thought about how amazing he'd just made me feel. After two orgasms, I was spent and ready to go to sleep.

He crawled up next to me and smiled.

"Well, do you feel more relaxed, baby?"

When I started laughing, I felt a sharp pain in my stomach. *Holy shit. What the fuck?*

"Jeff, will you help me sit up?"

Jeff got up and helped me into a sitting position.

"What's wrong?"

I looked at him and smiled. "Nothing. I guess I just had a sharp pain in my stomach. It was almost like the Braxton Hicks contractions, but this time it seemed different, stronger.

"Do you want something to eat?"

I nodded my head and slowly made my way off the bed. Grabbing my normal attire from the last few weeks, I threw on a pair of sweat-pants and a T-shirt.

Jeff whipped up some scrambled eggs. Just as I was about to take a bite, I felt another contraction.

Oh shit.

I looked at Jeff with a panicked look on my face. His face went white in two seconds flat.

"Holy fucking shit. Contractions?"

I nodded my head.

"Shit! I didn't time it…you had the other one like what…twenty minutes ago?"

"That sounds about right."

"Fuck!" Jeff jumped up and ran into the bedroom. When he ran by the kitchen, I saw he was carrying my bag that we'd packed for the hospital. He never even stopped.

At one point, he just tossed my flip-flops at me and told me to put them on.

One landed on top of the fridge, and the other hit me square in the face. Luckily, I was able to catch it. The one on top of the fridge was going to be a challenge.

I stood up, dropped the one flip-flop I had on the floor, and then walked over and grabbed the broom. I was able to knock the other flip-flop off of the fridge. It landed on the floor, and then I slipped that one on.

I reached for my purse and pulled out my cell. *Oh yay!* I had a signal.

I sent a text to my mother: *Having contractions. About twenty minutes or so apart. Heading to Seton.*

Less than a minute later my cell went off.

Mom: *OMG! OMG! Dropping Matt off at Melissa's and heading to Seton. Tell Jeff to drive safe. No! Tell Gunner to drive.*

I let out a laugh and replied back with a simple okay. I picked up the land line and called Ellie and Gunner's place. Ellie answered, and I told her I was having contractions. She screamed in my ear and then screamed for Gunner, saying they had to leave to meet us at Grams and Gramp's place. Then, the bitch hung up on me.

Okay. I'm the one having shooting-ass pains, and I'm the one that's about to push a watermelon out of a hole the size of a grape. What the fuck are they all freaking out about? Why am I the only one who is calm?

Gunner would be calm. I could always count on Gunner.

Jeff came running back, going straight by the kitchen, before skidding to a stop.

"Oh there you are, baby! What are you doing? I sent a text to Gunner. We have to meet him at Emma and Garrett's house. So, um, let's go. We have a long drive. Have you had another contraction?"

I smiled at him and shook my head.

"Have you called Dr. Wyatt?"

"No."

He pulled out his cell and looked at it. "Fuck!" He ran over to the land-line and started to dial.

"Oh yeah, hi…she's um…she's having contractions."

Oh dear Lord. I rolled my eyes.

"Who? Oh yeah, Ari…Arianna Johnson…she's my wife….well shit, you know that. Oh, sorry. I didn't mean to swear, but I kind of have to go now…we have a long drive…twenty minutes…two...yeah...okay. No, I'm not driving... No! Of course, I'm not going to make her drive…okay, yeah …I'm calm… sure. Who? Ari? Yeah, she's just standing here leaning against the kitchen island smiling at me… I think she might be in shock…she's too calm if you know what I mean. Okay, right…on our way."

Fuck a duck. I would have given anything to have recorded all of that. Damn.

***

By the time we got to the hospital, I was having contractions every ten minutes. Ellie went with Jeff to check us in while Gunner stayed with me. A nurse came up and had me sit in a wheelchair.

"Gunner, thank you for staying so calm. With freak number one and freak number two over there, I'm glad I could count on you to stay calm."

"Sure, Ari. You know there's nothing I wouldn't do for y'all."

Just then, Heather and Josh walked in. I knew the moment I saw Heather with the glow on her face, they had made love. *Thank God. It's about damn time.* She smiled as she walked up to me, and I saw Josh look over at Gunner and smile. *Damn boy looks like he's walking on cloud nine.*

She kissed me and asked if there was anything she could do. I shook my head and gave her a bigger smile.

She leaned down and got up next to my ear.

"It was amazing, Ari."

"I knew it would be with that boy. Was he big? I bet he was big," I said as I winked at her.

Out of the corner of my eye, I caught Gunner say something in Josh's ear as he patted him on the back.

Heather laughed and shook her head at me. "You're nuts!"

Jeff came walking up with a nurse, and of course, I would have to have a contraction right then. I tried to hide it. *Oh my god, it hurt like hell.*

Jeff dropped down to his knees. "Ari, just focus and go to your happy place."

"Why the fuck do you keep saying that to me?"

Gunner and Josh started to laugh, and Jeff snapped his head up and gave them a dirty look.

"We learned about it in Lamaze class. Don't you remember, babe? You were supposed to pick a happy place where you could escape to."

"The only happy place I'm going to is the place where this baby is out of my stomach, and I'm drinking a damn margarita. That is my happy place, Jeff."

"Good, babe…just go there."

I just stared at him.

"Baby, please don't tell me that again, okay? Because if you do, I'm gonna grab you by the balls until you feel the kind of pain I'm about to feel."

Jeff started laughing. "God, I love you, Ari." He leaned forward and kissed me right on the lips…fast and hard.

***

I was finally in a room, and the contractions were coming faster and stronger. Everyone had left the room, except my mother and Jeff.

Dr. Wyatt walked in with that damn smile on his face. "How are you doing, Arianna?"

I wanted to tell him to fuck off. Instead, I smiled. "Good."

"So, I hear you want an epidural, Arianna?"

"Ah, yeah, that would be really awesome if that could happen…like before the next contraction."

Too late.

"Coming faster are they? Let's take a look at how far along you are, Ari."

Dr. Wyatt looked up at me and smiled.

"I hate to be the one to deliver this news, Ari, but you're at ten centimeters. The baby is crowning. You're ready to push."

"What? Oh no… no, no, no, you have to push him back in! I'm not ready yet." Panicking, I looked over at Jeff and my mother, who both had goofy-ass smiles plastered on their faces.

"I wish I could, Ari, but it looks like your little guy is ready to make an appearance."

Then, another contraction hit me. *Oh god.*

"Jeff, come on over to the right hand side of, Ari. You might want to take her hand."

Jeff let out a laugh. "I think I'll pass."

I snapped my head at him, and he stopped laughing.

"I'm only kidding, baby." He took my hand and kissed the back of it.

My mother was on the other side of me, stroking my head.

"Are you really sure you couldn't just push him back in enough for me to get the epidural?"

Dr. Wyatt just laughed and winked at me.

Does he think I'm kidding?

"Alright, Ari, I need you to give me a good strong push when the next contraction starts."

***

Motherfucker. If I was told to push one more time, I was going to scream.

"One more good push, Ari, and I think we'll have it."

I leaned up and pushed as hard as I could.

"Shit," Jeff muttered.

I realized I was squeezing the hell out of his hand.

Good. I hope it broke.

Then, I felt an instant relief.

"Here, Jeff, time to cut the cord." Dr. Wyatt said.

Lying back down, I looked up at Jeff and saw he was crying. The moment I saw him cry, I started to cry. The nurse laid a towel on my stomach and then placed our son on me.

He was perfect.

I glanced at my mother, who was crying like a baby. Then, I turned my head back to Jeff. He looked white as a ghost while he watched whatever Dr. Wyatt was doing.

Then he looked at me and our son.

He leaned down and kissed me so sweetly.

"I'm so proud of you, Ari. You did it baby." He looked at our son and smiled.

The nurse leaned in to scoop up our son, and then she walked with him over to a table.

"Can I go with him?" Jeff asked me.

"Of course!"

I watched as they did what they needed to do to our son. I glanced down at Dr. Wyatt, who looked up at me.

"You had a third-degree tear, Ari, so you're going to be pretty sore. I'll have them give you something for the pain, and they'll explain how to take care of everything before you leave the hospital."

He stood up, walked over to my side, and smiled.

"Congratulations, Ari, and you as well Susan. You have a beautiful, healthy baby boy."

After I thanked Dr. Wyatt, I wondered why I wasn't feeling any pain. One of the nurses came over and helped me to slowly sit up. I started to move.

"Holy shit." *There's the pain.*

"I'll get your pain medication, Mrs. Johnson."

I smiled at her. "Thank you, and please call me Ari."

***

I watched as one of the nurses walked up to Jeff, who was standing next to me now. She placed our son in his father's arms for the first time. Jeff had tears rolling down his face, and I couldn't help it, I started crying again.

Then, Jeff cleared his throat and spoke to our son for the first time.

"Luke, I am your father," Jeff said in his best Darth Vader voice.

My mother and I both busted out laughing.

"So, we agree on his name?" I asked.

"Yeah, baby, we agree on the name. Luke, it is."

Jeff kissed Luke on the forehead and then turned to hand him to me. The moment Jeff placed him in my arms, something happened. Something inside me changed.

I looked into those beautiful eyes, and it was like he was looking into my soul.

"Hey, little bit. Well, I hope you're ready for a ride, baby boy."

He just stared at me, and I stared back at him. He was perfect. He had a perfect nose, perfect lips, and perfect ears. I pulled back the blanket, counted all of his toes, and then looked at every finger. I kissed both of his hands and then looked up at Jeff. He quickly wiped away a tear that was running down his face.

"Are you happy, Ari?"

"I've never been so happy in my life. What about you?"

"I feel like I'm on cloud nine, and I'm scared to death to wake up if this is a dream."

My mother laughed, and we both looked at her.

"Enjoy it now. In a couple days, you'll wish it was all a dream when he wakes you up every two hours."

The nurse, who was standing there, started to laugh.

"Oh my gosh, Mom, really?"

My mother moved to stand next to me, looking down at my little man.

"He truly is beautiful, Ari and Jeff." Shall I have the others come in? You know your father is probably about to die."

"Sure," I said with a smile.

My mother left the room, and the only person who came back in with her was my father. He walked up to Jeff and shook his hand before he came to stand next to me. He gave me a kiss on the forehead and looked down at Luke.

"Daddy, meet Luke Drew Johnson."

"Mon petit-fils belle."

"Yep, you're beautiful grandson."

"Et ma belle fille."

"I love you, Daddy."

"Mom, would you like to hold him next?"

"Oui, I would."

My mother held Luke while my father looked on.

Jeff leaned down and whispered in my ear.

"Are you hungry, baby? Do you want me to go get you something to eat?"

Oh, I could have jumped him and started kissing him that very moment. Just the fact that he asked if I was hungry turned me on.

"I'm so hungry that I'd eat my horse right now if I could."

***

Gunner, Ellie, Josh, and Heather all came into the room and took turns holding Luke after I made them all wash their hands twice.

Jeff was back with Rudy's Bar-B-Q. *Oh my gosh, it smells so good.*

I'd been hinting to everyone for the last hour that I was exhausted. I finally ended up just telling everyone to get the hell out.

"Are y'all driving back to Mason tonight?" I asked.

"Yeah, I think so unless y'all want to crash at my place," Heather said.

Gunner looked at Ellie and smiled. "I think we'll just head to a hotel tonight. I'm too tired to drive. Oh, wait. Shit, we took your truck Jeff."

"No worries, Gun. I got your truck keys from your dad, and I followed Heather here in your truck. I figured you were going to need it," Josh said.

Gunner walked up to Josh and slapped him on the back.

"Dude, you rock."

***

When the last person was out the door, Jeff collapsed onto the sofa that pulled out into a bed. I would have thought he had just given birth to an almost eight-pound baby. He fell asleep in less than two minutes. The nurse walked in, looked at him and smiled.

"It's from worrying about you. It totally wears them out."

"Uh huh."

She let out a giggle. "Do you want me to wake him up, so I can open the sofa bed?"

"Nah, he's alright."

"Ari, I'm going to take Luke for a few hours to the nursery. When did you feed him last?"

"Just a few minutes ago."

"Great. I want you to get some sleep, okay? If you need to get up, make sure wake up your husband or call me."

The moment she left the room, I closed my eyes. I drifted off into a deep sleep, dreaming about Jeff and Luke riding by the river while I followed behind them. Right behind me was a little girl, a bit older than Luke, riding on a white stallion. She had brown curly hair and emerald green eyes. When I turned around to look at her, she smiled at me, and I felt my whole body get warm. A feeling of complete peace took over.

"Don't worry, Mommy. I'll never leave y'all."

My little angel would always be with us.

CHAPTER FIFTY-EIGHT

HEATHER

Josh and I decided to head back out to Mason the day after Luke was born.

After we'd left the hospital, we had gone back to my apartment and did nothing but make love and talk until three in the morning. We woke up the next morning, went out for breakfast, and planned on heading out to the ranch. I had never in my life felt so complete and happy. It was the happiest I'd been since my parents passed away. Being with Josh was beyond amazing.

I called Jeff to see if there was anything they needed for Ari or Luke before they got home. I made a list of a few things, and Josh and I hit H-E-B before heading back to Mason

Josh's cell phone died yesterday afternoon. We stopped and bought a charger, so it could charge on the way out to Mason.

We were just walking out of H-E-B when my cell phone rang. I looked at the caller ID and saw that it was Ellie calling.

"Hey, Ellie! Have you seen Luke and Ari today?"

"Yeah, they're both doing wonderful, and I think they might get to go home today. If not, then they'll be heading home tomorrow for sure."

"Okay, well, I'm heading back to Mason right now with Josh, so I'll be sure to cook up a few meals. I know Ari asked if I could stay a few extra days to help out, so I probably will."

"Um, Heather, I need to tell you something."

"Okay, is everything alright?"

"Is Josh not answering his phone?"

"His battery died yesterday. He just bought a charger, and it's charging right now. Why?"

"Jim has been trying to get a hold of him. They came back a few days early from their trip."

My heart started pounding. Lynda was back and probably trying to get a hold of Josh.

"Okay…"

"Heather, Lynda was in a car accident yesterday when she was heading over to Josh's apartment."

I stopped walking. *Oh god, no.*

"Is she."

"She's in the hospital, but she's banged up pretty bad. She's been asking for Josh."

I looked at Josh. He had been smiling, but now, his smile faded.

"Which hospital?"

"Brackenridge."

I handed Josh the phone and started to walk toward my car. I heard him talking to Ellie…and I heard the panic in his voice.

"I'll have Heather take me over there right now."

Josh hung up with Ellie and walked up to me. "Can you please take me to Brackenridge? I'll figure out a way to get my truck later."

"Um, sure. Yes, of course."

He helped me put the items that I had picked up in my car, and then he jumped in on the driver's side. I walked around and got in. I looked at him, but I didn't even know what to say.

***

The ride over to the hospital was completely silent. It was clear Josh was not going to talk to me.

He looked over at me and gave me a small smile.

"Will you come up with me?"

"Why?"

"I need you with me, Heather, I'm not sure how bad she is, and I don't know if I should say anything about us."

"Josh, of course, I'll come up with you, but Ellie said she was in bad shape. I don't think now would be the time to tell her you want to break things off."

Josh slammed his hand on the steering wheel and cursed.

"There is always something that gets in the damn way."

***

As we walked into the hospital, he took my hand. He held on to it until the elevator doors opened, and he dropped it before he walked out.

Jim and Michelle were standing at the nurses' station. Michelle turned around and saw Josh coming toward them. She walked over to him, gave him a hug, and started to cry. Josh looked at me. He looked so confused.

"We've been trying to get a hold of you," Michelle said.

"I'm sorry. My phone died. We left Mason in a rush yesterday when Ari went into labor, and I didn't grab my charger."

"Where were you last night, Josh?" Michelle asked.

"By the time we left the hospital, it was late and."

"He crashed at my apartment since he drove in with me from Mason," I said as Josh turned to look at me.

Michelle smiled at me and then turned back to Josh.

"She's in bad shape. She has a broken leg, a few broken ribs, a concussion, and her left eye is black and blue."

Shit.

Josh grabbed my hand right in front of Michelle, and he asked if I would go in with him. Michelle looked a bit confused, and it was not lost on me when she looked down at our hands.

"Of course, I'll go in with you if you need me to," I said.

We walked into the room and I tried to take my hand from Josh's, but he held on to it tight. Lynda looked over at us, and immediately, she looked down at our hands and then back up at Josh. She tried to smile, but I could see the hurt in her eyes. Although she was hurting, I still didn't trust her, especially not after she'd lied to me about Josh asking her to marry him.

"Josh…" Lynda said.

He let go of my hand and walked up to the side of her bed.

"Hey, I'm so sorry this happened to you, babe."

My heart slammed into my chest when he called her babe. She tried to smile at him. When she glanced at me, I smiled. If looks could kill, I would have been on the floor in two seconds flat.

Then she looked back at Josh.

"I had a dream. You left me…" She glared back at me.

Oh.My.God. She knows. Somehow, she knew Josh and I had been together.

"What?" Josh asked.

"I had a dream on the plane on our way back. I woke up in a panic, so when we landed, I ran to my car to try to get to you right away." She started to cry or at least attempted to cry and then she called out in pain because of her ribs.

Oh, she's good.

"Lynda, please don't be upset."

"I was trying to get to you when I had the accident. Please don't ever leave, Josh. P*lease don't ever leave me.*"

Josh put his head down on the hospital bed, and Lynda looked up at me. The look she gave me showed me exactly what type of person she was. She knew exactly what she was doing.

Then, she gave me a smirk.

"Heather, can I talk to Josh alone, please?"

"Oh, um... Yeah... sure."

I left and sat in the waiting room. About fifteen minutes later, Josh came walking out, looking white as a ghost. He sat down next me and put his head in his hands.

"Motherfucker."

"Josh, you have to know she's trying to make you feel guilty. She knows we've been together."

"I can't leave her right now, Heather."

"What?"

"I just can't walk away from her. You heard how upset she is. She'll be devastated."

"Oh my god Josh, can you not see she just came up with that stupid story because you walked into that room holding my hand? She's playing you and you're falling for it. Can I just call a Rebecca here?"

"Heather, stop. She's in such bad shape. How could she come up with a story that fast?"

Michelle clearly saw our conversation was not one to interrupt because she turned away and walked the other direction.

"I just need more time. I need to help her heal and get in a good place mentally before I just leave her."

I shook my head and stood up.

"I knew this was going to happen. I knew there would be some reason why you wouldn't leave her. I knew it was stupid to be with you while you were still with her." I tried not to cry, but I felt a tear slowly slide down my face. I turned away and started to walk to the elevator.

Josh called out for me, but I didn't stop. I hit the down button and thanked God the doors opened immediately. I could hear Josh telling Michelle that he would be right back. I got in the elevator and tried to hit the main floor button as fast as I could. Then, I saw him as he started running toward the elevator.

Shit! Close, you damn doors. They started to close, but Josh stuck his arm between the doors and they opened back up.

He got in, reached over, and hit the button to close the doors. As the elevator started to descend, I backed away from him, but he came at me and kissed me. I pushed him off of me.

"Stop. You can't do this to me, Josh! You can't."

"Just give me a couple of weeks. Please, Heather, you're the only person I want to be with, but I can't leave her right now. I'd be a dick if I walked out on her and left her like this."

I knew he was right, but I also knew that Lynda was going to do everything in her power to keep Josh.

"She's going to trick you into staying with her, Josh. I don't trust her.

I felt sick to my stomach.

"Please, princess, just give me some time. I promise that we'll be together. I promise."

He pulled me to him and kissed me with so much passion that it felt like he was trying to pour his love into my body. Then, he pulled away and smiled at me.

"I love you, Heather. I love you more than anything."

"I love you, too, Josh. I probably need to get back to Mason. What about your truck?"

"I'll see what time Gunner and Ells are leaving, and I'll catch a ride back with them to get my truck. Can we spend some time together before I come back to Austin?"

As much as I wanted to say yes, I shook my head.

"I don't think it would be right, not while you're still with Lynda."

He looked down and stared at the ground. When he looked back up, he had tears in his eyes, and my heart was breaking all over again.

"Please wait for me, Heather. *Please*."

I smiled, leaned over, and kissed him softly on the lips.

I turned and walked out of the elevator. I left the hospital and headed toward my car.

I didn't start crying until I pulled out and drove away.

The worse feeling came over me. Lynda was not going to give up on Josh without a fight.

I also knew she wasn't going to fight fair.

CHAPTER FIFTY-NINE

JEFF

I walked into the Oasis with Luke in my arms and Ari at my side. My baby boy, the love of my life, was two months old.

Ari looked beautiful, and just by looking at her, I would have never known she had a baby two months ago. She'd been riding Star and Sweet Pea bareback for weeks, and she seemed to be in heaven now that she could ride again.

I looked around for Gunner and Ellie.

"There they are!" Ari said, pointing to where they were standing in the waiting area.

We walked up to Gunner and Ellie and saw Jack, Grace, Emma, and Garrett with them.

"So, the gangs all here now," Garrett said with a wink.

"Let me hold that baby," Emma said as I handed Luke over to her.

Grace and Emma walked over to a bench and sat down.

When I put my hand on Ellie's growing belly, I instantly felt the baby kick. Ellie and I both started to laugh.

"Still not going to find out?" I asked.

"Nope."

"Ells, have you talked to Heather? How is she doing?" Ari asked.

Ellie's smiled faded, and she looked at Gunner.

"I don't know. Lynda now seems to be having some kind of mental breakdown, so Josh still hasn't called it off with her. Heather is trying to act like she's okay, but I know she's dying inside. She went on a date the other day."

"What? Why would she do that?" Ari asked in a panicked voice.

I pulled Ari closer to me and held on to her.

"I think she's lonely, Ari. She's so confused on what she should do. She loves Josh, but clearly, Lynda is not going to give up that easily."

Ari said, "I think it's time we kick some ass. Stupid bitch. Why does she want a guy who she knows wants to be with someone else? Douche-twat. Oh, sorry, Gunner. I know she's your cousin."

Gunner laughed and held up his hands.

"Hey y'all!" Heather said as she walked up and hugged everyone. "We're in a back room on the second floor."

We all followed Heather into one of the larger rooms. I knew a few of the people, but most were friends of Heather's aunt, uncles, and cousins or friends of Heather's parents.

***

We talked, we laughed, and celebrated Heather's graduation from UT. With the absence of her parents, I could tell that this happy occasion was very emotional for her family. Despite any sad thoughts, her grandfather seemed to be very proud of Heather.

I leaned over to Gunner. "Josh isn't coming, I take it."

"I talked to him earlier. Lynda had some kind of breakdown, and he couldn't leave her."

"Dude, does he know she's playing him for a fucking fool?"

"Jeff!" Ari said as she punched me in the arm. "Don't swear in front of the baby."

"He's two months old, Ari. I'm pretty sure he isn't going to know what fuck means."

Just then, Matt who was sitting on the other side of Ari, called out, "I wanna be a mudder."

Ari quickly turned and started to tickle Matt before she whispered something into his ear.

She turned back and glared at me. Gunner let out a laugh, and I had to bite my cheek to keep myself from laughing, too.

Heather's uncle stood up to make a toast. As he was talking, Heather let out a gasp. She was staring straight ahead, and we all turned to see Josh standing in the doorway smiling at Heather. She got up and walked over to him. He whispered something in to her ear, and the next thing I knew Heather flew into his arms.

I turned around to see everyone watching them.

Then, louder than she meant to, Ari said,

"Shit, it's about fucking time."

Right on cue, Matt started singing,

"I wanna be a mudder fuckin' cowboy!"

Ari, Sue, and Grace all said at once, "Matthew!"

CHAPTER SIXTY

ARI

December

"Can you believe he's six months old?"

Jeff let out a laugh as he crawled after Luke on the floor.

"Nope. The little monster is fast as shit."

I tried to keep up with them as I videotaped Jeff and Luke.

"So, should we go shopping for more toys for Santa to bring?"

Jeff looked up at me with the biggest smile on his face. I swore I'd never seen a man who loved to go shopping for toys like Jeff did. I think he liked the stuff more than Luke.

"Do you even need to ask that, Ari? Hells yeah, my little buddy needs more stuff. Don't forget. I want to find something really cool for Matt."

"As long as it doesn't make too much noise. The drum set you got him drove my mother and father insane."

I saw the smile spread across Jeff's face, and I knew he bought that thing just to piss off my father.

Just then, there was a knock on the door, and Jeff jumped up to get it.

"Heather! What brings you here?"

"Hey! Just wanted to come for a visit."

Heather walked into the living room and immediately went down to the floor as Luke crawled up to her and got in her lap.

"Oh my gosh, you're getting so big, my little man!" She looked up at me and smiled.

I knew something was wrong. Her beautiful blue eyes were…dead. I hadn't seen her sad in months. Josh had left Lynda at the end of August after he'd had enough of her crazy bullshit. Heather got a job teaching first grade at the elementary school in Fredericksburg while Josh's furniture business was growing in Austin. I knew they tried to see each other as much as possible and Josh was ready to move the business to Fredericksburg just to be with Heather.

"Is everything okay?"

Just then, the phone rang.

Jeff ran into the kitchen and picked it up.

"What? Right now? You have to take her to Fredericksburg, Gunner! No, not Austin…don't drive…meet me at the main house. Dude, calm down. We'll be right there."

He hung up the phone, looked at me, and then to Heather on the floor.

"Ellie's water just broke."

Heather and I both let out a scream, and then Luke screamed and clapped his hands. I reached down and grabbed Luke. *It's about time!* Ellie was overdue and ready to pop any day.

"Let me change his diaper really quick," I said.

I grabbed a few things for Luke while Jeff and Heather were getting baby food ready in the kitchen. We had a plan. When Ellie went into labor, Jenny and Aaron were going to watch Luke for us. I grabbed my cell and did a fist pump when I saw I had a signal. I called Jenny, told her about Ellie, and said we would drop off Luke in a few minutes.

By the time we got to Emma and Garrett's place, Emma was sitting on the porch with Ellie.

Heather and I ran up, and I fell to my knees next to my very best friend, who had a huge pregnant belly. I could look at Ellie from behind and never known that she was pregnant, but when she turned around, she was all baby in the front.

"Hey, baby, how are you feeling?" I asked.

"Fine, Emma here is distracting me with a story, so I'm okay."

Emma who rolled her eyes, and I let out a giggle.

"Ellie needs to take some deep breaths, girls. Can you stay with her while I go in with Garrett? He's about to beat the hell out of my grandson."

"Ah…okay." Heather said.

I looked at Ellie as she shrugged her shoulders.

"Ells, are you okay?" I asked.

"No, I want to have the baby in Austin, but I don't think I'm going to make it, so we have to go to Fredericksburg."

"Alright, babe. Why are we just sitting on the porch? And why is Garrett about to beat the hell out of Gunner? I think we should probably be on the way to the hospital, honey, don't you?"

Ellie let out a laugh. "Yeah, I think we should...oh shit, here comes another one."

I looked at Heather. "Can you go into the house and see what the fuck is going on?"

Heather nodded and went inside.

"Ellie, baby, just take deep breaths. Come on, let's walk over to Gunner's truck. Can you get into the truck?" I pulled her up and held on to her as we made our way to Gunner's truck.

"Yep," Ellie said between breaths.

"Is your bag in the truck, Ells?"

"Yeah, I put it in there the other day because I was worried I'd forget it."

Sounds like Ellie.

I helped her into the truck. "Do you need a pillow or anything?"

"Nope, I just need Gunner. Please, Ari, can you go get him? I can't breathe."

I smiled at the thought of how only Gunner could calm Ellie down.

"Okay, baby, I'm going to go get his ass right now. He'll sit back here with you while Jeff drives. Heather will follow us."

"Sounds good, but I really think we need to hurry."

I jumped out of the truck and started to make my way back to the house. Jeff came walking out with Gunner, and I stopped dead in my tracks.

"What the hell happened?" I asked, confused.

Gunner was holding a bag of ice to his head. When he pulled it away, he already had a huge black eye.

"Stupid bastard passed out and hit his eye on the table," Garrett said as he threw his head back and laughed his ass off.

Gunner turned and looked at him.

"Thanks, Gramps, thanks a lot."

"Okay, boys that's enough. Gunner get in that truck with Ellie." Emma said. She turned to Heather. "I called Grace and Jack, and they're leaving from Austin and will meet us at the hospital."

After we got Gunner in the truck, Jeff and I jumped in.

Ellie turned to Gunner. "Are you sure you're okay?"

Jeff looked over at me and smiled. I'd never known Gunner to be nervous or scared of anything. I thought back to when I'd gone into labor and how Jeff reacted. Jeff reached across and grabbed my hand.

I turned around to see that Ellie had her head on Gunner's chest. He was softly singing to her. My heart started pounding. Ellie was about to have the baby she so desperately wanted.

As Jeff drove to the hospital, I looked out the window at the beautiful country side. Then, I thought about Heather.

Something was very wrong, and I needed to talk to her as soon as possible. Right now Ellie and the baby were my main concern.

"Gunner, will you please stop singing?" Ellie asked.

"Sure, baby, but I thought you loved it when I sang to you."

Jeff and I looked at each other.

"You're driving me fucking nuts with that song. Just please stop."

I let out a giggle. Jeff smiled as glanced at Ellie and Gunner in the rearview mirror.

He reached over and turned his iPod on. Keith Urban's "A Better Life" came on.

"Yes! I love this song." Ellie called out.

Jeff looked straight ahead and let out a small laugh.

"Let the fun begin," he said as he squeezed my hand.

CHAPTER SIXTY-ONE

GUNNER

Ellie seemed to be so much more relaxed after they gave her the epidural. My mom and dad made it, and they were in the waiting room with Gramps and Grams.

Of course, Gramps and dad laughed their asses off when Gramps retold the story of me passing out and hitting my eye on the table.

I tried to explain many times that I'd tripped and got knocked out when I hit the table, but it didn't matter. Gramps changed the story every time he told it, and he'd already told three nurses, a doctor, and one intern.

A young guy walked into the room with one of the nurses. I smiled at both of them while they walked up to Ellie and looked at me.

"Mr. Mathews, Mrs. Mathews."

"Please call me Ellie."

"Ellie, it is," The young guy said.

He couldn't have been but a few years older than me.

"Gunner," I said as I reached out and shook his hand.

"I'm Dr. Johnson."

Ellie let out a laugh. "Hey, that's my maiden name!"

I took a step back. "You're the doctor? Like as in the doctor who's going to deliver little bear?"

"Little bear? Is that what we call the baby?" Dr. Johnson asked.

"How old are you, dude? Have you ever even delivered a baby before? Are you even out of medical school?"

"Gunner!" Ellie said as she gave me a dirty look.

Dr. Johnson let out a laugh. "Well, Gunner, I'm thirty-three years old with three kids of my own. Yes, I've delivered my fair share of babies. And I've been out of medical school for five years now."

Ellie shot me another look.

I sat down in the chair and just stared at the doctor.

"I'm sorry. I don't know what's wrong with me. You just look really young. Please forgive me."

He let out a laugh and looked at the monitor.

"Ellie, can you feel the contractions at all?"

"I can feel pressure."

"Okay. Well I'm going to take a look to see how you're coming along, okay?"

Ellie nodded her head.

After a few minutes he stood back up and smiled.

"Ellie, are you ready to get this show on the road?"

Ellie smiled. "Yes."

"Then, let's get little bear out and into the big world, so he can meet his mommy and daddy."

I jumped up. "What? Now? We're going now?"

Dr. Johnson looked at me as he took a few steps toward me. "Dude, it's going to be alright. Take deep breaths and just be there for your wife. I've got the baby part down. I wouldn't want you to pass out again." He winked at me before he turned to the nurse and started talking to her.

Damn it, Gramps. What? Is he just walking around telling everyone?

***

For the next three hours, I stood next to Ellie while she exhausted herself from pushing. Finally, at two minutes after four, I heard the first cries from our baby.

"Well, your little bear is a girl. Congratulations, y'all." Dr. Johnson said as he held up our baby for us to see.

When I looked at Ellie, she was crying. I felt the tears rolling down my face as I looked over at little bear. She was the most beautiful thing I'd ever seen in my life.

Dr. Johnson asked, "Mr. Mathews, would you like to cut the umbilical cord?"

Speechless, I just nodded my head with a smile.

***

A nurse took the baby over to a table to clean her up. While the doctor was fixing up Ellie, she kept looking around him to watch what the nurse was doing.

After the doctor was done with Ellie, he helped her to sit up.

The nurse came over, holding my sweet baby girl.

"Dad, your daughter would like to meet you face to face."

I held out my arms as the nurse placed my little bear gently in them. She looked up at me and yawned. My heart was pounding hard in my chest. I couldn't take my eyes off of her. Her beautiful blue eyes embraced me heart and soul. She was just staring up at me. In that moment, I knew that she would always trust me to take care of her and to love her unconditionally. I'd die before I'd ever let anyone or anything hurt her.

Ellie was now sitting up all the way, and I looked over at her. She had tears running down her face. I turned and slowly put our baby girl in her arms.

They just stared at each other, like they knew what the other was thinking. I was in awe of the exchange. The baby didn't even cry. She just stared up Ellie.

"Hello, Alexandra Eryn Mathews. I've waited a long to time meet you, baby girl," Ellie said.

Ellie looked up at me and smiled.

Then, she turned to the nurse. "When can we all go home?"

"We want you to stay at least overnight. If all is going well and she's eating enough, y'all can go home tomorrow."

***

Later that night after everyone had finally left, Ellie and I sat on the sofa with Alex sound asleep in my arms.

"I didn't think they would ever leave!" Ellie said with a laugh. "I'm exhausted."

"Are you hungry, sweetheart?" I asked.

I continued stroking Alex between her eyes and down her nose. She must have liked it because it put her to sleep fast.

"I'm starved, but you're not going to find anything open in Fredericksburg this late at night. Oh wait! McDonald's! I could really go for a Big Mac...and large fries...oh, and a giant-ass sweet tea."

I laughed and leaned over to kiss her. I stood up and gently put Alex down in the bassinet. Then, I turned and helped Ellie up and back into bed.

"You got it, baby. One Big Mac and large french fries coming up."

I turned toward the door to leave, Ellie called out,

"Sweet tea! Don't forget the sweet tea, Gunner!"

CHAPTER SIXTY-TWO

HEATHER

By the time we left the hospital, it was well after midnight.

Ari called Jenny to let her know we were on our way back. Jenny begged Ari to let her and Aaron keep Luke all night.

"I don't know. I've never had him gone overnight before. You promise to bring him home first thing tomorrow morning? Okay, I guess it'll be kind of nice to sleep in a little in the morning for once."

When Ari hung up, Jeff expressed his happiness. "Hells yeah baby, we're having sex all night long. Don't worry, Heather, I'll find some ear-plugs for you."

Ari and I both laughed.

I pulled up, and Jeff jumped out of my car.

"Jeff, can you give me and Heather a few minutes, please?" Ari asked.

"Sure, baby, y'all take your time."

Ari and I got out of the car and headed toward the house. We walked up to the porch and sat down.

"What happened?" Ari asked.

Heather sat back and let out a sigh. "Josh and I had a fight."

"About?"

"Lynda. What else? Ugh, Ari, she is something else. She won't leave him alone, and he feels like he owes her something. It drives me crazy."

"Have you talked to him at all since you got here?"

"No. When everything happened with Ellie, I forgot about it. He was supposed to go to some Christmas party at his mother's law firm. I was supposed to go with him, but then we started fighting, so I came here instead. I tried to call him from the hospital, but it went straight to voicemail. I sent him a text telling him about Ellie and the baby, but I guess he's pissed. He must have turned off his cell phone. Every time I try to call, it goes straight to voicemail."

"It has to be hard for him. Baby, you know he loves you. He told Jeff that he's moving to Fredericksburg next month."

I looked over at Ari and smiled. "Yeah, I still can't believe he's going to move his whole business just to be with me. He's doing so well. I hope this doesn't cause him to lose any business."

"It won't, Heather. Don't worry. He loves you and wants to be with you. Don't worry about Lynda either. After Josh is out of Austin, she'll see that he's truly yours, and she'll move on."

"God, I hope so."

Just then, Jeff walked out onto the porch and looked at Ari and me with concern etched on his face.

Ari jumped up.

"What's wrong? Luke! Is Luke okay?"

I slowly stood up. Jeff was looking at me. Something was wrong.

"Ari, Luke is fine, baby. He's fine."

"Jesus, Jeff. What's wrong then?"

"I just got a phone call from Josh's mother Elizabeth…"

My heart started pounding.

Just then, my cell phone went off, I must have gotten a signal right then. I pulled it out of my pocket to see I had three missed calls…from Elizabeth. She must have called when I had no signal, and they just now all came through.

I looked up at Jeff.

"Heather, Josh has been in a car accident."

I took a step back and fell into the chair. All the memories of my parents' accident came flooding back to me.

"Baby girl, I'm going to drive you into Austin, okay?" Jeff said.

I nodded my head and looked at Ari, who was kneeling down next to me.

She looked up to Jeff.

"How is he, Jeff?"

Jeff cleared his throat.

"He's in critical condition, and, um…he's in surgery right now."

I jumped and ran to my car. I had to get to Josh right now.

Jeff came up behind me and grabbed me.

"Let me go, Jeff!" I screamed, kicking and pushing for him to let me go.

"Heather, calm down. Let me drive you to Austin."

"Let me go! Oh my god!" I fell to the ground and started crying.

Jeff held on to me as I cried hysterically.

Ari dropped to the ground next to me and put her hands on my face. "Heather, look at me, sweets. Let us take you to Austin. It's going to be okay."

"I can't lose him. Oh god Ari… I can't lose him, too."

Jeff picked me up and put me in the backseat of his truck.

Ari jumped in next to me and held on to me. She just kept repeating herself. "Baby girl, everything's going to be okay. It'll be okay."

It was my parents' car accident all over again. Images of me in the backseat of my uncle's car while Ari held me flashed through my mind. Even then, she did the same thing, telling me everything was going to be okay.

But it hadn't been okay. My parents had left me.

If I lose Josh…I'll lose my whole world.

EPILOGUE

HEATHER

It was just supposed to be another day at the lake. I knew he was bringing her. Ari told me. I watched as they laughed and kissed each other.

Each moment that passed, I died a little more inside. Every now and then, he would look at me. I tried to smile when he did, but it took every ounce of energy I had to smile at him and act like I was happy that he was with her. When I did manage a forced smile, he would give me a weak smile in return.

***

As the day went on, I hated her more and more. She did this. She knew that he was mine, but she went after him with everything she had.

She won.

When I walked up to the bon-fire, Ari reached out and grabbed my arm.

"Maybe you and I should take a walk, Heather."

"Why? It's getting cold, and I just want to sit by the fire."

Ari looked back over at the fire. I followed her eyes and saw Josh and Victoria hugging. My stomach turned, and I wanted to throw up.

Then, it happened. He dropped to one knee and held out a ring box. Victoria's hand flew up to her mouth as she let out a small scream.

My eyes moved from looking at her to looking at Josh. When he glanced over at me, I wanted to scream no.

I couldn't move.

The next thing I knew, I felt my legs going out from underneath me, and all I heard was Ari calling out my name.

Faithful

Coming Summer 2013

Stories from those touched by Fragile X

"Your son has Fragile X syndrome"….

When I first read those words my heart broke, honestly I was devastated. Of course I took to the computer to learn all I could and was soon presented with a rough road ahead of us. A genetic disorder that causes mental impairment, cognitive delays, developmental delays, ADD, hyperactivity, sensory processing disorder…all words and phrases I was bombarded with that brought me to tears that weekend…Logan was just 18 months old at the time he was diagnosed.

When you have a child every parent thinks about how their child's life is going to play out….their first steps, first day of school, getting their drivers license, their first date, graduating high school, getting married, and even having children of their own. It's strange how one little sentence can destroy every hope and dream that you had for someone that means everything to you. But I soon realized that all those hopes and dreams I had for him were still there, they weren't what I thought they were but they were still there. So I now have new hopes and dreams for him…better ones! Because he works so much harder that most everyone else to achieve little things he has taught me to appreciate EVERYTHING. First steps didn't come until he was 19 months old… but that made them all the more special when they did happen. I vividly remember the first time when he was 6 years old and walked up to me and said "Hi Mom!" all on his own with no prompts. All moments that people take for granted every day. So here we are now at 7 years old, his speech is slowly emerging, his motor skill are improving, he's starting to write his letters and his hyperactivity is calming down a bit. He still can't tolerate a kiss on his beautiful face or going to crowded places but the one thing that he has never had to put any effort into is smiling! He breathes life into every room he steps into and will have you grinning in an instant. He understands everything you tell him and he loves everyone with his whole heart! He's all things NFL and for some reason he runs around the house yelling "Go Steelers!" A master at the iPad and obsessed at looking for his grandpa's house on Google Earth, Logan surprises me every day of my life. I have my moments for sure, just as any parent would whether your child has special needs or not. Some days I'd love to hide but then I look at Logan and think about how he puts 100% of his trust and love in me to help him along his path and how he never ever gives up...that's enough for me. Everyone can take a lesson from Logan, he sings his heart out, his love knows no limits and he lives in the moment and he will literally stop and smell the roses. His big brother Gavin and I laugh and smile very single day because of Logan. So yes that diagnoses changed my life but I wouldn't have it any other way...

By Ari Niknejadi

For more information on Fragile X please visit www.fragilex.org or contact the National Fragile X Foundation at 800-688-8765

■■■

By Alexandra Louk –

My younger (I would say little but the kid is huge) brother has Fragile X. He was diagnosed when he was 5 and I was 9. The first thing people tend to ask it "What's it like to have a brother with special needs?" and my response is always, "What's it like to have a brother/sister without special needs?". My brother Jakob is my best friend; he is always there for me no matter what and can always brighten my day. Being away at college has been hard but I try to call him when I can and I always bring him little presents when I come home. Our sibling relationship is pretty normal. We fight and wrestle and then we fight over our parents' attention. He is protective over me and doesn't like when I bring guys home, even though he might not fully understand everything he knows I am his sister and boys can hurt me and make me sad. When he is upset sometimes he will come and try to curl up in my lap like he used to. Even though he is 6'4'' and 250 lbs. I don't care he is my baby brother and I love him. Having a brother with Fragile X is hard sometimes but I honestly wouldn't change a thing about him. He keeps my secrets and never tells my parents on me, and when we hang out I spoil him rotten and have a hard time telling him no. My brother is a Special Olympics Bowler and Ice Skater, he plays hockey and baseball, and he watches sports with me. So for me having a brother with Fragile X may not be easy but I wouldn't trade it for anything.

Playlist for Saved

A Thousand Years – Christina Perri – Jeff asks Ari to marry him.

Dirty Dancer – Enrigue Eglesias – Jeff and Ari at The Driskill Hotel first time they make love

Me and You – Kenny Chesney – First time Ari and Jeff make love

The Only Way I Know – Jason Aldean – Josh and Heather dancing in Marble Falls

Over – Blake Shelton – Josh and Heather dancing in Marble Falls

Red – Taylor Swift – Heather's feelings for Josh

Circles – Christina Aguilera – When Ari gives Rebecca the finger at Hula Hut

Red Hot Kinda of Love – Christina Aguilera – Heather dancing while drunk, flirting with Josh

Wipe Your Eyes – Maroon 5 – After Ari finds out she is pregnant and Jeff takes her home to their house

Everything – Lifehouse – Ari feeling lost after she finds out she is pregnant

Woohoo – Christina Aguilera – Ari singing in the barn

Our Little World – Susan Ashton – Gunner and Ellie dancing on their porch after returning from their honeymoon

Like I Am – Rascal Flatts – Gunner and Ellie making love after talking about having kids

Hurt – Christina Aguilera – Gunner and his father talking on the porch

Scream and Shout – Wil I Am – Ari dancing at the kitchen sink

Blank Page – Christina Aguilera – Jeff with Ari before they make love in the barn

Let There Be Cowgirls – Chris Cagle – Ellie, Ari, and Heather dancing

Lift Me Up – Christina Aguilera – When Heather finds the text Josh sent Lynda

Better Dig Two – The Band Perry – Lynda fighting for Josh

Cookie Jar – Gym Class Hero's – Josh Dancing with Lynda at the honkytonk

Toxic – Britney Spears – Ellie at the gym

Shut Up – Christina Aguilera – When Ari sees Rebecca at the gym

Cowboy – Kid Rock – Jeff in the barn

All I Need – Christina Aguilera – Gunner dancing with Ellie on Ari's birthday

Club Can't Handle Me – FloRida – Girls dancing at Ari's birthday

My Girls – Christina Aguilera – All the girls dancing at Ari's birthday party

There You Go – Pink - Josh and Lynda dancing at Ari's party when Heather gets upset

It Will Be Me – Faith Hill – Gunner dancing with Ellie in their room at the Driskill Hotel

When She Says Baby – Jason Aldean – Jeff and Ari dancing at the barn dance

You Save Me – Kenny Chesney – Jeff and Ari's wedding song

Desnudate – Christina Aguilera – Ari dancing at the wedding reception, driving Jeff insane

These Days – Rascal Flatts – Josh thinking about losing Heather

She Thinks My Tractos Sexy – Kenny Chesney – Pregnant Ari dancing in the kitchen

Breathe – Faith Hill – Josh and Heather make love for the first time at the ranch

Daylight – Maroon 5 – The day after Josh and Heather spend the night together when Lynda comes back

Run – Matt Nathanson – Ari and Jeff after Luke was born

A Better Life – Keith Urban – Jeff plays in his truck while taking Ellie and Gunner to have their baby

Say Once More – Amy Grant – When little bear is born

You Could Be Happy – Snow Patrol – Heather on her way to Josh after his accident

Made in the USA
Lexington, KY
06 August 2013